What People Are Saying About
MUCH ADO ABOUT CORONA

"*Much Ado About Corona* weaves a fascinating, entertaining, and sometimes very sad story, full of irony and subtle humour. The protagonist's narrative is full of sarcasm, openness and directness. Heartwarming and outright hilarious." —*Dr. Éva Székely, retired psychologist, author of* **Never Too Thin**

"I enjoyed *Much Ado About Corona* immensely. The police interaction was bang on and the subtleties are not so subtle and portray an authentic realism to me. Constable Mackenzie is a tragic character." —**Retired Constable Leland "Lee" Keane, Royal Canadian Mounted Police**

"Sometimes fiction is the best way to get the truth across. Shakespeare and Charles Dickens knew that and so does John C. A. Manley. He has crafted a ripping story of courage, awakening and love (with some good laughs thrown in) all in the time of COVID. As with the truth, you won't want to put *Much Ado About Corona* down." —*Patrick Corbett, former writer, director and producer (credits include CTV's W-5, CBC's Beachcombers and NBC's Dateline)*

"I have high praise for *Much Ado About Corona's* characterization, pacing, condensed truth and irony, and just the right amount of humour." —*Nowick Gray, author of* **Chameleon: The Virtual Reality Virus**

"I felt there was no more data I could absorb about COVID-19 without going crazy. Hence, it was refreshing to read a page-turning fictional account; it seemed more real than another non-fiction article, book, or blog post. Living in a profession where so few seem to see what is going on and are blind to the horrors we are participating in, reading *Much Ado About Corona* was very cathartic." —*Andrew Brannan BScN, RN, Canadian nurse*

Turn page for more reviews..

"I've commented many times how history will be written to falsely show how our government 'saved' us from extinction. *Much Ado About Corona* slowly brings forward the invisible truth one piece at a time. The novel flows well, has an original story, maintained my attention and has an unexpected good ending." —*Vincent Gircys, retired Ontario Provincial Police officer*

"I think *Much Ado About Corona* is at the cutting edge of modern literature; not fakey, establishment funded, postmodern, Avant-garde, garbage, but the actual cutting edge of genuinely creative and highly relevant writing." —*Jordan Henderson of Jordan Henderson Fine Arts*

"At the end of each chapter I am very curious and it is hard to put the book down." —*Father Anthony Hannon, founder of* **In Viam Pacis Retreat Centre** *and* **To Prepare His Way** *YouTube channel*

"The dialogue is believable and unforced, the family relationships neatly sketched in few words, the characters brimming with vivid life and individuality. Absorbing reading. And so many original, quotable lines! *Much Ado About Corona* is indeed a page-turner; very well-written. And there were moments when I was laughing aloud." —*Sean Arthur Joyce, author of* **Diary of a Pandemic Year**

"I predict Much Ado About Corona will stand as a testament to what we the resistance collectively endured in the name of truth and freedom... This novel will open many eyes." —*Dr. Gary Magder, DDS*

"What a fantastic read. Superb story-telling! Absolutely riveting for a COVID truth-seeker like myself. Well-placed humour, irony, injection of COVID evidence-based science and dismantling of the false narrative made this a powerful read for me." —*Ron deGagne, practicing member of the Association of Professional Geoscientists of Ontario*

Much Ado About Corona

a dystopian love story

John C. A. Manley

Blazing Pine Cone Publishing
Ontario, Canada

"Cashless" by Sean Arthur Joyce (seanarthurjoyce.ca) reprinted with permission from *Diary of a Pandemic Year* (Chameleon Fire Editions 2021).

Edited by Patrick Corbett, Sean Arthur Joyce (seanarthurjoyce.ca) and Nowick Gray (hyperedits.com); book formatting/design by Nowick Gray and John C. A. Manley.

Cover art and illustrations by Jordan Henderson (jordanhendersonfineart.com).

Cover design by Alerrandre (fiverr.com/alerrandre).

Published by Blazing Pine Cone Publishing (BlazingPineCone.com)

ISBN 978-1-7781231-0-8

Dedicated to my father,
Thomas Joseph Manley (1928-2022),
who passed away in a
COVID-restricted long-term care home
before this novel was completed.

And to all the men, women and children
who have suffered, died
and been permanently injured
due to the mandates.

And to all those who have bravely stood
for truth, freedom and human dignity,
despite being shamed, ostracized and abused
by their government, the media and their communities.

Author's Note

The events and characters depicted in this novel are fictional; while the information regarding COVID-19 and related public measures are based on facts that can easily be confirmed by referencing the books and websites listed at the end of this novel.

Moosehead is a fictional town but is situated in a geographically accurate location on the French River, south of Sudbury, on the border of Northern Ontario. Sudbury General Hospital is a fictional hospital that does not exist and is not related or representative of the former hospital bearing the same name.

The novel seeks to reflect, in an honest and balanced way, the multicultural reality of twenty-first-century Canada. I have done my utmost to properly reflect this diversity, particularly concerning the Indigenous, English, and French populations, utilizing sensitivity readers. Such depictions are by no means offered as perfect representations, but, rather, artistic renderings.

Nothing in this novel should be taken as legal advice and is in no way inciting unlawful activity. Readers, as always, are advised to exercise due diligence as to the legality of public health orders in their region, seek peaceful resolutions to tyrannical governance (whenever possible), and, above all, to follow their conscience, remembering that just because some bureaucrat made an edict law, does not mean it is right or even legal.

Prologue: Mountie 019

A field somewhere in Northern Ontario, Canada, December 26, 2020...

I'd never flown in a plane before, much less a helicopter. When I was sixteen, Mathéo and I took the train to Toronto to see a Leafs game. Even for the grade eight trip to Quebec we traveled in one of those two-storey coaches with the tinted windows.

Now, strapped to a yellow cot, wrapped in some sort of emergency, crinkly, subzero sleeping bag, I stared at the air ambulance that awaited me. It was painted orange with the letters ORNGE on the side—as if they left out the A to save money. From above its windshield extended a metal spike like a unicorn's horn. Except this orange, flying unicorn had only three legs—two in the back and one in the front—disappearing into a foot of snow.

Through the haze of pain, I could barely see the evergreen trees that surrounded the field, serving as a barrier against the howling wind. The dark night was lit by the headlights of many police vehicles and the red and blue light bar of an ambulance.

Overhead, the blades of the medical copter were whipping in circles—making the cold December air even colder. At least it numbed the excruciating pain in my chest a little. On the unicorn's tail, a tiny vertical propeller was also spinning like a windmill in a hurricane—proving how the seemingly inconsequential can alter the direction of the large and powerful.

"Here we go, buddy," said the Mountie who was holding the front end of the cot.

Instead of the iconic Red Serge of the Royal Canadian Mounted Police, he was suited in a thickly insulated black uniform. Rather than a brown, felt, wide-brimmed hat, he wore a military-style helmet bearing the ironic identification number 019. His white face mask matched his white eyebrows.

"You'll be warm in a minute," promised Mountie 019. He spoke in the groggy and grizzled voice of a man who had done too many back-to-back twelve-hour shifts.

The side door of the chopper slid open. With the grace of a

gymnast, a thin, feminine figure dropped down onto a patch of frosty grass. Someone had cleared away the snow, making a path across the field to the emergency landing area.

Like the medic holding the back end of my cot, the woman approaching also wore a blue face mask and a round flight helmet with dome-shaped headphones. The bulging helmets, glowing body cams and one-piece flight suits made them both look more sci-fi than medical. Their epaulettes, however, proved they were not from outer space—each heralded a Canadian flag with a red maple leaf.

Mountie 019 introduced himself to the approaching paramedic. "I'll be overseeing transport of the prisoner."

Prisoner. It seemed too harsh, too hard to believe. *Me.* I still lived with my parents in a two-streetlight town no one had ever heard of. I went to Mass every Sunday—at least until they made church illegal. I must have groaned or moaned or something because Mountie 019 retracted his statement.

"Uh, I mean accused." Icy vapour escaped from the edges of his face mask as he chuckled. "You know, in the academy, we're taught to call those in custody our 'clients.'"

"*Clients!*" exclaimed the medic behind me. "That's a joke."

"No kidding. God, I need to retire."

They all laughed in the way people do when they want to banish anxiety, guilt or confusion. I, however, did not laugh. Could not laugh. And if anything was funny, it was that they felt I needed this RCMP paratrooper to watch over me. It hurt enough to simply breathe; I was no threat to anyone. At least the black-clad Mountie no longer had the Remington assault rifle hanging from his shoulder. He'd traded it in for a modest fifteen-round Smith & Wesson sidearm.

The female medic looked down at me and asked, "How're you doing?"

Her eyes were a pretty blue. But I knew not to trust them.

From behind my head, the male medic warned, "He's a confirmed COVID case."

No! I'm not, I wanted to scream. But I didn't dare. The inferno of pain in my chest was burning too strongly.

"Can you tell me your name?" the female medic asked me.

I closed my eyes.

"Vincent," answered Mountie 019, as if he was reading from a notepad. "His name is Vincent McKnight. Age twenty-four."

"Oh," she replied. "Is he the one we saw on—"

"Yes, ma'am." He didn't sound happy about it.

"Is he... *the moose?*"

"That's the other guy, I think."

No, I'm the turtle and my shell is broken.

As they hoisted me up into the helicopter I screamed—the pain moving into the realm of sheer agony. Without a pause, they slid my cot headfirst into the warm chopper like a coffin into a funeral truck.

Mountie 019 buckled up in the seat beside me, all the while watching me intently. His gaze wasn't one of a guard watching his prisoner. Instead, his eyes looked confused and bewildered as if asking, *how did a kid like you end up in such a mess?*

The answer, of course, involved a woman.

At twenty-eight some would say she was just a girl. And she would say that such juvenile labels were part of the grand plan to keep adults behaving like easy-to-manipulate children. She was certainly not a child. And in as little as six months, between her and this so-called pandemic, I had been forced to grow up real fast.

PART ONE
To Be or Not to Be a Turtle

"Love makes your soul crawl out from its hiding place."
—*Zora Neale Hurston (1891–1960)*
American author and anthropologist

1. No Face, No Service

Friday, July 3, 2020, Moosehead, Ontario, Canada...

Hands on hips, she stood behind the counter glaring at me. "No face, no service."

"*What?*" I blurted, as the door swung closed behind me, jingling a bell. "You mean: No *mask*, no service—right?"

"No *face*, no service," she repeated. "This is a bakery, not a bank."

The overwhelming smell of fresh sourdough penetrated the polyester fabric stretched over my nose, mouth and chin. I took a few slow steps toward the counter which separated us, shaking my head in non-understanding.

"A bank?" I replied. "What're you talking about?"

The twenty-something girl, with bright blonde hair, raised a hand mirror from the countertop and aimed it at me.

"You look like a bank robber." She spoke with the slightest hint of a Germanic accent.

The mirror reflected my brown eyes peering over a bright green face covering. In a mask-muffled voice I replied, "I think I look more like a turtle than a robber."

"Well, you're acting like a turtle, hiding behind a green shell."

She lowered the mirror and rested her unmasked chin on her knuckles, elbows propped up on the countertop. Underneath, rows of dark crusted bread, sprinkled with rolled oats, lined the display.

"Do you always keep a mirror so handy?" I asked.

"Ever since people started auditioning for the bubonic plague."

"Well, if you haven't noticed," I said, gesturing to either side of me, "we *are* in the middle of a pandemic."

Her head turned slightly right and left, looking to either side of me.

"I don't see any bodies piling up," she replied. "All I've seen this year is a regular cold and flu season. And we'd be over it by now if turtles like you weren't so scared of catching the sniffles."

I felt oddly irritated (though at the same time attracted) by this blonde lioness. She also wore green, but not a mask. Her short-sleeved dress fit so well around her trim body I suspected she must have made it herself. The leafy green garment topped by her blonde hair reminded me of a...

"Hey, if this green mask makes me a turtle," I jested, "then I'd say you look like a dandelion."

"Suits me." She removed her elbows from the counter and stood tall. "Dandelions aren't afraid to be in the open air."

"Yeah, well, plants can't catch COVID."

"No. Just really sick and old people."

"Uh-huh," I said.

I felt like calling her a covidiot but she was way too pretty: Big, blue and unblinking eyes dominated a lightly tanned face. Her pursed lips—it appeared as if she was restraining them from making further comment—had no lipstick. Her impractically long hair was held back by a braided portion that wrapped around her forehead like a golden diadem, reminding me of some medieval damsel—except this damsel was not in distress.

"COVID's hitting more than just old folks," I said. "Hundreds of thousands have died. Don't you watch the news?"

She sighed. "Hundreds of thousands? Do you know how many people die each year from the old-fashioned flu?"

I hadn't a clue. And even though half my face was covered, I'm sure my eyes betrayed my ignorance. Avoiding her question, I asked my own, "If you can't trust the World Health Organization, then who can you trust?"

"How about evidence-based science?"

"Uh, I think scientists work at the WHO."

She walked out around the counter, revealing the rest of her green dress, draping all the way down to her brown sandals, barely allowing me a glimpse of her ankles. Those sandals stepped toward me, coming dangerously close to breaching my COVID bubble. Instinctively, I backed away.

"I said evidence-based science," she persisted, "not the words of scientists bribed, blackmailed and bamboozled into propagating mass hysteria. Because if you look at the facts, eight thousand Canadians died from the flu in 2018. Every year, on average, about 650,000 around the world die with the flu. Nothing has changed. Our government is lying to us."

"You're one of those... conspiracy theorists, aren't you?"

"Ha!" she laughed. "Flattery will get you nowhere."

"All I want is some bread."

"Well, as they say in Italy: 'Niente sorriso, niente pane.'" Her Italian accent was rather convincing. She made another step closer. "No smile, no bread. *Capito?*"

I stepped backwards again, hitting the door, jingling the bell. She was about half a foot shorter than me, but nonetheless intimidating.

"I really doubt they say that in Italy," I muttered.

"Probably not," she admitted, swaying side to side for a second.

"And most stores won't even let me inside without a mask."

"Forcing medical treatment on people is against the Nuremberg Code," she said, taking another step closer. "I'm surprised a big, strong guy like you would put up with that kind of abuse."

I felt like prey. Part of me wanted to run, to open the door and never come back. I'd tell Grandad I couldn't get him the bread he wanted because the place was run by a COVID denier. But I knew he'd just laugh at me. He'd already warned me that the baker was a "real hoot."

"But masks save lives," I protested.

The Dandelion looked me straight in the eyes. "And how do you know that?"

"The sc-science..." I stuttered.

"You've actually looked at a scientific study?"

"Uh, no..."

"Well, I have. Fourteen of them, actually. Every randomized controlled trial ever conducted on *human beings*—not mice or mannequins—shows that masks don't stop people from getting sick or dying from the flu."

"Ah!" I said, raising a finger, "but COVID's far worse than the flu."

She slid even closer, leaving barely six inches between our noses. "All right, Mr. Science, if a mask can't even stop the humble flu, how's it going to hinder your killer coronavirus?"

I reached my hand up to adjust my mask; but then pulled it away, remembering we aren't supposed to touch them.

"Masks do work," I said firmly. "I don't know which

conspiracy website you get your information from, but—"

"*The Journal of Infectious Diseases,*" she interrupted. "In March, the CDC reviewed every study ever conducted on masks and found... they did nothing."

"Well..." I said, drawing out the word, "nothing wrong with a placebo. Stops people from freaking out."

"Freaking out over the common cold?"

"It's *not* a cold," I insisted, taking a deep and tense breath. "You think you know better than the experts?"

"Experts like Professor Ioannidis?" she asked.

I didn't respond.

"You do know who Professor John Ioannidis is, don't you?"

I sighed the sound of prey that had tired of the chase, ready to suffer its demise.

"Professor Ioannidis. One of the world's leading epidemiologists. Stanford University. He says the SARS-CoV-2 death rate is in the ballpark of the regular flu season."

"All right! All right!" I held up my hands. "Grandad's waiting for his bread."

Her face softened and she took a step back. "Who's your grandad?"

"The old Indian with the long white hair," I said, happy to change the subject.

"You mean Paul, the Anishinaabe Elder?"

"Yeah," I said, taken aback by her familiarity. "Though, he's more specifically Ojibwe."

"Dokis band?"

"Uh-huh," I said with a nod, though I truly could not remember which band he belonged to. "To me he's just Grandad."

That made her smile. "Can I call him Grandad, too?"

I paused, stumped on how to respond. "He'd probably be okay with that."

"You don't have him in quarantine, do you?"

"Kicking and screaming."

"Shame on you, Turtle!" She waved her index finger. "That's why I haven't seen him since March. Under house arrest."

"He's at the nursing home, actually. We're just keeping him safe."

"He's as healthy as a horse," she said.

"He's eighty-seven."

"That proves it."

"Anyway, now that the lockdown's lifted, I was actually heading over there today—as soon as you sell me some bread, that is. I have an appointment"—I pulled out my cellphone and glanced at the time, 10:38 a.m.—"in thirty minutes. He told me he really misses your bread. So, I thought—"

"If his jail sentence is over, why doesn't he come and get his own bread like he used to? I'd love to see Grandad again."

"Well, it's not safe enough yet," I sighed, feeling a heaviness in my upper chest. "They're only allowing them on the front lawn to meet with family."

She rubbed her face with both hands, as if trying to hide from the world for a moment. "Four months locked in his room," she said through cupped hands. "It's inhuman."

"He says it's not been too bad." Not that I believed him. "He reads a lot. Memorizes Shakespeare. He's a bit of a loner."

"So am I," she said. "But four months of isolation sounds unbearable."

"They are just trying to take care of him."

She began twisting a strand of her hair tightly around her forefinger. "Oh, yeah, sure. If they call it *caring* then it must be okay. *Abusing* people is the new *helping* people."

She's nuts, I thought.

"That's not really what's going on."

It can't be.

She stared silently back at me. She didn't appear to be breathing. And neither was I.

When I could hold my breath no longer, I inhaled deeply and demanded, "Are you going to give me some bread?"

"Are you going to lose the facial inhibitor?"

I pulled on the top of the green cloth and let the spandex snap back into place. "Hey, my mom made me this mask."

Her blue eyes rolled up and to the left. "She also made your face."

"Oh, for Christ's sake!" I said, putting my hand to my forehead. "Do you have to be so difficult?"

"Do you have to wear a face diaper?"

More silence.

I needed her bread. But she didn't seem too concerned about getting my money. She obviously placed her protests above profits. I could've left. Called it a draw.

No, I thought. *All Grandad wanted was a loaf of her sourdough.*

I was running out of time. If I was going to be defeated, I decided, I couldn't let her win without some small victory on my side. Looking her in the eye, heart suddenly pounding, I said:

"I'll take off the mask on *one* condition."

She took a big step back, crossed her arms and said, "What's the condition?"

2. I Think I Hear My Pig Whistling

The Dandelion couldn't tell, but I was gritting my teeth and pursing my lips under the green mask. I wasn't usually this cocky or daring. But, as I said, I was feeling desperate to regain some stature—if not intellectually, then...

"I'll take off the mask," I began, holding up my thumb and forefinger, "if you promise to... give me a kiss."

Her eyes went wide, her face flushed.

"It doesn't have to be a French..." I added.

She spun around, her dress flailing out.

"A German kiss would do fine."

"Humph!" she snorted.

"Or Italian..."

"I don't kiss turtles!" she said.

Her voice almost shrilled with a mix of indignation and bashfulness. She stomped back behind the counter, turned sharply and faced me again.

At last, I had captured some ground. The Dandelion had retreated.

"I thought you believed in freedom," I said, taking a step toward her.

"What? Freedom to kiss whoever you want?"

"No," I replied calmly. "But if you want to be free to not wear a mask, shouldn't I be free to wear one?"

"But you're not free," she said. "You're brainwashed."

"I'm just trying to protect others."

"Then protect them from brainwashing. Even the Ontario Ministry of Health admits..."

Reaching under the cash register, she pulled out a small stack of stapled sheets and smacked them down on the counter. The cover page was headed with "Public Health Ontario" and "Santé publique Ontario" in green and white letters, followed by the title *COVID-19 – What We Know So Far About Wearing Masks in Public*. On the same page she had highlighted in yellow marker:

> Existing evidence demonstrates that wearing a mask within households after an illness begins is not effective at preventing secondary respiratory infections.

"Yeah." I shrugged. "We all know that. Masks aren't to protect the wearer. We are wearing them to protect those around us."

"Hmm," she said as she cast her eyes down.

"*Capito?*" I added, feeling confident that I was now regaining intellectual ground.

"Actually," she almost whispered, pointing to the report, "that's what it means by 'secondary infection.' When they tested having sick persons wear a mask it didn't reduce how often other 'secondary' members of the same household got sick."

Boy, she's one of those dandelions you could run over with a lawnmower and its head would just pop back up. "Well, that just means we haven't proven that they work." I crossed my arms. "Masks still might help. I mean, what's the harm, really?"

She closed her eyes. Was she praying for patience? Gently, she said, "They collect and breed bacteria that cause pneumonia and lung cancer. Dentists are saying they lead to tooth decay. And impetigo, the skin disease they cause, can lead to kidney failure."

I groaned softly.

"And they create an environment of fear," she went on. "Worse, they just don't cover your face, they also cover politicians' butts—making people think we are in a pandemic that never existed."

"All right, you win," I said, raising my hands in surrender. I may not have been well read, but I was a reasonable guy.

Returning to my previous and more successful (albeit somewhat pathetic) defense, I said, "Still, if you want a free country, then it's wrong to deny me bread just because I'm acting like a brainwashed sheep."

She stared back.

"Wouldn't you agree?"

I could hear a wall clock tick off ten seconds.

"*Fine!*" she finally blurted back with a grimace. "You're free to wear a face diaper if you want."

She stomped over to the front window and peeled away a sign which had been facing out toward the street. She held it up for me.

"'No Face, No Service,'" I read, scratching my head. "I could have sworn it said 'No Mask, No Service.'" I looked back at the window, but the only other sign was a HELP WANTED sign.

She tore her "No Face, No Service" sign through the middle and handed it over. "I'll write a new sign this evening. A better sign."

It felt like I had been handed a trophy. I folded the two halves and slipped them into my pocket.

Cocking my head to the side, while looking straight into her blue eyes, I asked: "Why are you so into freedom?"

She threw up her hands and retreated back behind the counter, while exclaiming, "Ich glaub, mein Schwein pfeift."

"Uhh... translation, please?" I suspected she had just sworn at me.

She spun around and said clearly: "I think my pig is whistling."

I nodded slowly. "Your *pig*?"

"It means I can't believe what I'm hearing."

"You're crazy."

"It would seem so."

She reached up to a wooden shelf built into the wall behind the counter. Most of the shelves were lined with jars full of jams and other spreads, but one ledge was filled with books. She pulled out a small brown hardcover.

"Why am I so into freedom?" she repeated. "Yeah! There must be something wrong with me! Voluntary servitude is so much more convenient."

She dropped the book on the countertop. The imageless cover contained the title *Discours de la Servitude Volontaire*, along with the author's name, Étienne de la Boétie.

"You read French, too?" I asked.

"*Oui, oui,*" she said. "*Et toi?*"

I shook my head.

"I'll translate." She picked up the book, flipped through the pages and then began translating:

> It is incredible how as soon as people become governed, they promptly fall into such complete forgetfulness of their freedom. So much so, that they can hardly be roused to the point of regaining it. They obey so easily and willingly that one might say that people have not so much lost their liberty as won their enslavement.

"We are hardly enslaved," I countered.

Switching to a heavy German accent, she began to shout, with all the gentleness of a drill sergeant suffering a toothache: "Stand on that dot! Six feet apart! Sanitize your hands! Don't let your kids go to the park! Mask your dog! Close your business! Stay home! Watch Netflix!"

I pursed my lips. I had been up till 1 a.m. the night before, binge-watching all three of the extended versions of the *Lord of the Rings* movies, back-to-back. At the time, I'd felt it was a commendable accomplishment. Sort of like I'd run a marathon without getting off the couch.

"You know what happens when you let government control us?" she asked.

"Civilization?"

She stared at me sternly. "My grandfather spent three years in a 'civilized' Soviet prison camp."

"Oh." I paused. "I thought you were German."

"I'm Canadian, actually," she said. "Born in Sudbury. My parents are German."

"And your grandfather was Russian?"

"No," she said. "He was captured by the Russians and sent to Siberia."

"Oh," I said again. "I can't imagine."

"Well, I can. And I think I can also imagine what tyranny

looks like." She picked up the hand mirror and aimed it back at me. "It looks like this."

I swallowed hard, suddenly finding it difficult to breathe. I stared back at my muzzled reflection—the green mask no longer a symbol of compassion.

"Do you truly believe that spit collector is saving anybody's life?" she asked.

Grandad always told me to be humble enough to admit when one was wrong; otherwise, you look like a fool. And in that looking glass, I sure looked like one. I reached up and pulled the straps away from my ears. I almost felt self-conscious revealing my mouth and nose to her, as if I was undressing.

In the mirror I saw my clean-shaven face. Irish genes from my mom's side of the family dominated over my Indigenous chromosomes. While I did possess dark black hair like my father, it was of a rather unruly variety. Left to grow long, it would make me look not like a brave Ojibwe warrior; but rather a bushy-haired, grunting caveman in some National Geographic documentary. So I tried to keep it short, like Martin Sensmeier in *The Magnificent Seven* (sans the mohawk). Nonetheless, after four months of lockdown, it was bordering on the barbarian.

"Doesn't that feel better?" the Dandelion asked.

That's when I noticed she was smiling at me from beside the mirror. Instinctively, the edges of my naked lips rose upward. A simple facial exchange I hadn't experienced with anyone in the previous four months of self-isolation and public masking (except possibly with my parents, who rarely smiled anymore). Smiling at people... it felt, well, normal. And kind of nice.

Maybe she's really not all that crazy after all.

But then she glanced at my reflection in the looking glass and began to... *sing*:

Nun schüttelt ab der Träume Flor
Und hebt euch frisch und frei empor
In Gottes hellen Morgen.

Okay, maybe she's a little bonkers.
"German?" I asked.
"*Ja*," she said with a nod.
"Translation, please?"

She cleared her throat and spoke in English:

Now shake off the veil of dreams
And lift yourselves fresh and free
In God's bright morning.

"Hmm," I said, looking at the limp green mini-veil in my hand. "Well, I guess this means you can't call me a turtle anymore."

"We'll see about that," she said and set the mirror back down. "But you certainly don't look like a thief anymore—which means it's safe to sell you some bread."

"What about that kiss?"

She shook her head and muttered, "Ich glaub, mein Schwein pfeift."

That darn pig of hers was whistling again.

"That's okay," I said, "you'd probably give me COVID."

Though, I must admit, I would have been willing to risk it.

A few minutes later, my black running shoes (with their now conspicuous green laces) were stepping back out onto the north side of Main Street. The bell jingled happily as I pulled the yellow wooden door shut behind me.

Before leaving she had made me promise not to be a turtle anymore. It was a promise I didn't keep for long.

3. My Naked Face

Standing on the sidewalk, I rotated my head, scanning the downtown strip. Face masks to the left. Face masks to the right. Face masks in front and... but not behind. Behind me was her Moosehead Artisan Bakery—the only place, among the town's forty-odd shops—to allow unprotected mouths and noses to come and go at will.

On both sides of Main Street, all I could see were turtles—at least twelve feet apart, marching single-file. I didn't see any green turtles like me, but plenty of blue and white ones—neighbours hidden behind 3M medical masks, making our rural town look about as friendly as a decontamination zone after a nuclear reactor meltdown.

One man, however, had refused to cave completely to the

institutional trend. Closing in on me was old Mr. Cooper. Instead of a medical mask, he sported a bright red bandanna. Between the oversized face covering, his crooked grey fedora, black wraparound sunglasses, a grey overcoat and matching dress pants, only his hands and a sliver of his neck revealed his light brown skin. I would not have known it was him at all, save for his trademark red bow tie, which perfectly matched his red bandanna.

My shoulders tensed like a block of ice had been pressed against them. Despite Mr. Cooper's shades, and his unorthodox face covering, I sensed an icy stare aimed at my naked face. Exiting a store without a face covering suddenly carried all the shame of fleeing a bank with a sackful of hundred dollar bills and wearing nothing but a pair of boxer shorts.

A young mother, with short, pink hair and a nose ring, dressed in torn jeans and a pink tank top, was pushing a carriage from the opposite direction. Her head bobbed to music flowing through earbuds. I gratefully noted she was not masked. Inside the stroller, however, a small child, maybe two years old, with curly blonde hair, wore a polka-dot mask.

The baby girl stared at me with wide, unblinking eyes. *Why do I have to wear this and not you?* her wordless gaze seemed to say.

And then there was Blake Chung, sweltering in his black bylaw uniform. Yellow patches on either arm gave him the aura of a cop. In reality, he was the younger brother of Quan Chung, who ran the Chinese restaurant and taught kung fu. Bylaw Blake, as we liked to call him, stood across the two-lane street, staring at a parking meter. His black mask matched his uniform and dark hair. And the stare he aimed at me with his almond shaped eyes felt just as dark, despite his white skin. He shook his head slightly, as he might when noting a parking meter twenty minutes expired.

My crime of nonconformity was undeniable. I had just walked out of a store with my face naked for all Moosehead to see. The atrocity of not protecting others from my lethal exhalations was being reflected back at me from two dozen scornful eyes.

My heart rate was increasing. My head drooped slightly. And

my arms crossed my chest.

Lanky Mr. Cooper was approaching at a surprising speed for a man in his eighties. His cane swung loosely at his side. It was as if some passion had arisen in him, giving him such strength that he no longer needed the cane's support.

Bylaw Blake, bent over his ticket book, scribbled madly. Was he writing my name down, followed by a dollar symbol and a three-figure fine?

I glanced back at the renegade bakery. That distracting Dandelion was no longer behind the counter, having retreated to her insulated bake room where she was likely baking up more far-fetched conspiracy theories.

With each step, Mr. Cooper appeared to swing his cane even higher. Was he building momentum to inflict corporal punishment?

Bylaw Blake was now tearing out the ticket from his black book.

And the woman with the muzzled infant veered the carriage onto the road in the path of an approaching Toyota Supra. Instead of honking, the 1,800 kilogram vehicle slowed in seeming understanding of her urgent need to bypass this anti-masker.

Slowly, I pulled my mask out of the back pocket of my jeans.

Maybe, I speculated, *if I just wore it around my chin, people would be happy.*

Looping it around my ears, I let it rest between the juncture of my jawbone and neck. It felt like a green snake tightening itself around my windpipe—threatening asphyxiation if I did not embrace its suffocating skin over my mouth and nose. Pulling at the reptilian mask, I stretched it out as far as the elastic would allow, seeking relief from its tightening grip on my air passage. And then, without thinking, I pulled the fabric up and over my airways. At least, I assume I did. For, suddenly, I was masked. *Had it slithered up there itself?*

The tension in my shoulders melted.

Somehow, bizarrely, I now felt like I could breathe.

Mr. Cooper's cane no longer swung madly at his side, but now rested on the ground, supporting his full weight, as he hobbled past me with a nonchalant, "Good morning, lad."

I nodded, feeling unworthy to respond.

Across the street, Bylaw Blake stuck the ticket he had been writing under the window wiper of a car. Slouching slightly, he turned toward the next meter, wiping his sweaty forehead.

Quickly I turned, heading west along Main Street, in the direction from which Mr. Cooper had come. Magically, the anxiety that had hit me hotter than the approaching noonday sun had vanished. The shade of the mask offered relief from the harsh rays of social pressure. I now felt welcome by my fellow turtles to merge in their stream of conformity.

As I walked, my mind sought to reconcile the out-of-touch world behind the walls of the Dandelion's bakery with the stark reality that surrounded me.

The lockdown had been lifted. But had we merely been let out of our domestic cells and forced to carry the world's thinnest ball and chain? A textile branding of our face, reminding us of the grave original sin we had all committed—the sin of being a hazardous human being, spreading disease and germs and carbon dioxide with each exhalation.

Upon reaching the vacant market square, I made a left onto Queen Street, passing more masked ex-convicts. Were we all on parole after four months of lockdown? We could roam about if we promised to stand, masked, six feet apart and never shake hands—hands which must be sanitized with the regularity of TV commercial breaks. There were other rules too—always changing, but always there. And if we managed to obey them well enough, maybe, just maybe, we wouldn't be herded back into our domestic cages, come winter.

Up ahead, I could see the Louis Riel Bridge crossing over the French River. Made of stone, the bridge featured ornate moose heads carved into both ends of its two flanking walls. It offered passage to the north side of town, where Grandad was waiting.

I hadn't seen my only surviving grandfather since February. He had been counted among the vulnerable and, without consent, forcefully protected within the claustrophobic walls of Moosehead's only nursing home.

Protected from people like me.

Stepping onto the bridge, I noted the black-and-white sign, protected under plexiglass, that Bylaw Blake had screwed into the masonry. It warned how only one person should cross the walkway at a time. Before the pandemic, I had walked, biked, and run over this bridge almost every single day since I was twelve.

And now, finally I was doing it again.

Visiting the man who taught me to skate, to fish, to enjoy reading, and to laugh when things got tough—seeing Grandad was never a chore. He was the one connection I had to the stories, beliefs and ways of my Ojibwe ancestors—a vague and distant heritage I only glimpsed through his presence. The Ojibwe were the second largest group of Indigenous people in the world. But most people can't even pronounce Ojibwe properly—me included.

Reaching the centre of the bridge, I stopped, staring over its edge at the rushing waters flowing south to Georgian Bay, on Lake Huron.

I felt my mask. Maybe these thin pieces of fabric are no more effective at preventing infection than Twitter is at preventing illiteracy. Still, the mask allows people to feel safe. Especially after months of CBC and CNN cycling images of ICUs, body bags and mass graves.

I scuffed my shoes on the bridge, mentally leaving behind the conspiratorial crap of that crazy Dandelion.

Grandad was waiting for me. I could see the green shingled rooftop of the nursing home in the distance on my left. To my right, up a hill, overlooking Brian Peckford Park, stood St. Jerome's Church. From its bell tower, the ding-dong of eleven o'clock resounded.

I was late.

I pulled up my green mask, which had sunk down to the tip of my nose, and broke out in a run, with the crusty loaf of sourdough tucked under my arm.

Things would be normal again, I lied to myself.

4. Ants in the Bathroom

Before the nursing home, Grandad and Grandma had retired to a cabin by Nepahwin Lake. They had the woods, the canoe, the wild animals, each other... and me, their only grandson, every weekend.

But then Grandma died. She died quickly, in her sleep, in the cabin, in the dark. They said it was a brain aneurysm. They said she didn't suffer. I don't know how they would know if she suffered or not.

And a few weeks after her funeral, a neighbour found Grandad unconscious on the floor of the cabin.

I was only twelve when it happened. Most of my youth is a blur. But that night, in 2008, when my parents told me what happened to Grandad, is one of those moments a little boy does not forget.

"Bless us, oh Lord and these thy gifts," I quickly prayed, as we had sat around our dining room table, "which we are about to receive from thy bounty, through Christ, Our Lord. Amen."

Mom and Dad added their own amens.

This was back when Dad was still thin and had only a few grey streaks in his pitch-black hair. In contrast, Mom had the reddest hair in Moosehead, and, while not fat, her face looked chubby compared to Dad's chiseled Indigenous features.

I'd just gotten back from hockey practice with a growling stomach. I reached unceremoniously for the bowl of potatoes, but Mom gently rested her hand on my wrist.

"Vincent, dear," she said.

I withdrew my hand and looked at her, my mouth agape.

"Grandad," she said slowly, "he had an accident today."

"*What?*" I had suddenly lost any interest in the mashed tubers. "Is he okay?"

"Yes." She nodded. "He's at Sudbury General." I must have looked confused because she added, "It's a hospital in the city."

"I know," I said. "But why is he there?"

"His blood sugar crashed," said Dad as he pierced two slices of roast beef and transported them to his plate. "Again."

"Why did it... crash?" I said, gripping the sides of my chair.

"He must have taken too much medication," replied Mom.

"But wh-what are we going to do?" I blurted. "I was going there with Mathéo."

"Not this Friday," said Dad. "Probably not any Friday." He took a deep breath, as Mom gave him a scolding glance. "Time for a retirement home." He began scooping potatoes onto his plate. "He can't live alone any longer." He passed the bowl of potatoes to Mom.

"Grandad can live with us, then," I said.

Our oak dining table had four chairs. Why couldn't Grandad have the fourth?

Dad grunted and starting spearing peas with the tip of his fork. He shot a glance over at my red-headed mother. She deflected the glance downward to my plate, as she filled it with peas and meat.

"Well," he began again. "Grandad's diabetic. We wouldn't be able to take care of him."

"But Grandma was able to take care of him."

Dad scratched the stubble on the side of his face. "Yeah, Ma was amazing." He picked up his knife and began cutting at a piece of beef. It sounded like he was sawing through the plate.

"I can help him." I smiled and imitated priming a lancet. "Mathéo's aunt showed me how to prick her finger and check her blood sugar with this little computer."

Without looking up at me, Dad asked, "Where would your grandad stay? This ain't a big house. Only two bedrooms."

"He could stay in the basement."

"It's just cement and cobwebs down there. It would take way too much work to renovate."

"I could help you," I said.

"I'm sure you could," said Dad. "But it's really... it's too expensive." He nodded toward my now full plate. "Eat up! It'll get cold."

I diverted my gaze downward, spying two peas that had rolled to the other side of my plate and were trapped behind a mound of potatoes.

"I know!" I said. "Grandad could share my room. We could get a bunk bed."

Dad chuckled, shoved the thoroughly severed piece of meat into his mouth and talked while chewing: "Dat's nice of ya, Vince." He swallowed. "But, you know your grandad lives differently than us. He's old and he's Indian."

"But aren't we Indians, too? I mean you and me. Not Mom."

Gazing at my arms, and Mom and Dad's face, I could see the difference. My father was darkest, I was a light brown, while my red-headed mother was as white as the napkin Dad was now wiping his mouth with.

"We're métis, aren't we?" I continued. "That's what Ms. Pace told Léo and me. It's French for 'mixed.'"

Dad snickered. "Everyone's genes are a little mixed up," he said. "But when it comes down to it, son, we can't be both Canucks and Indians."

I nodded rigidly and shovelled some potato into my mouth. After a few minutes of listening to our utensils clatter, Mom picked up the serving bowl of peas and asked if I would like some more.

I just stared at the bowl and said, "Mathéo says his Aunt Sofia hates the food at the ol' folks home. It's always cold. And there are ants in the bathroom."

"Ants, eh?" Dad mumbled. "I hadn't heard that myself." He shrugged. "Good source of protein, ants." He returned to sawing another slice of beef. "Eat up!"

My hand, still grasping my fork, began to shake. Mom reached across the table and held it.

"Maybe we can build him a wigwam in the backyard?" I suggested. "Grandad showed me how. You need birch, and, uh, juniper and..." I paused, trying to remember. "And willow."

"Oh, yeah!" Dad bent slightly forward with an anxiety-ridden guffaw. "The neighbours are just going to love that. Maybe we can tile it with reindeer hides and have a pow-wow."

I hadn't meant it as a joke, but I smiled, knowing I made Dad laugh.

"Maybe a rain dance, too," I added.

"Vince!" said Mom sharply, "We don't worship spirits."

"I thought we worshiped the Holy Spirit?"

"Yes," Mom said, with pursed lips. "*The* Holy Spirit, not *any* spirit."

"Not the spirit of rain, wind or..." Dad hesitated. "Or wolves!" Then he howled, tilting his head back. I giggled.

"Richard!"

Mom's body jerked, suggesting she was kicking Dad in the shins. His howling suddenly became a whimper.

"Vince," said Mom gently, "your father has worked really hard to fit in." Then eyeballing him with a frown, she added, "Even if he still has a ways to go."

Dad winked at me.

"We need to think of his job," continued Mom. "I know it's not right, but some people here don't take well to Indigenous people. I don't think it would be safe for any of us if Grandad—with the way he wears his hair and talks—was living here."

"Why would it be unsafe?" I asked.

"Well," she replied, "maybe unsafe isn't the right word."

"After all," cut in Dad, "this is Moosehead, not Thunder Bay."

"Thunder Bay?" I questioned.

"Yes, dear," said Mom. "It's a city on the—"

"On the north shore of Lake Superior," I completed her sentence. "Ms. Pace showed it to us on the map." I looked at Dad. "What do you mean Moosehead isn't Thunder Bay?"

Dad sighed. "Well, Thunder Bay, people call it the hate crime capital of Canada." He forked another slice of roast beef off the platter and onto his plate.

"Who do they hate?"

"Indians."

"Why do they hate Indians?"

"I don't know. I just know that there are some people, even in Moosehead, who won't treat you so well if they knew you were even a little Ojibwe."

I felt my body begin to tremble.

"That's not fair," I said, feeling a little nervous.

"Life's not fair," said Dad. "One out of four people murdered in Canada are natives."

"Richard!" Mom gave Dad a murderous look of her own.

"Hey!" said Dad, raising his hands out to the side, "he needs to know it's just safer and better if we try to look and act like everyone else."

I put my hand to my face, feeling my features.

"Don't worry," Dad replied. "You look more like John Wayne than Crazy Horse. Just don't rock the boat, son, and nobody will toss you overboard."

"Which is why," said Mom, her voice trembling, "I really think your grandad will feel more comfortable in the retirement home. There are a few of his people there. Like Mr. Cooper."

"Mr. Cooper's Indian?" I said in surprise. "But Mr. Cooper always wears a big red bow tie to church."

"Anyone can wear a bow tie, dear," said Mom.

"And he calls Indians pagans," I added.

"Well, pagan just means they aren't Catholic," said Mom, putting her hand to her heart.

"Yeah," said Dad, still smiling a bit. "A pagan isn't bad. They're just... different. They worship wolves and totem poles and dead ancestors. Not crucifixes and saints and doves."

"We do *not* worship doves," said Mom, tilting her head to the side.

"Matthew chapter three, verse sixteen."

"I'll look it up later," replied Mom, followed by a barely audible rumble in the back of her throat.

She moved some beef to her plate, while Dad was mashing his few remaining peas into his last lump of potato.

"But Grandad's not a pagan, is he, Mom?" I stated. "He's Catholic like us. He went to that school—"

Dad grunted and dropped his napkin on his plate. "Vince, you know we don't talk about those schools."

The howling humour had left his voice. He stood up, walked to the china cabinet and took out a long slender bottle. Expertly wielding a corkscrew, he stripped the foil, twisted the worm into place and pulled out the cork in under five seconds. Filling two wine glasses, he handed one to Mom, raised his own and said, "To the health and long life of Vince's grandad."

Mom took a sip and looked at me with shaky eyes. "He'll be fine, Vince. It's a good home."

"Can he come over for dinner on Friday?" I asked.

Dad sat back down.

"We'll see," he said.

5. Bloody Vegan Butter

And we did see, I reflected, as I waited out front of the nursing home. The only time my parents ever had Grandad over was for Christmas Day.

And every summer, Mathéo and I would kill the ants in his bathroom at the nursing home.

And every Sunday, he'd take me to the Green Dragon, next to the train tracks. Mr. Chung's all-you-can-eat buffet was the one restaurant in our two-streetlight town where he felt welcome. Not that we had many restaurants.

Grandad always ordered rice and mushrooms. I once asked him why. He told me how, when he was a boy, he always liked collecting wild rice from the river and foraging for mushrooms.

In the end, anything was better than the frozen dinners at the old folks home. Breakfast was even worse, which is why he had taken to buying bread at that bakery.

I looked down at the bag of sourdough resting on my lap. I wish I had asked Grandad earlier—I could have brought him loaves all through the lockdown. But I hadn't known until our last phone call. Pulling out my phone, I looked at the time.

11:15 a.m. I shifted my bum. The thin lawn chair wobbled beneath me. I had been sitting on that piece of molded plastic for ten minutes. I'd been late, but Grandad was even later.

Above, a canopy protected me from the harsh rays of a cloudless summer sky. Long grass curled over my running shoes. A few metres ahead stood a squat, plastic, black-and-white sign that read Moosehead Long Term Care Home. Behind it stretched the two-storey, red-bricked building with a turret on its left.

Another makeshift shelter, about twenty feet away, shaded an elderly resident chatting with a middle-aged woman. I didn't recognize either of them, but with the masks it was always hard to know.

I stared up at the second floor windows. Grandad's was the seventh from the right—his room for the last ten years. And it had become his cell for the last four months. At least, that's how that conspiratorial baker with the pretty blue eyes would put it.

"I used to go to that baker on the big road and buy a loaf of her bread," he had told me. "It's much better than the toast here. I asked the principal to get better toast once, but he got angry with me."

Principal? I knew he meant the manager of the senior's home. Grandad had long been showing shadows of dementia, but with each phone call over lockdown, the shadows had started to take more solid form.

"The baker also sells this butter," said Grandad. "It's made out of nuts. I wash my hair with it."

"*You what?*"

He chuckled. "I mean to say that I wash the bread with it."

Remembering the conversation, I slapped my head. With all her nutty COVID conspiracy theories I'd forgotten to get the almond butter.

"It's much *butter* than margarine," Grandad had said on the phone. Again, a vocab slip or a joke? I had assumed the latter and laughed.

But now, sitting under the canopy with only a loaf of bread to offer my elder, I wasn't laughing. I'd have to go back to the Anti-Masking Queen to get a jar of her bloody vegan butter and another dose of COVID conspiracy theories. Not that her far-flung thoughts about a fraudulent pandemic intimidated me as much as her lion-like demeanour, blue eyes and naked lips. Why was I so attracted to her smile? I'd obviously been staring at masked faces for far too long.

I looked over at the old folks home. *Where was Grandad?* I pulled out my phone again: 11:25 a.m. I had an 11 a.m. appointment. I was about to try calling him when the front door slowly opened by itself. Grandad's knees, calves and blue running shoes appeared through the passageway, followed by the rest of him.

He was sitting in a wheelchair.

Last time I'd seen him, back in March, he was walking up those steps after a Sunday dinner at the Green Dragon. Now, now...

Grandad in a wheelchair?

6. Nazi Nurse

There he was. My grandad. Four months had passed since last we were face to face, even though he lived just across the river, a ten minutes' walk away. Never would we have thought that the Ministry of Long-Term Care would decide solitary confinement was the best way to care for seniors.

He seemed thinner, his shoulders jutting out of his red plaid shirt. The skin of his face—protruding from sunken eye sockets—looked as stretched as the black mask pulled around his ears.

Claudia, a short, chubby Latino nurse, wheeled him forward onto the landing. He looked directly at me and raised his hands.

"Don't shoot!" he shouted.

My head shot around but I saw no gunman.

"You look like a train robber," Grandad called out.

He laughed as his hands came back down slapping his knees. Claudia shook her head and began rolling him down the ramp.

"Ha!" I laughed, standing up. "A train robber! Well, I've already been called a bank robber, today."

"Good to keep your options open," said Grandad. He tugged at his own mask. "Maybe we can partner up? I'm ready for some adventure."

I smiled a muzzled smile. "With the way the job market's going, it may be our only option."

"As long as we don't run into Zorro," said Grandad.

Grandad had read me all the Zorro novels when I was little.

"Zorro might side with us," I said. "After all, he wears a mask, too."

Claudia brought the wheelchair to a halt under the wide canopy. I wanted to run to him, shake his hand, give him a hug. Instead, I remained seated six feet away from where Claudia had parked him.

"Grandad, you've never even used a walker." I outstretched my hands. "What's with the wheelchair? You sprain your ankle?"

"Oh," he said slowly, looking for words. "I was walking but..."

Claudia cut in, "It was taking too long for him to get to the elevator. You wanted him to be any later?"

"What?" I said. "He had the whole morning to walk to the elevator."

"We can't have residents in the hallway too long," she replied, as she stuffed a stray black hair into her tight ponytail.

"But what's happened to him?"

She sighed. "It's a little room. Not much space for exercise. But now that lockdown's lifting, he'll get his sea legs back."

"I could have walked here," said Grandad with a quiver of his head. "She's as impatient as a jackrabbit."

"Just trying to keep you safe, Paul." Claudia patted the air above his left shoulder with her gloved hand. "Okay!" She looked at me. "Remember to keep your mask on and to social distance." She glanced at her phone. "Fifteen minutes."

"Fifteen?" I said. "But you didn't get him down here until just now."

"Hey!" she almost yelled. "I'm already working an extra shift this week. And we have Sofia scheduled for this spot at 12:00. I need time to sanitize your chair."

"All right, all right." I shook my head. "Thanks, Claudia."

She turned her plump frame around and marched over to the other visiting area—most likely to tell them their minutes were numbered.

I inhaled and exhaled, looking at Grandad. He gazed back like he was staring across a lake to someone on the farther shore.

I held up the paper bag and said, "I got you the sourdough bread you were missing."

"Terrific!" he said jovially. And then, after a pause, more somber, "Every prisoner gets at least bread and water."

"Oh, it's hardly that bad," I said, with a weak chuckle.

"No, not right now," he acknowledged, his head rotating, taking in the green freedom all around him.

"House arrest is fine by me," I said in a forced upbeat tone, "as long as the house has air conditioning. Boy, it's humid today." Under the green cloth, my face was itchy with sweat.

Grandad nodded and quoted, "So every bondman in his own hand bears the power to cancel his captivity."

"Shakespeare?" I asked.

"*Julius Caesar*. Act 1. Scene 3."

His increasing dementia prevented him from remembering basic nouns, but it did nothing to inhibit his ability to quote a four-hundred-year-old British playwright.

"Did I ever tell you I used to act in Shakespeare plays?"

"No," I lied.

"At the school. Father Milburn, in the evenings, would help us put on a play. First, we did *The Tempest*. I was Gonzalo." He cleared his throat and then quoted:

Beseech you, sir, be merry. You have cause,
So have we all, of joy, for our escape
Is much beyond our loss.

"Those were the first words I learned to say in English."

Of course, I remembered. Grandad had already read the entire play to me when I was ten.

"Then we did *Othello*." He laughed. "I got to play Cassio. That was so much fun. The next year we did *Much Ado About Nothing*. And then..."

He paused. His eyes squinting then relaxing, as if he didn't even realize he had stopped mid-sentence.

"So it wasn't all that bad," I said.

"What wasn't?"

"The res school. Father Milburn. He sounded like a nice guy."

"Oh, yes. Much nicer than Sister Tam. Good people everywhere. Even... there. I really liked acting in the plays."

He loved it so much that his eldest son, my Uncle Tomas, became an actor with the Shakespearean Festival in Stratford, Ontario. At least, before he ended up in Hollywood.

After a bout of awkward silence, I said, "Well, at least the lockdown's over."

He closed his eyes and said nothing.

The heat made Grandad's long white hair frizz out, despite being wrestled down by a long silver braid. When I was really little, I didn't get why my Indian grandad had longer hair than my Irish grandma. He said his long hair gave him a long life. And when Grandma died, I actually believed him.

"Let me smell the birch," he said.

"Birch?" I asked.

He pointed to the bag.

"Oh, the bread," I said, and handed the loaf over. As our hands neared each other, I saw how much browner his skin was than mine—even though I had surely been getting far more sun.

"Remember to keep your distance," hollered Claudia, positioned at the top of the stairs like a soldier on watch. "Or you'll be suspended from future visits."

I snapped back my hand. "Sheesh," I said looking in her direction. "I'm just handing him bread."

Claudia put her hands on her hips. "Hey! Not my rules. Ministry's. You think I want to be Nazi Nurse?"

Part of me suspected she did.

"Sorry," I said loud enough for her to hear me. Then I added in a German accent, "You're just obeying orders."

"Next time," she called back, "if you have something for Paul, give it to me." She pointed at her chest. "I can sterilize it and then give it to him."

Grandad rolled his eyes, his back to Claudia looming on the steps above.

"*Entiendo*," I said.

She vanished back inside without another word.

Grandad raised the unsterilized paper bag to his nose and inhaled. "Mmmm. Did you meet the baker?"

"You mean the nutso conspiracy theorist?"

Grandad chuckled.

"She thinks the government is turning into some tyrannical monster, faking the pandemic and controlling our minds."

Grandad snickered. "Isn't she dandy?"

"A dandelion."

"She's a smart woman," said Grandad.

"Do you know her name?" I asked.

Grandad was silent, his eyes cast down. He sighed. He set the bag on his lap. "No, we talk about more interesting things than names." He pointed to the grass, as if seeing the ghost of a dandelion left over from spring. "Dandelions don't live long, but they live fully. They stand tall and proud. It's a good name you've given her."

"A better name would be Stinging Nettle."

Grandad chuckled. "Aren't all women that?"

"Humph!" I leaned into the plastic lawn chair, tipping it back on its rear legs.

"So, when are you going to get married?" asked Grandad, slowly.

The chair suddenly tipped back onto the ground as I sprang to my feet, exclaiming, "*Married?*"

This time Grandad's chuckle erupted into laughter, as he slapped his sore knees once again.

"Grandad!" I exclaimed, as I swept up the fallen chair. "She's one of those covidiots. I see them on Twitter and Facebook ranting about how lockdowns are here to destroy the economy and turn us into some East German regime. She probably thinks this is some big population reduction program headed by Bill Gates.

Euthanize the elderly and the minorities. Then sterilize the rest of us with the vaccine. This nonsense is all over social media."

I was talking faster now, as Grandad sat silent, eyes fixed on me. He would sit there and listen to whatever I had to say, as if I'd been clasping a talking stick. He would let me hold it all day long.

"They think that the measures are purposely hurting children by not letting them outside. Making them commit suicide or die of a weakened immune system. These anti-vaxxers even think the vaccine might kill the kids." My voice rose as if I were a lawyer at the end of my closing speech. "This is Canada, not North Korea. Our government isn't *that* bad." I paused and inhaled, trying to calm myself. "They wouldn't hurt children."

Grandad's eyes suddenly cast down again toward his sore knees.

"Crap!" I said. "I'm sorry, Grandad. I forgot."

But even the dementia wouldn't let him forget.

7. Ojibwe Dejá Vu

Grandad rarely spoke of it. But he knew government could and had hurt children. He was one of them. In 1945, "pale-faced strangers with beards" came to his family's camp near the town of Minaki in Northwestern Ontario.

"The fish bellies came," said Grandad, speaking now with sudden clarity. He sat up in his wheelchair. A cool breeze fanned the grassy lawn of the nursing home. "I'd never seen the flying machines up close," he explained. "Only in the air. It was so much bigger than I thought. But it came down and landed on the water like a duck. The fish bellies came out. They had guns. They took Memengwaa. They took me. They shot at my father. They took us into the sky. I thought they would take us to their heaven."

Instead of heaven, he and his sister were brought to hell: Cecilia Jeffrey Indian School, on Shoal Lake. They called it a school. But it was during World War II and there was little money available for educating the native people. Grandad said they earned their daily bread working in the shop, making furniture. The buildings were so overcrowded and unclean, tuberculosis was as common as the cold. Grandad had only been ten. His sister was just seven. He survived, she did not.

There wasn't much known about how Great-Aunt Memengwaa died. Grandad once showed me the records, which he kept in a file folder, yellow with age. One document said she had TB. Another said she had an accident on a staircase.

"The government," said Grandad, "took child away from parent, and parent away from child. They made us build chairs all day. All day I sawed wood and hammered nails. Over and over. And if I made a mistake, Sister Tam hit me so hard I'd fall on the floor."

I sat back down in the chair and leaned forward with my elbows on my knees. "But the government wasn't trying to kill you; just, well, assimilate you."

"Assimilation," said Grandad with a bob of his head.

"It means to help people fit in."

"It means extermination," he responded with no lack of wit. He then sang quietly, "No more Indians jumping on the bed."

I sat back down on the floppy chair.

"Never doubt what evils are possible in this world," said Grandad slowly. "And what good it will bring out in those who try to stop it."

"Five minutes!" yelled Claudia.

Turning, I saw Claudia pushing the other resident, in her wheelchair, up the ramp. I shot her an annoyed look before turning back to Grandad.

"Listen, Grandad, I'll be getting my own place soon. When I do, I told you, you can come and live with me. I'll break you out of here."

Grandad smiled. "You lost your job."

"Yeah," I said. "But plants will open again. They all need welders. Until then the government is sending me cheques."

"That's what they did to us, too." Grandad nodded slowly. "They took our life away; then sent us money to buy stuff from their stores."

I intertwined my fingers together. "I saw a Help Wanted sign today. I'm not sure how much it pays."

"Better to earn less money than get more free money."

A blue jay landed above on the canopy. It whispered a soft

conglomeration of clicks, chucks, whirrs and whines.

"Hear that, Grandad?" I said. "A little bird just told me things will get better. The government makes mistakes, but I don't think there's any malice. Call me naive, but I'm staying positive."

"I remember," he said, his eyes gazing into the past, "people from the village told us that warriors in red suits and shamans in black robes were taking the children. They had holy books and said they were saving the kids from going to hell. My parents didn't believe the people from the village. They didn't believe anyone could do such a thing because they'd never steal children."

He paused and pulled down his mask. I saw his beardless face, and puckered lips. "They didn't prepare. They didn't protect us. We could have hid. We could have fought back."

Grandad's eyes refocused as if coming to the present. "I don't know if Dandelion is right about the things she says about this new disease. The government may be protecting us. There are good people everywhere—even in government. But they have so much power. And scaring people only brings them more power." His eyes became wider. "Don't be scared, Vincent. You are not a boy anymore. Make government prove what they say."

He inhaled and started humming a tune I did not know. I listened, not sure where he was. When the humming died away he added:

"Find out what she knows. Find out what is true. Not what you *wish* was true. Be brave."

I squirmed on the wobbly seat. "She says I'm a turtle hiding in my shell."

"*Miskwaadesi*," he said.

I raised an eyebrow. "Huh?"

"Turtle," he translated.

My Ojibwemowin was limited to a dozen words.

"My people tell how the whole world was sunk by water gods who became jealous when Geezhigo-Quae became pregnant."

"She's the one who lives on the moon, isn't she?"

"She was..." And suddenly his eyes glazed over again. "She was on the moon." He was searching for words.

I frowned. *Why does he go in and out like this?*

"She was going to bear the first children for Manitou," I

continued for him, having heard the story many times. "The water gods feared her children would be too powerful. They flooded the earth so her kids would have no land on which to live. But Geezhigo-Quae smeared dirt on the back of a turtle and it became North America."

Grandad smiled and nodded. "Miskwaadesi carries the burden of the world on his shell. He can't hide from it. It goes with him everywhere."

"So, you're saying I should take it as a compliment?"

He cocked his head and furrowed his brow in non-understanding.

"Being called a turtle, I mean."

"Sorry! Time's up." Claudia called out as she marched down the front steps.

I looked at my watch. "I thought you were Latino?"

"What's that supposed to mean?" She gripped the handles of Grandad's wheelchair.

"Latinos are always late, not early." I held out my cellphone, showing her the time.

"Hey!" said Claudia, in a tone that almost felt like a slap. "I have only two designated areas and twenty appointments."

"All right, all right," I said, holding my hand up. "Book me for the same time tomorrow." Then directing my eyes at Grandad. "I'll see you then."

"No can do," said Claudia. "Weekend's booked solid."

"When's the next opening?"

"Wednesday."

"*Wednesday?*" I exclaimed.

"Two tents, eighty residents," snapped Claudia. "You do the math."

"All right," I conceded, "Which time on Wednesday?"

"I don't know. Call the front desk."

I sighed and crossed my arms.

Claudia pulled back on Grandad's wheelchair and spun him around. As she headed for the ramp, I walked beside him, putting my hand on his shoulder.

"Unless I have a job by Wednesday," I said, "I'll see you then. Either way, I'll call you tomorrow."

"Six feet," barked Claudia.

I withdrew my hand from his shoulder.

"Bye, Miskwaadesi," said Grandad raising his hand. "Thank you for the bread."

"Sure thing," I said. "If you need anything else, just let me know."

"Does she still have that spread?" he asked. "The one made of nuts."

I gulped. "Yeah, sure. I can get that."

As Grandad was pushed up the ramp, I could hear him chuckling to himself.

8. Masked, Muzzled and Muted

Nuts! Grandad needs some nut butter. That's what I was mentally reciting to myself the next morning as I marched toward downtown Moosehead. I'll just get in, get the almond spread, and get out, I told myself. I don't need to chit-chat about the Corona World Order.

At the same time, a part of me was looking forward to seeing her. Alright, a big part of me was looking forward to seeing her. Honestly, the mere thought of her was causing a warm, aching feeling in the centre of my chest. I'd only felt like this about Emma Boissonneau, who I dated back in high school. She was a real Métis. My parents didn't approve. Dad said she made me look too Indian. In the end, her family moved north to Timmins.

But even without Emma, I had still felt a little "too Indian" and never asked another girl out. Instead, I lost myself in work, sports and movies. The only dates I had were with Grandad at the Green Dragon.

Part of what I think attracted me to the town's new baker was how out of place she seemed. That said, I did feel inadequate before this bold new Dandelion on the block. She probably read more books in one week than I read in a year. She could actually quote studies, rather than merely believe in "the science." And she owned a business, while I had become just another COVID welfare bum.

Still, when I'd left the bakery, she had smiled at me. It almost seemed like she didn't want me to go. Sure, she never gave me that kiss, but I had never expected her to. I was just trying to save face, before revealing my face.

As I made my way down Magder Road, I broke into a light jog, passing a row of postwar bungalows. Seventy-something Patricia Young, with her ghost-white hair and black face mask, passed me on the otherwise empty sidewalk. My mask was in my pocket. I didn't know if she would resent me for opening my mouth to say good morning, so I nodded and smiled. She just glared.

In the middle of the road, Jeff McLean, my neighbour, was walking his dog, Stormy, with one of those retractable leashes. Parallel to mutt and master, twelve feet away on the opposing sidewalk, walked his wife, Sarah, wearing a pink mask. They talked loudly back and forth to each other.

"I didn't mean to forget it," I overheard Jeff saying. "I mean, we share the same bed, for God's sake."

"You always forget your mask," she shouted back. "I'm going to start putting extras in your pants pockets."

"I'm just walking the dog..."

Turning left onto Main Street, I yanked my green mask out of my pocket as I passed The Green Dragon. Mr. Chung had a placard on the sidewalk announcing, "We're open for take-out and curbside pickup." I glanced through the front window, but it didn't look like he was open quite yet. Sitting on the inside of the restaurant's windowsill was an Apartment For Rent sign.

Picking up my pace, I continued past the town square, where arrows and dots created a maze around socially distanced stalls of the much diminished Saturday morning farmer's market. Above the half-empty square stood the two-storey town hall. It was made of grey stones, taken from a local quarry in the early 1900s. A black, wrought-iron bust of a moose stared at me from the middle of a small rose garden that fronted the building. Someone had strapped a blue medical mask around its snout, the loops extended with string, wrapping around its antlers.

As I neared my destination, across the street, on my right, I spied Harry's Barber Shop. Harry sat on his front steps, newspaper on his lap, cigarette in his mouth, white mask around his neck. He was heavyset with crewcut white hair.

I waved.

"Hey, Vince!" he called out, cigarette bobbing at the corner of his lips. "Your hair's looking a little shaggy."

I tugged at the visor of my baseball cap and called back, "Not, today, Harry. Too many errands."

Getting a cut with Harry was one thing I hadn't missed over lockdown. My hair would always smell like tobacco after a trim. But what's a guy to do in a one-barber town?

"Next week!" I promised.

"No worries," he called back, his head already back in his paper, his cigarette close enough to ignite the newsprint.

My pace slowed as I approached her shop.

Moosehead's Artisan Bakery, said the wooden sign above the entrance. The door immediately opened with a jingle. I froze, expecting the Dandelion. Instead, green sandals stepped out, followed by tanned legs, a summer dress, blue purse and ruddy red hair.

What was her name? I asked myself. *Susan?* Her husband had died two years earlier. It had made the front page of our weekly twelve-page paper.

At her side was her blond-haired son. In his one hand he held his mother's hand, in the other dangled a slingshot.

His name was Josh. Ten-year-old Joshua Henderson. I hadn't forgotten. Couldn't. The front-page article had told how Josh had been in the back seat during the accident that killed his father. They had been driving at night, on Highway 69, passing a crossroads, when an eighteen-wheeler slammed into the side of their car. Josh's dad was killed instantly. Or, at least, so the newspaper said. I don't know how they claim to know such things.

"Hey, guys," I said.

"Hi, Vince," Josh's mother replied.

The boy just stared and grinned.

No, not Susan, I realized, *her name's Sandy. Sandy Henderson. Dr. Sandy Henderson, in fact.*

"Say hello, Josh," said Sandy, as she turned to her son, moving her hands in the air.

"Hello," he replied.

His voice sounded slightly odd. That's when I noticed the hearing aids and remembered what else *The Moosehead Gazette* had reported. While Josh had survived the car crash, safely fastened into a child's seat in the back, he had suffered major hearing loss.

An inflating airbag, the article stated, could reach 170 decibels. That would have been louder than letting a firecracker explode beside his little ears. In fact, I was surprised to read that air bags didn't use compressed air but were inflated by igniting nitrogen gas. The bang of four exploding "nitrogen bombs," along with the crunch of imploding metal, had left Josh half-deaf and half-orphaned.

"Hey Josh," I said, speaking louder and slower, while pointing to the slingshot in his hand. "That your slingshot?"

He stared back at me, mutely.

"It's hard for him to understand you," said Sandy, slowly. "The mask hides your lips and muffles your voice."

Immediately I pulled the muzzle down around my neck. "Oh, yeah, sorry, I—"

"You look dumb with a mask on," said Josh.

"*Josh!*" exclaimed Sandy.

"It's true. Dumb means you can't speak. They don't look like they have mouths."

Both my eyebrows bounced upward as I laughed. "From the mouths of babes."

"I'm not a baby," said Josh, raising his unloaded slingshot.

"No, you're not," I said slowly and clearly, pointing again to his slingshot. "What's the sign for slingshot?"

He holstered his weapon in his back pocket. Fingers splayed or pinching each other in what seemed to be an intentional pattern, he moved both hands apart and then back together and then apart again. I tried to imitate him, which made him laugh.

"Actually," said his mother, "that's the sign for an arrow. That's what he wants for his birthday tomorrow. A slingshot looks like this."

She raised her left hand in a V-shape, while her right hand pulled back at an invisible string.

"Hey, that makes sense," I said, imitating the simpler sign, but aiming at Josh. "This sign language isn't as difficult as I thought."

"No, it's not," said his mom. "It just takes patience."

Something she had in abundance. When her husband died, she closed her medical practice in Sudbury so she could focus full-time on homeschooling Josh and helping him cope with the loss of his father and the loss of his hearing. She had bought a house in Moosehead with *cash*—her late husband had one of those one-million-dollar insurance packages.

"Maybe you can teach me more signs," I said to Josh.

He shrugged.

"Or maybe you can show me how to hit the bull's eyes with a bow and arrow."

"Yeah!" he said.

"On the subject of signs," said Sandy. "You gotta check out Stefanie's new sign."

"Whose?" I asked.

"Stefanie's," she repeated and pointed to a large, handwritten poster taped to the inside of the bakery's front window.

"Stefanie's my hero!" Sandy said with a laugh.

"We got to go, Mom," said Josh.

"Sorry," she said to me. "We have an appointment with Harry."

"Uh, yeah, no problem," I said. "I hope you get your bow and arrow for your birthday, Josh."

And I repeated the sign for the arrow. For the first time he smiled at me.

"Bye," he said. "Don't be a dummy."

Sandy silently signed him a reprimand as they started across the street to the barbershop. Harry snubbed his cigarette in the hibiscus planter beside his steps, greeted them both and ruffled Joshua's blond hair. As he held open the door for them, he slipped up his mask.

Stefanie, I repeated to myself. *So that's the darn Dandelion's name.*

I turned back to the bakery's front window and began to read her new sign.

By the time I finished the lengthy public service message, I realized: Either Stefanie had completely lost her grip with reality, or the rest of us were lemmings walking over the edge of common sense into the abyss of self-annihilation.

9. New Normal Drivel

The new poster was much larger than her No Face, No Service sign. The Dandelion had promised she would make a "new and better sign." The new message was certainly more verbose and daring:

NEW NORMAL DRIVEL

COVID-19(84): common cold hyperbole

stay safe: be afraid

mandatory masking:
forced face diapering and smile suppression

contact tracing: invasive surveillance

stay at home: decay at home

social distancing: anti-social madness

forced vaccination: big pharma profiteering

PCR: Plainly Crooked Results

shelter in place: wilter in place

sanitization: a germophobic ritual

flatten the curve: prolong the scamdemic

14 days: 14 months...

Prolong the scamdemic? I thought. *Boy, she does have guts.*
Nonetheless, I found myself nodding at a few of the points. As soon as I'd finished a second reading, the bell over the door jangled and the Dandelion's head poked out. She was wearing a purple dress. Her braid wasn't wrapped artistically around her head like last time, but trailed down her back.

"How do you like the new sign?" she asked.

A bit tongue-tied, my heart rate increasing, I followed her example, skipping any greetings. I pointed to the line about vaccinations.

"So you really think this is just one Big Pharma money-making scam?"

She stepped out and let the door close. "Mr. Gates did say he wants everyone in the whole wide world vaxxed."

"That'd sure be a lot of customers," I admitted.

"And not once. Not twice. But boosters for life."

"Hmm," I said. I hadn't heard it would be more than two jabs. Maybe three.

"Can you think of any other product that boasts such a marketing opportunity?" she asked.

"Food." I tilted my head toward her bread shop.

"Yeah, but I sell sourdough bread, and not everybody likes sourdough—for reasons I cannot understand."

"Maybe it's too sour," I replied.

She ignored my comment and continued, "But imagine if I could get the government to force everyone in the world to eat *my* sour bread? Whether they liked it or not."

I smiled. "You'd never do that."

"No, I wouldn't. But can you say the same for the big pharmaceutical companies? Seven point six billion customers served with zero marketing costs. Rather hard for a greedy oligarchy to resist."

"Oligarchy?" I immediately wished I hadn't exposed my ignorance. Fortunately, she wasn't snobbish about it.

"That's when you have a few people ruling over a lot of people," she explained. "Telling you what to do, what to eat, what medicines to take—"

"And what colour toilet paper to wipe our bums with," I blurted out. I felt immediate regret at exposing the crudeness of my humour; followed by immediate relief as she laughed. Oh, how I loved her laugh. So playful for such a serious dandelion.

"The oligarchs probably already own all the toilet paper companies."

I cleared my throat and changed the subject from Greek political terms I probably couldn't spell to the official purpose behind my expedition. "Hey, Grandad wanted some nut butter to go with the bread. And I thought I might try a loaf, myself."

She tilted her head toward the entrance and opened the door wide. "Then come on in."

That's when I noticed another sign taped to the bottom inside of the yellow front door. The eight by ten printout was upside down. I tilted my head to read Mask Wearing is Mandatory in big letters. The headline was followed by the image of a mask and some text about stopping the spread and respecting exemptions. The notice concluded with a logo consisting of a circle (representing a head) poised above a V-shape (indicating two arms raised in energetic joy). Beside the exuberant logo were the words:

Public Health
Santé publique
Sudbury & District

"I'm shocked to see you'd post such a thing," I said, snapping at the mask around my neck.

"If I don't, the fascist health unit will shut me down. So, yeah, I posted their stupid mandate on the entrance like they ordered. They never said I had to put it at eye level or even which side of the door."

"Wow!" I said, sincerely impressed and slightly intimidated. "I can see why Sandy says you're her hero."

"If anything, she's my hero," Stefanie replied. "Sandy's been one of the few doctors speaking out against the COVID lies— even though the College of Physicians is threatening to take her licence away."

"Oh," I said. I hadn't realized she had been speaking out. "Well, good thing bakers don't need a licence."

"Not yet, at least," she said, still holding the door.

As soon as I entered, she scooted past me and behind the counter. Over twin speakers of a pink stereo on the shelf behind her, piano notes sounded a melody akin to a frog hopping wildly from rock to rock along the crest of a waterfall. Accompanying the daring frog, a solo tenor bellowed words in German.

A CD player? I thought. *Boy, she's old-fashioned.*

Above the spinning disc were shelves of jams and spreads.

"Grandad likes the almond butter, right?" she asked.

"Yeah," I confirmed.

"Crunchy?"

"I don't know," I confessed. "He didn't say. But he says he washes his hair with it."

She gave me a lopsided grin. I returned a shrug.

"Well, we *butter* go with smooth then," she advised. "None left here, but I have more in back." She held up her index finger. "*Un minuto.*"

"*No problemo,*" I replied in Spanish. I was eager to show I knew a few non-English words to compete with her multilingualism.

"It's actually *problem-a*, not *-o*," she corrected.

Okay, I would stop trying to impress her with my nonexistent linguistic skills.

"Righto," I said.

She vanished through the beaded doorway.

As I waited, I rolled my neck in a circle, taking a deep breath. I didn't just feel relieved, I felt a bit happy. I wasn't sure why. Maybe because she didn't seem all that bonkers. After all, how could she run a store if she was crazy? Regardless, her slender form and big blue eyes certainly compensated for a few farfetched conspiratorial speculations.

And, anyway, I considered, *if it wasn't for people like her, we might all have the Canadian Armed Forces patrolling the streets by now.*

In fact, earlier that week, on the news, I'd seen a clip of a soldier in Peru, dressed in green camouflage gear, rifle over his shoulder, German shepherd at his side, keeping curfew in a region ironically called *La Libertad*.

Leave it to Latin America to turn a pandemic into an opportunity for a military state, I reflected, *Fortunately, we live in Canada: the true North strong and free.*

I turned around to look out through the front window. Much of the view of Main Street was blocked by Stefanie's New Normal Drivel poster. The poster was also hiding the upper half of the person reading its controversial commentary. Judging by the hips I assumed it to be a man. And judging by his attire, I assumed this was serious.

I swore and took a step back.

He wore a black vest, covered with pouches, one of which had a coiled wire running out of it, like you'd see on an old-fashioned landline telephone. Below the vest were black cargo pants. Around the thin waist was a belt loaded down with accoutrements in black cases. One of those black cases appeared to hold a pistol.

Moosehead did not fund its own police department. We relied on the Ontario Provincial Police (better known as the OPP) to enforce the law on the rare occasion a crime actually took place in our small town. Cops usually only stopped by to grab a bite to eat on their break. Something, however, told me this cop wasn't standing out front of the Dandelion's bakery because he wanted some almond butter on rye.

10. Two Masks Against None

The male tenor sank into an emotionally drawn out series of incomprehensible words in German. The CD died away, sounding as if the piano keys were, one by one, running from the scene. Its furtive finish was replaced by the jingling of the bell over the front door.

The cop entered, joining me in the small retail area at the front of the bakery. His dark peaked cap was fronted by a golden heraldic badge. The badge displayed the words Ontario Provincial Police—encircled by trilliums, maple leaves and the Royal Crown.

Removing his cap, and tucking it under his right arm, the OPP officer revealed a balding crown, with straggly white hair holding on around the sides. Both his body and his masked face (what I could see of it) were thin. He looked weary and worn, yet walked tall and erect.

"Good morning, lad," he said, nodding at me, as he halted at the other end of the counter. He had a gruff, but amiable voice.

"Mornin' officer." Unthinkingly, I slipped my green mask back up over my mouth and nose, feeling like a guilty shoplifter slipping a candy bar back onto the display rack.

"Thank you kindly," said the cop, gesturing to his own mask. "I'm not that old yet, but I'm getting there. Can't be too safe."

"Yeah," I said, quickly and awkwardly.

"You never know who's gonna be vulnerable, eh?" he continued. "Or, for that matter, who's infected."

"Yeah," I repeated. "Having no symptoms could be a symptom of COVID."

"Ha!" he laughed out loud. "That's funny. But too true."

I relaxed a bit—even though he was close enough (six feet, to be exact) that I could easily tell which compartments on his loaded duty belt held the taser, pepper spray and the holstered gun. On the rear of the belt hung a shiny pair of handcuffs.

"Boy, it smells good in here, eh?" he said.

Rubbing his hands together, he surveyed the breads, buns and cookies under the glass display case, below the counter.

"Yeah," I said, glancing at the entrance to the bake room, the beads still swaying a bit.

"You mind if I ask you a question?" said the cop.

Before I could respond, Stefanie emerged.

"Last one left—" she began to say, raising a jar triumphantly in the air, but stopped abruptly upon seeing the officer.

"Howdy," said the cop, nodding his head.

"Oh... good morning, Constable."

She shot a look at me (and my green mask) before her eyes returned to the cop (and his black mask). Two masks against none. She set the nut butter down on the countertop and took a graceful step backwards. I had a clear view of them both in profile. The lanky yet imposing cop must have been a foot and half taller than the short dandelion.

"Good morning," he replied. "Or maybe I should say, *guten Morgen,* eh? Being that folks say this is the finest German bakery north of the French River."

"Well," responded Stefanie, brushing loose strands of blonde hair behind her ear, "I rather doubt there are many German bakeries in Northern Ontario to compete with for such accolades."

The cop chuckled, as his head darted back and forth scanning the area. "Darling, I was looking for some hand sanitizer." He rubbed his hands together in the air, as if Stefanie might be deaf and required a game of charades.

"If you need to wash your hands," she replied, "you're welcome to use the sink." She gestured to a small basin and faucet mounted into the wall behind the display counter. Running the water, she washed her own hands, wrists and forearms, before pulling out a paper towel.

The cop let his hands drop to his side. "Maybe I'll just avoid touching anything."

"How may I help you, then?" she asked. "As I can assure you my hands are quite clean."

He tilted to his right, looking around Stefanie, toward the

swaying beads. "I need to talk to your boss."

"You're speaking to her. I'm the owner," she said and extended her hand over the counter. "Stefanie Müller."

This time the cop took a step backwards, almost dropping his cap, staring at her outstretched hand as if she'd pointed a gun at his chest. I was glad I was wearing a mask, so he couldn't see the amusement that won over my otherwise tense expression. I was inwardly chuckling not only at his germophobic reaction, but at the unfathomable image of this beautiful dandelion aiming a gun at this towering old cop.

"Oh," he said, without shaking her hand. Instead, he pulled out a notepad and pen and began scribbling. "Stef-an-ie Müller. Very nice to meet you."

"That's Stefanie with an *f*, not a *p-h*,'" she said, tilting forward slightly, as if proofreading his note taking. "And there's a diaeresis over the *u* in Müller."

I'd no idea what a diaeresis was. If the police officer shared my ignorance he didn't admit it. Once he finished jotting his note, he gestured with his head to the front window. "Well, I need to talk to you about that sign. The one in the window."

"The Help Wanted sign?" she said with a raised eyebrow. "I really think you'd be overqualified."

He released another laugh—quite a jovial one, which didn't suit his weary eyes and muzzled countenance. In fact, he laughed so hard, the smell of coffee on his breath penetrated his mask and found its way to my nose, six feet away.

"Oh dear," he finally said. "Trust me, I'm the last person you'd ever want working in your kitchen. I couldn't boil Kraft Dinner if my life depended on it." He turned and looked at me, shaking his head. "I think one of the reasons my Patty took pity and married me was so I wouldn't spend the rest of my life living off canned soup and bread."

He turned to me. Was he grinning behind his mask? I clasped my right wrist with my left hand behind my back like a cadet awaiting instruction. I felt relieved he hadn't continued asking about the poster Stefanie had on the front window.

He then returned his gaze to the glass display. "Not that I'd mind living off such magnificent loaves as we have here." He looked back at her, his eyebrows raised in a V-shape, as if they were acting as proxy for a masked smile. "No yeast, I assume?"

"Never," she said, with a definite hint of pride. "Everything is one hundred percent sourdough starter."

"Twelve-hour ferment?"

"Twenty-four," she replied. "At least."

"Organic?"

"Of course."

He leaned forward a bit, and almost whispered: "Spring water?"

"No, not pure enough," she replied. "I only use distilled."

He whistled. "Masterful."

"Would you like to try a sample?"

"A sample?" he said gravely. "No! No, thank you." Then returning to his jovial tone, "I'll buy a whole loaf! Even with this darn mask, my nose knows quality when it sniffs it."

"Well, I hope your tastebuds agree," she said, looking as uncertain about the situation as a chicken waiting on a fox. "Rye? Pumpernickel?"

He aimed his forefinger at one of the large loaves, his thumb cocked up. "Pumpernickel, please!" And when he had said "please" the whole hand jerked up and back as if he had shot the loaf with a bullet.

"If you can't eat it fast enough, it freezes well," said Stefanie, smiling faintly, as she used metal tongs to move the bread into a paper bag.

"Don't worry about that," said the cop. "This will disappear fast enough in my house."

She held out the loaf for him to take, but he waved his hands in the air. "Could you put it all in a box for me?"

"Of course," said Stefanie. She pulled up a small cardboard box from beneath the counter. "Anything else?"

He pointed to the shelf behind her. "What kind of jams you got there?"

She turned and read the labels. "Black currant. Gooseberry. Morello cherry. All from McDuffy's Organic Farm."

"One of each, then," he said, as if any other option would be unthinkable. "The missus grew up on toast and jam. Not sure if she's ever tried gooseberry, though."

"Oh," I cut in. "My grandad and I used to collect gooseberries in the woods. They taste like sour grapes."

"Oh, forgive me," said the cop, turning to me. "I was butting in line."

"No, no," I said, crossing my arms. "Not a problem. I'm in no rush." I pointed to the jar of almond butter on the countertop. "Just buying something for my grandad."

Stefanie looked at me wearily from the corner of her eye as she placed three jars of jam in the cardboard box on the countertop beside my almond butter.

"Here, let me pay for that," the cop offered. "Least I can do for holding you up."

"Oh, thanks," I said.

"My pleasure." He pulled out his wallet. "What about some bread? You want pumpernickel, too? Or can you handle a dark rye?"

"Uh, gee." I hesitated. "Is there any wheat? I'm pretty new to this whole artisan thing. I grew up on bannock."

"Bannock, eh?" said the cop, giving me a penetrating glance. "Ojibwe? Cree? Odowa?"

I gulped. "A little Ojibwe. Back a few generations. My family's mainly Irish."

"Well," said the cop, matter-of-factly, "You know, if we go back far enough, we all come from Indigenous people of one land or another." He turned to Stefanie. "A whole wheat loaf for the handsome young Métis, Fräulein Müller."

"Okay," said Stefanie.

With the ease of a potted dandelion at sea, she placed a crusty loaf into a brown bag and handed it out for me to take. I started to advance, but the cop suddenly outstretched his arm.

"Remember," he said to me, "six feet apart." Turning to Stefanie he said: "Fräulein Müller, if you could please set it on the counter, for our friend to pick up after I've paid and you've stepped away from the counter."

I could hear her inhale and exhale deeply, as her eyes closed and then opened. Without responding, she set the bread down beside the almond butter. Sliding over, she punched keys on the cash register (which looked as old as the cop).

"$41.89," she said. "How would you like to pay?"

"Plastic, of course," he said.

He pulled a red Scotiabank card out of his wallet. Stefanie set the debit machine down on the countertop. He came forward and tapped his card over the screen. After it beeped a confirmation, he grabbed his box of bread and jam, and shot back to his previous position, inhaling deeply, as if he had been holding his breath for the entire transaction.

Stefanie offered him a printed receipt. He silently shook his head, as if she had offered him an arsenic tablet.

"Well, thank you," she said. "I hope your wife enjoys her toast and jam."

"Ahem," he said from behind his black mask.

Then he just stood there with the box of bread and spreads under his left arm, cap still under the right.

"Thanks again," I said, holding up the bag. "My grandfather loves this bread."

"No problem, my friend. It's the little things that count in these trying times, eh?"

He paused. Silence hung in the air like a thick morning fog, making it hard to breathe.

"Just like," he continued, "it's such a small thing, asking us to wear a mask, eh?"

And he nodded at Stefanie's unmasked and reddening face.

11. Constable Corona

Stefanie crossed her arms over her purple dress and stared across the countertop at the constable.

"I know masks are uncomfortable," he continued, as if he was shooting the breeze with old friends. "A hassle to keep clean. But it's a way of showing we care for those who are not as well off as us, physically. The elderly. Like your grandfather." He nodded at me. "Or the disabled, like my wife." He paused. "We need to keep the weaker members of the herd safe. It's what separates humans from the beasts."

I could see the tension forming around Stefanie's jaw as a second wave of masking rebuke was descending upon her: yesterday me, today Constable Corona.

"But I understand. Masks aren't pretty," he continued, sounding like he was talking to a larger audience than just us two. "And you, my dear, have such a, how do you say it, *ein schönes Gesicht?* I certainly wouldn't want such a beautiful face hiding behind a mask. What about you?" He signalled to me.

"Um," I stuttered. "Well, no. I mean, I'd rather look at her. Her face. I mean, who likes looking at masks?"

"Exactly!" said the cop. "It's a sacrifice all ways round. There's no doubt about it."

"But if she doesn't want to wear one," I found myself unexpectedly adding, "if she doesn't think it's helpful or safe, then she should have the freedom to choose what she wears in her own store."

Did I just say that? I asked myself. I saw her look at me. She wasn't smiling, but, somehow, her eyes signalled appreciation; while the cop's eyes, above his big black mask, signalled disdain. My hands started to shake. I could hear Dad, in my mind, whispering: "Don't rock the boat. The Indian is the first to be thrown overboard."

"Ahem," said the cop, nodding his head at me. "So that sign in the window—with its clever comments: 'Shelter in place; wilter in place...' Did you think it was funny?"

My mouth may have opened, but no words came out. Instead, the German music—still playing over the stereo—filled the void:

Ach, wie ist mein Arm so schwach!
Was ich hebe, was ich trage,
Was ich schneide, was ich schlage,
Jeder Knappe tut mir's nach.*

"It's a simple question," said the cop. "Did you find her sign funny?"

"Umm." I looked from him to the Dandelion. "Well, not really funny. More... interesting."

He turned back to facing Stefanie. "I assume it was your creation, Ms. Müller? Did you think it was funny?"

---

* Oh, how weak my arms are!
What I lift, what I carry,
What I cut, what I hammer,
Any fellow can do as well.

"I wasn't trying to be funny, actually."

"Ah!" he exclaimed. "But humour is what's going to get us through these dark days." His voice turned to one of a Baptist preacher. "We are living through a Biblical plague. You could have the virus right now. And not wearing a mask, like you are, you could pass it to him." He nodded in my direction. "And then he could pass it on to his grandfather and his grandpa could…" He paused and his voice suddenly became clipped. "Die."

Stefanie immediately responded, "I don't think—"

"Now, you wouldn't want that to happen," interrupted the cop, "would you?"

"I don't think there's any risk of that happening."

"Well," he countered quickly, "far-fetched opinions don't make you exempt from the law."

Suddenly she squatted down behind the counter. It almost appeared as if a trapdoor had opened and saved her from the looming interrogation. Instead, after a few seconds of rummaging on the shelf under the cash register, she bounced back up, holding a small, black device. It had a clamp which she attached to her dress, and a lens which now faced outward. She pressed the button on the front face of the bodycam. A green light activated.

"I'm sure you understand if I film the rest of this interaction? Beginning with your name and badge number?"

"Ah, excuse me." He took a step forward, pulled out his wallet and, unintimidated, held his OPP badge up to the camera.

"Constable Justin T. Mackenzie," he said, sounding like our best buddy again. "I'm new to Sudbury. Transferred from Toronto. Please forgive me, I should have formally introduced myself, Ms. Müller."

"You can call me Stefanie."

"Stefanie," he said in a soothing voice, reminiscent of a Mr. Rogers on Paxil. "Stefanie with an *f*." A pause. "Now, where is your mask, eh?"

"Phooey!" she said with a shake of her head. "I stopped wearing diapers when I was eighteen months old."

"Hey, I get it," he replied with a shrug of his shoulders. "Working in the back there with those hot ovens. Last thing you want is a mask making your face all sweaty."

"Indeed," she countered, "breeding bacteria in a moist environment at the gateway to our respiratory system doesn't sound ideal for keeping people safe from lung infections."

Without a pause he replied, "Indeed, one needs to use common sense and change the mask frequently."

She shook her head. "Why bother? There's never been a single randomized controlled trial showing that masks stop people getting sick. Put a mask on five thousand people and no mask on the other five thousand—five weeks later, there's *no difference* in infection rates. Certainly no difference in death rates."

"Well, let's leave the data to the experts to interpret," he said, rolling his eyes. "I mean, how qualified are a cop and a baker, eh?" He cocked his head toward me. "Of course, I don't know about our friend here..." He turned his head to face me. "Mr. Métis, are you a doctor, by any chance?"

"Welder," I mumbled.

"Welder, eh?" he said. "Then you must know all about the importance of wearing a mask, eh?"

"Well..." I said, "we wear *helmets*, not masks."

Stefanie sighed.

"Well, then," Mackenzie said, snapping the strap on his own mask. "Compared to wearing a full-blown welding helmet, these things are nothing, eh?" His voice suddenly picked up in volume again, sounding a tad nervous. "I mean, all these things we are doing look pretty silly. I get it! Standing on dots, keeping six feet away..." He took a step to the right, increasing the distance between me and him by another three feet. "And wearing these— what did you call them?—face diapers." He chuckled. "You know, I used to call them dog muzzles."

And then the schizoid humour suddenly evaporated from his voice.

"But I'm sure they thought the guy who invented the first toothbrush was off his rocker, too." He let out a hoot. "And didn't they all make fun of the man who came up with washing our hands before we eat?"

"They did worse than just laugh," said Stefanie. "Dr. Ignaz Semmelweiss was thrown into an insane asylum and beaten to death by his guards."

"There you go!" said Mackenzie. "We've made progress.

Instead of locking scientists up when they tell us to tweak our habits, most people willingly follow the science."

He gestured over to me, with my mask (neither one of them could see me pursing my lips so hard they must have turned blue).

"Semmelweiss," responded Stefanie, calmly, "tested his theories about personal hygiene. He proved that less babies died if doctors washed their hands between working with cadavers and delivering newborns. We have no such proof for masks."

"Then how do you explain the drop in COVID cases?" he said, his voice sounding calm but already weary of the debate.

"Every summer colds and flus dwindle," said Stefanie. "Sunshine. Fresh air. Warm weather. People exercise more, eat better."

"Yes, of course, those help, too. But Canada's Public Health Agency, the CDC, and the WHO all agree that these new discoveries will help keep people even safer. Especially those who can't exercise or get outside."

This time Stefanie laughed out loud. "New discoveries? Face coverings aren't new! They are as old as bloodletting and about as useful. Simply getting to bed earlier would help people far more than hiding their face behind a germ-catcher. Yet, I haven't heard any of these esteemed health experts say more than a sentence about sleep, nutrition or exercise. They're like a plumber who can't change a shower head."

"I agree," said Mackenzie, holding up the box of bread and jam. "Good food, exercise, sleep. It's Health 101. The reason they aren't talking about these basics is simple: broccoli and an extra lap at the pool ain't gonna stop a super-virus." He paused, as if he'd said something profound that needed time to sink in. "That's why everybody else is wearing a mask. For some reason, you just don't get it."

I wanted to say something to support the lone Dandelion. But, standing there with a mask over my mouth would make any defence look lame. At the same time, I started to doubt her innocence. I mean it's not like they had put us all in concentration camps. They just asked us to keep our distance, stay home and relax. They even sent me 2K a month in Canada Emergency Response Benefit payments (CERB for short).

"So, while your sign may be cute," he continued, sounding like a professor ending his lecture, "it will discourage people from following public health measures."

Without a pause, she countered, "Since these measures are not really about health, I think that would be a good thing."

"You are, of course, welcome to your unique opinion," replied Mackenzie softly, almost sadly, as he pulled out his wallet and stared at the inside flap for a second. "But there's been enough deaths." He slapped the wallet shut, frustration creeping into his voice. "And your sign is bordering on murder."

12. Green, You Hateful Colour

It was so obvious that Constable Corona hadn't dropped by just to catch up on his groceries.

"*Murder?*" exclaimed Stefanie, her mouth not closing when she had finished repeating the one-word accusation.

I took a deep breath, not sure whom to side with. Even if some of these corona measures did help prevent the spread, could he really say she was murdering anyone? That's like saying driving a car is murder, because it might result in a fatal accident. Still, he was the cop. He knew the law.

"Now," said Mackenzie, reverting back to a gentler voice. "I don't think you mean to murder anyone."

Her voice rising, Stefanie said, "If anyone is murdering anybody, it's the public health unit—"

Mackenzie put his peaked cap with the golden OPP badge back on his head. "I understand," he said. "The poster was just a joke. A little new-normal shenanigans. If you would kindly take it down, we can forget all about it."

"I'm not taking it down."

"I strongly recommend that you do. It would be in your best interest."

Her eyes squinted at him. "The Charter of Rights and Freedoms hasn't been torn to shreds, has it?" she asked, slowly.

He cocked his head. I heard a bone crack. "Of course not."

"Then I won't be tearing up my sign."

Both were silent as the CD continued with a guttural verse in German, the piano churning away like a waterwheel.

Mackenzie's voice became tense, as if he was trying to contain an outburst. "If we don't flatten the curve, more people will die."

"How can changing a graph on a computer screen stop anybody from dying?"

"I don't have time for stupid questions."

"Or maybe you don't have a smart answer. Because flattening the curve won't save people's lives. All the WHO ever claimed was it would slow down the spread of the virus."

"So hospitals don't get overrun," he grumbled.

"Do the hospitals look overrun to you?" exclaimed Stefanie, making no effort to calm an impending outburst of her own. "My mom's a nurse at Sudbury General. She's reorganizing closets and catching up on paperwork, because they've cancelled all the elective treatments. She says the only thing overwhelming doctors is boredom."

"One lucky hospital," said Mackenzie. "Look south of the border."

"You mean where doctors and nurses have so much time on their hands they are making dance videos?"

"And why do you think that is?" he said. "It's because of things like masks and lockdowns."

"No, it's because people are scared to go to the hospital."

Mackenzie sighed loudly. "Your sign is costing lives. Call it free speech if that helps you sleep at night. But take it down if you give a crap about the sick and elderly."

Stefanie walked out from behind the cash register and stood within two feet of the cop. He held his ground.

"My grandmother died during the SARS outbreak." Any nervousness in her voice was dissolved into fury. "Oma would never have expected families to go bankrupt because she might catch a common cold virus. So don't use the elderly to justify your police state."

"You realize," he said coldly, "that even though I can't make you take down that sign, I should be writing you a ticket for not wearing a mask. $880."

"Then why don't you?" she said.

"Enforcement is a last resort. I, more than anyone, do not want a police state."

"So if we just do whatever the police tell us, then they won't have to force us. Sounds like a police state, either way, to me."

Me too, I thought.

"Canadians are a reasonable people," countered Mackenzie, keeping his voice calm. "The police would rather focus on education."

"Then please educate me on why reasonable people would expect others to wear a medical device on their face that has been shown to provide absolutely no benefit and many harms?"

He took a deep breath. "Are you going to make me write you a ticket? I really don't want to. I'd like us to be friends."

"Friends don't force people to do things against their will."

"Friends aren't selfish, either."

"Oh!" She gasped in sudden anger. "Who's the one being selfish? You're the one telling me to wear a petri dish on my face for *your* protection. Ordering me to stay at home for *your* safety. All for your benefit! I haven't asked anything of you—other than to leave me alone. So, you tell me—who's being selfish?"

He put the box of food on the counter and pulled out his ticket book and a pen.

"Relax," she said. "I'm exempt from wearing a mask."

His eyes rolled to the side in disbelief, as he gestured to me, "Hey, do you believe she really has a medical exemption?"

"Umm," was all I managed to mutter.

"Ethical exemption!" interrupted Stefanie. "In good conscience I will not foster fear in the population, against a nonexistent pandemic, with an ineffective and unhygienic germ collector. Acts of conscience are covered by the Charter. And informed consent is required by the Nuremberg Code."

The music suddenly increased in intensity as Mackenzie's forehead tightened.

"It's true," he said, slapping the ticket book shut and tucking it back into a pouch on his vest. In a much louder, and less gentle voice, he continued, "It's true the law can't force you to do the right thing. Can't force you to respect or care for others, to look beyond your personal perspective, preferences and desires."

"Phooey!" she spat, then spun around and walked back behind the counter, before facing forward again. She glanced down at her bodycam to make sure its green light was still shining.

"If you have no more shunning and shaming to share with me, I thank you for your purchase and wish you a good day."

Everybody fell silent, including the tenor on the CD.

"*Guten Tag!*" she repeated in German.

"So very sad," said Mackenzie, as the piano began to rumble again. "I think your heart's in the right place." He picked the box of bread and jam off the counter. "But your head is in its own little world." He turned to go. "Maybe you just need some time to reflect." As he passed me, he said, "I hope your grandfather stays safe and well."

I may have nodded slightly, but didn't say anything. He turned and headed out the door. As soon as it shut, I turned to face her. She glowered at me. Me and my mask.

"Yamamoto or Craig wouldn't have misused their badges like that," she said. "They're too busy actually protecting people from crimes, not pushing this psy-op."

"Psy-op?" I muttered, feeling more shock at what had transpired than confusion at her larger vocabulary.

"Psychological operation," she clarified, clearly annoyed with my ignorance. "Mass brainwashing."

"Maybe it is," I conceded, almost indifferently. "I don't know. But, regardless, people believe in it."

"Yeah!" she said. "*Blind* believers! Nothing to do with science, evidence or logic."

"Well, who are you to make fun of their beliefs?" I said. "Yesterday, Grandad was just telling me that we all live on the back of a turtle. Are you going to put up a sign making fun of his beliefs?"

She pursed her lips, and swayed back and forth a little before saying: "Ojibwe don't send cops around to ticket you if you don't believe in Turtle Island. They don't force people to wear a mask or stay at home."

"Either way," I said, feeling like I'd gained a little ground. "Making fun of these COVID measures is just going to enrage people." My voice sounded shaky. I was feeling short of breath; but I refused to pull down the mask. "Your customers—they'll feel offended. You could go out of business ticking off most of Moosehead."

"Whatever." She nodded her head toward the front window. Constable Mackenzie was leaning over the roof of his cruiser, jotting down notes. "Your overlord has left the building. You better go open his police car door for him."

"It's not like that," I blurted. "I was keeping an eye on you. I just think—"

"Yeah, you really looked like you were sticking your green neck out for me."

"Well, maybe the cop had a point. Maybe a few precautions won't hurt."

"Then get out of here! Stay safe! Social distance yourself. Go hide in your basement. Binge on Netflix. Cash your CERB-itude cheques."

With that the Dandelion growled. Reaching out, she grabbed the jar of almond butter, holding it up as if she were going to throw it at me. I ducked, as she slammed it back down on the counter, spun around and charged through the dangling beads.

Outside, I heard the cruiser door slam and its engine rev.

The beads leading to the bake room ceased rattling.

The tenor on the CD died away into a melancholy tone, like a man dying from sadness.

Suddenly, it was just me, standing there alone, wearing a mask.

I broke the encroaching silence by calling out, "Any chance I can buy a jar of that gooseberry jam? To go with the bread?"

"No face, no service!" she hollered back. Her hand shot through the beads and twisted a knob of the CD player, pushing the volume to the max as the next track erupted. Piano keys re-sounding, the tenor bellowed:

Ach Grün, du böse Farbe du,
Was siehst mich immer an
So stolz, so keck, so schadenfroh...*

With a sigh, I turned around—clutching the loaf of bread

---

* Oh green, you hateful colour, you,
Why do you keep staring,
So mocking, so proud, so pleased by my pain...

under my right arm, gripping the nut butter in my left hand—and ambled out onto the sidewalk. Even after the door closed behind me, I could still hear the taunting music shooing me away.

13. Why I Wear My Mask in the Shower

I walked briskly back down Main Street, hanging a right at the Green Dragon. Once on Magder Road, I pulled down the damp green mask and broke into a run. I felt like I was being chased by the voice of that German opera singer. I hadn't a clue what he was singing, but, somehow, it reflected how unsure I felt about anything and everything. As I raced past our next-door neighbour, Jeff McLean, mowing his front lawn, I couldn't help noticing he was now wearing a "Blunt Wives Matter" face mask.

I turned onto the driveway of my parents' small two-storey home, clambered up the white porch and through the front door. Once in the hallway, I kicked off my shoes. Entering the kitchen, I dumped the bread and nut butter on the table, before continuing down the short hallway.

"Hi, dear!" said Mom as I passed her sewing room.

I stopped, turned and leaned in the doorway.

"Hey, Mom," I responded, catching my breath.

She stood over her Bernina sewing machine, sliding a spool of thread into place. On her right, limply draped over a chair, was a decapitated penguin costume. Behind her, hanging on racks, were two dozen other mascots and get-ups ranging from dinosaurs to Donald Duck.

"How does this look?" she said, holding up a red face mask.

"It matches your hair," I said. "But it seems a little below your skillset, Mom."

She dropped it and gave a nervous laugh. "That's what I thought, too."

She looked glumly at her cutting table. Arranged and folded neatly, the surface must have contained a hundred cloth masks of various sizes, colours and styles.

"So many Etsy orders are coming in." She put a mug of coffee to her lips and sighed. "And then I promised to make more for St. Jerome's bazaar." She pulled a lever on her sewing machine and sat back down. "I can't keep up."

I started bouncing from one foot to the other, as I stretched my neck, glancing at the colourful assortment of face masks. I pointed to one with the word "PLACEBO" sewn across its front.

"Who ordered that one?"

"That was Father Shostakovich," said Mom with a sigh. "He actually asked for one that said 'HOAX.' Can you believe it? But I talked him out of it. Sometimes I think he might be a bit of a... you know."

I shrugged my shoulders and raised my eyebrows. "A what, Mom?"

"A conspiracy theorist," she muttered quickly, as she made the sign of the cross. "God bless his soul. He grew up in World War II, Croatia, you know. He can't help it."

"I'll pray for him, Mom." I brought the PLACEBO mask to my face to hide my big grin. "Maybe you could make me one, too?"

"Certainly not!" She flicked a switch on her sewing machine and it jerked into a steady hum. "I shouldn't even have made it for Father."

I started to bounce up and down on the balls of my feet. Mom looked up at me.

"What you humming?" she asked.

I didn't even realize I was. "Oh, just a tune I heard."

"It sure makes you dance."

"Actually, I really gotta use the bathroom, Mom."

"And I really have to finish twenty masks before the post office closes."

"After lunch, I'll help you pack them."

"You're a darling."

With that I sprinted to the end of the hall, up the stairs to the second floor, and into our cramped yellow bathroom which Mom always kept smelling like lemon. After emptying my bladder, I began to strip. A cold shower cooled my body down, but my brain still felt on fire. And my heart felt like it was bleeding. I looked at myself in the mirror. Between weights, running and hockey, I was muscular enough. But at that moment, I felt weak. The green mask still dangled around my neck. I always wore it in the shower. Seemed the easiest way to remember to clean it.

Don't be a turtle, said a voice in my head to the tune of that German music.

"Humph!" I said aloud, as I hung the mask over the shower rod to dry. "Time for some Netflix." Maybe a short movie would help calm me down.

I dashed to my room, slipped on jeans and a T-shirt, then descended two flights of stairs to the basement. The whole time, that German tune kept playing in my head. Except instead of German lyrics, it repeated, *Don't be a turtle*. Once in the basement, I promptly dropped my thin frame onto the couch and picked up the TV remote.

"Not even going to say hello?" said my father. He lay outstretched on the weightlifting bench.

"I thought you were sleeping."

"I was." He yawned. "Until you come stormin' down the stairs. Holy guacamole! You'd think a lion was chasing you."

"Something like that," I mumbled, as I selected "action" on the Netflix menu.

Groaning, Dad sat up on the bench. "You see your grandad?" he asked.

"Yesterday," I said grimly. "He looks thin. They seem so busy changing their PPE, I don't think they're making sure he eats enough."

"Ah," said Dad. "It's not like he's pumping iron." He slapped the barbell over the bench. It was loaded with sixty kilos. More than Dad could probably lift.

"I really wish you wouldn't nap on my exercise bench, Dad."

He rubbed his perpetually sore back and ignored my request. "If you don't think they're feeding him enough, maybe we should order him a pizza or something?"

I rolled my eyes. Grandad was lactose intolerant. "I bought him some bread from that bakery he used to go to."

"That German bakery on Queen Street?" asked Dad, with a quizzical look.

"Yeah."

Staring at the Netflix menu, I began to hum as I tapped the arrow button in tempo. Out of the corner of my eye I could see Dad running his fingers through his dishevelled hair.

"What you humming?" he asked.

"Uh, some German music. Opera or something. She was—it was playing in the bakery."

"Since when do you like opera?" He hauled himself off the bench, as if he had sixty kilos strapped to his back. Once standing, however, he glided to the minibar as if on figure skates.

"I dunno," I grumbled. "Just a catchy tune. Wondering what it's called."

Dad opened the bar fridge and pulled out a Molson. "You want one?" He waved the brown bottle at me.

"Dad, it's eleven o'clock in the morning."

"Yeah?"

"No, thanks." I shook my head.

"Well," said Dad, popping the bottle cap, "German opera, eh?" He took a pull of his beer. "I know a thing or two about German beer. But German opera... can't help you."

I kept on humming and pretended like I was actually paying attention to the movie options on the flatscreen. Dad reached into his jeans pocket and pulled out his cell. After setting down his bottle on the minibar he tapped the screen. Once it began to ring, he set it beside the bottle.

"Hullo?" said a voice over the speaker.

"Hey, Oskar, it's Rich."

"Hey, how're you liking quarantine?" Oskar had a slight German accent.

"Sitting on my ass, doing sweet nothing," said Dad whimsically. "Can't complain! Miss the team, though."

"I hear ya. We should all get together now that the lockdown's over, before we're back in the plant."

"Yeah, why not?" replied Dad. "But hey, listen Oskar, I got a German thing for ya. Do you know this tune? Vincent, hum it louder."

"Dad, it's not important."

"It goes like this," and he began a mocking imitation.

"That's not it," I said shaking my head and taking a deep breath.

Dad picked up the phone and spoke directly into it. "Oskar, I'm going to pass you to my son. He's a German opera singer."

He threw me the phone. I caught it and dropped it on the coffee table as if it were radioactive.

"German opera?" said Oskar, "Sing it to me, baby!"

"Oh, for God's sake," I mumbled. "It's just a tune I heard, goes like..." And I did a not-so-bad job of singing it in made-up German.

"Oh, that's easy!" said Oskar.

14. The Beautiful Maid of the Mill

"Franz Schubert," said Oskar over the phone.

It suddenly felt like a fog had cleared between my brain cells. The song on the stereo in the bakery was by Schubert. Not that I had any idea who Schubert actually was. A name I heard in school once. Maybe.

"Do you know what the song's called?" I asked eagerly.

"It's part of a series of songs. Together they're called *Die schöne Müllerin.*"

"Translation, please?" said Dad, bending over the phone on the coffee table.

"*The Beautiful Maid of the Mill*," said Oskar. "But it's not opera. It's just a solo with a piano. I saw Dietrich Fischer–Dieskau and András Schiff perform it at Schubertiade Feldkirch in Austria, like, oh, thirty years ago. High school trip."

"Can you tweet me a summary in 140 characters or less?" asked Dad.

"Oh, let's see," said Oskar. "Guy falls in love with pretty daughter of a miller. But she finds him too boring and runs off with a hunter. Guy drowns himself in the river."

"Ahem," said Dad. "I thought as much." He picked his cell up off the table, tapped the screen and put it to his ear. "*Danke*, Oskar, you've been immensely helpful." A pause. "Yeah, talk to Jeff and Michel. See if they wanna meet for drinks at Tilly's. Maybe grab a bite at Chung's." Another pause. "Yeah, maybe Vince can come and give us a recital!" I rolled my eyes. Dad listened to Oskar's reply and then concluded, "All right, take it easy, buddy."

The phone beeped and a moment of silence descended. Pulling out my phone, I began thumbing a note:

Die Shoon Moolleren. Franz Shoebert.

Dad came over, beer in hand. "Well, that confirms my suspicion." And when he said "suspicion," his voice slurred a bit. I scanned the minibar and saw two empty bottles already on the counter. *Were they from yesterday or today?*

"What *suspicion*?" I said, trying to pretend I didn't know what he was getting at.

"Hey, I've seen the pretty blonde who works at the bakery."

"She actually owns it."

"Beautiful maid of the mill, eh?" Dad moved the bottle from hand to hand. "And then you come back singing German opera."

"It's not like that," I said. "She drives me nuts."

"Of course she does."

"No, I'm serious. She's a bit of a... you know."

"A what?"

"A conspiracy theorist!"

Dad tipped his bottle back. "Well, nobody's perfect."

I sighed noisily and clicked through more movie listings, having reached the Rs, with *Rambo: Last Blood* being offered on the screen.

"What kind of conspiracies?" asked Dad. "She into Bigfoot?"

"No," I mumbled.

"Thinks the Queen's an extraterrestrial lizard?"

"She says the WHO is faking the pandemic."

"Oh, that," said Dad, sounding disappointed. After another pull of his beer, he asked, "So did you ask her out?"

"No, she kicked me out."

"Social distancing? Hmm. Doesn't sound like her thing. She's the one with that sign—No Face, No Bread—isn't she?

"She has a new sign, now." I paused. "This one got a cop knocking on her door."

"Oh," he said, followed by a barely audible burp.

"Dad," I said with sudden calmness. "Do you think it's a hoax?"

Dad turned, sauntered back to the minibar and tossed the empty bottle into the recycling bin. Opening the fridge again, he pulled out a can of Beck's. He stared at the label. "There! German beer. Want some?"

"Why not?" I said, reaching out my hand.

As he tossed it to me, he said, "Just don't think about it."

"Think about what?"

He pulled another can out of the fridge and set it on the counter. "Whether COVID's a hoax," he said. "Gotta go along to get along. Don't rock the boat because—"

"—the Indian's the first one they throw off," I completed.

"Still," he said, slapping his hands together, "she's a looker, so you might want to question it a bit."

"Question what?"

"The pandemic."

I sighed and slumped back in the couch, cracking the tab on the beer can. "I mean, she might be onto something," I confessed. "It's like we live in a Twilight Zone episode now. Three months without work. How long can that go on?"

"Ah," said Dad opening his can. "They'll just print more money. We may not get rich, but we won't starve. Don't fret about it. You have more important things to focus on, like how to land a date with the Beautiful Maid of the Mill."

"She's pretty mad at me," I said. "I doubt she'll even let me back in the store."

"Does she know your name?"

"No, we didn't get that far."

"Send in a résumé. She's had that Help Wanted sign on the window for months. Get an interview."

"Hmm," I said with a nod. Even when he was half-drunk, he always had some good ideas.

I was tired of scanning Netflix. I had reached the V's and found nothing I hadn't already seen or cared to see. I took a sip of the German beer.

"But how will I even get an interview?" I asked. "She'll slam the door on me once she sees me."

"Wear a mask!" said Dad, with a hearty laugh.

"Actually, that's what got us butting heads in the first place. She thinks masks are part of the hoax."

"No, not one of these COVID masks." He pulled out a 3M from his back pocket and dangled it from his index finger. "Get a real mask." With the same finger he pointed to the TV screen.

A smiling, black-and-white, full face mask was staring back at us. The listing said *V for Vendetta*. I'd already seen it. It was about a dagger-tossing survivor of forced medical experiments.

The hero takes on an evil British government while wearing a Guy Fawkes mask, a gaucho hat and a black cape.

"Ah," said Dad, swishing his beer can in the air, "she'll love the Guy Fawkes look. Read about him back in school. He tried to blow up Parliament because they wouldn't let him be Catholic."

"But I don't know if she's Catholic, Dad."

"Not the point," said Dad, sitting back down on the couch. "Fawkes is a symbol of freedom. It'd be like making fun of the masks. It's a mask to end all masks."

I looked at the white face on the screen, with its pointed goatee.

No face, no service, the Dandelion had said. Well, that mask definitely had a face.

I got up off the couch and sat on a barstool in front of Dad's laptop. After pulling up Google, I typed: "guy fawkes buy canada." The website gorillasurplus.com came up as the first search result with the following description:

The Guy Fawkes mask worn in V for Vendetta has become a popular symbol of protest thanks to vigilante hacker group, Anonymous. Whether you stand for anarchy, justice or freedom from oppression, wear your Guy Fawkes mask with pride. Freedom Forever!

"I don't know, Dad, seems kind of spooky. Might scare customers."

"Ah," said Dad, waving his empty can in the air. "Fawkes is a smiling, happy-go-lucky guy. They wear them every year in England."

"Says it'll be here by Tuesday."

"Probably take you that long to write a résumé," said Dad, tipping back his empty can. "Under skill set you can put opera singing. God knows you can't bake."

"I used to make bannock with Grandad," I grumbled. "And welding is sort of like baking. They both involve heat."

Dad crumpled his can and tossed it into the recycling bin.

"Well, it doesn't look like the plant's going to be needing a welder anytime soon. So why not give it a shot?"

I stared at the mask on the screen—its frozen smile daring

me to click the ADD TO CART button.

15. V for Vincent

Wednesday mid-morning, I sat in the kitchen alone. On the plate in front of me were two lightly toasted slices from the dense loaf of sour-dough Constable Corona had bought me, covered with peanut butter. After four days of sourdough, I was starting to enjoy the sharp taste.

Also on the table, the laptop streamed a video of the bread's blonde baker. The Dandelion's long hair, spilling out of her head like a golden waterfall, was tamed somewhat by another of her artistic braids wrapped around her forehead. Behind her I could see a large oven. She was holding a white book up to the camera. The cover displayed a black silhouette of a disintegrating coronavirus and the words *Corona Fehlalarm?* in red capital letters.

After visiting the Moosehead Artisan Bakery's website, I had found a link to her "coronacircus" YouTube channel with over fifty videos. I'd already watched ten.

"This little book has already sold a quarter million copies in Germany," she was saying on screen. "*Corona: False Alarm?* It's written by two German scientists." She started flipping through the pages. "Drs. Reiss and Bhakdi are saying what I've been saying since April. Things like calling everyone who gets tested positive for SARS-CoV-2 a COVID-19 case—that's just flat-out lying. Here's what they say..." She slowly translated:

> Each positive laboratory test for the virus was reported as a COVID-19 case, irrespective of clinical presentation. This definition represented an *unforgivable* breach of the first rule governing the study of infectious diseases: the necessity to differentiate between "infection" (invasion and multiplication of an agent in the host) and "infectious disease" (infection with ensuing illness.)

"In other words," she said. "Just because you might have some genetic fragments floating around in your blood, doesn't mean you're sick."

She continued translating:

> COVID-19 is the designation for severe illness that occurs

only in about 10% of infected individuals; but because of incorrect designation, the number of "cases" surged and the virus vaulted to the top of the list of existential threats to the world.

She closed the book and looked at the camera the same way a cat looks at a mouse. "Why aren't more people asking what's really going on here? Is the media just trying to jazz up the news? After all, it doesn't sound all that sensational to say that one thousand people caught the common cold today and nine-hundred-and-ninety-nine of them are going to do just fine. And the one who dies was at the end of his or her life with three other pre-existing health conditions."

She put down the book and her voice picked up a little fury.

"No, the regular cold and flu season isn't exciting enough. Let's say, instead, that there's a super-deadly respiratory virus ripping through society. It makes you wonder if—"

Suddenly, a raspy voice began singing along to a guitar. The music emanated not from the laptop but from my pants pocket. My cellphone's ringtone was, ironically, "Cellphone Vigilante"— a silly song by The Arrogant Worms, a Canadian band my old buddy Léo had turned me onto. Its lyrics tell the tale of a man dedicated to destroying people's cellphones if they answer them at inappropriate moments. Pulling mine out, I tapped the screen, while hitting the space bar on the laptop, pausing Stefanie's video.

"Hello?" I said.

"Hello, sir!" said a distinctly Middle Eastern accent. "This is UPS courier. I have package for Vincent McKnight."

I stood and looked out the window, seeing his mud-brown truck parked at the curb. "Why didn't you just ring the doorbell?"

"I can't do that, sir. I am in my van."

"Why don't you get out of your van?"

"Yes, sir. I will do that."

"Great."

"I will put your parcel on the sidewalk. Then I drive away. Then you can open your door and pick it up."

I grinned at Stefanie's frozen image on the screen. "Yeah, sure, do whatever you have to do to... stay safe."

"Thank you very much, sir."

He hung up and I tossed the phone on the table beside the plate of crumbs. Out the window I saw the van door open and a man with a red turban and a black face mask step out. He set a small cardboard box on the sidewalk. I moved into the front hallway and gripped the doorknob.

I hesitated—unsure if it was "safe" to go out yet.

Oh, for goodness' sake, I thought.

I yanked open the door. Instantly, the man yelped as if Frankenstein's monster had stepped out onto the front porch. He crossed his arms over his masked face and stumbled backwards toward the open side door of his van.

"Do you need a signature?" I yelled out to him as he turned and ran.

"No, no, sir!" He clambered up into his van. "Don't worry." He slammed the door and revved his engine.

I sighed as he sped away down an empty Magder Road. He seemed genuinely scared, which spoiled all the fun of his over-reaction. I sprinted across the driveway to the box. Taking out my keys, I cut the tape, pulled the flaps back and looked inside.

At that very moment the world felt lighter. Yes, there was a virus going around killing people. Or there were government mandates going around killing people pretending that the virus did it. One or the other. But, at that moment, there was just a smiling white mask staring up at me from inside the box. I picked it up, tore away the plastic covering, pulled its elastic band around my head, peered through the eyeholes and gazed upon our street lined with old homes and modern cars.

A boy on a bicycle was approaching. He stared for a few seconds, then yelled: "Awesome, man!"

I gave him a thumbs-up. I felt like a superhero.

Turning back to the house, I pulled at the plastic mask. It was a little harder to breathe with compared to Mom's green mask. Nonetheless, it somehow felt freer. I let it snap back into place. Stepping into the hallway, I opened the coat closet and pulled out Dad's fedora. He only wore it to church. And he only went to Sunday morning Mass when he didn't have a hangover. So, needless to say, it looked brand new. I placed it on my head. Turning to the mirror on the hallway wall, I admired my new countenance.

Not bad, I thought. *A bit bold, but certainly not a turtle in his shell.*

Remembering scenes from the *V for Vendetta* movie, I began kicking and punching the air, making use of Mr. Chung's martial arts training. I fought my way down the hallway, striking at imaginary coronaviruses floating in the air, veering to the left and returning to the kitchen. I spun in a circle as I moved toward the sink. Reaching out, I grabbed at the sheathed knives slotted in the sharpener hanging from the cupboard. With a spine-shuddering screech of metal against metal, I pulled out a nine-inch butcher knife and a twelve-inch boning knife.

"V for Vincent!" I declared out loud through the small slit in the mask as I slashed an invisible V in the air. I then spun around in another circle, chopping a hovering coronavirus the size of a bowling ball in half with the butcher knife. I was mentally emancipating myself from the subconscious turtle shell and emerging as a—

"Ah!" cried my mother, who had suddenly appeared at the kitchen entrance. I froze, the points of both blades pointed at her chest, as her scream lingered in the air.

16. U for Ungulate

"Mom, it's just me!" I dropped the boning knife on the kitchen table with a clatter and pulled off the fedora and Fawkes mask.

She put one hand on her chest and the other against the wall for support.

"Vincent!" she gasped. "What in God's name are you doing?"

The grinning white mask dangling in one hand, a wide butcher knife in the other, I said, "I'm just, umm, prepping for a job interview."

Mom moved to a chair at the table, sat down, and pushed the boning knife aside. "A job interview. Where? At the circus? An insane asylum?"

"Actually, the bakery."

"The bakery? What about your job at the plant?"

I shrugged, putting the butcher knife back in the sharpener. "Who knows when they'll be up and running. Grandad said it was time for me to get back to work."

"But a bakery? What do you know about baking bread?"

"Well, I used to help Grandma make bannock."

"You don't *bake* bannock." Mom reached across the table, took the Guy Fawkes mask and stared at it. "And you're going to wear this thing for your job interview?"

"I was trying to make an unforgettable impression."

"By dressing up as a psycho?"

"It's Guy Fawkes, Mom."

"I know who it is!"

She put the mask back down on the table.

"He's Catholic," I said.

"I don't care if he's the pope. He tried to blow up the House of Lords and kill the king. No son of mine is going to be going around looking like a lunatic. The pandemic is scary enough without you throwing knives around."

I grinned. "I was just going to bring the mask and hat, not the knives."

She shook her head, utterly unamused. "What in the world were you thinking? Why would you wear this to a job interview? *At a bakery*?"

"It was actually Dad's idea."

She snorted. "And how drunk was he when he gave you this sage advice?"

I shrugged. "It's just, you know, the owner of the bakery, she doesn't like the COVID masks much. I thought I could make a good impression with her if I wore another kind of mask. Not a medical mask. You know what I mean?"

"This is that German bakery on Main Street?"

I nodded.

"With that pretty girl with the long blonde hair."

She pointed to Stefanie's frozen image on the laptop.

I hesitated.

"I see," said Mom with a faint smile. "That's the place with that awful No Face, No Service sign on the front window, isn't it?"

"Actually, I got her to tear it up."

I reached into my pocket, where I still had the two halves. I unfolded them and placed them on the table.

Mom stared at the torn sign and said, "Good for you."

"But she has a bigger sign now. 'Stay at home, decay at home.'"

"Mother Mary!"

Mom's palms collided together in spontaneous prayer.

"She says masks don't stop COVID. That they're just a symbol of servitude—"

Mom waved both her hands in the air, palms toward me now.

"I don't want to hear it."

I didn't say anything more and reached across the table to pull back the Guy Fawkes mask, but Mom snatched it away.

"You call this piece of plastic a mask?" she said, holding it up. "I'll show you a mask!"

With that she rose, stepped out of the kitchen and marched down the hallway. I followed her red curls into the sewing room. She left Guy Fawkes' face hanging on the doorknob. Heading straight to the rack of costumes, she started sliding hangers aside until she pulled out a dark brown, furry suit, with hooves for hands and feet.

"Here!" She handed me the costume and then moved to the closet.

"What's this?" I asked.

"An ungulate," she said.

"A what?"

Opening its double doors revealed floor-to-ceiling shelves of three-dimensional felt masks that covered the entire head. Two dozen decapitated animals and cartoon characters stared back at us, including a rabbit, a dinosaur, Donald Duck, a bug-eyed alien and a moose with a big red tongue hanging out.

Mom said, "Ungulates are hooved mammals like cows, gi-raffes, horses and..."

Grabbing both antlers, she pulled the moose head off the shelf. I stared at its big white eyes, gaping jaw and massive over-bite. The left antler was torn and hanging.

"It's called Moosehead Bakery, isn't it?" she asked.

"Yeah, Moosehead Artisan Bakery."

She handed me the moose mask, saying, "I can hem it back to your size and mend that antler this afternoon."

"But Mom, isn't this the mascot you made for the football

team at St. Mike's?"

She waved her hand dismissively. "No team this year. COVID cancelled all that. You might as well use it."

I set the mask down on the cutting table and examined it.

"You're right, Mom, that sure is a mask." And the moose costume would certainly hide my identity better. Smiling, I added, "It's great, Mom. I think she'll love it."

"I'm sure *she* will," Mom said, smirking.

On the wall, above Mom's sewing machine, hung a wood-framed clock. The hour hand was approaching eleven.

"Oh! I gotta go, Mom." I kissed her cheek and spun around. "Appointment with Grandad at the Moosehead Gulags."

Or so I thought.

17. Trust the Experts

I sprinted onto the front lawn of the retirement home, swung off my backpack and dropped into the wobbly plastic chair under the canopy. Setting my pack on the ground, I was careful not to crack the glass jar of almond butter. As I wiped sweat from my forehead, I became aware that the other canopy shaded only empty chairs.

I glanced at my cell: 11:00 a.m. exactly. I stared up at the front entrance. *Are they going to be late again?*

The door immediately opened and Mathéo stepped out.

Huh?

He sauntered to the edge of the steps and halted. In a white T-shirt and white medical mask, he looked like a burly orderly at a psych ward. Mathéo was one of those guys who could eat salad, never do a single push-up, and still have all these bulky muscles. He wasn't exactly ripped, more a big grizzly bear no one would want to mess with, even though his heart was as soft as a teddy's.

Seeing his face covering reminded me to pull out my own. As I strapped it into place, I called up, "*Bonjour,* Mathéo!"

He looked down. "Hi Vince," he said in his Francophone accent.

I grabbed my backpack and sprinted up the ramp to where he stood on the landing, holding a metal thermos. "You visiting your aunt?"

Mathéo nodded. "She's sick," he said softly. "Cough. Low oxygen. They think she has COVID."

"Ah!" I waved my hand dismissively. "They call any little symptom COVID. Toenail fungus! Low blood pressure! What's next? A hangnail?"

I was surprised to hear myself say that.

Mathéo just stared at me.

"Come on, remember when this first came out and they called it Wuhan Pneumonia?"

He looked at me quizzically. "No, not really."

Neither had I. But one of the Dandelion's videos that morning had pointed it out.

"COVID-19 originally referred to people with severe respiratory trouble," I recited, sounding more intelligent than I possibly could have been at the time. "You had to be coughing up a lung for it to be COVID. Now someone can have COVID without even a sore throat."

"Hmmm." He was listening. The gears always moved slower in Mathéo's head.

"Kind of weird to have a disease with no symptoms, isn't it?" I asked.

"Well, *Tante* Sofia has a cough and a sore throat."

I shrugged. "And so have we all at one time or another. It's probably just a cold."

"Yeah." He looked back at the closed door. "I would have a cold, too, if they locked me up like that."

"No kidding," I said, speaking twice as fast as Mathéo. "Grandad's in a wheelchair now. COVID didn't do that to him. Lockdown did."

"In a *wheelchair*?" Mathéo didn't often look surprised. "He used to walk all the way to the library and back."

"Exactly."

"Well," said Mathéo, looking out at the road. "We do need to keep them safe."

"I'm not so sure we can." Actually, I was pretty sure we could not. "But we could do better at keeping them healthy and happy."

"Hmm," murmured Mathéo again.

He was never one to open his mouth unless he had something good to say (or eat). I pointed to the large thermos in his hands.

"What's that?" I asked.

"French Canadian pea soup. *Tante* Sofia's recipe."

Mathéo loved to cook. Even when we were little, and most kids brought sandwiches to school, Mathéo would unpack leftover quiche or lasagna that he made the night before. Unscrewing the thermos, he unleashed the aroma of split peas, celery, parsley and bacon.

"That smells amazing," I said. "Send my mom the recipe, would you?"

He screwed the lid back on. "Can't. *Tante* made me promise to never write it down. Côté family only. Taught generation to generation by word of mouth, memorized in French."

"Oral tradition, eh?" I replied. "Grandad's like that, too. I'm sure she'll love it."

He sighed. "Only if they let me give it to her. I tried going in. They told me to wait out here."

At that moment, Claudia pushed the front door open. This time she wore a visor plus a mask.

"Hey, sorry, guys," she said, "but we're in quarantine."

I shook my head. "Again?"

"No, not again." She stepped out fully and put her hands on her hips. "Before we were in *lockdown*. This time it's quarantine. This time someone's actually sick."

"*What?* Mathéo's aunt? It's probably just a cold or—"

Claudia pointed at me and shook her head. "Sofia could have TB for all you know. We're doing a PCR test. If it comes back negative then we can open back up."

"But you still wouldn't know if it's TB," said Mathéo slowly, his forehead a little furrowed.

She rolled her dark brown eyes, but didn't respond.

I filled my chest up with air, trying to stay calm. It didn't work.

"You're not saying I can't see Grandad?" I said on the exhale.

"That's exactly what I'm saying."

I looked up at the sky. "This is crazy! He's had enough lockdown."

"Hey, you wanna kill off the whole home?"

I looked her straight in the eye. "How do you know it's not these masks you make them wear?" I pointed to my own. "How often do you clean them?"

She just stared back, her jaw set in her chubby face.

"Once a week with their clothes?" I pressed.

She didn't answer.

"These damp rags breed germs. Surgeons change them every two hours. A friend of mine says they give people bacterial pneumonia."

"And is your friend a surgeon?" Claudia responded, crossing her arms.

"No." I hesitated. "She's a baker."

Now Claudia was glancing up at the sky. "Okay. Thanks. I think I'll stick to the medical experts."

"Like Bill Gates?" cut in Mathéo, in a quiet voice.

Claudia snorted and gestured toward the thermos. "I can bring the soup to Sofia."

"*Merci*," said Mathéo curtly, handing over the thermos.

"Hey, I don't make up the rules."

I put my bag on the ground and began unzipping it. "I know, I know, you don't wanna be Nazi Nurse." I pulled out the jar of nut butter. "Can you give this to Grandad? He may need help opening it. It says you need to stir it because all the oil will rise—"

"Yeah, I'll get it to him."

I then pulled out half of the sourdough loaf Constable Corona had bought me. "And here's some more bread for him. It's been in the freezer. Needs—"

"Yeah," she interrupted, taking the loaf, "the kitchen will figure it out."

Jar in one hand, thermos and bread in the other, Claudia elbowed the wheelchair button and the front door eased open.

"Hey, I'm sorry, guys," she said. "Trust me, I wish things were different. Check out the website tomorrow. We'll post the results of the test. Like you said, it's probably just a cold."

"And if it's not?" I asked.

She leaned on the open door. "We have a contractor ready to spray the building."

"What, with chemicals?"

"They're Health Canada approved."

I glanced at Mathéo, who looked like the gears in his head were picking up speed. "It's an airborne virus," he said, "not a bedbug infestation."

"Hey, I told you, I don't take medical advice from bakers, and the same goes for French chefs." The automated door began to close slowly on her. "Guys, I know you care. Just let the experts take care of your folks."

She turned and entered the building.

"Hmm." Mathéo crossed his thick arms. "*Qu'est-ce qu'on peut faire?*"

I grumbled, turned and sprinted back down the ramp, along the side of the building, stopping below Grandad's second floor window. Picking up a pine cone from the lawn, I flung it at the glass. It took three tries before Grandad appeared and slid the bottom half of the window open.

"Grandad!" I called up. "Pack your bags! It's time to clear this nuthouse."

18. Standing Hungry

From the other side of the screen window, Grandad said something. But between his room being on the second floor, and his voice being so soft, I couldn't understand what he was saying.

Pulling out my cell, I tapped on "Grandad." It rang twice before I saw him bring a phone to his ear.

"Don't break my window," he said immediately.

"I need to break you out of there," I shot back.

"'Having my freedom, boast of nothing else,'" said Grandad in a British accent.

"What?" I called back.

"*King Richard the Second*. Act 1. Scene 3."

I pulled my mask off and switched to speakerphone.

"I once broke out of school," he said.

"Let's do it again!"

"The penguin would have to come with me."

"*Penguin?*"

"Easier to tame than cats."

"*What?*"

"I helped bury a cat once. In the school. The cats go to heaven too. Father Milburn told me. He held funerals for all the cats that died at the school. Sister Tam said it was a waste of time. She said just stick a cross in the ground."

A wave of frustration rose in me. Mathéo started walking down the ramp.

"The prime minister called me yesterday. He wanted to know if I liked the food. I told him... I told him..." His voice wavered.

Was it the dementia or was locking him up again making him go bonkers?

I started to pace. Mathéo was crossing the lawn, heading my way, his black curly hair looking a little crazy in the hot afternoon sun.

"I brought you some nut butter," I said into the phone, looking back up at the window.

"Nut butter?" said Grandad, sounding distant, confused.

"You said you wash your hair with it."

He chuckled. "Oh, yes. That's terrific!" And when he said "terrific" he sounded gleeful, lost in some blissful oblivion.

"I'm joking. It's for your bread."

"My head?"

"No, your bread."

"Oh, I ate all the bread. Breakfast. Lunch. Dinner. Can you bring more? There is this blonde baker in New York. I think she's German. Maybe Dutch."

Boy, he's really out of it today, I thought. *Haven't seen him this bad.*

"Actually, I'm trying to get a job at her bakery."

"Really?" said Grandad. "That would be a good person for you to work with. Miskwaadesi and Dodoshaabo-jiibik."

"Dodoshaabo-jiibik." I repeated. "Is that how you say dandelion in Ojibwemowin?"

"Yes, it means, it means milk root."

"I doubt she drinks milk," I said. "I suspect she's a vegan."

"What's a vegan?" said Grandad.

"Someone who doesn't eat meat," I responded.

"Strange."

"Yes, she is."

Mathéo was now at my side. He waved up at Grandad. Grandad pressed his hand to the screen.

"Yeah," I continued. "So, if I get that job I might be able to afford my own place. You can come and live with me. Get you out of this prison."

"Yes. Yes. I'll be leaving soon." He chuckled. "Very soon. Me and your big friend, there. We have work to do, places to go."

I looked at Mathéo. He shrugged.

"Yeah," I said. "I saw a For Rent sign at Mr. Chung's. You can have rice and mushrooms every night."

Grandad didn't say anything. Just stared.

"You remember Chung's, right?" I said. "The Green Dragon."

"Oh, yes," he said unconvincingly.

I paused, not sure what to say.

Grandad broke the silence with a cheerful, "Hello, Vince!" He raised his hand again, as if he'd just seen me.

"Hmm," said Mathéo. "My aunt's more like that now." He pulled off his mask and stuffed it in his back pocket. "She just suddenly stops making sense." He tilted his head side to side. "If I ask about the past she makes more sense. Things that happened long ago—that's where they live now."

I nodded glumly and turned back to Grandad. "You said you broke out of the residential school, once. You never told me that before."

"My sister had died. And I wanted to see my mother again." Mathéo was right; his voice suddenly sounded more present and coherent. "They found me in a tree in the woods. Fish bellies took me back." He paused. "Told me the savage must be crucified and resurrected as a good Christian. Kill the Indian, save the child."

He paused. I thought he was done, but then he continued.

"Sister Tam put me in the basement. No food. No light. And a bucket to pee and poo in. After three days, she took me to the refectory. Made me stand in the middle watching everyone eat breakfast. Then, again, at lunch. I watched. Standing hungry. Barely able to stand."

"Grandad." My knuckles were white, gripping the phone. "Those weren't Christians."

"Sister Tam made me read the Bible out loud over and over again, while everyone ate."

"Sociopath."

"They ate bread. I ate the Word."

"Grandad," I murmured.

"'For I was hungry and you gave me something to eat,'" he began to recite. "'I was thirsty and you gave me something to drink. I was a stranger and you invited me in.'" He sounded like he was crying. "'I needed clothes and you clothed me, I was sick and you looked after me, I was... I was...'"

"J'étais en prison, et vous êtes venus vers moi," Mathéo finished while I stared blankly. "I was in prison and you came to visit me."

A long silence slid by.

"Grandad?" I finally said, not sure what else to say.

"Then Father Milburn came for me. He told me to promise Sister Tam that I would be a good Christian and not run away. Then she would leave me alone. Then she would give me food. Mother Mary would be my mother now."

I felt my bowels clenching.

"I never tried to escape again."

My heart pounded like a hummingbird was trying to escape my ribcage. Mathéo pulled his mask out of his pocket and used it to wipe his cheeks.

Grandad withdrew from the window. "I need to feed the penguin, now."

My hand holding the phone was shaking. "I'll get you out of there, Grandad."

He chuckled. And hung up the phone.

On a tree branch, jutting out past Grandad's window, black wings suddenly descended. A crow cocked its head to the left and right, and let out two gawks. That guttural sound enraged me. I picked up another pine cone and whipped it at the bird. It missed and ricocheted off the bricks. The crow looked at me with its yellow eyes, gawked and lifted back up into the air.

"You okay?" said Mathéo, putting a hand on my shoulder.

"I'll get this job. Get enough money. Get a place to live. Chung has an Apartment For Rent sign. And I'll get Grandad out of there before they kill him."

Mathéo's lips parted, as if he was going to say something but couldn't. He was staring a few windows farther along the red-brick wall of the geriatric penitentiary, where his Aunt Sofia lay sick in bed, all alone.

19. German Sherbert

That evening, I lay on the weight bench, in the basement, alone. Above me, at the end of my outstretched arms, I gripped a twenty-kilo barbell with twenty-kilo plates on each end. Sixty kilograms total. I could lift more, but not safely without a spotter. (Dad was usually too tipsy and Mom wouldn't let anyone in the house from outside of our bubble.) I held the weight for as long as I could, transferring into the metal bar the frustration and turmoil swirling around in my heart.

Die schöne Müllerin blared over the giant speakers that flanked the TV. I'd listened to four versions on YouTube before finding the one the Dandelion had been playing in the bakery. Surprisingly, the singer, Ian Bostridge, wasn't German, but English. He'd also written a book on seventeenth-century witchcraft. And the pianist, Mitsuko Uchida, was also not German, but born in a seaside town near Tokyo. Her father became the Japanese ambassador to Austria, where she moved at twelve. By the time she turned twenty-one she had won first prize in the Beethoven Competition in Vienna.

Yes, I had been doing my homework.

And then there was the composer, Franz Schubert himself— died when he was only thirty-one from typhoid fever. Despite passing so young, he composed over 1,500 songs, symphonies and overtures (whatever an overture was). I was already twenty-four and couldn't say I'd created much of anything that would be remembered if COVID-19 (or some real disease) took my life.

Across from me, on the bar counter, were two stacks of printouts—lyrics in German on the left, English on the right. I'd highlighted my favourite parts. Memorized a few lines. I'd even been soliciting unpaid tutoring from Oskar. Every day I called him up and he helped make my pronunciation *"etwas verständlich"* (somewhat comprehensible).

I let the weight descend slowly to my chest and then thrust

it back up. Suspending the barbell in the air, my eyes skirted over to the open laptop on the bar counter, displaying my sparse résumé.

I'll be lucky to get a polite email back. What the hell am I doing? I know nothing about baking. I could only remember four ingredients in the bannock recipe. *Maybe that was all there was? Maybe Grandad would know?*

I wanted an excuse to call him; to check on him. I set the barbell on the rack, pulled out my cell, and tapped on his name. But the phone just rang. He didn't have voicemail or an answering machine. *Napping,* I guessed.

I got up, my sweaty shirt sticking to my back, plopped down on the barstool and emptied a one-liter water bottle. Then, rubbing my clean-shaven face, I reviewed my skimpy employment history on the laptop:

- 2010–2013: Delivering newspapers for *The Moosehead Gazette.*
- 2013–2016: Busboy and dishwasher at the Green Dragon's Chinese Buffett.
- 2016–2020: Welder at Sacro's Automotive Plant.

Under Education, I had a high school diploma and a year of trade school.

She's probably been to some fancy European university, I thought. She spoke five languages; while I barely passed grade nine French. I doubted I could even spell ten words in Ojibwemowin.

I opened the internet browser and typed:

www.mooseheadartisanbakery.ca

Clicking "ABOUT," an image loaded of Stefanie Müller standing in front of another shop, in some other town. Above the front entrance, a wooden sign hung which read *Bäckerei Sonnenblume.* Below the photo it read:

I spent four years apprenticing at my granny's Sunflower Artisan Bakery in Germany, where my father, brother and sister live. Granny died in spring of 2019. Her bakery was sold. I returned to Canada in the autumn, where my mother works as a nurse at Sudbury General. Having become used to small town life in Europe, I had no desire to return to the big city. With money Granny left me, I moved to Moosehead and opened Moosehead Artisan Bakery in November 2019.

Just in time for lockdown, I thought.

"Vince, you down there?" hollered Mom.

I heard footsteps trudging down the basement stairwell. I turned. Mom appeared, a mended moose mask in hand.

Immediately she cocked her ear and said, "What're you listening to?"

"Franz Schubert."

"French Sherbert?"

"It's German, Mom."

"German Sherbert?"

"No, German classical music."

"Since when do you listen to opera?" She stared down at me, her large, black glasses slipping forward on her sweaty nose.

"It's not opera," I corrected. "It's a *Lied*."

"A what?" she hollered.

Grabbing the remote, I lowered the volume.

"A *Lied*, Mom," I repeated. I picked up the printout beside the laptop and read, "A *Lied's* a term in the German vernacular to describe setting poetry to classical music to create a piece of polyphonic music."

"Polyphonic?"

"It's where they mix melodies and tones."

My mom approached and put her hand on the back of my neck. "Are you okay, dear? You're not getting COVID, are you?"

"Maybe typhoid, but not COVID," I said with exasperation. "I'm just trying to get ready for my interview at the German bakery."

"With the German girl?"

"She's actually Canadian."

"And very pretty."

I tilted my head and ran my hand through my sweaty black hair. "It's the only place hiring."

"And for good reason." Mom pushed her glasses back up her nose. "You better not be bringing home any COVID or you're quarantined in your room for two weeks, young man."

I chuckled, not really sure if she was joking or not.

"I need to earn a living," I said, apologetically.

"Your father doesn't mind unemployment." She looked around the basement. "Do you know where he is?"

I paused. "Ummm."

"That's what I thought." She walked toward me on the stool. "Oh, well. Might drink less with his buddies." She handed me the moose mask. "Moosey's all fixed up."

"He looks fantastic!" I took the mask, feeling the costume rolled up inside. "Thanks so much, Mom."

"Try it on! Make sure it fits."

I set the head on the counter and unrolled the costume.

Mom's phone began to beep. She pulled it out and looked at the display. "Oh! I almost forgot, Father Shostakovich is offering confession tonight."

"Is it over Zoom?" I asked, only half-jokingly.

"Absolutely not!" she said, bonking me over the head lightly with her fist. "They would never offer any of the Holy Sacraments over the internet."

With that she turned and headed back up the steps saying, "Any problems, I can mend it in the morning."

"Thanks, Mom!"

Suddenly remembering, I sprinted to the stairwell.

"Hey, Mom! Do you have any green ribbon?"

She turned around, at the top of the stairs. "I have all kinds of ribbon. Bottom drawer on the left in the sewing room."

"I just need a little."

"Help yourself!" Her phone beeped again. "I gotta go confess my sins."

"What did you do?" I called back. "Let your mask slip below your nose while shopping at Fabricland?"

"Oh, you!" she exclaimed with a chuckle, before vanishing out of view.

I slipped my legs into the fake fur and pulled up the moose costume. A perfect fit.

Turning to the moose mask on the bar counter, I said, "Well, Moosey, I guess it's now or never."

Sitting back down at the laptop, I clicked on the bakery's contact page, clicked on the Dandelion's email address and began typing:

> Please find attached my résumé. I'm a hard worker. Learn quickly.

I winked at Moosey and continued typing:

> And I don't wear one of those useless COVID masks. Available for an interview any time of the day or night. Vince.

As I hit send, Ian Bostridge sang over the speakers:

> Ist das denn meine Straße?
> O Bächlein, sprich, wohin?[*]

The next morning, I rolled out of bed into my smartphone's inbox. A message from stef@mooseheadbakery.ca awaited me:

> Your résumé is a little weak. But you get good points for the volunteer work at the old folks' home. And I appreciate the fact you went to trade school instead of going in debt with a university degree.

That was all it said.

Was that a polite way of saying, Thanks, but no thanks?

Instead of cold cereal that morning, I found myself kneading together flour, water, salt and baking soda. Once I had the dough rolled out and frying in butter on the pan, I started tapping a reply:

> Just saw your message. Am making some bread for breakfast.

I flipped the flatbread. It felt stiff and made a clunk when it hit the pan.

> I thought I'd drop by today if that's OK? To talk about the job.

Five minutes later, I was sitting at the kitchen table with Moosey's detached head staring directly at me. His red tongue hung out, as if he was ready to slurp up my plate of rigid

---

* Is this my path, then? / Oh brook, tell me, whither?

bannock.

"Hell!" exclaimed Dad.

He'd just sauntered into the kitchen. I turned. He was still in his pyjamas, black lines under his wide eyes. He pointed at Moosey. "I didn't think I was that hungover."

I chuckled. "No, don't worry, Dad. It's real."

"Of course it is."

He shuffled over to the coffee maker.

"What're you eating?" he asked, as he sniffed the air.

"The driest bannock ever made by human hands."

"Of course you are."

I used my tongue to loosen a wedge of dough stuck to the roof of my mouth.

Dad poured coffee. "You see your grandad, yesterday?"

"No. They wouldn't let me. The home's in quarantine again."

"Of course it is." He sighed, picked up his coffee and shuffled back into the hallway.

While sipping some orange juice (to moisten another glob of the bannock) the phone beeped. I tapped on the email:

OK. 4:30 p.m. Interview. Remember: NO face mask.

I grinned at Moosey. "Don't worry. She wasn't referring to you." And I slid the remaining dry bannock toward his gaping mouth.

20. Interview with a Moose

By 4:25 p.m., my heart was pounding. I stood at the traffic lights at Queen and Main Street, mere footsteps from her shop. Overcast skies made the furry costume tolerable. Nonetheless, sweat was forming on my back. My hands held the moose mask, which gazed forward, eyeless. Passersby were making an extra effort to social distance from its antlers.

"Time to make a fool of myself," I proclaimed out loud and lifted the mask over my head. I peered out through the vertical slits in the eyes and took a slow, deep breath.

Am I really doing this?

Suddenly, it felt as if an invisible hand was pushing against my back, marching me toward a humiliating destiny.

The Dandelion was standing at the window, inside the bakery, flipping around an Open/Closed sign. She looked at me, froze for a second and then broke out in laughter so loud I could hear it through the pane of glass. With a mix of hesitation and hope, I swung open the door, loudly jingling the bell.

"Now, that's a mask!" she said, her slight Germanic accent becoming less slight for a second. She was wearing a green apron, covered with flour dust.

Raising a hoof in the air, I said in the best moose voice I could muster, "But, not a stupid COVID face mask."

"Indeed!"

I bowed. "Moose extraordinaire... at your service."

She giggled and put her hand to her mouth.

Letting the right hoof flap open, I extended my hand, presenting her with a rolled up sheet of paper, tied in place with a bright green ribbon. "My references."

Exposing my other hand, I pulled the green ribbon off as I sang the one line I was able to learn after three days of practice with Oskar:

Nun schlinge in die Locken dein
Das grüne Band gefällig ein,
Du hast ja's Grün so gern.[*]

To which she sang back, with far better pronunciation and melody:

Dann weiß ich, wo die Hoffnung wohnt...[†]

"*Ja,*" was all I could respond, having reached the end of my German.

Again, she laughed, before blurting out: "You're hired!"

I jolted back at the unexpected acceptance. Reaching up, I pulled off the mask. "You do know who I am?"

She tilted her head to the left with a grin. "The turtle who

---

[*] So now wind into your curls
The green ribbon, if you please,
Since you like green so much.

[†] Then I'll know where hope resides...

thought he was a moose."

"Or a moose who thought he was a turtle." I chuckled, self-consciously.

"Either way, you seem to be coming out of your shell."

"Lovely ladies have that effect on me."

I blurted that out, much to my own surprise.

"Phooey! You can knock that off, right now." Her voice was stern, but still amused. "I'll be your boss. And there's nothing lovely about bosses."

"Forgive me." I set the mask back down over my face. "Awaiting orders, Captain Dandelion." I saluted and stood to attention.

"At ease, Mister Moose."

I relaxed my shoulders and arms.

"Hmmm. Your mask idea solves a dilemma I've had."

"It solved a dilemma I had, too."

She squinted. "Customers are not coming into the store as much."

"Well, that New Normal Drivel poster probably isn't helping." I tilted my antlers toward the front window.

"Well, it's staying up," she declared, putting her hand on her hips. "But that's why I wanted someone to start delivering bread to customers' doors. That way, the germaphobes—too scared to enter an enclosed space with other bio-hazardous human beings—can have their order dropped off at their self-imposed prison door." She paused. "It's just..." She paused again.

"They'd want the delivery guy to be wearing a mask."

"Right! And I don't want to give into the face mask nonsense."

"I've noticed," I said in my muffled moose mask voice.

"So, if you're willing to wear your moose costume when making deliveries..."

I tipped my antlers forward in acknowledgment. "If Captain Dandelion so commands it."

Inside, though, I felt a pang of fear grip my chest. *Delivering bread dressed like this? Forget about a COVID quarantine facility, they'll send me straight to the looney bin.*

"Well, then, you got the job," she said. "At least, a trial run. See how you do."

"Would I also be helping out around here?"

"I think you'll be too busy with the van. Restaurants as far away as Sudbury have been wanting bread delivered. I just didn't have the manpower."

"Well, now you have moosepower," I joked. Inwardly, though, I wasn't amused. I was rather hoping to spend more time with her, not all day in a van. "Well, that's the shortest job interview I ever had."

"Don't be too flattered," she said. "I've had an ad on Kijiji for three months and you're the first person to apply. Seems most are all too happy living off corona welfare cheques."

"It has been a cozy crisis." I shrugged my furry shoulders.

"Well, nothing cozy about this job. And, until orders pick up, all I can afford is $10 per hour."

"But that's lower than minimum wage," I protested, feeling even less amused.

"I know," she replied. "That's what I can afford but not what I'm going to pay you. I'll give you $15 an hour."

Now I felt quite confused. "But that's more than minimum wage."

"I know," she said again. "But I'm not going to let the government dictate how much I pay you. Since I can't pay you less than their mandated stipend, I'll pay you more."

"Well, that's one way to outsmart the bureaucrats," I replied.

$15 an hour, I thought to myself. *Eight hours a day. That would be $120 a day. Not bad.*

"But it'll have to be part-time," she clarified.

Okay, more like $60 a day.

"Six days a week."

About $360 a week. $1400 a month. $600 less than the government is already sending me. And now I'd have to work for it. And the flat Chung's renting is going for $900.

Nonetheless, I found myself saying: "Great, when can I start?"

"Eight o'clock, tomorrow morning."

Ah, forget about sleeping in, too.

"Can't wait!" I lied.

"Deal!"

She extended her hand. I extended my hoof.

"Welcome aboard, Vincent."

"Friends call me Vince."

"Well, as I said, I'll be your boss." She crossed her arms over her dusty apron. "So, I better call you Vincent, then."

I gulped.

"Anyway," she continued, "my fiancé's going to be jealous enough that I hired such a cute moose."

Fiancé? I suddenly felt like I had dropped down an open manhole. A manhole I should have seen coming.

"You're... you're engaged?" I said slowly.

"You better believe it." She pulled out the necklace hanging around her neck, revealing a ring with a green stone. "I can't keep it on my finger with all the kneading."

I looked at the engagement ring so intently I began to see double.

"It's green," I said.

"It's an emerald," she said.

"No diamond?"

She smiled widely. "Green, as you've observed, is my favourite colour."

Staring at the ring, those words from Schubert's *Lied* played back in mind:

Ach Grün, du böse Farbe du,
Was siehst mich immer an
So stolz, so keck, so schadenfroh...*

$400 less per month. Super early. Stupid uniform. And she's almost married.

"That's great!" I forced myself to utter in a tone resembling enthusiasm. "What's his name? Maybe I know him. Does he live with you?"

"Josef's his name. He lives in Bavaria."

"Bavaria?"

"It's a state in Germany—"

"Yes, yes, I know." Actually, I had thought it was a country. "Is he a baker, too?" I tried to sound interested.

---

* Oh green, you hateful color, you,
Why do you keep staring,
So mocking, so proud, so pleased by my pain ...

"Paramedic."

"Oh!" Another pause. "Well." Pause again. "Must be real busy these days with COVID and all."

"Actually, he says they hardly get any calls. Not for COVID. Not for cardiac arrest. Mainly corpses. People are just too scared to call until it's too late."

"Oh," I said. "Well, I bet there's plenty of need for a paramedic around here."

"When he moves to Canada he was planning on helping me run the bakery. I actually bought the delivery van for him. As a paramedic, he's used to lots of driving."

Ah, I realized. *I'm just a placeholder.*

Glad I was wearing a mask to hide the increasing tension that must have been showing on my face, I asked, "So, when's the wedding?"

She sighed. Took a few steps back. Looked at the ground. "May."

"Ah, still a good ten months away." I felt a little relief.

"No, last May."

"Oh." Confusion. "Why did you postpone?"

"Why do you think?"

She suddenly sounded angry. *At me? Was it a stupid question? This moose mask was getting as hot as a baker's oven.*

In a softer voice, she continued, "He can't enter the country with all these stupid COVID restrictions."

"But he's your fiancé."

"Yeah, but he's not Canadian." She looked away. "We've appealed five times. Even that good-for-nothing MP argued it out in Parliament—more for his own publicity, I suspect."

"I'm sorry." And I meant it. In more ways than one. "Well, this can't last forever."

"Yeah."

That's when I noticed on the wall, beside the counter, a series of photos. One was of her with a white-haired lady who wore giant, red-framed glasses—I assumed this was her grandmother. Another was of her, at what looked like age ten, beside a slightly older girl with curly black hair, who I assumed was her sister. Behind them stood a thin, blond-haired man on one side, and a chunky woman with shoulder-length, curly black hair on the other; I assumed these were her parents. The third framed photo was of her embraced by some blond guy with long sideburns, surrounded by trees full of golden leaves. They both appeared to be laughing.

I pointed to the last photo. "Is that Josef?"

She turned her head to the wall. "Yes. Just before I left Germany last fall." She smiled, cheeks giving way to slight dimples.

"Looks like a good guy." I tugged at one of my antlers. "I hope he likes mooses."

"Actually," she said with a pause, "he hunts game."

"Ah, I see."

"I'm trying to get him to go vegan."

I nodded. Immediately, I remembered a line from her stupid German *Lied*:

Was sucht denn der Jäger am Mühlbach hier?
Bleib, trotziger Jäger, in deinem Revier!*

"Well," she said after another pause. "I still have some things to do before I can call it a day."

"Absolutely. Umm. I'll see you tomorrow. Eight a.m."

Insufficient pay. Stupid uniform. Early hours. And lots of lone moosing it around the Greater Sudbury District in a bread van designated for her sideburn-strutting European fiancé. Even if I wasn't dressed as a cartoonish ungulate, I would have felt like an idiot.

"See you tomorrow," she said, her smile fading.

"You bet," I replied with no smile at all—just a stupid snout, with nostrils so wide they hung over the front lip.

Turning, I pranced out of the bakery, wondering how I got myself into such a predicament. Little did I know, by accepting that incidental delivery position, I'd actually stepped across the threshold of a rabbit hole—a rabbit hole that would lead to far more life-changing circumstances than early hours working for a conspiracy theorist engaged to a moose-hunting paramedic.

---

* What is the hunter doing at the millstream?
Bold hunter, stay in your forest preserve!

PART TWO
The Taming of the Moose

"The fear of freedom is the fear of assuming responsibility."
— *Joost A.M. Meerloo (1903–1976)*
Dutch American psychoanalyst

21. Health Canada Approved

I slowed the van to a halt in the driveway of 118 Rothwell Road and turned off the ignition. In the back of the van were fourteen green bins full of baked goods. I had the windows sealed and the air conditioning blasting, trapping the smells of sourdough, cardamon and cinnamon inside the enclosed space.

On the dashboard rested a clipboard with the list of orders. The Dandelion Luddite printed everything out, even though I told her she could just send it to my phone. She told me she'd boycotted smartphones and that they were part of the grand plan to enslave humanity. She said she would never call me on one. Just like she would never expect me to wear a face mask.

But a moose mask... well, that was different.

Looking over my shoulder, I could see antlers extending above the bins. Glancing down, I looked at the fur costume I was wearing. Even with the AC blowing in my face, I was already sweating.

Why are you doing this? I said to myself.

I didn't need the money. The plant would be reopening soon and my bank account was holding a four-digit balance for the first time in my short life, thanks to free government money and nowhere to spend it.

You know why you're doing this, I responded to myself. *Yes, it's hard to meet girls these days—but maybe I could check out some online dating sites.*

After all, Stefanie would soon be the wife of a German paramedic. Weren't all Germans like six foot six? And this one liked to hunt elk in his spare time; except now he was coming here for our Canadian moose. I was obviously wasting my time, if not risking my furry neck. Still, I knew she needed the help. It was only four hours a day. And what else did I have to do?

I looked at the clock—9:10 a.m.—and yawned. This was normally the time I'd be rolling out of bed, not rolling into someone's driveway looking like I was auditioning for a kids' TV show. In fact, that morning, walking to my first day of work, my neighbour, Jeff McLean, stopped me on the sidewalk.

"Hey! It's the moose from *Cucumber*," he announced to an

otherwise empty street.

"Cucumber?" I asked.

"When I was a kid, there was a show called *Cucumber* on *TV Ontario*. Had two actors. One of them was dressed as a moose, the other a beaver, teaching kids about science."

Science. I shook my head, as I now stared out the driver's side window of the parked van. An older fellow was sitting on the neighbouring porch, reading a newspaper. He was all alone, wearing a blue medical mask. *Sure seems like their generation could have used a few more TV shows teaching them science.*

I looked at the clipboard. Fifteen orders. Three hours to make them. Not all were in Moosehead, so I'd have to get moving. Looking at the top of the list, I read, Valerie Young. I swallowed.

"Best get it over with," I grumbled to myself.

Two loaves of rye and a box of oatmeal raisin cookies, said the list. Bin #3.

I opened the door and dropped onto the driveway. The bread van was as conspicuous as my costume—bright yellow, like a dandelion, with the words "Eat Real Bread" in big black letters. I walked around, opened the rear doors and grinned at Moosey's big white eyes, devoid of irises.

"Ol' Mrs. Young," I said to Moosey with a groan. "Better you than me."

Thirty seconds later, Moosey was ringing the doorbell with my hoof-covered hand. Mrs. Young's house was huge. The garden out front was normally thick with flowers. This year it was thick with weeds. Two arched iron doors with double-glazed glass made me feel as if I were standing on the steps of royalty. Instead, a dusty plaque on the limestone wall informed me I stood on a designated heritage site, belonging to the first mayor of Moosehead, dating back to 1885. The wraparound porch was painted bright green and looked like it hadn't been swept since 1885. Beside the lordly doors was an ornate, round side table. On its walnut surface was a clear plastic squirt bottle, sitting in a puddle of hand sanitizer.

After a long wait, a hoarse feminine voice on the other side of the door called out: "One minute!"

In the frosted windowpane, I could see a short, slender

figure rushing a black mask onto her face. The door finally opened, revealing Valerie Young. She had white curly hair, pale skin and a drooping jaw, which her mask could not hide. Instead of greeting me she just stared.

"Good morning, Mrs. Young," I finally said, tipping my antlers. "Moosehead Artisan Bakery. I have your two loaves of—"

She cut me off and pointed her index finger, with a red-painted nail, directly at my snout. In a creaky, almost nervous tone, she asked, "Is that mask... *Health Canada approved?*"

"Yes, of course," I replied instantly. "But for interim emergency use only."

Before she could respond, I handed her the paper bag with the two loaves, atop the cardboard box of cookies.

"Have a great day," I said quickly and made a dash for the van.

Just as I reached for the driver side door, the older fellow on the neighbouring porch yelled out: "Nancy! Get me my rifle. There be a moose running wild right here in Moosehead."

"Hey!" I said, spinning and pointing my hoof directly at the man. "Moose hunting season doesn't start until September 18."

I actually had checked on ontario.ca the night before. Not that I was afraid he'd fire; sadly, public humiliation scared me more at that precise moment than death. Still, I didn't wait to find out. Within seconds, I was pulling out of the driveway, the moose mask riding shotgun. Sweat poured down my forehead as I backed out onto Rothwell Road. That's when I realized my oversight. Grabbing the clipboard, I looked at the payment column. Valeria Young was a COD. She hadn't paid over the internet like all the other customers.

I hit the brakes, but didn't open the door. No, I was too embarrassed to go back. I looked at the clipboard again. $18.50. With a sigh I pulled out my wallet. Extracting a twenty dollar bill, I slipped it into the money purse laying in the cup holder between the two bucket seats. I looked at the time: 9:15 a.m.

Just great! I thought. *I've already lost the first hour's wage before I even earned it.*

I pressed back down on the accelerator, sending both the van and my heart rate racing toward the next drop-off.

22. Chef Facemask

Two hours later, I was parked at the rear entrance to Le Papillon—the closest thing Moosehead had to fine dining. They made the creamiest French onion soup and the fluffiest crêpes this side of Quebec. Or, at least, so they claimed. I leaned the clipboard against the steering wheel and glanced at my cell: 11 a.m. Still an hour to go and this was the last order of the day.

Opening the door, I stepped out. The backs of shops lined the north side of the parking lot, and a steep incline on the south side dropped down into the French River. I walked around to the passenger door, unbuckled the moose mask and slipped it over my perspiring head. Pulling two loaded bins out of the back of the van, I headed for the rear door of Le Papillon. The outer door was open. A wave of heat was pouring out through the inner screen door.

Mathéo was a prep cook here. I'd rather hoped he was working today. After two hours of strangers gawking and laughing at me, I'd welcome his familiar face and sedate personality.

Despite the heckling, I realized, it hadn't been all that bad. Kind of fun, really. People were all stressed out with case counts and I had delivered not just food but a good laugh.

Looking through the screen door, I could see steam rising from two bubbling pots on a gas stovetop. Standing at a table, in front of the burners, with his back to me, was a large man chopping so fast it sounded like machine gun fire. He was dressed in a white chef's uniform. He wore one of those tall, cylindrical hats—what did they call them, a toque?

That toque looks just as silly as what I have on my head, I thought, feeling a little relief.

"Hey, Mathéo!" I hollered through the screen.

The knife froze in midair, as the man looked over his shoulder. He had bushy eyebrows, a white mask and not much in common with Mathéo other than his size and uniform. Turning around, however, I saw he had black buttons along his chef coat. Mathéo had told me that black meant a real chef, while white buttons were for students.

"Oh, sorry, I thought you were Mathéo," I said.

"*Hé! Un orignal!*" he gasped.

I guessed that *orignal* was French for moose.

"*Oui, oui,*" I responded quickly.

Without putting down his knife, the chef turned around and walked toward me. Both the white apron hanging around his waist and the white mask around his mouth were splattered with red... *sauce?* At least, I hoped it was sauce.

"Delivery moose!" I announced, a tremor to my voice.

He just stared at me, his large chest expanding. Behind him, one of the pots spluttered.

"Moosehead Artisan Bakery." I lifted the bins up, speaking quickly. "I have your order. Ten baguettes and six dozen almond cookies."

Without replying he yanked open the screen door, ducked his head down and peered into my snout.

"*Bordel! Quel con!*" he said shaking the thick blade. "You think I'm stupid? You're not wearing a mask."

Sweating ever more vigorously, I slowly tried to clarify, "I'm not wearing a mask?"

"Not a face mask," he said. He passed the knife from hand to hand as he rolled his sleeves up to the elbows. "That costume is not going to protect anyone from anything."

"Yeah, well," I said, daring the same comeback I used with Mrs. Young, "it's approved by *Santé Canada*." Standing taller and prouder than a quadruped could, I waited for him to laugh.

"*Imbécile!*" he hollered, as he turned his back on me and began to walk away.

"Hey!" I snapped back, "it's not like your skimpy mask's any better."

Spinning back around, pointing the tip of his knife to his sauce-splattered mask, he said, "Mine is at least covering *ma bouche.*" He then pointed the knife at the tip of the limp tongue hanging from my moose mask. "While that is a runway for your corona-infected spit."

I took a deep breath, then said through a clenched jaw: "Do you want me to just leave your order here on the ground, then?"

"*Dieu non!*" he exclaimed, as if I had offered to surgically implant a grenade in his abdomen. Slamming the screen door tightly closed, he added, "If you guys are going to mock public health rules, you and your bread can go to hell." He sliced the air with his chopping knife, while his French accent thickened.

"Enough people have died already."

I glanced down at the bins. "There's nothing to worry about," I said. "The bins are sealed tight. It's quite... *safe*."

Chef Facemask stomped back to the prepping table, bringing his knife down and sending one end of a carrot shooting into the open flames beneath his bubbling pots.

"The only thing that would be safe," he said, head bent downward toward his orange victims, "is if you get the hell away from my *resto*."

"You're joking," I said.

He had to be joking.

"I have immune-compromised customers," he bellowed. "I won't risk their lives taking orders from *un orignal stupide* who doesn't understand basic science."

"Yeah, well," I responded through clenched teeth, "you're already blindly *taking order*s from *bureaucrates stupides* who don't understand basic science. Ask Sudbury's public health officer to show you proof this virus even exists."

Stefanie, in one of her videos, had said they never isolated the virus.

Chef Facemask picked up the remaining half of the carrot he was slicing and flung it at the door to a large steel fridge.

"The only officer I'm calling is a police officer. To arrest you for trespassing. Endangering lives."

I paused, probably not breathing. Then, shaking my antlers, I turned around and headed back toward the van.

As I retreated, I heard him yell from the screen door, "And make sure she refunds my order or I swear I'm adding moose stew to the menu."

I had had enough.

"Screw you!" I yelled back, without looking.

I heard the screen door open.

"What did you say?" he demanded.

I turned around. He was bigger than me, but could he fight as well? I sure felt like finding out. Then I shook my snout. What was I thinking? First day on the job and I get in a fight with a COVID-crazy cook wielding a six-inch chef's knife, with nothing but felt antlers to protect me. Who did I think I was, Moose Lee? Yeah, that would impress Stefanie as I called her from the

ER on the smartphone she didn't want me to use.

"*Je suis désolé,*" I apologized.

Then I sniffed the air.

"Is something burning?"

Burnt carrot, I assumed.

The chef looked back over his shoulder, said a word I certainly didn't learn in grade nine French, and rushed back into his hot kitchen.

I retreated to the van, set the bins on the ground and opened the rear doors.

My heart was racing.

And then, suddenly, it stopped.

"*Boo!*" said a high-pitched voice.

I jolted back, stunned to see the tip of a unicorn's horn sticking out of the van, pointed directly at my snout.

23. The Little Shop of Heroes

"*Mon Dieu!*" I blurted out.

The unicorn giggled with delight.

My God, I was speaking French and seeing mythical creatures. Was wearing a felt mask in July leaving me delirious with heat? Or...

Her two small hands held the unicorn mask in place on her petite shoulders. The girl was sitting, cross-legged in the back of the van on one of the empty green bins. After the tense situation with Chef Facemask, her little "boo" had stunned me like a taser.

From behind me, an explosion of laughter mingled with her giggling. Turning my masked head, I saw a skinny guy, in jeans and a blue T-shirt, wearing a rubber mask over his entire head. The mask was hairless and green, with long fangs which suffered a serious overbite. It might have startled me too, if the wearer wasn't holding his belly, almost doubled over.

"Oh, bro!" AJ called out, "how I wish I could have seen your face."

At once I knew it was AJ Howey. And in the van, giggling even harder, was his little sister, Cindy. The Howeys lived in the countryside, but AJ worked in town. In fact, he worked at the shop directly behind him—The Little Shop of Heroes—where all the *nerdz* in Moosehead hung out.

"Very funny, guys," I said, pulling off my furry mask.

"I scared you, didn't I?" asked Cindy. She lifted her unicorn mask to reveal a wide grin, spooky green eyes and golden blonde hair.

I smiled at her. "Maybe," I admitted. "Now, get out of there." I reached out my hand and pulled her out of the van and onto the cracking asphalt. "I gotta start locking the door."

Removing his monster mask, AJ said, "We saw a moose pull in and couldn't resist." He then quickly fastened around his ears a face mask emblazoned with the words "The Tragically Hip"— his favourite rock band, for reasons I would never understand. He then slipped his big, black framed glasses over his nose, pinning the face mask in place.

"And you guys just happened to have a unicorn and monster mask handy?"

"Monster?" exclaimed AJ, looking at the rubber mask. "This is an orc."

"Of course it is," I responded.

"We're playing DnD today," said Cindy, jumping up and down.

"D and D?"

"Dungeons and Dragons! It's like a board game where you get to pretend you're somewhere else, being something else. I'm gonna be a halfling!"

"You look more like a unicorn," I said, pointing to her mask.

"Roger didn't have a hobbit mask," said AJ, walking over to us.

Roger Gygax was the old geezer who ran The Little Shop of Heroes. Skinny guy, with coke-bottle glasses, hunched over all the time like he spent his whole life reading comic books. When he wasn't selling superhero stories, he had what they called "gaming" going on (whatever that meant). I never liked chess growing up; and Dungeons and Dragons seemed to fall into the same geeky category.

"Well, you make for a very pretty unicorn," I said, setting my moose mask on top of the green bins at my feet.

"And you make an awesome moose, bro," complimented AJ, as he walked toward us. "Feels like Disney World has come to

Northern Ontario."

Cindy set her unicorn mask inside the open van. Looking at me with wide green eyes, she asked, "Can I please try on your moose mask?"

I held it up over her head. "Might be a bit big for you."

She reached up and pulled the felt mask down, gripping the base of the antlers to stop it from falling off her shoulders.

"I'm going to go scare Josh now," she said and dashed toward the comic book shop.

"Hey!" I called out, "I need that. It's my, uh, uniform."

But she vanished in the back door.

"Ah, just give her a minute," said AJ. "Her attention span lasts about as long as a gnat's hiccup." He then pointed to the unicorn horn sticking out of the van. "Anyway, you can always wear hers."

"I think I'll wait," I responded with a lopsided grin. "I'm ahead of schedule anyway."

Remembering my final delivery, I glanced over at *Le Papillon*—half expecting Chef Facemask to come charging out, brandishing two skewers in each hand. I was really regretting letting Mom talk me out of the Guy V. Fawkes costume. A pair of kitchen knives of my own might come in handy after all.

AJ mirrored my glance, saying, "Sure sounded like Christophe didn't appreciate the superior artistic stature of your... *face* mask."

"I wouldn't say he was impressed."

"Ah," said AJ, waving the limp orc mask, "even before COVID he was always throwing ladles and yelling at Mathéo for putting too much cinnamon in the tortiere. We could hear him through the walls. I don't know how Mathéo puts up with the guy. Or, for that matter, stays alive."

"Ah, Mathéo's invincible," I said. "You could shoot him in the stomach and he'd probably just digest the bullet."

The door to The Little Shop of Heroes burst open. Out ran a short moose, followed by Josh who was aiming a plastic bow and arrow at her retreating back.

"Moose!" he yelled, in his slightly muffled pronunciation.

He released one of the suction cup arrows, which bounced off Cindy's back and fell to the pavement.

"Ah!" she exclaimed. "I've been hit." She spun dizzily, before dropping slowly to the ground, first on her bottom, then collapsing on her back, arms splayed out.

AJ ran over to her. "Hey, careful, Sis. You don't want to damage Vince's mask." He squatted, sat her back up and lifted the elongated snout off her head.

Her eyes were closed as she mumbled, "Your only sister has been shot in the back and all you care about is the smelly mask?"

Josh's shadow cast over her, as he aimed another arrow at her chest.

AJ put out his palm. "Don't shoot, Josh," he pleaded. "She's no longer a moose. Your magic arrow has transformed her back into a halfling princess."

Josh immediately released a second arrow, which bounced off her T-shirt.

Cindy reached out and pulled at AJ's mask. "He can't see your lips." Then she turned her head to face Josh and said, "I'm no longer a moose. You can't be a noble archer *and* shoot a beautiful princess."

Josh let the bow drop to his side. "Sorry," he signed by rotating his right fist in a circle over his sternum, before turning and running back into The Little Shop of Heroes.

As soon as the shop door shut behind Josh, the kitchen door to Le Papillon swung open and Chef Christophe stepped out. Acting like we didn't exist, he leaned against the brick wall, pulled down his mask and lit a cigarette. AJ put a hand on Cindy's shoulder and ushered her to the other side of the yellow bread van.

"Secondhand smoke, no problem, folks," he grumbled. "But how dare you don't wear a face mask, eh?"

I followed them, getting out of view and earshot of Chef Facemask.

"Better put on your face mask, Sis," said AJ. "Before Christophe reports us."

She pulled a pink face mask out of her pocket. "It's hot out. The mask feels icky. And Vince is not wearing one."

I raised my eyebrows as I took the moose mask from AJ and put it back on my head. "There," I said in a muffled voice. "I've got the biggest mask in Moosehead."

Cindy's fat lips stuck out rebelliously. "That doesn't count! I can see your mouth."

"Since when have mouths become a crime?"

"Since the WHO said so," countered AJ. "Or Doctor WHO, as I like to call them. After all, the world is starting to look like a far-fetched science fiction series with some really cheesy props." He tugged at his own mask. "One big B-movie."

"*The Invasion of the Face Snatchers*?" I suggested. "You know you don't have to wear them. They don't work. And anyone can claim an exemption."

AJ adjusted his Tragically Hip face mask and said, "I hear you, bro, but parents are scared to let their kids come here." His voice lowered to a near whisper. "Just between me and you, Roger's on the verge of losing the place. Curbside pickup may have worked okay for Le Papillon, but comic books and role-playing games aren't hot take-out items."

"Isn't Roger getting help from the government?"

AJ shrugged. "Whatever the gov sent him barely covered the rent. I'm practically working for free, bro. Under the table, lunch money. I don't want to see this place go under. Especially when the winter comes, where are kids supposed to go in Moosehead? And, I mean, it's not like Roger's living the high life."

He gestured to the metal fire escape leading up to an apartment above the shop. Roger lived up there alone. He had been married. I barely remembered his wife. She was Mr. Chung's sister and helped him run the Green Dragon Chinese Buffet. The restaurant business must have brought in more money for poor old Roger than his comic book business. When Chyou died of cancer, around the same time Grandma died, Roger sold their house and moved into the apartment above his comic book shop.

"Maybe," I ventured, "he needs to find some additional revenue streams."

AJ raised an eyebrow. "Like?"

I bent down, opened the bin, lifted out one of the cardboard boxes of almond cookies that Christophe had rejected and handed it to AJ. "Try a sample! No wheat. No dairy. No sugar. No eggs. No nuts."

"But you said they were almond cookies," corrected Cindy.

"Well, no peanuts."

AJ pulled out one of the large cookies and pulled down his mask.

"A free sample," I insisted, "compliments of Moosehead Artisan Bakery. See how they sell. If Roger wants more, just let me know and I'll talk to the boss."

Taking a bite, AJ asked, "Don't we need a permit or something?"

I waved my hand, the hoof flapping at the side of my wrist. "Ah! All public health cares about these days is if people are wearing masks and standing six feet apart."

"But what if they don't sell?"

"Then just give them to the kids for free. I'm not charging you for them."

AJ looked uncertainly at the bin.

"Can I try?" said Cindy. Her hand reached into the box before I could reply.

"These are good," admitted AJ, taking another bite. "Aromatic smell."

"Cardamom and maple syrup," I said.

"Yummy!" said Cindy.

I closed the cardboard box and set it back into the bin with the other five dozen. Picking up the bin, I handed it to AJ just as the door to The Little Shop of Heroes swung open again, and a short, chubby kid with curly hair and round glasses stepped out. He was wearing a Harry Potter face mask with the words: "No one should live in a closet."

"DM!" he called out. "We've all filled in our character sheets. We're ready to start playing."

"Okay, Ferris," said AJ. "We're coming."

"I'm not Ferris," he said, "I'm Mialee the elf wizard."

"A thousand pardons..." AJ offered a half bow. "Mialee the Magnificent."

The boy disappeared back into the shop.

AJ turned to his unmasked sister. "At least," he pleaded, "put on the unicorn mask."

Cindy grabbed the horn of the disembodied unicorn as I slid the other bin of rejected baguettes into the back of the van, before I closed *and* locked the rear doors.

Turning to AJ, I asked, "Why'd he call you DM? Did you

change your initials?"

"It stands for dungeon master," explained AJ.

"And I'm assistant dungeon master," cheered Cindy. "We're like referee storytellers."

"We determine who lives and who dies," said AJ, in an ominous voice.

"Well, have fun, I guess," I said, twirling the keys of the van in my fingers. "I hope everybody likes the cookies."

AJ's brow furrowed as he extended the bin of cookies back to me. "Why don't you explain your money-making scheme to Roger," he said. "I don't want him to think I stole these or something."

I took the bin and was about to protest.

"Yeah! Come on Mr. Moose," said Cindy, running toward the back door. "We'll show you the dungeon."

"What *dungeon*?" I asked hesitantly.

24. The Dungeon Before COVID

"Bro," responded AJ, "you've never seen the dungeon?"

"I try to avoid dungeons, prisons and jails," I said. Then, remembering the encounter with Constable Corona, I added, "Especially, these days."

"Ah, you gotta see the dungeon," said AJ. "Come on, it'll only take a minute."

"Well, I am ahead of schedule," I acknowledged.

Cindy, with her white unicorn mask, held the back door open to The Little Shop of Heroes, as I followed her older brother into a cramped storage room. Cardboard boxes filled every available space on the metal shelving unit to our right. And on our left was an open bathroom door and another closed door. I barely noticed any of it in passing. Wearing a moose mask certainly results in tunnel vision.

AJ passed through into the main retail area. I followed. I'd only been inside the place once or twice, growing up. Books (even comic books) and board games weren't really my thing. I spent my summers playing soccer and winters playing hockey. Still, the museum-like aura of the place inspired a sense of respect for my friends' fantastical obsessions. Lining the right wall were racks of comics. On the left were glass cases displaying miniature wizards, elves and dwarves, holding staffs, swords, and battle-axes. Wooden boxes of older comics, sealed in plastic wrappers, covered two rows of tables in the centre of the space.

"If it wasn't for this place," said AJ, slapping me on my furry back. "I'd probably be illiterate and doing time in juvenile detention. I started with comic books. Worked my way up to DnD manuals. Now I'm writing a novel."

"I thought you were writing a screenplay?"

He shrugged. "I'm also inking a comic book. What can I say? I'm full of talent."

Roger was at the front, behind the checkout counter. At least, I assumed it was him. Starting with long boots, he was covered head to toe in a red and blue Spiderman costume. Instead of a germophobic face mask, his entire head was enclosed in a red mask decorated with a black spiderweb pattern. His two large, white arachnoid eyes were directed at a short kid with a comic rolled up in one hand, his mother holding the other. Both mother and son wore blue medical masks as they stood on the other side of the cash register.

"Where are Josh and Ferris and the other kids?" I asked.

"Come see," called Cindy.

I followed her voice back into the rear storage room. Cindy was pointing her unicorn horn at the door beside the bathroom. Looking straight on, I could see it was made of thick dark wood, held in place by iron bracings. A black, antique key, with an O-shaped handle, hung out of the oversized keyhole.

"*Shh!*" said Cindy, putting her left index finger to her lips, while her right one pointed to a sign above the door:

BEWARE OF DRAGON
(Has not been fed!)

"I put that up to keep public health away," said AJ, from behind.

I rolled my eyes. "Well, it might slow them down."

Cindy was jiggling the oversized key in the antiquated lock, groaning as she tried to get it to turn. Finally, the lock clicked and she heaved open the door with a little help from her brother. It squeaked loudly as if it had purposely not been oiled. On the other side of the medieval portal was a landing with a flight of stairs descending to the right. Cindy, still wearing her mythical mask, ran down the wooden steps. I could hear children below, greeting the unicorn.

AJ followed. I took up the rear.

"Be sure to close the door," said AJ. "And lock it."

I pulled the door shut and twisted a latch until I heard the lock click again.

"I can't believe you've never seen the gaming room, bro," said AJ, as we descended.

"Board games are boring games," I grumbled. "Not my thing."

"Dungeons and Dragons is not a game—it's an alternative, higher reality."

"I guess it's some people's cup of tea," I mumbled.

"Cup of tea?" gasped AJ. "DnD is magic potion served in the skull of a goblin."

"Of course it is. Just, you know, not everybody likes drinking out of a vessel which once contained a monster's brain."

AJ twitched his head. "Over twelve million DnD players in North America are cool with it."

"That many?" I said in disbelief. "You'd never know it."

"When something gets taboo people keep their heads low. When it comes to role-playing games you're either labelled a nerd, a geek or a satanist."

"Yeah," I said, "my folks thought it was too occult."

"What did they mean by *occult*?"

"You know, supernatural stuff."

"Like walking on water, then turning the water into wine?"

"Well, Dad would say wizards and stuff are pagan."

"Pagan?" asked AJ.

"It means, supernatural stuff that *isn't* Catholic."

AJ shrugged. "You can construct any character you want. A medieval monk is hardly unheard of. Most of the ridicule comes from people who don't know anything about RPGs."

"RPGs?"

"Role-playing games," clarified AJ. "Please, pay attention."

"I'm trying," I said as I lifted the moose mask up enough to see the next step on the steep and poorly lit staircase.

"You know," continued AJ, "modern-day fantasy was practically invented by a Catholic."

"You mean C.S. Lewis?"

"Actually, he was Anglican," corrected AJ. "I was thinking of J.R.R. Tolkien."

"He wrote *Lord of the Flies,* right?"

"*Rings,*" corrected AJ.

"Whatever," I said. "He's the old English dude with the pipe."

"English dude?" said AJ. "Dude! He might be a saint one day. There's a Facebook group petitioning the Holy See for his canonization."

"What, are they going to make him the patron saint of hobbits?"

I paused on the final step as AJ turned aside into the basement. Standing at the foot of the staircase was a knight in rusty armour. Well, at least the trappings of a knight. A gaping hole on the right side of the breastplate, where an arm should have been, revealed the suit of metal was empty.

Hanging above the amputee knight was a bell the size of my head. It was made of thick iron and looked so old I doubted it could move at all. A cord was attached to the lip of the bell, extending upward through a metal pipe protruding through the ceiling. All these antiques explained why Roger had to sell his house.

"Welcome to the dungeon before COVID," said AJ.

He pulled off his Tragically Hip face mask and slid one of the loops onto the end of a sword fastened to the wall. Four other face masks already hung on the blade.

Stepping off the staircase, I saw two wide bookshelves on my right, against the rear wall of the basement. They were half-empty, containing mainly books, two large silver goblets and, thankfully, no goblin skulls. Despite the archaic appearance, the space was well-dusted and clean. It looked more like a shrine than a dungeon.

Ferris, breathing heavily, ran past me, and took refuge behind the suit of armour. Josh, with his quiver full of toy arrows strapped to his back, fired one at Ferris. He missed, instead hitting the armoured knight in the heart, where the suction cup tip held. Ferris reached around, removed the arrow and slung it back at Josh. But Josh had already retreated to the rear of the basement on the other side of a large wooden table, where a short boy sat, wearing a plastic knight's helmet and faux chain mail. Across from the short boy sat an even shorter unicorn. And on the boy's right was...

"*Léo?*" I said.

Hardly a kid, and certainly not short, my six-foot-two friend sat there with a grin and raised eyebrows. Léo was more Indigenous than me—but, unlike me, he didn't try to hide it. His family were Métis—an equal mix of French settlers and First Nations. We were the same age, but he was taller, broader and cockier.

"Hey, *niijii*," he said.

Niijii was Anishinaabemowin for "friend."

"Léo?" I repeated.

"Yeah, it's me. Time to come out of the closet, I guess."

He leaned back in his chair, holding up a thin, wide book. The cover displayed the Dungeons and Dragons logo with the title *Manuel des joueurs*.

"You're a DnD nerd, too?" I said.

"No, I'm an elven bard from the planet Abeir-Toril." He removed from his pocket a miniature figurine and set it on the table. It even looked a bit like him, with skin a shade darker than white and long black hair flowing down its shoulders.

"Actually," he corrected himself, "I'm a half elf, half human. You can tell because my ears aren't as pointy."

Speechless, I shook my masked head slowly. Suddenly, dressing up as a moose felt down to earth.

Cindy took off her unicorn head. "Mr. Moose, you don't have to wear your mask down here if you don't want to," she said.

"I guess you guys aren't worried about COVID," I replied.

"It's safe down here," said the boy with the plastic knight's helmet. Even though I couldn't see his face behind the visor, I assumed it was Walter. His dark arms gave him away—only black kid in Moosehead. "Those aren't ordinary stairs." He pointed behind me, lifting up his visor to reveal an Afro pushing at the edges of his knight helmet. "That staircase is a portal through time, bringing you a thousand years before COVID."

"Is that so?" I said.

At that moment, behind me, I heard the door at the top of those magical stairs squeak open.

"Ah, here comes our full-blooded elf," said Léo.

He rose from his seat, as I turned to see the real reason for his interest in DnD walking down the steps.

25. Beauty and the Bard

"The Lady Bindu has entered the Dungeon Room. All rise," announced Léo.

Walter and Cindy both slid their chairs back and stood up from the table, rolling their eyes. Josh and Ferris ignored Léo, continuing to shoot arrows at each other. AJ and I were already on our feet, as we watched the last person I would have expected descending the creaky staircase into their corny catacombs.

Bindu Chatterjee was wearing a long white dress which contrasted with her dark East Indian skin. Her black hair, usually in a tight ponytail, now hung long and loose.

Léo pulled out the wooden stool to his right. "Please, my lady," he said to Bindu in an accent that sounded *somewhat* British. "May I offer thee a seat?"

She held up her hand. "My dear bard," she replied, in a far more convincing English dialect, "may I remind you that the Queen of Ayodhya, my mother, would not permit me to accept such an offer from a man such as yourself who has not received her unattainable blessing."

"Hmph!" I said with a chuckle as I rubbed my snout. There was more truth than fantasy in what Bindu had said. While Mr. Chatterjee was rather laid back, Mrs. Chatterjee was as flexible as a frozen iron pipe.

"I understand, my lady," said Léo with a frown. "The queen is wise to set such incomprehensibly high standards for one so fair, wise and beautiful as thee."

Both her parents became baptized Catholics upon moving to Moosehead from India, long before any of us were born. I suspect their conversion to Christianity was more to fit in, rather than from any divine calling. Regardless, they still adhered to many customs of their homeland. Her mother, especially.

Passing me, Bindu smiled and said, "A moose. How quaint."

I had heard from Bindu's brother that their mother had arranged Bindu's marriage to a medical student in Sudbury, after consulting the family's Vedic astrologer. Apparently Bindu was Aries rising and her future groom had a moon in Scorpio. So, it was destined to work out whether Bindu liked him or not.

Bindu sat down beside Cindy, in front of the unicorn mask. "Greetings," she said, giving Cindy a hug. "I do look forward to sharing adventure, fellowship and... *music* with thee all." Turning to Léo, she added, "I trust you brought your lute?"

While Léo's current apprenticeship as a plumber should lead to a decent income, someone who fixes toilets was not quite what Queen Chatterjee had in mind for her only daughter. Especially when Léo was more enthusiastic about his hockey stick than the plumber's wrench. But even more dear to Léo's heart than smacking a puck was plucking his lute substitute.

"Yes, of course, my lady," he replied, pulling up a guitar from behind his stool. "If it pleases my lady, I have prepared a song for thee."

"Please, no," muttered AJ, putting his hand to his heart. "Not another one."

"That would please me much," consented Bindu, folding her hands on the table, beaming a smile at Léo and his "lute."

"Let me turn off my hearing aids, first," said Josh, putting his hands to his ears.

Léo began to strum the nylon strings of his classical guitar, and I began to wonder: Was the underground DnD club a way for this East Indian Juliet and West "Indian" Romeo to meet in secret, chaperoned by unicorns, dwarves and wizards? Every guy in Moosehead knew that the beautiful Bindu Chatterjee was forbidden from being alone with anyone of the opposite sex. It hardly mattered that she was in her mid-twenties. Her father, affectionately called Baba by all the residents of Moosehead, was a gentle man. Her mother, however, was quite willing to go to jail, if need be, to save her daughter from even the most innocent of premarital relations. Hence, any aloofness Bindu showed toward Léo, I assumed, was more for his protection than her own.

Bindu's endangered lover began to sing to the tune of Don McLean's "American Pie":

Oh, my, my, Princess Bindu I spy,
First time that I beheld her face,
I was ready to die.
Oh, so beautiful, like drinking a sunset sky,
Won't the queen let her be my elven bride?
Won't the queen let her be my elven bride?

Bindu put her hand over her face, hiding an embarrassed laugh, as AJ groaned and Cindy applauded.

"If I may," said Bindu, reaching out her hand.

Léo passed her the guitar and pick. She began to pluck with less skill, while singing a few octaves higher:

Mata's singin', no, no—you she's fixed to deny,
Maybe in time my bard will climb,
But now you're too small a fry.
So my dear Léo, I don't want to lie,
Mata rather I wed a rich guy.
Mata rather I wed a rich guy.

With a final flourish, Bindu ended the recital and everyone erupted in applause (even AJ). Everyone except the moose (I just stood there mutely and in shock).

"Bindu," I said, when the cheers died away. "I never would have thought... You, you play these fantasy games?"

"I participate, yes," she clarified.

"But you're a lawyer. Or almost a lawyer."

"Yes, and as an 'almost' lawyer I like a game with lots of rules. I like the rule of law. I like the predictability of there being rules we all play by. Quite unlike what has happened in our country, where public health officials can just make up stuff and pretend they're laws. And people are gullible enough to go along."

Did she just call me gullible?

"So you don't think the COVID restrictions are justified?" I asked.

"Complete violation of the Charter of Rights and Freedoms," she said without hesitation. "You can tell they are fraudulent by how fast they rushed them through. It takes years for the publisher to make even minor changes to the rules in Dungeons and Dragons, yet it took only a month for governments to make the most outrageous and widely sweeping changes to civil law."

Wanting to change the subject, I said, "I didn't realize there were so many rules to the game."

"This is just the Player's Manual," said Léo, pointing to his French copy. "There's also the Monster's Manual and the Dungeon Master's Guide."

"And we're playing the fifth edition, which isn't as strict," explained AJ. "The third edition, sheesh, that had *way* too many rules. Only a lawyer could keep up."

"You guys are nuts," I said.

Under my mask I was smiling.

"On the subject of rules," said Bindu, pointing a finger at my felt face. "No masks in the Dungeon Room." She spoke in the same tone a teacher might scold a student for wearing a hat in class. "No exemptions."

I set the bin of cookies down on the floor and lifted the moose mask away. Immediately I felt the coolness of their dungeon hideaway. Sensing a current of air, I looked up and over. On the rear wall, above the bookshelves, were two open ground windows that I assumed looked out into the back lot where the van was parked. Each window was about two feet high—enough for someone to crawl through if they had to. Oddly, neither window let in much light, despite the glass pane being swung open wide. In front of each window were two small fans drawing in fresh air.

Putting my mask down on top of the bin, I asked, "Does Roger know you're not wearing masks down here?"

"Sure, bro," said AJ. "I told you, he doesn't buy into the whole face diaper fantasy. He just has us wear them upstairs to keep the Karens happy."

"Just don't tell anyone," said Ferris, as he ran past me again, Josh firing another arrow.

"No worries," I said. "I'm no snitch."

I turned my attention to the wooden game board. It looked even less interesting than a chessboard—containing nothing more than grid lines. It wasn't even checkered. I was expecting model castles, moats and drawbridges.

"Not much of a landscape," I commented.

AJ tapped his forehead. "The landscape is in our..."

"Imaginations!" exclaimed Cindy and Walter together.

Ferris plopped down on the stool beside Walter with an arrow wedged under his armpit. Josh had finally got him. "I've been hit!" Ferris cried out, and then promptly fell face first on the table, the arrow's fletching sticking straight up.

Josh cheered and began retrieving arrows from the floor, returning them to the quiver on his back.

"Let's get this game going," said AJ. Facing Josh, he twisted his right index finger back and forth between the extended middle and index finger of his open left hand, as if he was turning the ignition on a car.

I didn't know AJ could sign. Though, for that matter, I also didn't know he led an underground youth group. Retrieving a small wooden box from the shelf, AJ set it on the table and opened it.

"Mialee the Magnificent," announced Ferris. He extracted from the box a tall figurine, with a long beard and crooked wooden staff.

Josh sat down in a chair at the end of the table. I assumed he got the head seat so he could easily see everyone's lips.

"Here I am," he said, removing a miniature archer, wearing a long green cloak with brown boots up to its knees.

Cindy pulled out a purple pouch, spilling its contents onto the table: an assortment of multicoloured dice. Just one of the dice had six sides. Another, the shape of a pyramid, had only four. The rest displayed numbers as high as twenty, many surpassing my geometrical vocabulary to properly name.

"I get to roll the dice," said Cindy, picking up a yellow die with pentagon-shaped sides. "I use them to see whether they win or lose their battles."

"What do they get if they win?" I asked.

"Experience points!"

"So, what, whoever gets the most points wins the game?"

"No, it's not like hockey," grumbled Léo. "The dungeon master dude just keeps on coming up with more and more adventures... until you die."

"Sounds great," I mumbled.

"Bro, you should give it a try," said AJ. "We're not far into this campaign. We can easily introduce a new character."

"Ah, looks kind of low-tech," I said, holding up one of the

pencils. No video screens. No controllers. No one even had cell-phones on the table. Stefanie would probably love the joint.

"Once you get into it you don't even notice," replied Léo.

"Maybe another time," I said. "Anyway, it already looks like you're past capacity. No social distancing, no masks, you didn't even sanitize the dice—aren't you afraid you'll be thrown in COVID jail?"

"By whom?" said Léo. "Bylaw Blake? Roger's his brother-in-law."

"I was thinking the police," I responded. "You know, Yamamoto."

"Yamamoto?!" exclaimed Léo as he slapped the table, causing the dice to jump.

The entire group erupted in laughter again.

"Yamamoto?" cut in Bindu, as the others were regaining composure. "Yamamoto's dungeon master on Friday nights."

"The dungeon master?" I looked her in the eye to see if she was pulling one of my four moose legs.

"Yeah, the guy who runs the game," explained Walter. "Like AJ. But with better voices."

"I do admit," conceded AJ, "Yamamoto's kobold voice makes the hairs stand up on the back of my neck." He picked up Léo's manual. "But he's rather by the book. Stickler for the rules. Not much improv."

"Obviously not too by the book..." I said, my voice trailing off again. "I'm surprised this would be his thing."

"His girlfriend dumped him after the first week of lock-down," explained Léo, clasping his hands behind his neck, "so he had nothing better to do on a Friday night."

"You guys met all through the lockdown?"

"AJ missed a few weeks," said Léo. Then, switching to a goofy, high-pitched voice, he taunted, "His *mommy* wouldn't let him come out to play."

AJ slid off his glasses and rubbed them on his shirt. "Ma wouldn't even let me out for fresh air," he remonstrated. "And we live in the middle of a freakin' cornfield."

"We were about to launch a campaign to break him free," said Ferris, "but—"

Clang!

I looked up at the ceiling.
Clang!
That rusty iron bell was swinging slowly back and forth.
Clang!
"Oh, oh," said Cindy.

26. Experience Points

Clang! The old rusty bell had life left in it. It wasn't loud, but it was moving—apparently being pulled back and forth by the cord ascending to the upper floor.

Clang!

"*Frack!*" exclaimed AJ.

"What does that mean?" I asked.

"It's a bad word from *Battlestar Galactica*," said Cindy.

"No, I mean the bell. Why's it ringing?"

They ignored my question. AJ looked to the kids.

"Everybody stay calm," he said in a frantic whisper.

"We are calm," whispered back Cindy. "You were the one who said frack."

"Remember we've trained for this moment."

"*Trained for what?*" I said.

"Keep your voice down," warned Léo.

The bell clanged again. Was it part of their game?

Walter looked at me and whispered, "A flesh-and-blood kobold has breached the premises." Then he let his visor fall back down over his face.

"A *what*?" I asked, trying not to laugh.

"This!" said Ferris, pulling out another figurine from the wooden box. It was red, scaly, with two horns growing out of its head. The monster's face looked like a cross between a wolf and a lizard.

"Kobolds are not very strong, but very clever," added Josh. He patted his left bicep, shaking his head, then tapped his forehead, nodding.

"Uh-oh!" I chuckled. "Well, you better roll some dice and cast a spell before he gets ya."

"Negative, Mr. Moose," responded Walter. "This is for real."

He rose to his feet and began signing to Josh—whether in

true American Sign Language or spontaneous charades, I didn't know. In fact, everybody was now signing to everybody else—silent hand signals that would not be heard by their approaching red, scaly imaginary monster. All now standing, they began clearing the table of everything but the grid—hastily moving miniatures, dice, paper, pencils, manuals and the unicorn head to the shelves on the rear wall.

"Grab the face diapers!" AJ said to me in a hushed tone. He was pointing to their face masks hanging along the dull blade of the long sword fastened to the wall.

I just stared at him, trying not to laugh.

"Kobold's coming!" urged AJ.

"Uh-huh," I responded, smirking.

Bindu rushed past me to collect the masks herself. The bell clanged once more and then stopped. Bindu crunched the masks into a ball.

"Kobold!" she repeated. "As in Constable Kobold."

"*What?*" I asked, getting out of her way as she fumed past me.

"Kobold's codename for cop."

"I thought you said Yamamoto was cool with your DnD underworld?"

"It's not Yamamoto," said Léo. He was running his fingers along the edge of the left bookshelf against the rear wall.

"I bet it's that new cop," said AJ, joining Léo at the bookshelf. "The old guy."

I shuddered.

"You mean Mackenzie?" I exclaimed.

No one responded. The kids were sliding stools and chairs under the table as if they had rehearsed the drill a thousand times. Bindu was sweeping madly, making more of a mess than cleaning anything up. AJ and Léo were now pulling forward one side of the bookshelf until it was at a forty-five degree angle. I walked toward them.

"What the hell?" I said.

Instead of a solid wall behind the shelf, there appeared a hidden alcove. The windows and wall above the shelves was only a façade; the brickwork descended one third the way down, enough to make it look as if the shelves were pressed against the wall.

Pointing to the three-foot space between the shelves and the real subterranean wall, Léo whispered, "Women and children first."

Immediately the kids filed in, vanishing behind the unmoved shelf on the right.

"Has it really come to this?" whispered Bindu.

She followed the kids but remained standing exposed before the opening on the left. Léo moved beside her, both their backs against the wall.

He put his hand on her shoulder and said, "Don't worry, I'm right here with you."

She rolled her eyes, removed his hand and replied, "Remember, if we are caught together in here, Constable Kobold is the least of your worries. Mata will surely have you castrated."

"Yes, my lady."

On the back of the shelf two metal handles had been screwed into the wood. AJ grabbed them and started to pull. I stared back, mouth agape.

"Vince," he gasped, "grab your antlers and get in. There's enough room."

I shook my head, approached the shelf and started pushing it from the outside.

"I'll cover for you guys," I said.

"No!" protested Cindy. "You don't have enough experience points."

"Actually, I've already done a round with Constable Kobold. I can handle this."

I sounded braver than I actually felt.

"Vince," whispered Léo, as I pushed the shelf forward, "I just want you to know, if you don't make it... you'll always be remembered. I'll always be your *niijii*, in this life or—"

"Oh, for goodness' sake," I muttered, pushing the shelf flush with the other, feeling like I was sealing them into a crypt.

Of course, with the real windows behind them, fake ones in front and the two fans, they wouldn't suffocate. But suddenly I felt like *I* was about to suffocate as I heard the iron key jiggling in the old lock at the top of the stairs.

27. Constable Kobold

The key continued to jiggle in the lock at the top of the stairs as if the bearer was finding it difficult to open—or was buying us time.

"What's happening?" I heard Josh's voice say nervously from the other side of the bookshelf.

"Shh!" sounded Cindy loudly, as if she was yelling it in his ear.

Half a minute later, the old hinges at the top of the stairs began to squeak.

"Beware... of the... dragon," I heard the gruff voice of Mackenzie reading aloud. "You know there are laws against owning exotic wildlife?"

"Ha!" laughed Roger nervously. "The only dragons down there are three-inches high and made of plastic. I really just use the space to store stuff that didn't sell."

"Hmm," said Mackenzie. "Like I said, I've heard more's been going on down there than just storage. And, looky here, you've left the light on."

"Are there laws against that now, too?" asked Roger.

The wooden steps began to creak with their weight.

"Be careful," warned Roger.

I could see a pair of boots descending, gingerly.

"What? Your dragon might eat me for din—"

Mackenzie's voice and movements stopped abruptly. He was now standing at the bottom of the stairs, wearing his usual black uniform, peaked cap still on his head, mask around his face, staring at a...

"Ha!" he exclaimed. "Forget about a dragon. You got yourself here a moose—unless I took too many painkillers this morning."

I had put the moose mask back on and was holding the bin of cookies at chest level.

"Don't shoot!" I said.

Mackenzie chuckled. "Don't worry," he said. "Hunting season doesn't start until September 18."

Roger came up around him, still wearing his Spiderman costume.

"Hey, Roger," I said as casually as I could muster. "Saw you were with a customer. Didn't want to bother you. Just delivering your order. A half-dozen boxes of almond cookies. AJ said you wanted them down here where it's cooler."

"Of course," said Roger, pointing to the bookshelf. "You can unpack 'em on the shelf like usual. But first, I'll take a box up now for the front desk. We're all out."

I handed him a box as I crouched down by the bookshelves and began to unpack the bin. Mackenzie was advancing around the table, inspecting the game board.

"What's the grid for?" he asked, pointing.

"Oh, that?" said Roger, standing on the other side. "Goes waaay back. I used to play a lot of military strategy games in my teens."

Mackenzie nodded. "Back when I was a kid, I subscribed to *Strategy & Tactics*. You know it?"

"Of course," confirmed Roger, "new wargame in every issue. I was with them from issue eighteen when Dunnigan took over—running it out of a windowless basement in New York's East Side."

"Well, at least, your basement has some windows," said Mackenzie, gesturing to the open ones over the bookshelf. "Strange you feel the need to keep two fans going."

"Gets musty down here, otherwise," said Roger. He opened the box of cookies, releasing the aroma of almond and cardamon. "Care for a cookie, Officer?" His hand, covered with the black-on-red web pattern of his Spiderman costume, extended the box across the gaming table.

"Well..." began Mackenzie. He pulled out his wallet and dumped out three loonies (the bronze-plated, one-dollar Canadian coins imprinted with the image of a loon). He let them fall to the old wooden table, clinking together. "Those cookies do smell good."

He pushed his payment across the table and pulled a cookie out of the box. In order to eat, he had to pull his mask down, allowing my first glimpse of his wide mouth and stubby moustache. Immediately after taking a bite, he let the mask snap back into place.

"Oh, you don't have to pay," said Roger, waving his red hands over the loonies.

"No, best I do," Mackenzie mumbled, mouth full of almond

flour. "Otherwise, it might look like Spiderman is bribing an officer in the middle of a criminal investigation." He stared at the remaining cookie. "Mmmm. Tastes like something the missus would make. Who baked these?"

Roger turned to me.

Trying to avoid the question, I responded in a nervous voice: "Criminal investigation? Has someone been murdered?"

"No, no," said Mackenzie, pulling the mask down and filling his mouth again. "At least, not directly. Rumour has it there's some type of meet-up group happening down here, exceeding capacity limits, not wearing masks, no social distancing."

"Only things I've seen are a mouse and a spider," I said with a forced chuckle. "And they're keeping six feet apart."

Mackenzie followed with an equally artificial laugh. "And the only thing I see is a lone moose. Sorry about this, guys. You know how it is. If they report it, we gotta come."

Roger shut the cookie box and said, "So, case closed?"

Pulling down his mask one last time, Mackenzie shoved the other half of the cookie into his mouth. "Well, let's just say I'll be keeping an eye on the joint." He winked. "But, for now, innocent until proven guilty." He extended his hand over the grid board, cookie crumbs falling.

"Ah," I said waving my hoof, "even before COVID those nerds had been playing all those games online now."

"Too true," confirmed Roger. "And many weren't even doing that much. Last year, there were nearly nine million on Twitch *watching* other people play Dungeons and Dragons. Just watching."

"Doesn't look like much of a spectator sport," I said.

Mackenzie backed away and toward the bookshelf. "Well, soon enough," he said, "it'll be safe for people to get together again."

I cringed, realizing four kids and three adults were squeezed together in a space the size of a closet on the other side of the very bookshelf Mackenzie was now resting his elbow and forearm on.

"Until then," he continued, "kids not being able to play some board games is hardly a big sacrifice if it saves lives. Let's just be grateful they have the virtual version to tide them over."

"Virtual isn't cutting it," protested Roger. "Kid's Help Line is seeing three times as many calls. Suicides are up. Teenage eating disorders have doubled. The stats are in... kids shouldn't be isolated."

Mackenzie nodded and crossed his arms. "Well, at least we won't have any more kids killing themselves because their character died in the game. You ever see that Tom Hanks movie?"

Roger shook his head. "If the death of a fictional character causes such a meltdown—don't blame the game, get the kid some help."

"You could say the same about kids who can't handle a little lockdown."

"A little lockdown?" I blurted out. "It was three months! That can't be healthy for kids."

"Healthier than getting COVID," shot back Mackenzie.

"But kids don't die from COVID," I replied.

"It's for their parents and grandparents."

"Abuse the kids to protect the grownups?"

"It's hardly child abuse," said Mackenzie. "And growing up without a mom or dad is hell."

"Constable," said Roger slowly, "you didn't have to follow stay-at-home orders during the lockdown. You don't know what it's like to be alone."

"*Alone?*" said Mackenzie, sharply. "God, I can tell you what it's like to be alone." He let his arms fall to his side, his right hand hanging beside his firearm. "When this whole goddamn pandemic started, my wife ended up in the ICU for a month. I was stuck in a big empty house. No idea if she'd be coming home. Not even allowed to visit her." He paused and took a deep breath, causing his mask to suck into his mouth. "So, hell, I know what it's like to be alone. And, more to the point, I know what it's like to have a loved one get COVID. And if that means some kids can't sit around a table tossing dice, then tough."

Mackenzie lifted a fist and slammed it back down on the shelf. I'd have sworn I heard one of the kids yelp from behind, but the fans muffled it enough that Mackenzie didn't seem to notice. Instead, he grabbed a handful of dice from off the shelf and whipped them at the game board, some ricocheting onto the floor.

"Look," he growled, "I'm not convinced there's not been something going on down here in your Little Shop of Heroes."

He then picked up one of the figurines from the shelf—a bearded man, wearing a cloak and brandishing a sword.

"You think these are heroes?" he said, looking like he was ready to throw the figurine at us. "The doctors and nurses on the frontline of this pandemic are the real heroes. Risking their lungs every single day to save those who got this damn virus because people were too full of themselves to put up with a little pseudo quarantine."

I would have let him just burn himself out, but knowing the kids were only a few feet away, I had to speak up.

"There's absolutely no proof that lockdowns stop anyone from getting sick."

Mackenzie stared at me with tense, unmoving eyes over his black mask.

"Just look at Florida, Texas, South Dakota or Sweden..." My voice trailed off as I tried to remember the name of that African country Stefanie had mentioned in one of her videos. She'd showed a clip of the president saying how even jackfruit juice produced a positive COVID-19 test. "Or Tanzania! No lockdowns and even less deaths. We can't ignore that."

Mackenzie snorted and thumped the miniature warrior down on the shelf. "We'll leave the statistical analysis to the medical experts—not a... delivery moose."

"Medical experts?" questioned Roger. "Really? Looks more like we're taking orders from the Chinese Communist Party."

"You got something against Chinese people?" said Mackenzie.

I sighed. Roger clenched his fists.

"My wife escaped Communist China," he said. After a pause, he continued, "Can we wrap this up? You've completed your investigation."

"Actually, I haven't," he said, now looking up and down the shelves, pulling a few books out and then sliding them back into place, as if looking for a secret passageway.

"Yes, you have," said Roger, adjusting his Spiderman mask. "It's time to leave."

"Just a moment," said Mackenzie, scanning the frame of the

bookshelf. "I think my spidey-sense is tingling."

"Get out!"

Roger's old, weak voice suddenly sounded like the roar of the dragon which the sign on the door had warned about.

It even made Mackenzie turn his head.

"You don't have a warrant. I've been very patient. It's time to go."

"Got something to hide?"

"I've got a store to run."

"I'm hardly in your way."

They both stood there, mask to mask. Without thinking, I unzipped the front of my moose costume, reached into my pants pocket and pulled out my cell. Tapping the camera icon, I started recording.

"Constable," I said, remembering what Stefanie had done in the bakery, "name and badge number, please."

Mackenzie didn't say anything, but immediately slipped on a pair of sunglasses.

Roger, in a calm but firm voice said, "You either return to the retail area and buy a comic book for your grandson... *or you get out.*"

Through the phone's display it looked like I was watching a movie, with the friendly neighbourhood Spiderman facing off with New York City police.

"Or what?" said Mackenzie.

Holding my breath, I forced myself to dial three numbers.

"911. What's your emergency?" said a female voice over the speaker phone.

Mackenzie's wide eyes locked with mine, staring directly through the open sockets of my moose mask.

"I, er, I," I began to stutter. "Little Shop of Heroes. Main and Queen Street, Moosehead. A, er..." I glanced at the three loonies Mackenzie had left on the table. "A customer is refusing to leave after making his purchase and is loitering in a non-retail area. I guess you might say he's trespassing."

"Can you provide a description?"

"Hard to say, he's wearing a mask, hat and sunglasses. Kind of shady looking. I think he has a gun, too."

Mackenzie pulled up his utility belt and immediately made

his way for the stairs.

"Wait," I said to the operator. "I think he's leaving."

One foot on the first step, he paused, pointing a finger at the black spider insignia on Roger's chest. "I'll be watching your Little Shop of Freaks." Then snubbing his masked nose in my direction, my camera still aimed at him: "And, I think I can guess where your moose came from."

Roger trailed him up the stairs, Mackenzie threatening to sue if anything ended up on YouTube.

"Is everything all right?" said the operator.

That's when I heard Cindy's voice whisper from behind the bookshelf, "Can I come out now? I want to go home."

28. A New Normal Criminal

Ten minutes later, I was sitting in the van and emptying my second bottle of water. Stefanie had equipped me with a six-pack of the same distilled water she used to make her puritan bread and sourdough starters. Even the bottles she supplied were made of stainless steel—BPA-free plastic wasn't good enough.

Josh and Cindy had both been rather shaken up after being let out of the secret alcove. It must have been weird for Josh, in the dark, unable to hear much of what was going on. Ferris and Walter, on the other hand, were all high-fives. And Léo, well, he probably could have spent all day in that cubbyhole with Bindu. In the end, AJ decided it best to send the kids home, each with a box of cookies.

Over the van's speakers, Ian Bostridge was singing out the words to "*Ungeduld*," the fifth song in *Die schöne Müllerin*. I had borrowed the CD from the bakery's stereo that morning. I could discern little of what the German lyrics were saying, but the emotional outpouring carried across by the melody felt appropriate for the moment.

Having quenched my thirst, I reclined back in the driver's seat, reflecting on my first day at the new job. Not what I expected at all. In a matter of an hour, I had gone from being a corny delivery moose to a new-normal criminal. I glanced at the moose mask buckled into the passenger seat. Had Moosey become the mascot for the Moosehead Underworld?

The dashboard's clock glowed 11:50 a.m. Lifting the clipboard, I gulped. That bin of cookies I had just donated to Roger's Little Shop of Heroes cost $92.33 (tax included). Pulling five twenties out of my wallet, I slipped them into the cash purse.

The baguettes that Chef "Facemask" Christophe had refused remained in the back of the van. I scanned down the list: La Papillon, $125.72. I stared into my now empty wallet.

Why was I doing this? I asked myself for the second time that day.

Over the speakers, as if in response, Ian Bostridge sang out in incomprehensible German:

Ich meint', es müßt' in meinen Augen stehn,
Auf meinen Wangen müßt' man's brennen sehn,
Zu lesen wär's auf meinem stummen Mund,
Ein jeder Atemzug gäb's laut ihr kund,
Und sie merkt nichts von all dem bangen Treiben:
Dein ist mein Herz, und soll es ewig bleiben!*

I sighed. I didn't care about comic books. And that dungeon game was the pinnacle of geekdom. But it was nice seeing kids, big and small, getting together without masks. In fact, it dawned on me that it's often only via a screen that we now see people without masks. Rarely in person. Face-to-face contact had become regulated to FaceTime.

Before I left, Roger told me:

"Vince, these role-playing games, they aren't just for fun, you gotta understand. They teach math, logic, problem solving, critical thinking, risk assessment. Kids work together as a team. They get to see the consequences of their actions play out in a safe way. They learn how to discern right from wrong." Then he pulled back his Spiderman mask, revealing his wrinkled face. "They learn how to be a hero without needing any superpowers."

---

* I'd swear it must show in my eyes,
Anyone could see it burning on my cheeks,
Anyone could read it on my silent lips,
Every breath proclaims it aloud,
And she doesn't even notice my anxious yearning:
My heart is yours and will ever remain so.

Chyou and Roger never had any children. Instead, Roger seemed to have adopted half the kids in Moosehead. And now he was providing for those same kids what the COVID restrictions had denied them. And he wasn't doing it for the money.

I sighed again as I fastened my seatbelt. Here I'd been accepting direct deposits from the government so I could sit on my ass, drinking Molson Canadians with my alcoholic father, watching Netflix A to V; while Roger struggled to keep the kids of Moosehead learning and away from the razor blades.

And then there was Grandad. While he was stuck in his one-room cell, eating microwave dinners and picking ants out of his ice cream, I was living in a three-floor house with a big backyard, feasting better than a medieval king on Domino's pizza and Häagen-Dazs ice cream.

And then there was the Dandelion, running that bakery solo, probably living off sourdough three times a day, so she could save enough cash to keep her landlord from writing an eviction notice.

I slapped my empty wallet shut and turned the ignition.

Ten minutes later, after a stop at the ATM, I was carrying the bin of baguettes up the front steps of Moosehead Long Term Care. I pressed the buzzer and waited about three minutes before Claudia came to the door.

Her eyes went wide when she saw a cartoonish moose standing on the front steps.

"*Un alce!*" she blurted, with a hint of delight I didn't think she was capable of.

"*Sí, señorita,*" I responded, extending the bin. "*Pan para todos los residentes.*"

She just stared. Thinking I may have mucked up my Spanish, I clarified.

"Fresh-baked bread. A donation from Moosehead Artisan Bakery. For all of the residents." I felt like saying "the prisoners" but held my big red tongue.

29. Moose Lee

As I entered the rear of the bakery, my antlers snagged on the doorframe. I had just parked the van in the narrow back alley. Stefanie stood on the other side of the kneading table. She held a phone, with a long cord stretching around a tall metal rack. Twelve baking sheets were slid into each slot on the rack. Each sheet was covered by a towel. Underneath I could smell the fermenting dough of unbaked loaves.

"Oh, looks like the lone moose just walked in," she said into the phone. "Okay... thanks! Let me know how it goes. We'll talk soon. Bye."

She followed the long cord around the rack and set the phone back in its cradle on a desk in the corner. The cramped corner, she had told me that morning, was her "office." The office consisted of a desktop computer with a large display, beside a printer/scanner sitting atop a four-drawer filing cabinet.

"You don't trust cordless phones either?" I asked, the moose mask making my voice sound even more weary than it already was.

"They're even worse than cellphones," she replied, turning around to face me. Her lips were pursed and her blonde hair tied back in a ponytail. She was wearing a purple dress and a yellow apron covered with flour. "Cordless base stations are like setting up a mini cell tower in your home."

"I'm beginning to suspect you're a Luddite," I said.

She glanced down at her windup wristwatch. "And I'm beginning to suspect you're late," she countered. She didn't sound angry, but a little frazzled.

"Sorry," I replied, "there were some... hang ups."

"Issues with the moose mask?"

"You could say that," I admitted, not knowing where to start or how much to tell. "Moosey sure got some laughs. Well, Valerie Young didn't laugh, but she... And, um, then there was Christophe at Le Papillon. He wasn't too happy. Hey, what does *papillon* mean, anyway?"

"Butterfly."

"Well, he's more like a wasp. He wouldn't accept the order. Wants a refund. Said we're *imbéciles*."

"I know," she said flatly. "He already called and gave me an earful *en français*."

"Oh. Je suis désolé."

"Not as sorry as I am." She put her hands on her hips, walked around the table and right up to my snout. "I was doing him a favour baking those baguettes at the last minute. His regular supplier couldn't deliver—staff were self-isolating or something. He was in a tight spot. I even consented to use *yeast. Yeast!* And those cookies! Almond flour he wanted. Do you know how much almond flour costs? He has some nerve."

"Don't worry," I interrupted. "I already sold the cookies."

She looked at me sternly. "You... *sold* them?"

"Yeah, more or less," I said carefully. "They're with Roger Gygax—he runs the comic book shop."

"You *sold* them?" she repeated in disbelief.

"Paid in cash. Same with the baguettes. The old folks' home took them. Claudia's having the kitchen make some French onion soup tonight... or at least, reheat some. It'll probably come out of a can—Campbell's if they decide to be classy. But at least Grandad and company will get some fresh-baked bread."

"You're trying to tell me that stingy, government-subsidized, ant-infested, quarantine-crazy nursing home bought $125 of *organic* French baguettes?"

Avoiding a direct answer, I held up the change purse. "All the money's in here." I unzipped the purse and handed it to her.

She looked inside and shook her head. "Vincent," she said gently, reaching out and shaking an antler, "take off that mask."

Guiltily I lifted it up. She immediately leaned forward on her toes and kissed me on the cheek. It lasted half a second and felt like eternity.

I must be hallucinating, I thought. *Heat exhaustion.*

"What..." I began to ask, words failing.

"After Christophe finished expanding my French vocabulary," she explained, "Claudia called, thanking me for the 'donation.' And then that was just Roger on the phone. He told me everything. How you hid the kids and stood up to Mackenzie."

"Did you just kiss me?" I said, awestruck.

"Did I?" She immediately scooted around to the other side of the kneading table. "Well, we did agree you'd get at least one peck if you took off that dirty green face mask, remember?"

I didn't remember her agreeing, but I wasn't going to argue.

"Roger says you're a real hero. The kids are calling you Moose

Lee."

She just kissed me, I repeated to myself.

"You know, like Bruce Lee."

"*Moose Lee?*" I shook my sweaty head. "But all I did, really, was what you showed me. I filmed Constable Kobold when he—"

"Constable Kobold?" she asked.

"It'll take too long to explain," I responded.

"Well, it was super sweet what you did. And super brave. If more people would rebel like you did, this 'pandemic' would be over in fourteen hours."

"I wasn't trying to rebel. I just didn't think it was right—that cop stopping them from playing their geeky board game. It wasn't hurting anyone—except maybe Hollywood profits. Can you imagine kids needing nothing more than their imagination and some dice to entertain themselves? It's insane what the cop was trying to do."

"Well, that still makes you a hero."

"Thanks."

Silence.

"Umm," she said, putting her hands to her lips, "forgive me if I was a bit exuberant there. Remember, I did live four years in Europe."

"No, no, *no problema*. Anytime."

"Hmph!" she said, her sweetness melting away into a businesslike tone. "Now, regarding *el dinero*. You don't have to cover the bill. It's not your fault Christophe's joined the dark side."

She tossed the change purse back at me. I caught it with one hand, holding the moose mask in the other.

Stefanie added, "The unsold items would have gone to the soup kitchen."

"I didn't know Moosehead even had a soup kitchen or any really poor people for that matter."

"We do now," she replied. "CERB cheques weren't enough for families with mortgages."

I suddenly felt ill.

"I really don't want the money back," I said. "I bought some baked goods for my friends, Grandad, and his neighbours. It made me feel useful for the first time in the last three months. Sitting at home, pretending I'm saving the world, was getting kind of depressing."

"Stay-at-home and save lives," repeated Stefanie, mockingly.

"Wear a face mask and protect others," I parroted.

"New-normal acts of phony altruism," she said. "Remember when charity meant actually reaching out and helping people?"

"Exactly!" I said, tossing the change purse back. "So, please, let me cover this. Trust me, I have a lot of quarantine karma to burn off."

She nodded her head and smiled. "I wasn't sure about hiring you, but I must admit you're showing potential... *Moose Lee*."

I smiled back, a warm sensation expanding in the centre of my chest, happy to know I had pleased her.

"Does that mean I'm no longer a turtle?"

"Let's not rush things."

Removing a towel from a plate on the kneading table, she revealed a pyramid of sandwiches, cut in fours. Pale green cucumbers peeked out between the dark rye slices.

"Cucumber sandwich?"

I was hungry.

"I make my own mayo," she added.

"Of course you do," I responded, dryly.

"Dill weed, vinegar and flax seeds. The flax is why it looks brown instead of white."

"Just like your bread," I said. "Let me clean up."

I set the moose mask down on the table, grabbed my backpack from a shelf and scooted over to the restroom. Once I closed the door, I stripped off the fur, changed my sweat-drenched T-shirt and gave my head a mini-shower with the sink's faucet. Exhilaration filled me. I'd gone from Moosey to Moose Lee in less than three hours.

Dripping with water, I returned with a growling stomach to the unconventional lunch. Upon sitting, she slid an empty plate in my direction.

"Cucumbers will cool you down," she said, taking a sandwich from the stack.

"Thanks!"

I said a silent prayer and took a hungry bite.

"Listen," she said, "if that costume's too hot, we can find some other way to outwit the maskers."

"No, no," I said, shaking my head. "It's not a problem. Portable sweat lodge!"

"All right. Just remember to stay hydrated." She lifted a pitcher full of yellow liquid and clinking ice cubes. "Lemonade? I made it with mint leaves and stevia."

I nodded, mouth full of sourdough. "Please." I had no idea what stevia was.

She filled a glass and slid it in my direction.

"These are good," I said, raising the sandwich in the air, pleasantly surprised. "Fresh bread, fresh cucumbers, fresh lemonade. I feel like a king."

She smiled. Maybe even blushed. Suddenly all the humiliation of prancing around town in a fur suit felt worth it. My beautiful boss had made me lunch, christened me Moose Lee and bestowed a kiss upon my sweaty cheek. Indeed, Roger's little shop was a place where heroes were made.

"Did Valerie Young give you a hard time, too?" she asked, before biting into a crunchy cucumber that had slipped out of her sandwich.

"Oh, her," I said, a bit cockily. "She just pointed her knobby old finger at me and said, 'Is that mask Health Canada approved?'"

Stefanie put her hand to her mouth, as she laughed out loud.

"What did you say?" she asked, reaching across and putting her hand on my wrist.

"Well, I said—"

Suddenly, the computer in the corner interrupted my punchline with its speakers blaring a familiar ringtone. Stefanie leapt off her stool, landing in front of the keyboard and slapping the spacebar. Skype appeared on screen, displaying an incoming call. Moving the mouse, she clicked on the green icon of an old-fashioned handset.

Blond hair and long sideburns blinked on-screen.

"Josef!" she exclaimed. "*Na, alles gut?*"

He looked just like he did in the photo. The photo on the wall she had showed me the day before. The photo of her with her arms wrapped around the fiancé I had conveniently forgotten existed.

"*Schatzi!*" he called out from across the Atlantic.

The Dandelion responded in gleeful German.

Mr. Sideburns responded back in more of their guttural language.

And Moose Lee ate in forgotten silence.

30. Mr. Sideburns

For several more minutes, Stefanie continued to converse in high-speed German with her hunk of *side*burning love. Boy, with those sideburns halfway down his cheekbones and his wave of blond hair, her fiancé looked like the German reincarnation of Elvis Presley. With the angle of the webcam sitting on top of her display, she was probably blocking Mr. Sideburns from glimpsing me at all. She certainly seemed oblivious of my presence.

"Oh!" she suddenly exclaimed, as she rotated on her five-star office chair to face me. "I'm so sorry! Vincent, I didn't mean to ignore you. Vincent, this is Josef. Josef, Vincent."

I stood up, wiping my hands on a napkin and nodding toward the webcam. I felt relief that I had not become permanently invisible.

"Hey there, Josef."

"You don't look much like an elk," he said jovially, his accent thick.

"Oh, yeah?" I reached over and slipped the snout and antler back over my head. "How's that?"

"*Ha!*" he laughed. "*Ja, da legst Di nieda!*"

Did he just insult me?

"That's amazing, man. Boy, it must be hot, though."

I shrugged my sweaty shoulders and lifted up a quarter triangle of a sandwich. "The cucumber's cooling me down." I passed the sandwich over the red carpet of the mask's hanging tongue and into my human orifice.

"Stef," he said, "you'll go broke feeding this beast of burden."

That's when the phone rang.

Stefanie reached across the desk for the receiver. Josef's gaze followed her. It was a little disconcerting—it almost appeared as if Josef was the computer itself, gone full-blown AI, chaperoning our first day of work together.

"Moosehead Artisan Bakery," said Stefanie into the phone. "Oh, hello, Mrs. Young."

I coughed and put the plate down.

"Is that so?" said Stefanie, turning in my direction. "Yes, of course. You can pay next time." Then she looked at me. "Don't worry about it. It was his first day on the job."

I took off the mask and wiped my sweaty forehead with the sleeve of my shirt. Lifting up the glass of lemonade, I took a swig as if it was a shot of something far stronger. It did have a bitter-sweet licorice-like taste, probably caused by that mystery stevia ingredient she said she added.

"Oh, I don't know about that," she continued with Mrs. Young. "I'll ask him for you." Putting her hand on the mouth-piece, she said to me, "Pat Young would like to know if the moose does birthday parties."

After a second of silent stupefaction, I attempted to verify that I wasn't hearing things: "Birthday parties?"

"Her grandson is turning six this week. She wants to know if you can deliver his birthday gift and card, since she's not allowed to see him."

"Umm, sure. Why not?"

Returning to the phone, she said, "He'll drop by Monday morning to pick up the delivery." Another pause. "Sure, he can deliver it on Wednesday, with a box of two dozen raisin oatmeal cookies." Another pause. "No, sorry, we don't do cakes."

As she finished making her call, I could feel Josef's webcam-facilitated blue eyes—from a thousand miles away—studying me carefully. I continued to gulp down the cooling lemonade.

When she hung up, Stefanie said to me, "Well, if Mrs. Young likes the costume, then we know it's a success."

Josef chuckled uneasily. "Well, I'm glad you finally found some help..." His voice buffered a little and his image distorted. Part of me was hoping the connection would drop. "I just ... no animal rights groups... involved." His Skype feed suddenly came clear again. "How I wish I could be there to help."

"Yeah," I said, imagining how he must feel. "I'm sorry the pandemic got in the way of the wedding."

"*Pandemic!*" he exclaimed. "It wasn't no pandemic that can-celled our wedding. It's those bloody bureaucrats running your country."

"Yes, of course." I gulped and shook my head. "I can't believe they wouldn't let you come. They're just..." My voice trailed off.

"Trying to keep everyone safe," he grumbled.

"*Donnerwetter!*" snapped Stefanie. "They'll use that line to justify whatever they want. Bankrupt businesses. Deny kids an education. Ban parks. Put grandads in solitary confinement. Even stop people from getting hitched."

Josef responded with some angry words in German; to which Stefanie followed with equal fervour.

"Maybe if you got married over Skype first?" I suggested. "Then Josef would be a citizen and could—"

Stefanie tilted her head backwards as if looking to the sky. "I am not getting married over the internet," she proclaimed. "It's going to happen in the woods with birds arriving in spring, rabbits coming out of their holes and green leaves budding." She looked wistfully at Josef on the screen. "It's what we planned."

"It'll happen," said Josef. "*Das versprech' ich Dir!*"

I sat back down and picked up another quarter sandwich. "Boy," I said, before filling my mouth, "my mom would nail me to a cross if I didn't get married in church."

The Dandelion turned side to side on the office chair. "I don't care much for religious organizations."

"I imagine you wouldn't," I said, right cheek bulging with dough.

"But, hey, Vincent, do you go to church?" asked Josef. "Doesn't bother me if you do. I'm just asking."

"Well, lately, it's been streamed. But, yeah, I usually go with my folks. Well, at least, my mom. Actually, this Sunday is the first time since lockdown the doors are opening. Father Lacombe wanted to wait longer, but we got this new priest now who said it was time for a real service."

"I see," said Josef, and then fell silent.

Stefanie's eyes were cast down, looking at her knees.

I suddenly felt uncomfortable, like I'd just admitted I voted Liberal at the annual meeting of Canada's National Firearms Association.

31. It's World War III, Mr. Elk

The Dandelion and her sideburned fiancé stared at me. I felt like I was roasting inside the bakery's massive oven behind me. They obviously didn't think much of people who attended church.

With the large French population around Greater Sudbury, the area attracted a lot of Catholics. Even though Moosehead was prominently English-speaking, it was still prominently English-speaking Catholics. For elementary school, I had attended École St-Antoine, a fifteen-minute yellow bus ride away, in nearby Noëlville; but for high school, St. Michael's was located on the other side of the hill that St. Jerome's—Moosehead's only church—stood on. All my friends were Catholic. Sure, we didn't read our Bibles every night (or even every week). I hadn't said a rosary in over a decade. And lately, with the lockdown, we hadn't even been taking Holy Communion. Nonetheless, I wasn't used to being the outsider when it came to religion.

"You didn't strike me as the churchgoing type either," Stefanie said.

The fermenting loaves of sourdough, on the rack beside her office corner, suddenly smelt extra pungent.

"Well," I replied, pointing to the moose mask and mocking indignation, "I don't wear the moose head to Mass."

"Mass? You're Catholic, too?" She sounded even more disappointed.

"Is that a problem?"

She bit her lower lip. "It's just that I thought you were..."

"Anglican?"

"No."

"Gay?"

She burst out laughing.

"No," explained Josef. "She thought you were Ojibwe. Like your grandad."

"Oh," I said.

The image of Grandad in the window of the old-age home flashed before me. *Kill the Indian, save the child. They put me in the basement. No food. No light. No bathroom...*

I shook his words out of my mind and replied, "You thought I do sun dances and vision quests? That kind of thing?"

"Yeah."

"Dad wouldn't have any of it. Heathen woo-woo, he says."

"Is your grandad Catholic, too?" asked Josef.

"Ojibwe Catholic, he says. He'd go to Mass and all that until Grandma died. He said there's only one Great Spirit and it didn't matter much which name we gave it."

"Strange," said Josef, leaning into the camera. "Why would he go along with the religion of his conquistadores?"

I shrugged. "The world changed. He adapted."

Closing my eyes, I saw a seven-year-old boy, standing, hungry, watching the other children eat. *They asked if I would be a good Christian now.* I opened my eyes and put down the sandwich that had been loitering in my hand.

Josef was shaking his head. "I don't know how native peoples can belong to a church that almost wiped them out."

"It's just how it is with any big organization," I responded. "You're going to have bad and dumb people do bad and dumb things."

"Sounds like German government." Josef grinned. "They know masks don't work but they're having police dogs attack people who don't wear one."

"Really?" I said. "That's crazy." I picked up a fallen cucumber, and crunched down on it. "Still, you don't go and abandon civilization. We still need government, just better government."

"Well, that's what the QAnon is trying to do," said Josef.

"QAnon?" I'd never heard the term.

"It refers to people who follow Q," said Stefanie, swivelling her chair away from the webcam so Josef couldn't see the smirk that stole over her face.

"Q?" I repeated. "Wasn't he that cocky, all-powerful, transdimensional alien from *Star Trek*?"

Josef laughed. I'm not sure if he was laughing at what I said or at my ignorance.

"Q might as well be from *Star Trek*," said Stefanie, who wasn't laughing. "Q is the head of a made-up secret military organization which people like my lovable but gullible fiancé believe will overthrow the Corona World Order."

"Hey, hey," cut in Josef. "The US military's just waiting to make their move. Letting things get bad enough before they take down the Deep State."

"Ich glaub, mein Schwein pfeift," said Stefanie, and then whistled like a pig does not.

"You'll see, *Schatzi*," said Josef. "You'll see. Trump won't let us down."

"So you think Trump's a good guy?" I asked Josef.

"He's no saint," admitted Josef.

"That's for sure," muttered Stefanie.

"But compared to every president since JFK, he's the only one standing up against the global elite."

Stefanie extended her left arm out to the side, cocked her head, and began moving an invisible bow across an imaginary violin with her right hand.

"You don't agree?" I asked her. "Are you rooting for Biden instead?"

Her barely visible, blonde eyebrows rose and held their position as if she was trying to discern whether I meant the question as a joke.

"Biden?" she said with an astonished chuckle. "It's like Corbett says, Trump or Biden, Pepsi or Coca-Cola, it's all the same."

"*Quor*bett? Is he Q?"

"Ha!" laughed Josef. "No, he's C. James Corbett is this bald Canadian journalist living in Japan. I admit he's pretty witty and smart, even if he's *totally* wrong about the Q movement."

Stefanie shook her head and said, "James Corbett runs an alternative media site called *The Corbett Report*. I'll send you a link."

She clicked on the mouse, temporarily minimalizing her QAnon fiancé to the bottom corner of the screen.

"CorbettReport.com," she said, as she composed a new email destined for my inbox. "James deals in facts; doesn't push hopium,"

"*Hopium?*" I asked.

"That's where the government tricks people into thinking that some military coup or womanizing president is going to save the day, so the people won't bother saving the day themselves."

"Ah!" exclaimed Josef, as his face filled the screen once again. "This is a war between powers far greater than any of us.

We need to stay alert and not get caught in the crossfire."

"War?" I repeated. "Crossfire?"

"World War III, Mr. Elk," said Josef. "It's begun. And these sociopaths are set on exterminating most of the world's population."

I had thought the Dandelion was a bit bonkers, but her future husband sounded completely unhinged.

"Kill us off?" I said. "I'm willing to believe they've overreacted with these measures, made a big mistake; but—"

"The COVID hoax is hardly a mistake," said Josef. "It's going exactly as they planned. Well, almost as planned. Check out Event 201. Last year, Bill Gates hosted a closed-door meeting with world elites in New York, rehearsing how they would react to a, get this... *a coronavirus outbreak*. Then a few months later... *surprise!* Now the world's flipping out over a coronavirus—on track to kill millions with lockdowns. And New York, where they held their pandemic preparedness meeting, is leading the way with deaths by ventilators—"

I wrinkled my forehead. "Ventilators? Come on. Now you're just talking nonsense. Ventilators keep people alive."

Stefanie swivelled her chair to face me. "Only two out of ten survive a ventilator and all the drugs that go with it."

"Yeah, but that's why they are on the vent, because COVID made mincemeat of their lungs."

"Then why only in Italy, Wuhan and New York were they using so many ventilators?"

I shook my head, not getting where she was going.

Stefanie turned back to the computer and began typing. "Google Erin Olszewzski. She's a nurse from Elmhurst Hospital."

"Elmhurst? That's the one with the line of refrigerator trucks filled with corpses, isn't it?"

"Watch her video on Journeyman Pictures' YouTube channel. I'm emailing you the link right now. You'll find out why New York had so many deaths. It wasn't COVID. They were putting people with anxiety attacks on ventilators—wrecking their lungs."

I could feel my appetite vanishing as I swallowed the last bite of my sandwich. I wasn't sure if I could take anymore of their "alternative news." Josef, however, was only getting started.

"And I just saw a vid of Dr. Bryan Ardis testifying before the German Coronavirus Investigative Committee," he added. "He says hospitals, especially in America, have been mandated to give their COVID patients Remdesivir."

"*Rem-des-a-what?*" I asked, knowing I didn't want to know the answer.

"It's a drug that causes kidney failure. That's why they've been putting so many patients on dialysis."

"I thought that was because the virus fried their kidneys?"

"You ever hear of the common cold giving people kidney failure?"

I didn't respond.

"They know Remdesivir causes kidney failure," explained Stefanie. "It's a known side effect. Without kidneys the patient can't go pee, so their body starts filling up with fluid."

"Look at this," said Josef. Suddenly the image of him on the screen was replaced by two black-and-white X-rays. "The one on the left is how lungs look when full of pneumonia. Kind of like cauliflower. The X-ray on the right is when it's full of edema, but no infection. Looks like a skating rink."

I stood up, walked toward the display and squinted at the ghostly images of an organ we normally only felt, but never saw.

"They're not dying of respiratory problems," Josef said angrily. "They can't breathe because they're drowning in their own bodily fluids. If the Remdesivir-induced kidney failure doesn't kill them, then the ventilator will."

In a flash, the X-rays were replaced by Josef and his blond sideburns filling the screen. "Time to wake up, Mr. Elk! COVID-19 is code name for mass murder."

32. Corona World Religion

I'd wondered why the United Sates, especially New York, had had so many more COVID deaths than Canada. If anything, the weather was colder on our side of the border. I'd figured we should have suffered more. Or, for that matter, what about Sweden, which was even farther north and didn't even have a lockdown?

I took a step away from Josef's tense face, which morphed into large cubes for a second, as Skype struggled to maintain the transatlantic connection.

"But why would they purposely murder patients?" I put my hands out as if holding a globe at chest level. "These are doctors and nurses, after all. What would be the point?"

"Why did the Catholic Church kidnap Indigenous children?" said Josef, leaning into the camera. "They were priests and nuns, after all. What was the point?"

"Hey!" Irritation suddenly filled my voice. "We didn't kidnap them. The Mounties did that. We just schooled them. And the Presbyterians did the same. So did the Church of England and the United Church and..."

"Phooey!" said Stefanie. "You have to do some serious mental gymnastics to not think they weren't all complicit in child trafficking."

"They believed they were saving the kids' souls," I defended. "And maybe even their lives. I mean, living in the bush ain't easy. Grandad remembers. His uncle got his leg bashed up really bad and couldn't ever walk again."

Josef frowned, sympathetically. "I'm sure some of their abductors and wardens had good intentions."

To which Stefanie added, "But a few good intentions can blind one to a mountain of evils."

"Yeah, but..." I stammered. "I mean, some of these priests— back in the 1700s—they left the comforts of France to teach the Gospel to the Indians around the Great Lakes. Living in wigwams. No hot water. Freezing winters. Blackflies and mosquitos instead of quiche and baguettes. It's not like they did it for their own benefit."

Josef and Stefanie looked back at me, blankly.

"Back in grade seven or eight, we went on a school trip to this shrine in Midland." Thinking Josef might not know Midland, I explained. "Midland's a town south of here on Georgian Bay. They have a shrine dedicated to eight Jesuit missionaries who were killed while preaching to the locals. Iroquois poured boiling water over them, cut off their noses, tortured them to death..."

"Hmm," said Josef with a snicker. "Maybe those Jesuits

should have taken such a reception as a sign not to push their religion on others."

"They didn't want the Iroquois to go to hell," I almost yelled, taking another step back.

Stefanie's eyebrows raised. "You really believe they would go to hell if they didn't get baptized into your church?"

"Well, no. Of course not." I walked over to the moose mask and tugged at an antler. "But those missionaries probably did."

"Just like today," said Stefanie, "people are bullying others into these new-normal rituals because they think everybody is going to COVID hell if we don't comply."

"In order to sell salvation," added Josef, "you first must convince people of their damnation. Get them scared. Then you can justify whatever you want in order to save them."

"And what better way to scare them," said Stefanie, winding a lock of hair around her forefinger, "than inducing kidney failure with a toxic drug, letting their lungs fill up with fluid and then blaming it on a respiratory virus?"

"But most doctors and nurses wouldn't poison their patients intentionally," I said. "I'm sure there's a few evil ones, but you're talking about hundreds if not thousands of doctors and nurses—"

"—just following orders," completed Josef in his thick German accent.

"*Befehl ist Befehl!*" added Stefanie. "An order is an order, as all those doctors and nurses said during the Nuremberg Trials."

"*Befehl ist Befehl!*" repeated Josef.

Then we all fell into a silence so profound I'd swear I could hear the microbes fermenting the sourdough loaves on the rack.

I placed the brown felt mask back over my head. Speaking in the best moose voice I could muster, I said: "You know, for a baker and a paramedic, you're both deep thinkers."

Stefanie leaned back, letting her long hair hang over the back of the chair. "My grandmother always said: 'Du hast ein Gehirn. Benutze es.' You've got a brain. Use it."

"Hmm," I said in my deep ungulate voice. "My grandmother always said, 'Don't eat all the grass or it won't grow back.'"

The Dandelion put her hand to her mouth and laughed.

I immediately felt relief.

Josef grimaced.

"So," I asked, shaking my antlers with my hands, "are you going to fire me for being a Roman Catholic moose?"

She rolled her eyes. "Of course not. But the pope better watch out. COVID-19 is vying to become the New World Religion."

"Hey!" I exclaimed, "that's what Father Shostakovich was saying." I slapped my hands together and pointed at Stefanie, forgetting about Mr. Sideburns on the display beside her. "If there's a Catholic priest you're ever going to like, it's Father Shostakovich. He's new to St. Jerome's. During lockdown, he was caught holding Latin Masses in the basement of his church back in Ottawa."

Stefanie straightened her posture and said, "Good for him."

"The bishop sure didn't think so. Shipped him to out-of-the-way Moosehead, Ontario. And it's not like Father Lacombe needed the help. Especially these days."

"Shostakovich?" said Stefanie. "Russian?"

"Croatian," I corrected. "I heard his homily last Sunday on the Facebook feed. He was a kid in World War II. He said that after the war, Croatia went from fascism to full-blown communism."

I figured that would impress her, even though I really wasn't all that sure what the difference was between communism and fascism.

Stefanie nodded, swivelling her chair side to side again. "That would explain why he wasn't fooled by the government trying to disguise tyranny as a health and safety thing."

"Hey, he'll be doing the homily tomorrow."

"What's a homily?" asked Stefanie.

"It's what Catholics call a sermon. If you want to come with me and—"

"*Festhalten!*" Josef butted in. "Did you just ask my fiancé out on a date?"

I took a step back.

"Ah, no," I said quickly. "I didn't mean—"

Stefanie waved her hand at the webcam. "*Hör auf, Schatz!*"

Josef laughed loudly and leaned back in his chair, which rocked back and forth in synch with his guffaws.

"I just meant," I almost stammered, "you might want to attend and hear what he has to say."

She blushed a little. "Thanks for the offer, but..."

I waved my hands. "No, no. Forget I asked. But hey, I'll send you both a link to one of his videos. You'll get a kick out of him."

"Sounds great!" chimed Josef. "An old superstitious religion telling us why we shouldn't follow a new superstitious religion."

I didn't say anything. Just stared off to the side.

"Did you want anything more to eat?" asked Stefanie, softly, pointing to the remaining sandwich on the platter.

I would normally have eaten more. My appetite was usually robust and used to something more substantial than vegetarian sandwiches. But, not so surprisingly, all hunger had left me. The safe and ordered world I thought I lived in was being slowly dismantled.

"Umm, no, no, that was great. Your, ah, *vego mayo* was yummy."

She grinned. "I'll wrap up the rest. You can bring it to Grandad."

"Yeah, sure. He'll love that."

"I'll grab a bag."

She picked up the platter, said something to Josef in German and disappeared through the hanging beads.

I turned to the video screen. "Hey, well, Josef, I hope you can get here soon. I'll email my MP or MPP. Not sure. One of them. Maybe both of them. Asking them to get real and let you guys get married."

He just stared at me silently for a few seconds, before saying, almost in a whisper: "Watch it, Mr. Elk. Remember: she's my fiancé. If you forget, visa or no visa, I'll hunt you down like a—"

"Here you go!" Stefanie passed back through the beads with a brown paper bag in hand.

"Thanks," I said, taking the bag, one eye still on the Skype feed, where Josef was laughing at me again.

"Well," she said, "I hope it wasn't too much for the first day on the job."

Anarchistic pagans getting married in the woods, I grumbled, mentally, to myself.

"You mind if I leave the moose mask here?" I said, almost

sadly.

Euthanizing drugs and killer ventilators.

"Of course not," she replied.

Corona world religion.

"Great. I've had enough of being a moose for one day."

The whole town must be laughing at me.

"Don't worry, Vincent," said Josef. "We don't hunt elk in Germany anymore."

I need to get home.

"Good to hear," I said.

Get back in my shell.

"We already killed most of them off."

Watch some Netflix.

"*Jetzt reicht's aber!*" Stefanie scolded, slapping at his digital grin on the display.

As I headed out the door, gym bag around my shoulder containing a sweaty, furry costume inside, I glanced back. The Dandelion had her face up close to her fiancé's pixelated sideburns, jabbering in German again.

More German, from song fifteen of *Die schöne Müllerin,* played jealousy in my mind:

> Sahst du sie gestern abend nicht am Tore stehn,
> Mit langem Halse nach der großen Straße sehn?
> Wenn vom dem Fang der Jäger lustig zieht nach Haus,
> Da steckt kein sittsam Kind den Kopf zum Fenster 'naus.

Which is to say...

> Didn't you see her last evening standing at her door
> And craning her neck toward the highway
> When the hunter returns home merrily from the hunt
> No decent child sticks her nose out the window.

33. Fourteenth Sunday in Extraordinary Time

I took a deep breath. After twenty minutes of sitting on a hard wood pew, in a hot and humid church, my green face mask had become damp and suffocating. Beside me sat Mom wearing her Sunday best—a black mask with a white cross. We sat alone in the fifth pew from the altar. Dad, well, he wasn't able to make it.

Every other row had yellow caution tape barricading its entry points. In the front pew sat Mayor Hill and his family. Between the Hills and the altar roved AJ, holding a video camera. He was wearing an untucked, red, button-up shirt and a Jesus Over COVID-19 mask.

Since it wasn't Easter, Christmas, Advent or Lent, it was what the Church called Ordinary Time—the Fourteenth Sunday in Ordinary Time, to be precise. But nothing seemed ordinary about Sunday morning Mass with less than thirty physically distanced people disguised as bank robbers. Rather, it felt like the Fourteenth Sunday in *Extra*ordinary Time.

One of the few bearing his face was Father Shostakovich, who stood at the lectern closing the Bible he had just finished reading from. It was the first time I'd seen him in person, as he had only arrived three weeks earlier. He looked like he'd stepped out of scripture and had visited an optometrist: longish, curly snow-white hair above his round spectacles, and a grey beard descending halfway down his green and white robes. I tried to imagine what kind of mask could possibly contain such an explosion of facial hair.

"I'm glad you all braved this terrible pandemic to come together in Christ."

And when he said "terrible pandemic" he shuddered mockingly. His theatrics generated a couple of giggles from the congregation but otherwise a lot of confused and silent stares. I glanced at Mom. Her eyes darted back and forth nervously.

"And for all you in Facebook land," he said, waving at AJ's camera, "you are with us here, in spirit."

Scanning the church, I immediately spotted the Chatterjees, the only brown-skinned family in the parish. Otherwise, it was hard to recognize anyone—hidden as they were behind masks, scarves and...

A mosquito net? That was a first, I thought.

Four pews behind us sat a woman in a yellow dress, her face veiled by a green mesh hanging down from her wide-brimmed straw hat. I figured she must be a new widow, from the countryside.

Exercising face-covering exemptions were Sandy and Josh,

sitting two pews in front of us beside the confessional booths. Sandy's hands were flying through the air, signing everything Father Shostakovich was saying for her deaf son. It almost looked like her hands were dancing. I bet she never fell asleep during a sermon.

Otherwise, even Father Lacombe, who sat at the rear of the altar, gazed upon us over a green cloth mask that matched the green robes both priests were wearing. Previously, via one of his streaming Masses, Father Lacombe had told us the face covering was a natural extension of his liturgical robes. The draping vestments were meant to hide the priest's body, he said, putting the focus on the real reason for our gathering, Jesus Christ. The mask, likewise, hid his face, allowing him to perform the Holy Sacraments *in persona Christi*. But rather than seeing the Good Shepherd, he looked more like a thief in priest's clothing.

A half decade older than me, Lacombe was only a few years out of the seminary. He had short, brown, curly hair and, from what little skin was exposed around his mask, a clean-shaven face. I had wondered whether he always took his mask off to shave, or sometimes just shaved around the edges. His homilies were so boring, these were the types of questions that usually passed through my mind while he spoke in a lifeless monotone about the etymological significance of the word "kingdom" in the Bible.

One thing was for certain, Father Shostakovich's homily would prove to be neither boring nor monotonous.

"Before lockdown," Father Shostakovich began, still standing at the lectern, "St. Jerome's averaged about one hundred attendees every Sunday—so Father Lacombe has told me. But the church was built to hold five hundred. It's amazing that the government felt the need to lock you all out, considering you were more or less social distancing already."

I saw Mr. Chatterjee chuckle, while Mrs. Chatterjee shook her head. Both sported short hair, as if the couple went to Harry's for a trim together. Both were thin—too thin—like they worked too hard and didn't eat enough (even though they were probably the most well-to-do family in Moosehead). Mrs. Chatterjee was wrapped in a dark purple sari, which covered everything her mask did not, save her dark eyes. Mr. Chatterjee, or

Baba, as most people in town referred to him, somehow seemed more colourful than his wife even though he was wearing a white dress shirt, black tie, and a black mask.

"We must wonder," said Father Shostakovich, "what is the real motive behind Caesar telling Christians to keep their distance from each other."

He paused. I could see the back of Bindu's head nodding. Another sign that these were not ordinary times: she was sitting alone, two pews in front of her family. She was wearing a purple sari, like her mother, but it did not cover her head, and she was not wearing a mask.

"In today's Gospel," Father continued, "our Lord came to the temple and found that con artists, pretending to be merchants, had taken over. Did he stand passively by? No! He overturned the tables and grabbed hold of a—the Book of Matthew says— a 'whip of cords' and drove the evildoers out."

Mom began fidgeting with her hymnal.

"Yet, today, hardly anyone has put up a fight when corporately funded institutions like the WHO and the Bill and Melinda Gates of Hell Foundation have invaded not only our churches, but our schools, our parks, our places of business and even our homes."

Mayor Hill coughed—into his mask. *Gross!*

"Families have been separated," continued Father. "Grandparents sentenced to long-term solitary confinement. Children denied learning, play and friendship. And now they ask us to practise voodoo—wearing masks to ward off the premier's 'invisible enemy.'"

He pulled out from below the lectern a black plastic eye mask and stretched its elastic band around his head.

"Yesterday, I wore this to the library," he said.

I laughed so hard my own mask snapped up my chin and into my upper lip.

"The librarian told me this wasn't the kind of mask they wanted." He tossed it into one of the collection baskets stacked by the altar boy. "Oh, well. I tried."

More chuckles, cautiously bubbling up from the sea of parishioners, were suddenly stifled by the mayor's crewcut head rising in the front pew. He nodded down at his wife, who slowly stood, her blonde hair trailing down the back of her black dress. She signalled to their three children. As the kids rose and turned into profile, I saw both girls wore pink masks and the boy a blue. Their homemade masks looked like my mom's handiwork. The white crosses she had sewn on gave the appearance that each of their mouths had been taped shut.

Unperturbed by the fleeing family, Father smiled broadly. "What does it matter whether I wear an eye mask or a face mask?"

The Hills' footsteps echoed as they headed up the aisle to the front entrance.

"Why are we going?" said the older girl.

"Father Zorro might have COVID," said the taller boy in a whisper so loud the whole congregation surely heard it.

Father seemed unoffended, as he continued: "In May, the scientists were quite clear. The pores in masks are eight times wider than a virus. So what changed? Does this novel coronavirus suffer from gluttony? No, not at all. Instead of claiming masks could stop a microscopic virus, they said masks could stop spit. And that's all people needed to convince them to adopt this new-normal ritual."

The door of the church closed loudly. The Hills had left the building. Our congregation of thirty was now only twenty-five. And it would be even smaller before Father Zorro said Amen.

34. The Fictitious God of COVID

Father Lacombe appeared to be gripping both arms of his mahogany presiding chair. It was no secret that, next to the Chatterjees, the Hills dropped the largest cheques into the collection basket. Obviously, Father Shostakovich valued truth more than donations.

"Wearing a mask is like putting up a chain-link fence to protect your crops," he said with the surety of a dandelion. "It'll stop the occasional rabbit, but not the swarm of locusts."

Next, a middle-aged man I didn't know, wearing a face mask with the words PSALM 91, began to exit his pew, followed by what looked like his elderly mother. Lacombe shot up from his seat, strutted around the altar, and whispered something to

Father Shostakovich. Father Shostakovich laughed and turned back to the mic.

"Father Lacombe says I need to be more sensitive. Yes! He's right. We need to be more sensitive to the acts of evil happening under the guise of compassion and altruism. We need to be more sensitive to the poorest of the poor who will starve due to these lockdowns."

Father Lacombe crossed his arms and gazed downward.

"The United Nations says we are now facing a hunger pandemic. Some 270 million men, women and children are being pushed to starvation." He paused and closed his eyes. "We don't live in the Garden of Eden. Food is not falling from trees. We need to work."

Father Lacombe, still standing by his side, whispered something again, but Father Shostakovich shooed him away.

"We should be sensitive to injustice, but not sensitive to those committing the injustice. Jesus did not practise sensitivity with the Pharisees. In Matthew 23, the Prince of Peace called these hypocrites 'children of hell,' 'blind fools' and a 'brood of vipers.' And so, we must not be sensitive to the blind, hellish vipers injecting the deadly venom of indolence and apathy into healthy people."

Glancing over at Sandy, I saw her signing to her son—index and middle fingers were pointed outward like a forked snake tongue, as her hand slithered across the air in a wavy motion. Josh's eyes were wide. Church was starting to sound like a game of Dungeons and Dragons.

Mom, however, did not look amused; her hands were shaking. I put my arm around her and squeezed her shoulders.

Father Lacombe started to say something else but Shostakovich cut him off: "Thank you, Father Lacombe. I'm almost finished."

The younger priest bowed his head, spun around, vestments flailing out as he retreated to his throne behind the altar. Father Shostakovich held up the Bible and continued his intense homily in a surprisingly relaxed voice.

"Jesus says that the Pharisees 'tie up heavy, cumbersome loads and put them on other people's shoulders, but they themselves are not willing to lift a finger to move them.' Lockdown's easy for the wealthy enjoying mansions on large estates, but unquestionably harmful to a family living in an apartment."

"Amen!" exclaimed a voice from behind me—a familiar voice. "Hallelujah!"

Heads shot back in the direction of the woman wearing the green mesh. She obviously didn't know that Catholics remain silent during homilies. Still, Father Shostakovich didn't seem to mind the cheerleading. He only smiled and nodded to Ms. Mosquito Net.

"And Jesus said that the Pharisees appear to people as righteous, but on the inside they are full of hypocrisy and wickedness. In the same way, politicians don their virtuous face coverings for the camera but then wine and dine at private parties without masks or social distancing. As Jesus says, how will they escape being condemned to hell?"

He paused, his words making the humid air even heavier. I saw a few people adjusting their virtuous masks.

"Whether you wear a face covering or not is between your conscience and God. I will not judge you. But I believe masks, especially in church, are sacrilegious. Everything about them is counter to our faith. The putting on, and taking off, the washing and drying of them, is a ritual. A pagan ritual."

I saw Mr. Chatterjee reach behind his ears as if he might remove his pagan adornment, but after an askance glance from his wife—I could have sworn her eyes glowed red—he returned his rebellious hands to his lap.

"Now," continued Father, "some say they wear the masks to make others feel better. They don't believe in the mask, but suffer them for the sake of those who do." He paused, shaking his head. "Lies have nothing to do with charity—but come from the father of lies, the Devil himself. Instead, you may wish to ask yourself if you are really wearing the mask so others won't shame you?"

Oh, what the heck, I thought with a sigh and pulled the mask off my face, stuffing it in my pants pocket. At that very moment, Raj shot up from his pew like a volcano that no longer could remain dormant.

"Father Sasha-ko-vick," he said, butchering the new priest's name, "with all due respect, I am not being a Satanist by wearing a mask."

"Raj!" exclaimed Mrs. Chatterjee, in her thick East Indian accent.

Despite Raj outweighing his mother by forty or more kilos, she yanked him back down with the ease of a lion's paw, followed by harsh words muttered in Hindi. I didn't know if even Raj could understand Hindi, but we all got the gist of what she was saying to her twenty-four-year-old son. Never in all my years attending Mass did anyone ever speak out during a homily. Now, on this Fourteenth Sunday in Extraordinary Time we'd already had two interruptions: Ms. Mosquito Net's impassioned Baptist-like fanfare, followed by Raj denying his allegiance to Satan.

Father Lacombe raised both his hands. "Please! We are here to unite in Christ. A house divided cannot stand."

Father Shostakovich swept his hands out and said, "That's exactly what this new-normal nonsense has done. It creates a visible division to the point people shun those who do not look like them. Masks make you neither Mother Teresa nor Beelzebub. But to believe they do anything to stop disease is mere superstition; like carrying a rabbit's foot or tossing salt over your shoulder—"

Now old Bill Cooper, in his grey suit, blue latex gloves and red bow tie, shot out of his pew. "If you weren't a priest," he exclaimed, "I'd have some fine words for you."

Father grinned widely over his long beard. "You need not worry, I'm quickly becoming obsolete. Doctors are fast replacing the clergy."

Without responding, Mr. Cooper and his red bow tie (which perfectly matched his red mask) began marching down the aisle toward the rear entrance. Father Lacombe leaned forward, bringing his forehead to his hand, his arm propped up on the leather-bound armrest.

"Vaccinations have become the new baptism," continued Father, unperturbed. "And pills have replaced the Eucharist. Since the lockdown we stopped bringing Communion to the elderly in nursing homes, yet they still get their medication each day, don't they?"

A long silence ensued. I thought he had finished. No doubt Father Lacombe was praying so; but such a prayer was not to be answered yet.

"In the first century, Christians were persecuted by the Romans. Why? Not so much because they believed in Jesus; but because they would not offer sacrifices to Jupiter, Apollo and Vulcan. Rome feared that their gods would be angry. They saw Christians as a threat to the empire and everybody in it. And if we don't stand now, then those who are not willing to mask their face, to isolate from others, to get injected with an experimental therapy—to appease Caesar's fictitious god of COVID—may be deemed a threat to society."

I heard a muffled sound come from Mrs. Chatterjee. Was she crying?

"Enough!" Father Lacombe exclaimed. "I plead with you, Father Shostakovich, let us continue with the Holy Eucharist."

The older priest closed his eyes and folded his hands together. After a brief pause, he said, "God our Father, we pray that the Holy Spirit will fill us with courage to act with faith and freedom in your son, Jesus, who has already overcome this world. Amen."

With that, he turned toward the altar where Father Lacombe was looking heavenward.

"Let us celebrate the sacrament of Holy Communion," said Father nonchalantly, as if his homily had simply reminded us that we should eat fish on Fridays.

As Father turned away from the lectern, I felt a wave of relief pass over the twenty-three remaining members of our socially disintegrating congregation.

Well, I thought, stretching my arms out to my sides, *I don't think she'll be disappointed with that homily.*

I looked back over my shoulder at Ms. Mosquito Net, nodded, and flashed her a mask-free smile.

35. Ms. Mosquito Net

Twenty minutes later, Holy Communion was distributed. Before COVID, the congregation would normally proceed up to the altar in a line to receive the body of Christ. The new-normal version involved us remaining seated while a masked Father Lacombe used the sectioned-off pews as a "safe" pathway from which he distributed the host.

The thin wafers imprinted with the sign of the cross normally had a bland taste—being made with only white flour and water. That morning, however, they tasted of ethyl alcohol. I noticed that after Father Lacombe gave each of us the host, the altar boy trailing behind him would squirt some hand sanitizer into his palm before proceeding to the next person.

"Go in peace," proclaimed the well-sanitized Lacombe at the end of the Mass, "glorifying the Lord by your life."

"Thanks be to God," the congregation responded with audible relief.

Since Father Lacombe considered a live choir "too high risk," a recorded hymn played over speakers. The altar boy lifted a four-foot wooden cross and led Shostakovich down the centre aisle. Lacombe trailed twelve feet behind.

Once they passed, Mom immediately stood, brushed her hands and said, "I'm so sick of hearing about COVID, masks, and the whole thing."

I rose, grinning. "Hey, Mom, would you like to meet my boss?" I nudged her around and pointed to the mosquito netting four pews back. "Mom, this is Stefanie."

"Hello, Mrs. McKnight," said Stefanie, pulling the green mesh up and over her straw hat. "I'm so glad to meet you."

Boy, she was beautiful, I thought. Not gorgeous. No, she looked too real for gorgeous—rather a rustic, wild beauty. No makeup, no flair, just a wild dandelion beaming at us.

"Yes," said Mom. "Hello. Vince has said such wonderful things about you." Her sentiments sounded as stretched as the mask around her face.

I pointed at Stefanie, grinning. "That veil looks dangerously close to a face mask."

"Phooey! I thought veils and hats on women were a Catholic custom. Believe it or not, I do try to fit in."

"Other than for brides, I think that rule got shot down at the Second Vatican Council—along with Latin Masses."

"Humph!" She removed the hat, revealing her blonde hair tied up in a bun. I couldn't help noticing she now had that emerald ring around her finger—no longer hanging from her necklace.

"So," I said, a bit whimsically, "what did you think of Father's sermon?"

"You were absolutely right. He's a gem of common sense. Doubly impressive coming from a priest indoctrinated into a highly dogmatic, centrally controlled and historically repressive worldwide institution."

She grinned. I chuckled. Mom took a deep breath and squeezed her eyes shut. I shuffled from foot to foot, eyes darting from my mother to the Dandelion.

"Oh, Mrs. McKnight," said Stefanie, "I wanted to tell you that that moose costume you made... *it's incredible*! And it's really helped business. I mean, like really helped. I've never had so many orders on a Saturday. Phone's been ringing every ten minutes, and I may have to pause the website's shopping cart or I'll have more orders than I can fulfill."

"Shows how dull things have got with lockdown," I commented, "if one lone moose can cause such a stir."

"If you think you are too small to make a difference," said Stefanie, "you haven't spent the night with a mosquito."

"Did you come up with that?" I asked.

"Dalai Lama," she said, looking side to side. "I hope it's not a sin to quote Buddhism here?"

I shrugged. "Christians are pretty forgiving."

"Well, customers aren't. It's going to be a busy baking week. But I couldn't be happier. Honestly, sales were starting to sag before Moose Lee saved the day."

Mom opened her eyes. "I'm so glad to hear." She almost sounded happy for a moment.

"You did a great job with the antlers. And that tongue's hilarious. You're a master costume maker, Mrs. McKnight."

"Oh, please... please, call me Carol," said Mom, probably blushing under her mask. "Yes, the antlers weren't easy. Took three tries."

"Where did you learn?"

"My parents," said Mom. "They were costume designers for the Abbey Theatre in Dublin."

"Wow! Well, that explains it. Did you grow up in Ireland?"

"Only until I was twelve."

"But you don't have an accent," said Stef.

"Awful good of you to say it," said Mom, reverting to the musical lilt of her homeland and even pulling down her mask. "But I've had a donkey's years in Canada. It's me home now, you see, and I do not want to seem *arseways*."

We all laughed. For a moment, the world no longer seemed so *arseways*.

"Well," added Stefanie, leaning on the back of the pew in front of her, "suddenly everybody in Greater Sudbury wants fresh bread delivered by Moose Lee." She turned her smiling face toward me. "Are you willing to go full-time? I won't be able to keep up if this continues. I'll need help in the prep room, kneading, baking—"

"Oh, my!" said Mom, giggling and holding her hand to her mouth. "Vince baking bread! He can hardly make instant oatmeal without burning—"

"Ahem!" I cleared my throat. "We don't need to go there, Mom. In fact, I've been making bannock for breakfast as of late and it's been great. Doubles as a frisbee, it's been so dry and hard. I throw it over Jeff's fence and Stormy catches it in his mouth and swallows it whole."

Another round of laughter.

"So, are you interested?" asked the Dandelion, starting to sway back and forth.

Oh, yes, I'm interested, I admitted to myself as I stared back into her blue eyes.

"In the extra hours, I mean," she added, as if reading my thoughts.

"Hell, yeah!" I said aloud. "That way I can afford to rent Chung's place and still have money left over for food."

"Chung's?" asked Mom. "Renting?"

"There's an apartment available above the Green Dragon. I could get Grandad out of the nursing home. You know that's always been my plan. We'll room together. Between his pension and a raise, we can do it, I think. I need to talk to Mr. Chung."

"Oh," said Mom and she crossed her arms. "Yes, of course."

"I was actually taking Grandad there for dinner tonight."

"Oh," said Mom, again. "But aren't they... isn't his place in lockdown again?"

"Claudia's given me the go-ahead. Turned out that Mathéo's

MUCH ADO ABOUT CORONA – 163

aunt didn't have COVID. So Grandad's a free man."

"That's wonderful," said Stefanie. "I can't wait to see him again."

"Hey," I said to her, "if you want to join us for dinner—"

"Oh," she said, taking her hands off the pew and standing erect. "I'm afraid I, uh, I have a birthday party to attend."

"Oh," I said.

I felt disappointment and doubt. *A birthday party?* She didn't strike me as the partying type.

Suddenly the voice of Father Lacombe interrupted us.

"If you are not going to wear your masks, would you be so kind as to stand outside and talk."

Lacombe was now standing in the aisle at our side—and he didn't look much like the partying type either. He had removed his bright green and white robes and was now wearing a black cassock with a matching black mask.

"Yes, of course, Father," said Mom.

She pulled her black mask up over her red face, grabbed her purse and scooted past Lacombe and down the aisle. Much slower, I exited the pew, but didn't mask up. As I passed Father Lacombe his dark eyes followed me.

"If you are unable to follow the rules," he said, "you may prefer to attend virtually."

"What?" I exclaimed, smiling. "And miss out on the automated holy water dispensers?"

I laughed. He didn't.

Facing the altar, I dropped to one knee and made the sign of the cross. I made a point of doing it in slow motion, then rose and turned around. Stefanie had already vacated her pew and stood in the aisle with her mosquito veil draped back behind her wide-brimmed straw hat, making her almost look like a bride. A small part of me wished that engagement ring on her finger was from me and not Mr. Sideburns. A silly wish... I hardly knew her, really.

Gesturing to Father and the Dandelion, I said, "Father Lacombe, Stefanie Müller. Stefanie, Father Logan Lacombe."

"Good morning," she said, with a nod.

"Welcome to St. Jerome's," he said with as much friendliness as a socially distancing crocodile.

I pointed over Stefanie's shoulder toward the rear doors and said, "You gotta see these new holy water fonts. Infrared sensor. No touch. Kind of crazy-brilliant."

As we walked down the aisle toward the vestibule, I could feel Father Lacombe's stare burning into my back. Little did I know, his reproachful glare was nothing compared to what awaited us in the parking lot.

36. Touch-Free Holy Water Dispensers

As we entered the lobby, I turned and pointed to a wooden box mounted on the wall beside one set of doors leading back into the nave. The box was shaped like a crucifix, with a black label affixed to the bottom that read, HOLY WATER. Below it, a small ledge held a ceramic bowl to catch any drips from the high-tech font.

"You just put your hand underneath," I said to Stefanie.

The red LED at the bottom of the bulky cross turned green, followed by a barely perceptible mechanical hum and a drop of water falling into my hand. I had to let it run off onto my fingertips before making the sign of the cross on my forehead.

"Does it also bless the water?" she asked.

"No, I think the priests still do that."

"Is it supposed to protect you from evil spirits?" she asked.

"Not really. It's to remind us that we were baptized."

"You remember being baptized?"

"Well, no, I was quite young at the time."

"Doesn't it bother you that you were initiated into a religion without your conscious and informed consent?"

"Uh. I hadn't really thought of it that way."

That's when I noticed Raj standing by a twin dispenser at the other set of doors. Like his parents and sister, his East Indian skin was of the very dark variety—so much so that he could almost pass for an African with straight hair and thinner lips.

"Hey Raj," I said.

He was now wearing a yellow safety vest over top of his white dress shirt. I'd noticed the other ushers wearing the same. It was the type of polyester vest construction workers and late-night cyclists wear to avoid being hit by a passing SUV. I hadn't been keeping up on the Ministry of Health's latest guidelines, but I doubted even they would go so far as to suggest orange and grey reflective stripes could fend off SARS-CoV-2.

"Hey, Vince," Raj responded with far less flair than his getup.

Raj was a few inches taller than me and had broader shoulders. With his orange vest, his black mask, and his large build, he looked more like a bouncer than an usher. As he stepped toward us, I expected trouble. But instead of booting us out of the vestibule for not wearing masks, he patted the wooden frame of the touch-free holy water font.

"Made them myself," he said. "This is version three-point-O." I couldn't see his mouth, but I suspected he was smiling proudly.

"You made these?" said Stefanie. She sounded sincerely impressed.

"Needed something to do during lockdown."

He lifted the cross-shaped box off a bracket on the wall and flipped it over. It had no back panel, allowing us to see its innards. Along the horizontal width of the cross was a transparent container half full with holy water. The upper portion of the cross contained four AA batteries. A tube and wire ran down the length of the cross and connected to an infrared sensor at the bottom.

"Ingenious," said Stefanie.

"Thanks," said Raj, as he placed the dispenser back on the wall. "Give it a try."

Stefanie raised her hands. "But I'm not baptized."

"Oh, that's okay, pagans can use it to."

"Thanks," she said and extended her hand. Somehow, I imagined she took being called a pagan as a compliment. After massaging a large drop of water into her palms, she added, "Well, it does seem more sanitary than everybody sticking their fingers into the same bowl."

I shrugged. "I guess—like better ventilation and outdoor patios—a few good things might come out of this scamdemic."

Raj grumbled.

"And it's very creative," added Stefanie.

"That's what Pope Francis told us to be," Raj said, adjusting his crinkled orange vest, "to be creative when it comes to expressing our faith."

"I think he was, uh, referring to promoting the faith," I interjected. "Evangelization. Not sanitization."

"Well," said Raj, rubbing his palms together, "I've been promoting these babies—driven to all the churches between here and North Bay, showing them the prototype. They're taking to them like ducks to holy water. Just think, over 221,000 parishes in the world. Each needs at least two, probably more. We're talking half a million units. $50 each. That's $25 million in sales."

A smirk came across my face as I remembered the day I first met Raj. We were both twelve. He had been going door-to-door on Magder Road, selling cellphone charger holders he'd made out of plastic shampoo bottles pilfered from people's recycling bins.

"Sounds like a booming new business venture for you," I said.

"That's how my parents raised me," he said. "Work for no man and do something to make the world better."

"Well, I don't work for a man, but this lovely lady," I said, turning to Stefanie.

She cleared her throat. "I told you, I'm your boss, not a lady." She flashed her emerald ring at me.

"Got it," I affirmed, before turning back to the automated holy water font salesman. "Raj, this is Stefanie. Stefanie, Raj. You both probably have a lot in common, being that you're both entrepreneurs."

"Yes, well..." said Raj, awkwardly, his voice abruptly turning sour. "I doubt we have all that much in common. And I would appreciate it if you both stood a little farther back, since neither of you are masked and my parents aren't the youngest."

"Hey, didn't you hear what Father said? The masks are just superstition."

Raj raised his hand, palm outward—making him look more like a crossing guard with his orange vest. "When it comes to religion, I listen to priests," he explained. "When it comes to science, I listen to scientists."

"Which scientists?" shot back Stefanie.

"The ones who know what they're talking about."

"Can you be more specific? Names? I'd love to find a scientist who can make any sense out of all this unscientific behaviour."

"You've never heard of germs?" said Raj, patting his touch-free holy font again.

"You never heard of an immune system?" countered Stefanie. "I mean, have you ever heard of people getting sick from dipping their fingers in holy water?"

"People get sick all the time," said Raj.

"Exactly," snapped back Stefanie.

They both stared at each other. Obviously, entrepreneurship did not offer a strong enough connection.

"Maybe," said Stefanie, "everybody dipping their fingers in the same bowl helped strengthen their immune systems? Have you ever considered that?"

Raj took a deep breath, expanding his chest before puffing out his mask with a large exhale. "We're in the middle of the worst pandemic since the Spanish Flu—we don't have time to run a double-blind study to prove basic hygiene laws to people too ignorant—"

"So you don't care about science?" interrupted Stefanie.

"Raj!" said a thick East Indian accent from behind my back.

Stefanie and I turned to see Mrs. Chatterjee standing at the open doors to the church. Her dark purple sari blended almost seamlessly into her dark purple face mask. I wondered if she had sacrificed some of the silk from the hem of her sari to make the matching face covering.

"Raj, I told you not to talk to *those* people."

Those people? I was speechless. Raj and I were hardly the best of friends, but we'd been playing hockey together for over a decade. How many times had Mata stuffed the team with her fiery curries and crispy samosas after a game?

"Mata," I said, smiling, thinking she must not recognize me. "It's me, Vince."

She just raised a hand. "If you're not going to wear PPE, please, stay away from my children."

Children? I looked back at Raj. He was twenty-four—was he going to put up with this from his mother?

Instead of protesting, he closed his eyes and whispered to me, "Sorry, man."

"Ah! there you are," exclaimed the voice of AJ, sounding a bit out of breath.

He was now standing beside Mata at the front door, holding the tripod from the camera he'd used to stream the Mass. Even though he still had his Jesus Over COVID-19 face mask, he must have been standing a bit too close to Mata, because she immediately stepped aside.

"Father Shostakovich would like to talk to Stefanie," said AJ. "He's out in the parking lot. And, um, judging by the mob surrounding him, he could probably use her help."

37. Love Thy Unmasked Neighbour

St. Jerome's was propped up on the highest hill in Moosehead. Stepping out onto its stone steps, Stefanie, AJ and I had a clear view of the French River, the Louis Riel Bridge and Brian Peckford Park on our left. To our right, in the distance, I could see the green rooftop of Grandad's nursing home. The sky was clear, save for a few large, fluffy clouds, one of which looked like a giant, albino turtle. The turtle swam in front of the hot sun, casting a cooling bit of shade over us.

It would have been a beautiful moment, if it wasn't for the twenty masked parishioners in the parking lot surrounding Father Shostakovich.

"And if we are to love our enemies, then, certainly we must love our unmasked neighbours," Father was saying. "And we certainly shouldn't fear them giving us a disease that they don't even have to give."

Rather than a Sermon on the Mount moment, it looked more like the Spanish Inquisition—led by Mrs. Elliot. Mrs. Elliot was the science teacher at St. Matthew's Secondary. She had long black hair, which had always reminded me of a witch, and oversized, black glasses that normally slid down to the end of her nose, but were being held stationary by an oversized, black mask. Her right arm was raised, as if pointing to an invisible chalkboard, while she spoke with far more emotion than she ever did when teaching my grade ten biology class. Apparently, defending face masks excited her more than explaining how the Krebs cycle generates adenosine triphosphate.

"But the Public Health Unit says face masks are required," she insisted, tapping her invisible and soundless chalkboard.

"They can say whatever they want," replied Father, the corners of his mouth turned up, "but that doesn't make it a law."

"But we don't want to give anyone COVID."

Father's brows drew together as he leaned toward her, squinting. "My dear," he said gravely, "do you have COVID?"

Baba, who was standing at the edge of the circle with his daughter Bindu, began to laugh.

"That's the thing, Father," said Mrs. Elliot, "most of us wouldn't know if we had it."

"You can't tell if you have a deadly disease?" said Father, his voice losing its doomsday edge.

"I could be asymptomatic." She now appeared to be writing the word "asymptomatic" on her invisible chalkboard for Father not to see.

"A disease without symptoms," exclaimed Father, stretching out his arms. "That's like a rainstorm without water."

There were a few scattered chuckles, much like the first raindrops hitting a lake.

"A disease that doesn't make you sick," said Father, in a rising voice, "is like a clown who... can't do balloon animals."

Laughter erupted like thick storm clouds that could no longer hold back. AJ almost doubled over, supporting himself only with the tripod he was carrying. Even Mrs. Chatterjee's head was bobbing as she came to her husband's side. I saw Sandy signing, moving her palms apart as if holding a growing balloon, while Josh laughed.

Almost everyone was laughing, except for Father Lacombe. Again, I felt his glare. He was now standing before the open doors of the church, at the top of the steps, looking as stiff as the pope's pastoral staff, eyes fixed on his father superior.

"But Father!" exclaimed Mrs. Elliot, banging an imaginary ruler on an imaginary desk, "the PCR tests show that COVID-19 exists."

"Oh, for the love of God," said Father quickly, putting his hand to his forehead.

That's when the Dandelion could hold back no longer, saying, "We've actually no idea what the test is testing for."

Forty eyeballs turned to identify the strange new voice among them. She grinned back at them, unafraid. I felt both proud to be standing beside someone so bold and beautiful, while at the same time wondering how long it would take us to die when they burned us at the stake.

"They never isolated the virus," she continued, "just randomly tested for a fragment of DNA from the sputum of some guy in China."

"I see we have a guest," said Father, nodding at Stefanie.

"Vincent invited me," she replied, almost defensively.

Eyes veered in my direction. "She's my boss," I said quickly, generating a few chuckles. "At the bakery."

"Best sourdough bread in all Northern Ontario," Sandy professed loudly, waving to Stefanie.

"She's also," said Raj, who was now standing beside Father Lacombe at the top of the steps, "Northern Ontario's biggest conspiracy nut."

"Now, now!" said Father Shostakovich, raising a finger. "Nuts are good for the brain—full of omega-threes."

Crossing her arms, Mrs. Elliot looked at Father Shostakovich with a tense forehead.

"Father, with all due respect, please leave the science to the experts."

"Ah, but what did Einstein say?" asked Father. "Science without religion is lame. And religion without science is blind."

"We're just trying to keep everyone safe," an unidentified voice spoke out.

Bindu snorted. She was still maskless, standing beside her father, who had his mask under his nose. "If you want to keep others safe," she said loudly and clearly as if speaking to an assembled jury, "then stop driving your car. Eighteen thousand Canadians died last year in car accidents."

"And if you want to live longer," said Father, "then let people go to church. Study after study shows churchgoers have longer, healthier and happier lives; while masks haven't been shown to do anything more than virtue-signal one's way to a face rash."

"Well, I never..." began Mrs. Elliot. "Religion may need the help of science, but it has no business teaching it."

"And science certainly has no business preaching blind faith," countered Father. "We wear a cross around our necks to show our faith; but the COVID cult asks you to wear a mask around your face to signal your obedience."

"*Cult?*" gasped Mrs. Chatterjee. "Really! We're just trying to stop people from dying."

"But you can't!" Father almost hollered, his eyes growing wide and his patience thin. "Old people die! I'm going to die! You're going to die! Science can't promise eternal life."

"Mrs. Chatterjee," said Stefanie, "Father's right. All this new-normal pseudoscience is only causing harm. The restrictions are literally killing people. Especially the lockdowns."

"But," said AJ, pulling his mask down below his nose, "what about the virus? Without the lockdown, wouldn't COVID have wiped out humanity, leaving only a few immuno-superior survivors scattered across thousands of apocalyptic cities living off canned beans and Doritos?"

I shook my head and smiled. *AJ reads way too many graphic novels.*

Father raised a finger in the air. "They never said the lockdowns would stop the virus, only slow it down. And we've seen no proof they do even that."

"But Father, what do you want us to do?" asked AJ. "Break the law?"

38. The Untouchables Among Us

I saw Father Shostakovich take a deep breath, about to respond to AJ's question. Before he had a chance, Father Lacombe descended the front steps of St. Jerome's and was now standing among us in the parking lot.

"We would *never* recommend anyone break the law," said Father Lacombe, hastily. "That is not the place of the Church. We would only ask that everybody pray and follow their conscience." He looked awkwardly at his superior. "Would you not agree, Father Shostakovich?"

Father Shostakovich nodded. "Hebrews 9:14 says the blood of Christ will cleanse our conscience—making us wish to obey *God before man.*"

"Then let us end with that," pleaded Father Lacombe. He began gesturing people away with outstretched arms. With his black cassock, he looked like a crow learning to fly. "Please, we are gathered much too close, even if we are outdoors. Please go to your homes, and pray for guidance, remembering that the bishop has advised us all to cooperate with the public health regulations and to do our part as Christians to protect the sick and elderly."

"And remember," added Father Shostakovich, "even if you think someone is wrong, you still have to love them. Would you not agree, Father Lacombe?"

"Second Timothy, chapter two," quoted Father Lacombe, "'Have nothing to do with foolish, ignorant controversies...'" He then looked directly at Stefanie. "'And the Lord's servant must not be quarrelsome but kind to everyone, able to teach, patiently enduring evil, correcting his opponents with gentleness.'"

Lacombe's eyes, however, looked about as gentle as the front of a charging freight train. Stefanie met his stare with a smile.

Turning back to the crowd, he continued in a slightly more upbeat voice: "Thank you everybody for joining us today. If we all keep being safe, then we can enjoy many more Masses together and avoid any future lockdowns."

But Stefanie was not finished. "Why are you letting a bunch of politicians tell you how to practise your own religion?"

Father Lacombe didn't turn to acknowledge her.

"I think we've heard enough from you," said Mrs. Chatterjee, her thick East Indian accent sounding even thicker. "Are you even baptized?"

Father Lacombe raised his hand, "Please, let us be patient with her, she's new."

Bindu let out a big sigh. "Well, I've lost my patience." And she marched past Father Lacombe and up to Stefanie. She reached out her hands and said softly, "I told Father Shostakovich about the..."

My ears perked, but I couldn't hear what she said next.

Baba was watching Bindu and Stefanie intently as they joined hands. Beside him, his wife stared with eyes so wide I thought they might launch out of their sockets like twin cannon balls, striking Stefanie and Bindu to the ground.

"Bindu!" exclaimed her mother. Bindu was now giving Stefanie a hug. "Don't touch her! God knows where..."

Bindu said over her shoulder, "Mata, I thought you left India because you disagreed with the untouchable caste."

"Ah!" said Father Shostakovich. "Do you not see, the government is trying to make us all untouchables." He walked over to Bindu and Stefanie and clasped their hands. "I would very much like to speak with both of you in private about the..."

Again, I could not hear what came next.

"Well, she can walk home," said Mrs. Chatterjee to her husband with a huff. That's when she noticed Baba was now wearing his mask below his chin. "And for that matter... so can you!"

But Baba pulled out the keys, smiled, and headed toward their Honda Odyssey. Arriving at the passenger side, he opened the door for his fuming wife.

I spied Sandy facing Josh and putting her fingers to her mouth as she said, "Shall we go to the Green Dragon for lunch?"

Josh nodded eagerly and clasped his mother's hand, and they headed out of the parking lot. I suspected Josh liked Chung's Chinese buffet more for its name than anything else.

Mrs. Elliot slammed her car door closed. Her husband was already in the driver's seat reading a newspaper. In fact, he'd been sitting there the entire time, while his wife had tried to convince Father Shostakovich of "the science" behind masking and lockdowns.

Parked beside the Elliot's car was one of the Chatterjee's smaller ten-foot moving trucks. Raj, the church-to-church salesman, was opening the back door, revealing stacks of cardboard boxes—presumably containing more touch-free holy water dispensers ready to help stop the nonexistent pandemic from ravaging Northern Ontario parishes.

As the parking lot cleared, I heard others mumble about how Father Shostakovich was an old man who couldn't change with the times.

Mom was now standing alone. Walking over to her, I could tell she was visibly shaking as if it were a cold winter day.

"I'm ready to go home," she said.

"What about lunch?" I asked, imitating the sign for *eat*. "I promised you pizza at Trozzi's."

"Thank you, dear," she said, shaking her head. "I just want to go home. Could we get take-out?"

Stefanie then ran over to us, smiling. "Father Shostakovich wants to speak with you and me about the M—" Her eyes glanced at Mom, and her voice trailed off. "About my project to help those who have lost their jobs because of the phoney health measures."

I looked at Mom, who appeared to be backing away from Stefanie's presence.

"I wish I could," I said. "But I promised Mom lunch today."

A flash of disappointment crossed Stefanie's face, but she quickly smiled and said, "Thank you so much for inviting me. I don't think I'll be getting baptized, but it was a certainly a unique first date."

Date? Did she just say "date"?

She blushed. "I mean, outing." Her right forefinger and thumb suddenly clasped her ring.

In the bell tower of the church behind her, I envisioned Josef perched like a sniper, his hunting rifle aimed at my now racing heart.

"Have a nice dinner with Grandad," she said. "Tell him I said hi and hope he comes to visit soon. I'll see you tomorrow morning."

She put her palms together, as if praying, seemingly unsure what to do with her hands. Turning to Mom, she said, "It was so nice to meet you, Carol."

Mom nodded back and softly said, "Stay safe."

Stefanie feigned a smile, turned and jogged back toward the front steps of the church, holding her straw hat as her yellow dress fluttered. AJ, who was now maskless, saluted me as he held the door open for Stefanie, Bindu and Father Shostakovich.

What were they planning? Would they all be donning Guy Fawkes masks and planting dynamite under Parliament Hill? I shook my head. Such a mission might excite AJ, but it hardly seemed to fit with Father Shostakovich's ministry, while Stefanie wouldn't even harm a rabbit if she was starving to death.

Gazing down at the townscape below, I could see the third-floor apartments above the Green Dragon peeking over the roof-top of the town hall. I didn't know what Father and Stefanie were up to, but I knew what my mission was now that I had the promise of a higher salary: Free Grandad.

39. The Mask of the Green Dragon

"There you go," I said, slowing the wheelchair to a halt. "We made it!" I pointed to the sign above the front door of Mr. Chung's restaurant:

The Green Dragon
Authentic Chinese Cuisine

It wasn't easy convincing Claudia to let me take him out of the old folks' home. His release came with many conditions such as wearing masks at all times. We kept them on until we crossed the Louis Riel Bridge, out of her range of vision. *Nazi Nurse.*

Grandad looked up at the sign of his favourite restaurant but said nothing. I wasn't sure if he recognized it.

"Why don't we leave the wheelchair out here?" I asked.

"Won't someone take it?" he responded slowly.

"Ha!" I laughed and backed the chair up against the brick wall. "Here's your cane." I pulled out the brown stick I had wedged into the side of the chair.

"All right."

Grandad gripped the cane and tried to pivot himself into a standing position, but only fell back. I grasped his left arm and helped him to his feet. I marvelled at how much lighter he felt. He certainly had not gained extra weight over lockdown like Dad and Mom.

"There!" he said, with relief and satisfaction.

I patted his shoulder. "Don't worry, we'll have you doing one-legged squats by Christmas."

"Really?" Again, that voice of childlike wonderment.

With me still holding his one arm, I opened the front door with my free hand. The hinges squeaked. Grandad's cane clunked on the wooden floor as we entered. The restaurant was vacant. After all, it was only 5:30 p.m., the hour Grandad was usually served dinner at the old folks' home. The kitchen door, at the rear of the dining room, suddenly swung open. Mr. Chung appeared, holding a metal tray.

"Oh, Paul!" he said with his slight Mandarin accent. "Where you go so long?"

The old Chinese man, with night-black hair, dropped the tray into an opening in the buffet counter under red heat lamps, then practically sprinted toward us, abruptly halting six feet away, arms outstretched awkwardly. His grey goatee peeked out from below his face mask, and his stubby nose stuck out above it. Lounging smugly in the middle of the mask was a two-dimensional green dragon.

"It's so good to see you, so good to see you," he said. "How you doing?"

"Terrific!" said Grandad with sudden enthusiasm.

He then fell silent, cane wobbling under a shaky arm.

Mr. Chung turned to me. "And you, Vince? You look stronger. Bigger muscles, no?" He clenched his fists. "You working out?"

"Lifting weights. Had to get strong enough to bend the bars on Grandad's COVID jail cell. They tried to lock him up again."

"Yes," Mr. Chung replied, reflectively. "I heard, I heard they had an outbreak; but this looks like a break*out* instead."

Suddenly Grandad broke out in his Shakespearean accent: "Let us cry peace, freedom and liberty!"

He said it with such fervor and volume that it shocked Mr. Chung and me into silent awe, but a second later we were both rocking with laughter.

"Wow!" exclaimed Mr. Chung, applauding softly. "Where did that come from?"

"*Julius Caesar*," I guessed.

"Act 3. Scene 1," replied Grandad with a smile.

"Well, I so glad Caesar is free to dine at my humble establishment once again."

Grandad suddenly defaulted to a blank stare. After an awkward pause, Mr. Chung addressed me.

"You such good grandson." He looked like he was going to pat me on the shoulder, but instead gave me a thumbs-up.

"Ah!" I said, shaking my head. "Grandad was always taking me out when I was a kid. He taught me to skate, fish, canoe, hike. Geez, he practically taught me to read. I'm barely balancing the scales."

Mr. Chung formed his right hand into a fist and pounded it into his open left hand. He then bowed slightly. That's how he opened every one of his martial arts classes. The classes he held in that very restaurant on Saturday mornings before the pandemic. We'd move the tables and chairs to the side, and a few of us guys would get an hour of instruction with Moosehead's black belt.

"I sure miss Kung Fu Saturday," I said. "I saw AJ today, and he said the same."

Mr. Chung chuckled. "Ah, AJ. Great master of falling with style."

His attention suddenly veered to the squeaky front door opening behind us. I turned to see Mayor Hill entering with his wife and kids. All wore masks, though no longer with crosses emblazoned on the front.

Mr. Chung instantly pulled his Green Dragon mask up over his nose.

I took a deep breath, expecting the worst.

"I want to see what the fortune cookies have to say about the pawn-damn-ic," said the mayor's daughter, skipping to a long table at the front window. She was probably eight or seven.

"No fortune in a pandemic, you dummy," said her brother, a few years her senior.

Mr. Chung said to us, "One moment, please."

He stepped around and approached the mayor. "Welcome, welcome. Your usual table, Mayor Hill? Ah, Annabelle has already chosen one. You come, please, right this way. How you tonight, Mrs. Hill?"

The mayor puckered his forehead as he walked past Grandad and me. He was still wearing the same dark suit from church; but his bald head looked shinier somehow. I wondered if he oiled it. His wife was now wearing a red evening dress, revealing most of her back, down to her waist.

"Buffet or menus?" asked Mr. Chung, as they sat themselves.

The mayor gestured to Mr. Chung. He leaned forward and Mayor Hill whispered something to him. Mr. Chung nodded, then rushed over to the take-out counter, retrieved two menus, three colouring sheets and a cup of crayons. Bringing them back to the family, he said, "I let you look the menu while I..."

His voice trailed off. The couple was already staring at their numerical options. Mr. Chung dashed back to us.

"Um, Vince," he said, nervously. "The mayor says to remind you that you, please, put masks on indoors."

Grandad was staring at the kids, who were gripping the crayons in awkward fists. Without averting his gaze, Grandad asked, "How do they eat with masks on?"

"Oh, never mind," said Mr. Chung, swatting his hand through the air. "Once you sitting you don't need them on. Come this way."

He took Grandad's arm and walked him toward a small table at the farthest corner of the room, where he helped him into a chair. I took the other seat. A waterfall babbled on my left.

"Menu or buffet?" asked Mr. Chung.

"Buffet, of course," I said.

"Yes, of course!" Mr. Chung looked back nervously at the mayor's table. "But in honour of Paul's return, allow me to serve you, please. Just let me know and I get it for you."

"Rice and mushrooms?" I asked Grandad.

"*Manoomin*," said Grandad distantly. "When I was a boy, I would help my mother hull the *manoomin* after she and my sister collected it from the river. We'd dance all over the rice."

"I think that's a yes," I said to Mr. Chung.

"And then," continued Grandad, "we'd take some of the rice and roll it in mud, and throw it back into the lake, to grow more for next year."

"And I'll have..." I stood up to look at the buffet counter. "The Cantonese chow mein."

"We'd also find the mushrooms in the woods and caves," continued Grandad. "My father knew which were good, which were poison."

"Well, no poison in my mushrooms," said Mr. Chung with a jovial nervousness. "Anything to drink?"

"Two green teas," I said.

Mr. Chung nodded. "So glad you both back." And he headed into the kitchen.

I stood up. "I gotta go take a leak."

"That's terrific!" said Grandad, smiling.

I scooted across the back of the dining area, toward the corridor leading to the restrooms.

"Mask!" barked the mayor.

I turned and saw his shiny head turning as red as his wife's dress.

40. Standing Germs Only

I said and did nothing, just froze.

Pounding his fist lightly on the table, the mayor repeated even louder, "Put on a mask! for God's sake, what's the matter with you?"

More sheepishly than I would have preferred, I replied, "I'm just going to the washroom."

"I don't give a crap," he barked back. "If you're not sitting, you're wearing a mask."

"What if I'm sitting on the can?" I countered.

"What if I call the police?" he responded, pulling out his cell phone.

"I'm not breaking any laws."

The little boy laughed. "Are you stupid?" he said, pointing his crayon at me. "Wearing masks indoors is the law. Isn't it, Daddy?"

"That's right, son," said the mayor. "But it's not nice to call people stupid, even when they are acting stupid."

I felt like telling them, as Josh had told me the other day, that with their masks they were the ones who looked truly dumb. Instead, remembering Father Shostakovich's words from his homily that morning, I cocked my head and argued, "Actually, it's not a law, just a public health recommendation. Anyway, I'm exempt."

"Like hell you are," said the mayor. A blue vein bulged along the side of his bald head. "You don't look like you got COPD."

"Religious exemption," I stated. "I don't believe in invisible germs that can only hurt us when we're standing."

"Don't be a smart ass with me, kid. Even if you don't got the sense to protect your own pulmonary system, at least compromise a little and keep others safe."

"I thought I was compromising," I said, feeling braver (or more ticked off) than usual. "Just like you'd rather I wear one; I'd rather you didn't—and especially not your kids. It's disturbing to look at."

"What a hopeless, self-absorbed generation," said his wife. She looked at me with sunken eyes. "Christ, can't you use some common sense?"

"I thought common sense was washing our hands before we eat, which is what I was about to do. Enjoy your meal, Mr. and Mrs. Hill."

I smiled at them. Neither responded. But Annabelle turned toward me, pulled down her mask and smiled.

"Annabelle!" exclaimed her mother, as if her daughter had just lifted her skirt. "How dare you."

"But I was holding my breath," she sulked.

I couldn't bear it anymore and headed down the corridor. Once in the restroom, I hit the light switch and saw my face looking back at me in the mirror. No green mask. No turtle in his shell. I bet she would be proud.

A minute later, I returned, feeling an odd mix of fear and exhilaration. Stepping into the dining area, I immediately noticed the mayor's table was empty, a crayon rolling around in a circle. Mr. Chung had his back to the front door, holding it open, staring out into the street, where the Hills were opening doors to their Mercedes-Benz.

"Take-out?" called out Mr. Chung. "Or maybe Henry deliver something to your home?"

"We're going to Harvey's," said the mayor loudly, before slamming the car door.

"Why can't we stay, Daddy?" said Annabelle, as her mother ushered her into the back seat.

"Boy, you're stupid too," said her brother. "It's because that jerk used the bathroom without a mask. Now the bathroom gots COVID."

I heard more car doors close, the engine revved and they pulled away. Mr. Chung pulled his mask back down below his nose and sighed. I slid into my chair at the back. Two teapots and mugs were now on the table.

"Hey," I said to Grandad.

"He wasn't happy," said Grandad, sounding slightly amused.

Mr. Chung let the door close and headed straight for the buffet. A minute later, he presented us with two bowls, wafting ginger and soy sauce.

"Hey, Mr. Chung," I said. "I didn't mean to scare off your customers. I was just minding my own business."

"I know," he said softly. "But some people. The mask is very important to them."

"Well, don't worry. I think I can make it up to you. You know that Apartment For Rent sign you've had up on the front window since Christmas? After dinner, Grandad and I would like to take a look."

"Really?" said Mr. Chung.

"Yeah, I'm getting him out of the old folks' home before they kill him."

"But, Vince, I don't think he'd be okay living on his own."

I chuckled. "He wouldn't be. I'll be joining him."

"Apartment only has one bedroom."

I crossed my arms. "As long as it has a living room."

"Yes. Of course, of course." Chung bounced on his toes. "It's a bit small, but nice. Very nice. We just put in hardwood floors and repainted all the walls. Has great view of town hall."

"And, hey," I said, "if they lock down restaurants again, they'll be locking two of your best customers inside."

Mr. Chung chuckled.

"Either way, we'll probably end up patronizing your buffet on a daily basis. Because, as bad as the food is at the nursing home, I assure you, Grandad, my cooking is even worse."

Grandad didn't respond.

"Well, well," said Mr. Chung, with a little hesitation. "After you eat, I give you the keys. You go up. See if you like it."

At that moment, I heard the squeaky door swing open again and a cacophony of voices bustle into the dining area behind me.

"Excuse me," said Mr. Chung, with a little bow.

"No prob," I said.

I turned my attention to my large bowl of noodles, chicken, shrimp, bamboo shoots and water chestnuts, drenched in the Green Dragon's signature honey-garlic sauce.

"All right, Grandad, time for some real food."

He nodded, bowed his head forward and said his usual prayer. He always whispered it. I could never tell if it was Ojibwemowin or English. That's probably the way he preferred it. He then picked up a fork and began to eat. He ate so slowly. It was as if it took all of his mental acuity to move food from bowl to mouth.

Ten minutes passed. I was halfway through my large meal, and he had barely scraped the surface of his senior's portion.

This may take a while, I thought.

The front door squeaked again. One of the five rowdy men, now seated at the longer table near the front, hollered: "Ah, look, there he is. We were starting to wonder whether—"

"Be with you gentlemen in a minute," replied the voice of my father.

Before I had a chance to turn around, Dad was already pulling a chair out from an adjacent table and setting it down backwards against ours with a rattle.

"Holy guacamole!" he said, putting a hand on Grandad's shoulder. "Can't keep my old man in a cage, eh?"

41. The Scorpion Strikes

I put down my fork, pushing my near-empty bowl of noodles aside.

"Hey, Dad," I said, trying to sound nonchalant and happy to see him.

Grandad just stared at his son as if he didn't recognize him. Dad was wearing a black mask with the words WILL REMOVE FOR beside a drawing of a beer bottle. Dad pulled the mask down to his neck.

Grandad smiled and said warmly, "Richard!"

As far as I knew, Dad hadn't seen Grandad at all since Christmas. And I doubt Dad had called him much. Now, here were the three of us all sitting together at a table at the Green Dragon, just as I was getting ready to sign a rental contract with Mr. Chung. I doubted it was a coincidence.

"Carol said Vince was eating here tonight," Dad continued, sounding like he was beginning a stand-up comedy routine. "I thought he had a hot date with his new boss. 'That's my boy,' I said. But Carol, she says, 'No, she's engaged. Big green ring and all.' And I say, 'Hell, that shouldn't stop a McKnight in shining armour. Not like she's married. Still fair game.' But, no, Carol tells me he's dining with his... *Grandad."*

I leaned my right arm over the back of my chair, hand running through my short hair, and sighed.

Dad shook Grandad's shoulder again and jested, "You're not nearly as pretty as the baker, but you're looking good." He chuckled, somewhat nervously. "How are you doing, Paul? The home treating you well?

"Terrific!" replied Grandad, with that tone of wondrous oblivion.

"Good to hear! Good to hear! But, hey, must be nice to get out for a little break. Enjoy the warm weather. Was that your wheelchair I saw out front?"

"I'm not sure," said Grandad, looking at me.

"Yeah, it's his," I said. "Not that he'll be needing it much longer."

The door squeaked again. I turned to see Oskar, my German tutor, step inside. Despite his HOCKEY GRANDPA mask, I couldn't mistake him. Thick German accent, six foot three, with white hair no more than six millimetres long.

I hadn't thought the situation could get any more uncomfortable; but I had underestimated how strange my life had become.

"Ah, Vince!" he immediately exclaimed. "My protégé!"

Before I could say a thing, he put a hand to his stomach and bellowed: "Laß singen, Gesell, laß rauschen." *Sing on, friend, keep rushing.*

I took a deep breath and sang back the next line: "Und wandre fröhlich nach!" *And travel gladly along.*

Oskar raised his eyebrows and nodded at me. "Sehr gut!"

"Danke," I said, shyly.

"Hey!" hollered one of the other men at the table by the window. He was wearing a T-shirt with the Corona beer logo. "Knock it off, guys. Don't you know singing spreads bloody COVID?"

Oskar pressed a hand to his throat, shrugged, headed straight for the buffet and began shovelling rice onto a plate.

"Bravo!" said Dad, looking at me in awe. "You must really have it bad for this baker babe."

I waved my hand dismissively and poured some of the green

184 – JOHN C. A. MANLEY

tea. "I've always loved music."

Mr. Chung swung by our table.

"Richard," he said, "can I get you a drink?"

Dad looked at the watch he wasn't wearing. "Well, it's hardly six o'clock; but..." He swung an arm behind his back. "Hey, you've twisted my arm. How about a scorpion?"

"And would you like a menu or—"

"I'll do the buffet with those ladies over there." He cocked his head toward the other table, where Oskar was planting himself down before a mountainous plate of rice, chicken and broccoli. "I just wanted to make sure Vince's grandad was staying out of trouble." He slapped Grandad on the back, causing rice to fall off his spoon.

"Paul and Vince are looking at renting the flat upstairs," said Mr. Chung.

"Oh yeah, your mother said something about that. I thought she was joking."

"The only thing that's a joke," I said, "is the way they're caring for people in that long-term care home. If they keep up this kind of neglect, we're going to have to start calling them short-term care homes."

"Hmph!" said Dad with a heavy sigh.

"I get you that drink," said Mr. Chung, turning back to the kitchen.

"Vince, I get it," Dad said, in a louder than needed voice. "I know the old folks' home ain't Caesar's Palace. And it's not like we've ever been through a pandemic before."

"And aren't going through one now," I interrupted. "Ontario's had like three thousand respiratory deaths. Just like we did in the winter of 2018. And it's mainly happening in nursing homes."

"Exactly!" said Dad, leaning farther back in his chair. "It's those living in nursing homes who have always been the most vulnerable. And while we've been lucky so far, we got a second wave coming. I don't think having your grandad cooped up in a restaurant, with people singing opera, is the safest place for him."

I shook my head. "Even Claudia said he'd be safer here. If they ever do have an actual outbreak at the home, that's the last place you'd want him to be."

"Yeah, but if he gets sick and needs medical care, a nursing home is exactly where I'd want him to be."

I sighed and sipped my green tea, hoping it would calm me down. "Dad, you know they'll probably just lock him up in a room again, come fall. How's that any good for him?"

Dad shrugged. "God, I'd do anything to be left alone in a room with en suite dining, sitting on my ass all day, doing sweet nothing. Sounds like a helluva retirement to me."

He turned to Grandad, who seemed more focused on getting food to his mouth than anything we were talking about.

"Paul, how's your room? You got a TV? Netflix? Plenty of books to read? Crossword puzzles?"

"Grandad doesn't do crossword puzzles."

"Sudoku, then? It would take me the whole bloody second wave to get one of those solved."

"Dad, it's not a suite. It's a six by twelve cell. Dining? It's frozen food dried out in an oven and cold by the time they get it to his room. And you know Grandad hates TV."

Dad raised his eyebrows and yawned. "Bane of my childhood. The other kids got to watch *The Brady Bunch* and *Scooby Doo* and all we'd get was the complete works of William Shakespeare, the King James Bible and a bunch of psychedelic fables about living on the back of a turtle."

"It must have been a traumatic childhood," I said, crossing my arms.

"Hell, it was. I wasn't Indian. And I wasn't white. Didn't fit in anywhere. I was an inbetweener."

"Here you go, Richard," said Mr. Chung, setting down a ceramic bowl, decorated with tropical island scenes. Mint leaves floated on the blend of rum, brandy and orgeat syrup. A recipe I knew he loved.

"Oh-la-la!" said Dad. He took a long sip through the glass straw and then returned his attention to Grandad. "Paul. Tell me, how's your home? You liking it?"

Grandad's eyes darted back and forth. "It's terrific!" he said, instantly falling silent, as if waiting to hear if he had answered correctly.

I closed my eyes and took a deep breath.

"That's what I thought," said Dad. He turned back to me. "You're young, Vince. You got your whole life ahead of you. You need to be out running around, banging bakers—"

"Dad!"

"But your grandad, he's an ol' Indian shaman-like kind of guy. His room is his lodge. His teepee. His abode where he prepares for the last great journey to that—" and he switched to a fake British accent—"'undiscovered country from whose bourn no traveler returns.'"

Grandad put down his spoon. "*Hamlet.* Act 3. Scene 1."

Dad smiled and lifted up his straw. "To be or not to be... drunk." And he took another sip of the cocktail.

Grandad watched him for a second and then recited: "'O God! that men should put an enemy in their mouths to steal away their brains.'"

Dad chuckled. "*Othello.* Act 2. Scene 3."

"You remember," said Grandad.

"How could I forget? You drove that one into our heads hard enough."

Grandad winced at the scorpion bowl. Dad grinned.

"Sadly, Paul, my Irish DNA got the best of me. But I will admit..." He booted up his British accent again. "'I have very poor and unhappy brains for drinking: I could well wish courtesy would invent some other custom of entertainment.'"

I shook my head. "Sounds like you missed your calling as a Shakespearean actor, Dad."

He took another sip. "I'll leave the acting to your Uncle Thomas. I'll find my fulfillment watching you climb to stardom at the Metropolitan Opera, whenever they open back up."

I pulled my bowl back toward me and returned to my noodles, hoping Dad and his scorpion might move to the other table to eat with his buddies. Grandad continued with his slow and methodical conveyance of rice and mushrooms into his mouth.

After some time, and a final sip, Dad rose from his chair. "Well, I guess that settles that. Grandad stays at the 'terrific' nursing home, and Vince auditions with the Met."

And with that, he turned toward the buffet.

42. Unmasking the Dragon

Dad knew full well that Grandad's deteriorating mind had left him in a state of unrealistic positivity. No court in the world would deem Grandad capable of deciding something as basic and important as where to live.

"Hold up, Dad," I called out, dropping my fork on the table with a clatter beside my near-empty bowl.

Dad was halfway to the buffet. I could see his shoulders slump as he turned back to face us.

"Grandad," I said facing him, "how did you like having that tooth pulled last year?"

He blinked and then slowly said, "Terrific!"

"How about being dropped in a pot of boiling oil?"

This time he didn't answer.

"Come on, Dad. You know the old folks' home sucked before COVID; now it's intolerable." I stood up, stepped toward him and said softly, "How could you leave your father there?"

His face went blank as he stared back at me. "Hey, I know it's not paradise." He winked at Grandad. "Don't worry, Paul, that's coming soon." He turned back to me. "And, maybe if your uncle would choke up some of his Hollywood dough, Paul could have something better."

"Well, I'm offering him something better."

Dad looked over his shoulder, speaking out to Mr. Chung, who was adding more rice to the buffet. "Quan, how many stairs to that apartment of yours?"

"Well, I never counted."

"Second floor or third?"

"Third."

Dad looked back at me with tired eyes. "How the hell do you expect to get him up and down two flights of stairs?"

"Slowly," I replied, instantly.

Dad shook his head. "He's just gonna end up stuck up there in another prison."

"Well, at least he won't be alone."

"He's not alone at the home." His voice was getting louder. "The attendants are in and out of there all day long."

"More out than in. I grilled Claudia. They haven't cleaned his room since this whole COVID thing began. They've only bathed him a few times in four months. And when they bring him food it's done quickly, with masks and gloves."

"Yes, well, he's still safer. And not just from COVID. You gotta go to work. What are you going to do? Leave him alone. What if he has an accident?"

Mr. Chung cut in, "Henry, Melinda and I happy to help out. We can visit with him when Vince is out. Or he can come down here."

"Ah! ya got a restaurant to run," said Dad. "And while I'm sure there's no bat wings on the menu, I think we should remember that this virus originated from some wok in China."

I could see a vein popping in Mr. Chung's forehead.

"I know you Asians like to keep your old folks at home until they're mouldy," continued Dad in a voice that made me doubt that the scorpion was his first drink of the day. "Must save a ton of money on nursing care. But we have different standards here in Canada. And this all-you-can-eat railway leftover is not a safe place for someone in the state your grandfather's in."

"A state the nursing home put him in," I insisted.

"Ah," said Dad, swatting the air with his hand, "he had diabetes long before the nursing home. You were too young to remember. But that's how he ended up in the hospital in the first place."

"He ended up in the hospital because his doctor prescribed too high a dose of Glyburide."

Dad swore and then hollered over his shoulder to his pals at the table by the window. "Hey, Oskar! Forget what I said. My son's no opera singer, he's actually an endocrinologist."

Mr. Chung stepped forward. "Please, if you could keep your voices down."

"Yeah!" yelled one of the men, wearing a Vancouver Canucks T-shirt, holding chopsticks dangling with noodles. "Stop spreading bloody COVID all over the place."

"Listen, Vince," said Mr. Chung, looking at me. "Your father may be right. The stairs—"

"Mathéo and I can carry him in one of those transport chairs paramedics use, if we have to."

Mr. Chung folded his hands together. "Perhaps... finding a place on first floor or with an elevator—"

"Yeah, like the nursing home," cut in Dad.

"A year ago," I countered, in a tense voice, "Grandad could have done the stairs. He just needs to get moving again."

"Well," said Mr. Chung, turning to Grandad. "Paul, what would you like: Live here or back at the old folks' home?"

Grandad just kept on eating. Not as if he didn't hear the question; more as though he couldn't process it.

"It doesn't matter," said Dad. "Linda, Thomas and I have power of attorney. And I can guarantee you, Linda's not going to agree to this."

"I'll call Aunt Linda tonight," I said, staring Dad in the eye.

He pulled his black mask up so high it almost covered his shaking eyes. "Why don't you do that?"

He shoved the chair he had been sitting in back under the other table and turned to Mr. Chung, while pointing to the Vancouver Canuck at the other table. "Michel owes me. Put the scorp' on his bill."

Mr. Chung nodded but said nothing.

"And listen," Dad continued, "don't be messing in our family's business."

Mr. Chung's eyes narrowed, glaring at Dad in a way that reminded me of Mom's pressure cooker.

Dad laughed, pointed at the green dragon on the mask below Chung's nose. "And pull up that mask. Get with the program or go back to China."

Both of Mr. Chung's fists clenched as he said slowly, "I think it best you leave, now, Richard."

"Or what?" said Dad, taking a step forward. "You going to do some *ka-rat-he* on me? Think you're Bruce Lee or something?"

I knew Chung could have Dad fit for the ICU in under five seconds.

"No," Chung snapped back, yanking his green mask completely off his face, revealing his grey goatee and black moustache. "I give you COVID instead."

A moment of silence fell, as Mr. Chung's naked grin stared back at Dad's oversized face mask. Then Dad snorted, turned around and walked toward the front door, passing his buddies at the front table. "When you ladies are done with your spring rolls you can find me at Tilly's."

"What the hell?" exclaimed the guy with the Corona beer T-shirt. "You were the one who told us to meet here."

The door squeaked closed behind Dad.

I dropped back into my seat and pushed the soy sauce stained bowl aside. There was no way Aunt Linda would let Grandad out of the nursing home. She was a nursing professor at the University in Toronto. So even if Uncle Thomas agreed, he'd be outvoted. Grandad was going to die in that bug-ridden prison.

I looked at him and said, "Terrific!"

But even he knew I didn't mean it.

I couldn't pretend, I couldn't deny that something was diabolical about this new normal—where neglect was called caring. The Dandelion had lured my head out of the shell of blind acceptance and made me see the truth.

But what could I do? At best, I could make life a little better for Grandad.

I guess a little better was better than nothing.

I'd promised Nazi Nurse Claudia that I would have Grandad back to the old folks' penitentiary by sunset. I looked out the front window at the bright street. It was the middle of summer in Northern Ontario. The sun wouldn't set until well past nine. It wasn't even seven yet.

"Grandad?" I said.

"Hmm?" he responded with a content smile.

I smiled back and said, "How would you like to see my pet moose?"

43. Moose Don't Like Hay

I pushed Grandad's wheelchair to a halt alongside the black bust of the moose in front of the town hall. Thankfully, the wrought-iron snout wasn't covered by a face mask that evening.

"Is *this* your pet moose?" asked Grandad, with a slight frown.

"No, no," I answered, tapping its metallic antlers. "My moose is far more handsome."

Grandad looked at me with a furrowed brow and rubbed his chin.

"Hey!" I said, coming around to the front of his chair. "If you get to have a pet penguin, and Stefanie can have a pet pig, why can't I have a pet moose?"

"She has a pet pig?"

"It even whistles."

He shook his head slowly. "Moose don't make good pets," he warned. "You can't feed them hay or straw. It makes their stomachs sick."

"Oh, I just feed my moose cucumber sandwiches," I assured him.

"Shame on you!" said a voice from behind me.

Turning my head, I saw a grey-haired lady fast approaching, hunched over, as if her little red purse was full of bricks.

"Pardon?" I said.

She continued past us, veering off into the square. Stretching her arm out, purse dangling from shaking arm, she chastised me, "Bringing a senior out and about without masks on. Totally irresponsible!"

Grandad turned as much as he could in the wheelchair to face her. "We *are* wearing masks," he said, giving her a big smile, revealing his porcelain dentures. "They're invisible!"

Her sandalled feet paused their evasive maneuver as she squinted at Grandad's face, trying to confirm his fantastical claim. I also smiled wide through my imaginary face covering.

"Latest technology!" I confirmed. "Amazon's making them. Free shipping!"

"Retards!" she said and kept on walking.

Grandad and I looked guiltily at each other for a second, then broke out laughing.

"Invisible mask!" I said. "Oh, that's a good one, Grandad."

"No, it's true," he said. "My penguin bought it for me."

"All right," I said, returning to the back of his wheelchair. "Let's go see if my moose is whistling."

I hung a left onto Queen Street and then a right down the alley running behind the stores on the north side of Main Street. Passing the rear doors of Trozzi's Pizza, Home Hardware and the local Guardian pharmacy, I noticed that a vehicle was parked between every dumpster—rather busy for a Sunday.

"Bakery's closed today," I said. "Boss is out having dinner with friends. But I have keys. I don't think she'd mind me popping in to show you Moosey."

About a hundred metres later, I pointed out the delivery van with its vanity license plate: GRTBREAD.

"That's what I drive," I said, feeling a hint of pride at having a job again.

As soon as we cleared the van, I froze. Standing at the back door to the bakery was a man. At least, I assumed it was a man, based on his attire. Otherwise, there wasn't enough skin visible with which to identify his gender, much less his identity. Steel-toed work boots, blue jeans, a brown leather jacket, blue medical gloves, a white face mask, sunglasses and a baseball cap. The only human characteristic I could distinguish was his dark skin. He was standing there, patting his hand against his thigh, as if he had knocked on the back door several times, but received no answer.

What's this character doing here?

I could feel my heartbeat accelerating, as I halted and clamped the brakes on Grandad's wheelchair.

"Hey there, buddy," I called out, sounding more wary than I intended.

He turned toward us.

"Hey, Vince," he muttered, with a curt wave.

Facing us now, I could see he was wearing at least two face masks, maybe three. Nonetheless, I immediately recognized his voice.

"Raj!" I felt both surprised and relieved. "You're the last person... What are you doing here?"

"Trust me," he replied, advancing toward us, "this is the last place I'd want to be. Word's getting around what you're up to."

"What're you talking about?"

"Hey, Gramps," he said, nodding at Grandad and ignoring my question. "Long time no see. Your hair looks longer. How's it been goin'?"

"Terrific!" answered Grandad. "I'm here to see the moose."

"Moose? Well, she's not that bad," he said. "Not hard on the eyes at all... Too bad she's freakin' crazy."

"Raj," I interjected, "what's going on?"

"I don't know," he said. "That's my story and I'm sticking to it."

He reached into the breast pocket of his leather jacket and withdrew a black envelope.

"Make sure she gets this," he said. "Baba would've done it himself, but Mata'd kill him if he got caught."

"Won't she kill you, too?" I asked.

"Her favourite son?"

"You're her only son."

I took the envelope. It was sealed and unmarked.

"Is this for Stefanie?"

"Who do you think?"

"What's it for?"

"Like you don't know."

I just stared at him.

Raj adjusted his masks. "Just keep my family's name out of it, okay? My parents worked their asses off for three decades to build up Chatterjee Moving. Business was booming before COVID. Last thing we need is association with your lot hurting our reputation."

"I honestly don't know what you're talking about," I said.

"Perfect," he replied.

"But I'll make sure she gets this. She's out with friends right now, but I'll see her tomorrow."

"Whatever," said Raj, swatting his hand in the air. "I'm outta here." Nodding to Grandad, he added, "Stay safe, Gramps."

Grandad's light brown eyes looked at him intently, before asking, "You don't want to see the moose?"

"Absolutely not!" Raj snapped back, before aiming his dark sunglasses at me. "Remember, if anyone asks, you didn't see me."

"I won't have to lie," I said, grinning back at his head-to-toe coverings.

He strutted past us, heading back toward Queen Street.

"Are you so worried what other people will think?" I called out to his retreating back.

Without turning around he just slapped the air with his gloved hand. But I wasn't done with him.

"It's not like anyone is going to hunt you down if you don't wear a mask in the fresh air."

He swung around, still walking backwards and replied

loudly, "You don't know what it's like being the only immigrant family in a hundred miles."

"Stefanie's family's German," I pointed out.

"I mean non-European," he countered. "Other than the Kings, everybody's white in this one-horse town."

I released the brakes on Grandad's wheelchair and spun his darker Ojibwe pigmentation around to face Raj.

"Grandad's not white," I pointed out.

"White enough."

"And this is in fact a one-moose town," corrected Grandad. "Not one-horse."

"Very true," I agreed, cracking a wide grin. "I know of at least three horses. Léo's folks have two. And doesn't the mayor's daughter have one?"

"It's a pony," grumbled Raj.

"And it can whistle!" Grandad added.

I laughed. Raj didn't.

"Listen, Raj," I said. "I know it's not easy being a minority. But this is Ontario 2020, not 1920 Alabama. Baba runs the biggest moving company in Greater Sudbury. You guys have nothing to worry about. It's safe to show your face."

Raj walked back toward me. "Listen," he said in a near whisper, "Mata's freakin' about all this Wuhan virus stuff. We just need to lie low until the vaccine's out."

"All right," I said. "You guys do what you gotta do."

He paused, took a deep breath, and said, "Okay." He didn't take off his gloves but he did extend his hand. I reached out and shook it firmly.

"The arena's opening back up," I said. "You coming back to hockey?"

"Maybe."

He turned around, kicked a pop can into the side of a recycling bin and retreated down the alley.

I looked at the black envelope, tempted to open it up. Instead, I folded it and slipped it in the back pocket of my pants. Withdrawing Grandad's cane from the side of the wheelchair, I handed it to him and said, "All right, ready to hear a moose whistle?"

I helped him to his feet and pulled out my keys. As we neared the rear doors, I could hear voices on the other side.

Many voices.

What's going on?

I slipped the key into the lock.

Opening the metal door revealed no whistling ungulates, but six strangers. They sat on stools around the kneading table, chatting and eating from bowls. Stefanie was nowhere to be seen.

44. Psalm 146:7

The bake room smelt unmistakably like pea soup, with plenty of parsley and celery. Bowls of the yellow dinner were in front of each of the unknown guests sitting around the kneading table like a party of Goldilocks. In the middle of the table were a cutting board, a serrated knife and two loaves of sourdough, flanked by two jars labelled Pumpkin Seed Butter.

I recognized a few of the unmasked faces, but nobody I could name. Three women and three men. I assumed they were all married. One couple looked in their seventies, while the other two were probably only half as old. While I'd only worked in the bakery one day, I had never seen more than Stefanie in the bake room—not counting Josef's talking head on Skype.

That's when I noticed Mr. Sideburns himself on the computer display, chattering in German to a man sitting in the swivel chair before the display. I could only see the rear of the man. His hair was grey and he wore a black, high-collared jacket.

"Hey, look, it's Paul," said one of the ladies at the table, gesturing to Grandad. She wore red glasses on her very thin face.

"Hello!" said Grandad, probably as clueless as I was about her identity.

"Paul, it's Nancy and Phil."

The man beside her, Phil I assume, had bushy black eyebrows and red glasses that matched his wife's. He rose from his seat and pulled a foldout chair from against the wall and set it out.

"Please, sir, take a seat," he said to Grandad.

"Have you eaten, yet?" asked Nancy.

"I don't know," said Grandad, as he let Phil guide him into

the chair.

Who were these people? Where was Stefanie?

"Would you like some soup?" offered Phil. "It's pretty good, despite... well, you know, the missing contraband ingredient."

"Thanks," I said, "but we've already had dinner."

Nancy walked to the side counter and brought over a plate of cookies.

"How about dessert, then?" she asked. "The almond cookies are *delicious*."

Grandad didn't say anything but accepted a napkin and a cookie.

"Hold tight, Grandad," I instructed, patting his shoulder. "I just need a minute to sort all this out."

I circled around the table toward the office corner. As soon as I was close enough, I could see the face, and, more so, the enormous beard hanging over the cassock, of the man talking to Josef on Skype.

"Father Shostakovich!"

"Greetings, son," he replied with a smile. He leaned back in the swivel chair. An empty bowl of soup and a plate with discarded crusts were on the table in front of the keyboard.

"Hey, Mr. Elk," said Josef, with a salute on the display.

Ignoring Mr. Sideburns for the moment, I asked Father, "What, what are you doing here?"

"Psalm 146:7," he cited, leaning back in the chair and spreading his arms out to the side.

I shook my head.

"'Who executes justice for the oppressed; who gives food to the hungry. The Lord sets the prisoners free.'"

"*What?*"

"He's helping Stef run the soup kitchen," interpreted Josef.

"Just the type of thing I was trying to convince Father Lacombe to let us run at the church," added Father. "But the bishop said someone might catch a cold and wipe out the human race."

I glanced back at the group at the table, spooning up soup and listening to Grandad tell a yarn about a moose who wandered by his cabin one morning.

"The Moosehead Soup Kitchen," I muttered, remembering

what Stefanie had told me the day before.

"Now you know what happens to all the bread that doesn't sell," said Josef.

"Bless her heart," added Father, clasping his hands together.

"You mean she doesn't charge for this?" I asked.

"No, it's free," said Josef. "Lots of people are out of work. Government has stopped handing out those COVID cheques now that lockdown's over. But so many businesses went under, people don't have a job to return to."

"Where is she?" I asked.

"Upstairs, keeping a close eye on the chef," said Josef.

"*The chef?*"

"Yeah," he confirmed. "I don't think she trusts him." He yawned. "It's getting late here. Like past two. Vince, you think you can find my girl, so I can say *gute Nacht*? As stimulating as our conversation has been, Father, I can barely keep my eyes open."

Father smiled and replied in slightly choppy German, "Ein Vergnügen, mit Ihnen zu sprechen, Josef."

"Father, you speak German too?" I asked.

"I try."

"No," said Josef, "he speaks it really well. And despite being a minister, he speaks more sense than Dr. Anthony Fauci."

"Danke, sehr nett," said Father, with a slight nod.

"We were just debating," explained Josef, "the morality of the COVID vaccine being derived from aborted fetal tissue."

"What?" I said, running my hands through my short, black hair.

"They use cells from the hearts of aborted babies," explained Father, "extracted while they're still beating."

"That's crazy!"

"Well, not all the vaccines came from fetal tissue," said Josef. "And those mothers were going to abort them anyway. At least, their deaths weren't for nothing."

"Do the ends justify the means?" asked Father.

"Sometimes," said Josef. "Trump had to warp speed things. End the pandemic."

Now I was totally confused. "But Josef," I said, "yesterday, weren't you saying there was no pandemic? That it was all a hoax?"

"Yeah," he said. "It's just a hyped up cold and flu season. But that's not what the rest of the world thinks. If Trump's vax can cure the common cold, or at least serve as a darn good placebo, then people can relax. Otherwise, without the optics a vaccine provides, the cabal would keep us masked and in lockdown for another decade."

"Sweden wasn't in lockdown for even a week," countered Father.

"True." Josef yawned again. "Vince, can you find Stef before I lose this debate?"

"Sure."

I pivoted one-eighty on one left heel and then bulldozed through the hanging beads into the front retail area, only to encounter further proof that I had walked into an episode of the *Twilight Zone*.

45. The Silence of the Meese

Instead of the usual open retail space where, once upon a time before COVID, people would line up to purchase Stefanie's sourdough creations, there were four card tables set up, with four chairs at each and about as many kids. I recognized most of them from around town, but I only could name Cindy, whose bright blonde hair stood out at once, and chubby Ferris, who had the most cookies on his plate.

And in the middle of the four tables stood Moosey. At least, Moosey's felt head, set upon a skinny frame I immediately recognized as AJ.

"And so these guys came into my woods," AJ Moosey said to the kids, walking on the spot, knees rising high. "They had rifles and they were there to hunt... *moose!*" He clasped the mask's snout and gasped.

"*Nooo!*" screamed his young audience in unison.

"But," AJ Moosey continued, holding up his hand, "they had a little too much to drink, so their aim wasn't all that sharp."

He lifted up his hands, pretending to fire a gun that he couldn't hold steady.

"Bang! Bang! Whoopsie! They missed me... and *shot Ed.*"

The children looked at Moosey with open mouths. That's when I registered that they, like their elders in the bake room, were all unmasked. I hadn't seen so many young faces at once since February.

"'Ed's been shot!' the other men cried out," AJ continued. "So they pulled out a cellphone and called for help."

AJ switched to a nasally, high-pitched voice: "911. What's your emergency?"

In a deeper voice with a redneck accent, he responded: "'Um, yeah, we, uh, were, uh, hunting moose and by mistake, mind you, we uh, shot, um, our pal Ed. It, uh, doesn't look like he's breathin' any. I reckon he's dead.'"

Back to the nasally operator, AJ continued: "All right, sir, please remain calm. I need you to make sure he is really dead."

Back to the hunter's voice: "Uh, all right. If you say so."

This time AJ pointed his imaginary rifle down at the imaginary victim. "Bang! Bang!"

Cindy laughed loudly at her brother's comedy routine. The other kids stared silently with wide eyes. A girl with a doll hugged it tight against her chest.

"'Okay! He's dead. Whadda we do now?'"

The kids continued to gaze at AJ Moosey unblinking and motionless—his black humour totally lost on their innocent minds.

After a few seconds of awkward silence, AJ said in his regular voice, "Umm, well, can anyone tell me the moral of the story?"

Ferris, with his long, floppy, brown hair, raised his hand slowly.

"Oh, you don't have to raise your hand," said AJ. "I'm no teacher."

That's for sure, I thought to myself.

"Uh," said Ferris, "is the moral that you shouldn't shoot *mooses*?"

"Actually, we don't say *mooses*. Just moose. Sort of like fish."

"How are fish like moose?" said a girl with braces.

"Well, when there are more than one fish, we say fish, not *fishes*."

"But," countered the girl squeezing her doll, "goose sounds more like moose than fish."

"Right!" said AJ. "That's why we don't say gooses."

"No, we say geese," replied the girl. "So why don't we say *meese*?"

AJ looked across the room at me. "Vince, bro, can you help me out here?"

I didn't say a word, as I slowly shook my head, wondering how much more of the corona underground I could take. That's when I noticed butcher paper blocking the front windows, preventing passersby from seeing the illegal grammar class.

Lifting up the felt mask, AJ frowned at me. "I hope you don't mind me borrowing your moose mask."

Before I could muster a response, the door behind AJ opened, revealing the landing to the stairwell leading to the second floor, and the bard of Moosehead. Léo strutted forward, with his classical guitar hanging from his shoulder and his long, black hair tied in a ponytail.

"Move over, Moosey," he ordered, lightly bodychecking AJ to the side. "It's time for the main feature."

I inhaled and exhaled slowly, fearing what was coming next.

"Hey, kids!" said Léo. "Do you know the words to the 'Mounted Animal Nature Trail' song?"

A few kids cheered their assent.

Léo's pick began sliding along the nylon strings of his guitar as he began to sing about the popular hiking trail on Manitoulin Island—the world's largest fresh water island. Only a two-hour drive away, off the shore of Lake Huron, the trail features stuffed and rigid bears, dogs, cows and pigs. *The Arrogant Worms* made the outdoor exhibit world famous when the band released a song about the posthumous attraction. A rather twisted version of Old McDonald, the lyrics describe how each taxidermy animal goes... Well, being stuffed, they don't make any sound at all. Sadly, the kids weren't catching on.

"*Grrr!*" growled the kids, after Léo cued them for the mounted bear.

"No, no, no!" cried Léo, thumping his guitar. "The animals are *dead*! Death inhibits their vocal capabilities."

"You're supposed to say nothing," whispered Cindy to her peers. "Until we get to the crow. Because the crow is—"

"Spoiler alert!" interrupted AJ.

"Let's try again," said Léo. "And the pig goes..."

"*Oink! Oink!*" went the kids.

"*No!*" cried Léo, putting hand to forehead. "A stuffed pig does not go oink! It has no vocal cords, lungs or windpipe. What has lockdown done to you kids?"

"Guess that just shows," interjected AJ, "online schooling isn't cutting it."

I escaped into the stairwell, closing the door behind me.

"All right," I could hear Léo's voice, "Moosey, you stand here. Real still. Don't move." He strummed his guitar and sang, "And the moose goes..."

I had no clue what sound a moose makes.

Neither did the kids.

"Gotcha!" proclaimed Léo.

"The silence of the *meese*," said AJ.

Sounding like she was ready to cry, a girl said, "I don't like this song."

Obviously, Léo and AJ had a ways to go before they became professional entertainers of children. Still, I had to wonder how much I had been missing out on while hiding in my Dad's basement.

Apparently, a lot. A white piece of paper was taped to the wall with words written in scrawly lettering: "Fine Dining Lounge." A thick arrow pointed diagonally up the stairwell. From the top of the staircase I could hear violin music.

46. Life Without Bacon

I'd made it halfway up the stairs, when Bindu appeared at the top landing, carrying a plastic washbasin. She was dressed in a tweed blazer, white dress shirt and dark pants.

"Ah! I was wondering if you'd be showing up," she said to me.

"Bindu, you too?"

"Me too, what?"

"Uh, I just saw your brother," I explained. "Well, sort of. He was... undercover."

Bindu rolled her dark eyes. "Baba said he'd be sending something."

I pulled out the black envelope.

She looked at it and snickered. "He uses black envelopes so satellites can't see the contents inside." She cocked her head backwards. "Give it to Stef." She then scooted past me, as I pressed against the wall. "Don't bother knocking. Just go right in."

I glanced into the blue washbasin in her hands. It was full of mason jars.

"Canning?"

"No, it's leftover soup for people to take home."

I followed her back down the stairs and opened the door for her. As I reascended the stairwell, I noticed how the white paint on the walls was peeling and cracking, not boding well for the promise of fine dining at the end of the climb. Stefanie had not included the second floor in my job orientation tour the day before. The landing at the top had but one door, which I opened, leading into what I assumed must be Stefanie's apartment.

Entering, I found myself in a small room with what looked like more card tables, side by side, covered by a red tablecloth, with five chairs seating a family. The only light came from candles and the lighted kitchen on the other side of a partition. The drapes were closed, with an air conditioner humming in the window.

The rest of the apartment, what I could see in the dim light, was rather spartan. No couch. No TV. Just a desk, a chair and two shelves full of books. On the far side of the tables stood Stefanie, sawing away at a violin. She was wearing the green, short-sleeved dress from the first day we'd met. A bit screechy on certain notes, I immediately recognized the melody to be "Morgengruß", the eighth song from Schubert's *Die schöne Müllerin.*

No one seemed to have noticed my appearance. I skirted to the side and peeked into the kitchen to find myself once again staring at the back of a large chef. But this one was neither masked nor yielding knives. Immediately Mathéo turned around to face me.

"Vince," he said, unmoved, as if I had dropped by every evening for dinner. He was wearing an undersized apron with the words "COVID-1984" followed by "Let's Make Orwell Fiction Again."

"Cool apron," I said.

"It's all she had," he replied.

"I didn't even know you and Stefanie were friends," I said.

"Well, she does pay me," he said.

"To be her friend?"

"No, to cook."

He nodded toward the three pots he was stirring on the white stovetop with both his hands. His mop of short curly hair glistened with sweat and steam.

"What about your job at Le Papillon?"

"Christophe cut my hours back. It's not enough."

"*Je suis désolé*," I lamented. Pointing my nose at the pots on the stovetop, I asked, "Aunt Sofia's French Canadian pea soup?"

"Sans bacon or ham," he grumbled, banging a wooden spoon against one of the iron pots. "She won't let me use any animal products."

"Who? Aunt Sofia?"

The violin stopped with a squeal as Stefanie called out, "My kitchen! No greasy, fatty, slimy, dead, decaying flesh."

I walked past a frowning Mathéo, exiting the kitchen from the other end, coming out into the makeshift dining area beside Stefanie, as she let her violin and bow drop to her sides.

"Pas de jambon! Pas de bacon!" grumbled Mathéo.

"It keeps costs down," Stefanie hollered back. "Ham and bacon aren't cheap and we have mouths to feed."

"Ah, knock it off, Mathéo," hollered the bald man at the table. "Beggars can't be choosers."

Now that I was close enough, I was surprised to see that it was Tom Horowitz sitting at the table with, I assumed, his wife and daughters. He wore a white dress shirt and a purple tie that matched his wife's sleeveless dress. Tom was one of the accountants from the car plant Dad and I had been working at. He always wore a black suit to work, while we line workers wore blue coveralls. Usually, the suits and the coveralls didn't mingle much. No surprise he didn't recognize me, but his clean-shaven head and black, round glasses were hard to forget.

"Don't worry, Mathéo," called out his wife, "C'est excellent!" She lifted a slice of the day-old bread. "And I'm really lovin' this pumpkin seed butter."

"*Pumpkin seed butter*," spat Mathéo, banging his stirring

spoon again. "Butter comes from cows, not squash."

"Hey," I said to Stefanie, with a nod toward her stringed instrument. "You play the violin?"

She nodded back, saying, "When I can."

"How long have you been at it?"

"Since I moved back to Canada."

Ever since she left Josef behind in Germany.

She swayed back and forth for a second before asking me, "I thought you were out with Grandad?"

"Stefanie," interrupted Tom, "I want you to know, as soon as I find work—"

"Don't worry about it," she said, waving her bow in the air. "You were always good customers."

"Still, tomorrow, I have a job interview."

"At a pork farm," added his wife.

"Great," Mathéo said from behind the partition, "you can bring us some bacon."

"Dad's going to be a farmer," said one of the three girls sitting around the table. They all looked in their teens—too old for Léo and AJ's circus downstairs, I figured.

"Yeah, Dad's going to have to work for a living," said the older girl to her right, with about seven multicoloured bracelets jingling on each wrist. "No more desk job."

"Just don't come home smelling like a pig," said the third sister. Her hair was tied up in such a tight bun, I thought it must hurt.

"Oink! Oink!" said Tom, as he sliced another piece of bread from the loaf on the cutting board.

His wife nudged him and laughed. "This will be the most memorable birthday I ever had."

"It's your birthday?" I asked.

"'Fraid so," said Tom. "I wanted to take her out to Le Papillon but—"

"I refused," said his wife. "We can't afford that right now."

"So Stefanie offered us her fine establishment at a rate even Barb could not decline."

"It's like that birthday we had in our camper..." began one of the daughters.

Stepping closer to Stefanie, I whispered, "You didn't tell me that *you* ran the Moosehead Soup Kitchen."

"I'm trying to stay off the police radar."

"Good luck," I replied. "Constable Corona will be busting down the door before you know it. I can already hear the SWAT team's helicopter landing on the rooftop."

"I doubt he'd ever go that far," she replied, with a weak chuckle. "Anyway, an insider with the OPP emails me Mackenzie's work schedule every Monday morning."

"Insider?" I asked, grinning. "You mean Constable Yamamoto?"

She put her finger to her lips, before continuing. "Any night Mackenzie's off duty, we're on. No surprise COVID raids."

"Well, you sure surprised me. I was just swinging by with Grandad to show him the moose mask—"

"Grandad's here?" she said, poking my chest with the end of her violin bow.

"Yeah, downstairs, telling stories."

"Why didn't you tell me?"

She poked me again.

"You know those violin bows aren't vegan," I said. "Made with horsehair."

"Phooey," she replied, squatting down and setting the violin in a case on the floor. Loosening the ends of the bow, she wedged it into clamps in the case's lid. Once it was closed, she stood up, carrying the case in her right hand.

"I so want to see him," she said.

Heading through the kitchen, she passed Mathéo and shoved the violin case into his chest. "I'll be back in a few minutes. Until then, you're in charge."

"Hardly," grumbled Mathéo.

47. Milk Thistle

Stefanie rushed out the front door of her apartment—almost as if she was fleeing me, rather than seeking Grandad—and started down the stairs. I followed, pulling the black envelope out of my jeans.

"Hey, a, um, strange man delivered this today. Says it's from Mr. Chatterjee."

She paused on the stairs, took the envelope and opened it up. It contained several red fifty dollar bills with the face of Canada's tenth prime minister.

"Ah, Baba's such a sweetheart," she murmured. "We couldn't pull soup nights off without him."

"How long have these 'soup nights' been going on?" I asked.

She closed the envelope. "Since April. For families with kids, those CERB cheques weren't going far—not after you pay the mortgage and car insurance. And the nearest real food bank is in Sudbury."

We exited the stairwell and entered the front of the store to find all the card tables and chairs folded up and pushed aside. Léo was still playing his guitar, this time singing *Puff the Magic Dragon* to a less traumatized audience. Bindu was thumping a tambourine, keeping rhythm, as she and Léo stood in the center of the space. AJ Moose and the kids danced around them, swinging their arms and singing along. Stefanie skirted around the party and disappeared through the hanging beads behind the counter.

Passing AJ, I paused, slapped his furry back and said, "Can I borrow you and your antlers for a minute?"

"Sure, bro," he said.

When we entered the bake room, we found Father Shostakovich had rolled his swivel chair over beside Grandad. Seeing Father reminded me of Josef, who had asked me to fetch Stef so he could say goodnight. My head turned toward the computer display. "Call ended." I felt guilt at having not delivered the message.

My guilt quickly morphed into frustration as I watched Stefanie greet Grandad with a kiss on the cheek. Of course, I wasn't jealous of my eighty-eight-year-old grandfather, but it made me realize I had thought too much of the peck on the cheek she gave Moose Lee the day before.

She's just an affectionate person, I realized. *Europeans are like that. I'm nothing special.*

Father, Bill, Nancy, and the other two couples were all now paying close attention to the exchange between Grandad and Stefanie.

"I haven't seen you in so long," she said to him. "I miss you coming to my bakery."

Grandad was silent for a few seconds, then reached out, took her hand, and said, "Dodoshaabo-jiibik."

So he did remember her.

"Dodoshaabo-jiibik?" repeated Stefanie, slowly.

"It means milk thistle," I clarified, stepping forward with my arms crossed, glad to have the linguistic upper hand for once. "It's Ojibwe for... dandelion."

She squeezed Grandad's hand with both of hers. "I love it!"

AJ, who was standing beside me, still wearing the moose mask, squatted down beside Stefanie, putting his snout at eye level with Grandad.

"How do you say moose in Ojibwe?" asked AJ.

Grandad stared silently back at the moose mask, with its red tongue and bulging white eyes.

"Actually," I said, "English adopted the word 'moose' from the First Nations. The Ojibwe call them *mooz* with a Z sound at the end."

"*Mooz*," corrected Grandad, giving the "oo" more nasal resonance. "It means twig-eater." Then pointing at AJ Moosey he said to me, "You really do have a pet moose." Laughing, he slapped his knee with his free hand.

We all joined him, before a knock at the back door brought a sudden end to our mirth. Bill signalled to Stefanie, one of his bushy eyebrows raised above his red glasses. Another series of knocks followed, but this time to the tune of Twisted Sisters' "We're Not Gonna Take It." Stefanie smiled and nodded. Bill spun off his stool and opened the door.

And in strode three caped crusaders.

"Holy guacamole!" I blurted out, half-choked by a laugh.

This time Roger Gygax had crossed the line from Marvel to DC Comics, and was wearing a blue and grey Batman costume. The pointed-eared mask would not meet the face covering criteria the local health unit stipulated—it covered Roger's entire head *except* for his mouth, nose and chin. Likewise, the shorter woman by his side had a similar getup—albeit purple and yellow. Judging by her ruddy red hair escaping out the back of her hooded mask, I knew it must be Dr. Sandy "Batgirl" Henderson.

"Gary and Josh made me wear this," she said with a giggle.

As she spoke, she was signing to Josh, who stood by her side, with fists on his hips. He was wearing a black cloth eye mask, Robin's signature red tunic, green spandex briefs and a yellow cape. In his right hand, he held his plastic bow, and across his back hung a quiver full of arrows. He looked as much like Robin Hood, Prince of Thieves as Robin, The Boy Wonder.

"Howdy, folks!" said Roger. "I hope you don't mind us taking shelter here."

"The police are after us," said Josh. He formed his right hand into a C shape—I assume for "cop"—and positioned it where a badge might rest on his chest.

"With the WHO saying bats caused the scamdemic," explained Sandy as she pointed to the bat insignia on the front of her costume, "we are being hunted down."

AJ Moose sauntered over and took the grid board Bat Roger had tucked under his left arm. "Don't worry, you're safe with us... Batman."

When he said "Batman" AJ crossed both his clenched fists over his chest, making an X with his arms, while extending and retracting his index fingers, imitating bat ears.

Josh immediately responded by using his right thumb and forefingers to imitate the opening and closing beak of a robin.

Bat Roger cleared his throat and said, "Stef said we could move the DnD club here tonight." He winked at me through his Dark Knight mask. "Now that the old hangout is being watched by satellite."

Pressed against his right hip, half-covered by his dark cape, he was carrying the wooden box from the Dungeon Room.

"Dungeons and Dragons!" said Bill. "Cool!"

"Honey, it's for the kids," Nancy replied, putting her arms around his shoulders.

"Actually, all ages welcome," corrected AJ, giving Grandad a nudge. "What do you say, Mr. McKnight?"

"Oh," he responded. "I don't know the rules."

"Don't worry," I replied. "It's mainly improv."

"Kind of like life," said Father Shostakovich, still sitting beside Grandad, his big beard unable to hide his grinning face.

Too true, I thought, looking around at the room full of people improvising how to maintain humanity, community and dignity in those early days of COVID.

Grandad didn't end up playing any DnD. He just sat contently and watched. More families and a few single people showed up at the improv soup kitchen. Not all were hard up on money. I think they came for the company. Nobody, however, left without a mason jar full of leftovers, often including a note from Mathéo directing them to add ham when they returned home.

By nine o'clock, Bat Roger and I were washing dishes in Stefanie's kitchen.

"Boy, that soup was good," Roger said to me. "I haven't had a home-cooked meal like that since Chyou passed away."

"I bet you miss her," I said.

"Always," he replied, staring down at the pot he was scrubbing. "Don't be a lone moose, Vince. Life's better if you share it with someone. The sooner the better. The only thing I regret is that I didn't ask Chyou to marry me earlier. We would have had longer together. And maybe some kids of our own." He looked at me. "You want kids?"

I grimaced. "Not sure I'd want to bring kids into this world. Future's looking pretty grim these days."

"And it'll only get grimmer if good people like you and Stefanie don't raise some good kids."

"*Me and Stefanie?*" My eyes darted toward the webcam on the computer. "Stef's engaged to this big blond guy in Germany who hunts meese."

"Meese?"

Before I could explain, my phone rang. I looked over my shoulder, glad to see Stef wasn't in earshot. She'd instructed me to keep my "cancer-causing contraption" in airplane mode if I insisted on bringing it into the bakery. I dried my hands and pulled out the forbidden tech and silenced its telltale ringtone.

"Hello?" I said in a hushed voice, hand cupped over the phone.

"Where's Paul?" demanded Claudia, in her sharp Latino accent.

"Umm," I stuttered. "Please, hold."

I raced down the stairwell to the customer area where I had left them playing DnD. Grandad was now sitting in a chair beside Cindy. Cindy had both her palms up, pushing forward against the open air. She was grunting as if pushing a heavy weight.

"Then we all hid behind the shelf. Then Mr. Moose pushed it into place. It was really dark. Then Ferris farted and it was really smelly. Then Constable Covid came down the stairs. And then..."

"Grandad's right here," I said into the phone. "Do you want to talk to him?"

"No! I want him back here. It's past nine. There's only two of us on and we still have to get him ready for bed."

I sighed and promised to deliver him to his cell at Moosehead Penitentiary immediately.

48. This Covidian Cup...

I remember that summer so well for so many reasons. It was, of course, the first summer under the Corona World Order. It was also the summer I met the Dandelion. Two of the most life-changing events of my life.

But more than any other reason, I remember the summer of 2020 because it was the last one I ever spent in Moosehead.

As I pushed Grandad's wheelchair back over the Louis Riel Bridge toward the nursing home, I decided to make Claudia wait a little longer. After a hot and humid Ontario day, the evening temperature was pleasantly cool. The sun was setting over the French River and I positioned Grandad's chair so he had the best spot in Moosehead to view the sunset. On the hill on the left bank, I could just make out Father Shostakovich opening the big wooden door that fronted St. Jerome's.

I didn't ask Grandad if he had a good time. It would have been pointless words, like the ducks quacking on the water below. I felt immensely happy. And I'm sure he did, too.

I wish I could say that this is where my story ends. That the government made much ado about corona and then everything fizzled out. Sadly, I can't.

Yes, there were many more illicit gatherings of the unregistered, nonprofit Moosehead Soup Kitchen. Stefanie kept on baking more bread and cookies than she could sell, but with the help of Baba, she stayed clear of debt.

She and I even became short-lived characters in AJ's geeky board game. She became an elf named Dodoshaabo-jiibik who played the fiddle. I, like my Métis *niijii* Léo, took on the role of a half elf, whom I called Miskwaadesi. I only lasted two gaming sessions before I fell through a portal (rather intentionally) and could no longer participate in the campaign. Sadly, Stefanie's character perished the following week after drinking from the wrong goblin skull at a shady inn.

So, she returned to playing Schubert in the VIP lounge on the second floor, where I helped Mathéo cook pea soup and listened to him grumble about the ban on bacon.

Grandad, however, discovered a hidden talent for roaring like a dragon. It made the kids laugh, even though I suspected DnD did not involve quite as many encounters with dragons as Grandad portrayed.

There were lots of laughs. Even though, outside our haven of sanity, we could sense reproachful stares over multicoloured face masks—blaming us for the pandemic that seemed no more real than AJ's role-playing game.

Léo, the Bard of Moosehead, continued his secret courtship with the Lady Bindu.

Mr. Chung even brought back Saturday morning kung fu—but out in the middle of Brian Peckford Park, not in the dining area of the Green Dragon.

Stefanie began forwarding Yamamoto's emails to The Little Shop of Heroes, so AJ and Cindy knew when it was safe to run the Dungeon Room.

Roger had even drawn up plans, proposing to Father Shosta-kovich that they dig a catacomb-like passageway from the Dungeon Room to the St. Jerome's basement—in case the government made religious services illegal again. Father said he didn't think the bishop would approve.

Josef continued to help Father with his German. Over Skype each week they would debate everything from the divinity of the Catholic Church to the legitimacy of Donald Trump's vaccine rollout. About the only thing they agreed upon was that the pandemic was a hoax, but that seemed to be enough.

As summer's warmth started to give way to cool autumn

breezes, we hoped that the whole COVID con would blow away like dead leaves. Mega-rich companies would offer variations on an untested vaccine for those who believed being jabbed in the arm would make their lives better, and that would be the end of the so-called emergency. Politicians could pretend they saved the day, and we'd let them, knowing that they knew we knew what really had happened, and that they would never dare such a farce again.

Even Mackenzie never made an appearance for the whole summer or fall. It was like he avoided our small town altogether. It made me hope that the power-hungry elite would let the people of Moosehead live our lives in peace.

After all, we didn't want much.

No, we didn't want much at all...

We just wanted to enjoy multi-million dollar cinematic productions, involving casts and crews of thousands, streaming directly to our large-screen TVs with Dolby surround sound. We wanted technology so advanced and complex, it could feed us infinite streams of Tweets and TikTok videos from all over the world directly to the palms of our hands.

We wanted to be able to eat anything, anytime, regardless of season, environmental damage or health effects. Bananas in Northern Ontario. Factory-farmed meat, seven days a week. Pepsi and potato chips without heart failure or cancer.

We wanted big banks to loan us money so we could own homes we couldn't afford. We wanted the government to go into debt by building roads and highways so we could travel anywhere and pretend we were free. We wanted to be able to hop on a plane, and travel faster and higher than a bird, yet still complain about the lineup at security.

We wanted all of this, the simple, peaceful people of Moosehead.

I glanced down at Grandad, sitting in his wheelchair, staring out at the French River. He was born in the bush. All *his* family ever wanted was enough food and firewood to survive the winter. Yet, even with their few wants, the government didn't leave them in peace.

I sighed and closed my eyes, listening to a kayaker paddle underneath the bridge. I could feel an undercurrent of anxiety running through me—as it would for every moment of those last six months of 2020.

I knew that the Ontario premier—endowed with his emergency dictatorial powers—required nothing more than a graph on a computer to justify locking us up in our homes again. All our plump overlord needed was an inflated case count to empty businesses and schools.

Winter would return. Bill Gates had promised it would be a dark one. What I didn't know then was that it would be the first of the darkest winters the Great White North had ever seen. Standing on Louis Riel Bridge, I looked up at the steeple of St. Jerome's and prayed:

Please, God, let this covidian cup pass us by.

It felt as futile as Jesus' plea in the Garden of Gethsemane.

So much would be taken away. Everything, really, but that feeling I had in my heart. Love for the beauty of a summer night. Love for my grandfather who raised me to appreciate such natural beauties. And love for that beautiful Dandelion who would not permit me to hide in my shell. That feeling would be buried by fear at times, but never extinguished. She would be my light, a yellow flame in the coming darkness—igniting courage I would never have believed I possessed.

Below, a duck was now swimming circles not far from where the river bank met Brian Peckford Park. The duck looked up at me with its glossy green head and began to quack madly. Did he know? Was he trying to warn me what would happen in six months' time? How in that very spot, where he now floated, I would literally be sent racing into the darkness.

PART THREE
Maple for Measure

"A minority is powerless while it conforms to the majority."
—*Henry David Thoreau (1817–1862)*
American naturalist, essayist, poet, and philosopher

49. Moose Cratchit

"*Brrr!* It's another cold one in Greater Sudbury," said the host of CGIT FM.

I had the van's radio playing and the heat blasting as I sped down Highway 69.

"Expected high today of minus seven. Dropping below fifteen tonight. Seventh day in a row with freezing temperatures... yet no snow. Chris, do you think we'll get snow for Christmas?"

"I hope so, Bernard," said co-host Chris, in his perpetual on-air enthusiasm. "Only two days before Santa's sleigh is scheduled to be skidding over rooftops. Fortunately, the premier has put off lockdown number two until Boxing Day, so Santa will still be able to deliver his gifts. But Ol' Saint Nick is expected to mask up."

I sighed as I turned the yellow bread van off Highway 69 onto Route 64.

"Up next on 93.5 CGIT FM we have 'I Saw Mommy Kissing Santa Claus'—an unlikely possibility this year."

Ten minutes later, Route 64 became Queen Street West. It only took another minute before I passed over the Louis Riel Bridge, and Queen Street West became Queen Street East. I entered a mostly vacant downtown Moosehead, crossed Main Street, and hung a right into the back alley, coming to a halt behind the bakery. I opened the door and stepped out into the freezing air, tucking my gloved hands under the hooves of the moose costume. In the summer, the furry getup had me sweating like a marathon runner; now it couldn't keep me even remotely warm. I made a mental note to put on some long underwear after work before heading out for hockey practice.

I sped around the front of the van and opened the passenger door. Moosey's head sat on the front seat, staring blankly at the glove compartment. Mom had sewn a red Santa hat to one of the antlers. I picked up the mask and slid it over my head, trying to preserve my freezing earlobes. I made a second mental note to get my Eddie Bauer aviator hat out of the closet and onto my head.

I looked up through the mask's eyeholes at the late

December sky. The sun was just beginning to descend—if it had ever ascended at all—only a few days before the darkest day of the year. Despite the freezing temperatures, there wasn't a snow cloud in sight. Moosehead seemed trapped in some brown purgatory between the gold of autumn and the white purity of winter. Already we'd had a few snowfalls, but each time it had melted away in a day or two of icy rain.

I opened the rear of the van, pulled out three bins and slammed the doors shut. All three bins were full—quite unlike my savings account, which had dwindled from buying up too many unsold baked goods. I carried the rejected loaves to the back of the bakery, set the bins on the ground and opened the door that led directly to the bake room.

The large oven blasted a welcome wave of heat. "Little Drummer Boy" played over the desktop computer. *Pa rum pum pum pum.* Pressing my foot against the three bins, I slid them across the threshold. I followed, snagging both my antlers on the doorframe.

"Bad news!" I announced.

"Not many takers?" asked Stefanie, cutting gingerbread dough on the kneading table.

"The restrictions are killing the restaurants in Sudbury. La Lune only took two loaves, and Soup Surreal, five. Rachel said most people don't want bread with their take-out." I stretched my arms over my head and yawned. "Oh, and when I dropped off Roger's order, I couldn't help noticing Le Papillon..."

"What?"

"Chains on the door and a sign in the window saying Christophe hasn't paid the rent in three months."

She slapped a cookie cutter down as the last *pum* of the drummer boy died away on the speakers, before saying, "Well, we have enough Christmas cookie orders coming in. That'll keep you busy enough tomorrow."

"Ah, you're going to make me work on Christmas Eve?" I joked. "But Fräulein Scrooge!"

"You'll get Christmas off, I promise, Moose Cratchit."

"As long as I get some of those gingerbread men, too."

"You'll get a whole platoon. And Grandad, too."

Grandad. I hadn't seen him in two months. As Dad had

promised, Aunt Linda voted against any form of parole from Moosehead Long-Term Prison. I considered suing, but Bindu assured me I'd lose. Grandad had dementia. And his children had power of attorney. I assumed Bindu knew what she was talking about. She was completing her last year of law school at Lakeside University in Thunder Bay.

I'd kept on visiting Grandad each day until Halloween night, when one of the residents at the home had a positive PCR test and their doors were once again closed to humanity. I was limited to phone calls with my deteriorating Grandad and his ever-present penguin.

I reached for the amputated arm of a baked gingerbread man and popped it into my gaping moose snout. "Mmm. I can't believe they're vegan."

"And I can't believe you're still working here," she said, with frustration. "I'm really sorry I can't pay you more."

Those full-time hours she was giving me back in the summer (after the initial fanfare the moose costume generated) had long since disappeared. When Sudbury region was put into "orange alert," orders plummeted. Orange meant that restaurants could only offer take-out. And that most small businesses could only have one or two customers in their shop—unlike Walmart and Home Depot, who could have hundreds. Orders started lagging. Stefanie had to scale me back to part-time hours—showing up at 10 a.m. and punching out at 2 p.m. But I usually kept on working until there was nothing left to do.

"Ah," I waved a hoof. "Rather be here than hanging out at home."

"I thought turtles liked to carry their home with them everywhere they went."

"Do I look like a turtle?" My hoofed hands fumbled with the antlers and the Santa hat.

"Less and less, I must admit." She smiled at me, blinked, and then grabbed a spatula to scrape raw gingerbread men off the table.

I smiled. "All I can say is, thank God a bakery is considered an essential business. Trust me, the last place I want to be is at home when Dad's off work." I pretended to tip an invisible beer bottle back. "I'd much rather be here with you."

"I'm glad my company ranks higher than an al—" She stopped herself.

"Don't worry," I assured her. "You can say it. I won't be offended."

"I'm sure your dad's just doing his best to deal with this madness."

"Even if Dad was as sober as the Dalai Lama, I'd still rather be working here with you." To prove my sincerity, I cleared my throat and half recited and half sang a line from *Die schöne Müllerin*, as the Dandelion rolled out more of her almond flour dough:

Nach Arbeit ich frug, Nun hab ich genug
Für die Hände, fürs Herze Vollauf genug!*

"Your German is improving," she said, appearing to blush.

Six months of practice was paying off.

"So don't worry," I said. "I'm glad to be useful."

"Well, it's frustrating," she said, transferring gingerbread onto a line of waiting metal trays. "If I'm not paying you for all your hours, I can't be really bossy."

"Don't worry, you pay with leftover bread. Mom's freezer is packed." Then, kicking the three bins I had set on the floor, I asked, "On the subject of leftovers, should these go in the walk-in freezer?"

"Are there more in the van?"

"Two more."

She pointed to the bins at my feet. "Put those in the freezer. There won't be a soup kitchen until after Christmas. Might as well leave the rest in the van. It's so cold out there, they'll freeze. That way you can drop them off at the nursing home tomorrow. Claudia seems to appreciate them."

"You got it!" I began to unzip the costume. "Let me get out of this fur first. It's already getting too hot..."

"Wait!" said Stefanie. "Remember?"

I looked at her, blankly.

"Christmas photo shoot!" She pointed to a tripod and

* I sought after work, Now I have enough,
For my hands, for my heart, I have more than enough!

camera. "AJ left his gear here. Can you set it up out front? I just need a few minutes to get these cookies in the oven."

"Aye aye, Captain D." I saluted with hoof to antler.

I grabbed the camera and tripod, lowered my cartoonish moose head and charged through the beaded passageway, past the front counter, through the front door and back out into the bitterly cold weather.

Unfolding the tripod in the empty parking spot, I mounted and aimed the camera at the storefront. A wreath, which Mom had made out of real pine branches, hung on the door; and yellow lights framed the two windows flanking either side.

That's when I noticed the window no longer displayed Stefanie's "New (ab)Normal Drivel" poster. Instead, both panes were completely covered with a collage.

I pressed Moosey's snout to the window and began reading. What I read chilled me to the core more than even the bitterest of northern winters could muster.

50. How to Fake a Pandemic

Heralding the collage of computer printouts filling both windows of the bakery was a banner written in Stefanie's hand:

There is NO pandemic!
Hospitals are ALWAYS overrun in the winter.
Look...

From there, running left to right, were printouts of articles, with key sentences highlighted in yellow marker—beginning with a CBC article dated January 2020. That would have been two months before COVID found its way to Canada. The headline proclaimed: "Some of Ontario's biggest hospitals are filled beyond capacity nearly every day." What followed made my moose jaw drop:

Overcrowding has become so common in Ontario hospitals that patient beds are now placed in hallways and conference rooms not only at times of peak demand, but routinely day after day...

Going back another year, the next printout, from *Time*

Magazine, opened with:

> The 2017–2018 influenza epidemic is sending people to hospitals and urgent-care centers in every state, and medical centers are responding with extraordinary measures: asking staff to work overtime, setting up triage tents...

I shook my head. *And, right now, they say we're in a second wave? Yet not a single hospital in Canada or the United States has tents set up.*

The next article, also from 2018, read:

> University of Alabama Hospital Emergency, Critical Care, Ambulatory and Prime Care services have experienced a 50 percent increase in seasonal influenza cases in the past 72 hours alone. These events led Alabama Gov. Kay Ivey to issue a State of Emergency this evening.

Yet, no lockdowns, no social distancing...

Scanning to the right, the headline of a third 2018 article, from the *LA Times,* heralded the now familiar corona military cliché: "California hospitals face a 'war zone' of flu patients—and are setting up tents to treat them."

2018 was a bad year for the flu, I remembered. Certainly worse than COVID 2020. Grandad got sick. Heck, so did I.

Moving to the next row of printouts, I scanned a November 2017 article from France, which quoted the head of their ambulance association saying, "Emergency rooms are at breaking point..." Yet no mention of masks, no standing six feet apart, no Zoom Christmas.

"Look, Josh!" said a female voice to my right antler. "It's one of Santa's reindeer."

I turned to see Sandy and son walking toward me. Sandy was holding her gloved hands up by her head, palms forward, fingers outstretched like antlers, signing what I assumed must mean a reindeer.

"Ah, Ma," said Josh. "That's no reindeer, it's a moose."

Josh repeated what looked like the same sign, except he brought his hands out and away from his head.

"Maybe Santa will have a moose lead his sleigh this year," said Sandy.

"But he can't fly," said Josh, looking at me.

I took off the moose mask so Josh could see my lips and hear me better. "True. But I can drive a van. Can any of Santa's reindeer do that?"

"No," said Josh. "Which proves you are not one of Santa's."

"No fooling you," I said. "There may be hope for the future after all." I tilted my head toward the printouts on the windowpane.

Sandy nodded, saying softly, "We read them this morning. Stefanie's outdid herself this time. They're spot on. I've done my fair share of shifts in ER and know how busy it gets in the winter."

I squatted down to Josh's height. "So, what did you ask Santa for?"

"A real bow and arrow," he proclaimed.

"Oh! I hope not to shoot moose."

Josh shook his head, the pompom on his winter hat flopping back and forth.

"Josh beats me in darts all the time now," said Sandy.

"And," he added proudly, "I can knock water bottles off the fence with my sling shot all the way across our yard."

"Awesome!" I said. "You never know, these days, a skilled bowman might come in handy. I guess since you can't hear as well, your eyes have gotten to be pretty sharp."

"And so are real arrows," said Sandy, starting to shiver. "We better keep moving. Merry Christmas, Mr. Moose."

"Yeah, merry Christmas, you guys. I'll see you tomorrow. I saw you ordered some cookies."

"See you then," said Sandy.

"Bye, Mr. Not-a-Reindeer," said Josh, putting his outstretched hands to his head again.

They continued down the empty strip. I slipped the moose mask back over my freezing head and continued reading the conspiracy collage. A 2014 article from *The Dayton Daily News* read:

The Center for Disease Control and Prevention said this week that the flu has reached the epidemic threshold nationally and is widespread in 36 states.

Seemed like every year we had a "pandemic." Beside that printout was a January 2013 article from *CTV News*, with a quote from a Dr. Bill Dickout highlighted:

In our emergency rooms, we would normally see about 150 patients a week with influenza; now it's nearly 700.

The next row down began with a 2011 *Globe and Mail* article stating:

A surge in seasonal influenza cases in parts of the country has clogged hospital emergency rooms...

Another chill shot down my already chilled spine as I pictured a roundtable of rich overlords, sitting in some penthouse, smoking fat cigars, jeering, "I bet we can get people scared to death of the flu season if we give it a new name."

The next article was from 2009, the year of the swine flu pandemic. I had just turned thirteen and remembered some of the media hype. The printout from the *LA Times* read:

At Loma Linda University Medical Center near San Michaelino, emergency room workers have set up a tent in the parking lot to handle a crush of similar patients. In Chicago, ER visits at the city's biggest children's hospital are double normal levels...

It didn't stop there. A 2009 article from *CNN* quoted a Dr. Mark Bell, head of eighteen emergency departments in Southern California:

We have had a lot of nervous patients with minimal respiratory tract symptoms. It has caused significant amount of delays in emergency care. They're all walking well.

Déjà vu, I thought. *How many people are calling ambulances because they fear they'll die from COVID, when, last year, they would have just stayed home and eaten chicken soup?*

"Hi, Vince."

I turned to see Mathéo approaching, wearing an ushanka fur cap, the flaps tied under his chin and a green scarf over his mouth and nose.

"Hey," I said. "How did you know it was me?"

"Actually, I thought it was a reindeer at first."

I noticed he had a thermos in hand. "More pea soup for your *tante*?"

"Just coming back." He shook the thermos. "This is empty."

"How is she?"

"Sick again. This time they say it really is COVID. Four others got it, too."

"Ah, they'll be okay. I was talking to Grandad last night. He had a bit of a cough, sore throat." I shrugged and waved my hoof at the printouts on the window. "Happens every year."

He stood there and stared at me.

"You okay, Mathéo?"

"Yeah," he said, softly, tucking the thermos under his arm. "See you at hockey practice?"

"Five p.m."

"I'll be there."

Mathéo nodded, smiling faintly. "*À plus tard*," he said and he continued plodding along.

Squatting, I started reading the bottom row of the collage. It went back to 2000, with an article from *The New York Times*:

> This year's wave of influenza has become widespread across the nation, overwhelming emergency rooms in cities from Boston to Los Angeles, filling hospital beds and forcing postponements of operations as staff members turn to treating the rising number of flu patients...

I shook my head and looked at the next printout—a 1999 BBC article titled "Health Lorry used as mortuary as flu strikes hospitals."

> A hospital spokesman said emergency admissions were up 50% on last year, and fewer burials and cremations over Christmas and the New Year had created a body jam.

Going back to before my birth, a 1993 *LA Times* article read:

> An outbreak of Beijing flu has swept Los Angeles, boosting absenteeism at local companies, schools and government offices and sending droves of feverish people to doctors' offices and hospitals...

Stefanie's final printout dated back to 1978, *The Washington Post*, opening with:

> Influenza has hit the Washington metropolitan area with such force that the emergency room staff at the Children's Hospital National Medical Center has been overwhelmed and has called for volunteer help from other hospital staffers.

I couldn't take anymore.
We'd all been fooled.
Well, not all of us.
She hadn't.
And that's when the bell to the front door jingled and the Dandelion stepped out.

Pointing to the collage, I said, "How did you ever dig all these up?"

51. The Shreddies Deception

Stefanie was wearing a Santa hat, a yellow scarf and a pine green jacket. She held two metal trays stacked one on the other. The top tray was covered with Christmas cookies and loaves of bread.

"So you're enjoying my collage?" she asked, smiling at the info bomb covering the bakery's windows.

"'Enjoying is not the word I would use," I replied, watching vapour rise from my snout. "It's way too mind-boggling. How did you find all these articles?"

She grinned. "It was so easy even a moose could do it. Just Google 'hospitals overwhelmed by flu.'"

"I thought you said Google was a lying, spying, censoring monolithic shill for the overlords trying to rule the world?"

"Probably is," she responded flatly. "Yet, even they can't hide the truth."

"Humph!" I said, rubbing my hooves together to keep warm. "It reminds me of Shreddies."

"Shreddies?"

"You know, that square-shaped breakfast cereal?"

"Uh-huh."

"They were able to boost sales simply by presenting the squares tilted on their corners."

Her blonde eyebrows drew together.

"They started calling them *Diamond* Shreddies," I said, with a laugh of vapour. "It made all the difference. More people started buying them."

"But they must have changed the shape or taste or something."

"Nope. Exact same product. Just changed the name and the angle."

"Sounds like COVID-19."

"Yep!" I agreed, gesturing to the collection of news articles. "The cold and flu season got a new PR team."

She began to sway, I assume to generate extra heat. Looking over at the camera atop the tripod I had set up, she asked, "You know how to use the timer?"

I skirted over to the camera, extended my hand from under the hoof and began tapping its touchscreen menu. It began to beep.

"60 seconds!" I said, as I dashed forward to stand beside her.

"Here!" She handed me an empty tray, while she held another one packed with the baked goods.

"What do I do with an empty platter?"

"Put the moose mask on it."

"Huh?" I realigned my head to better see her through the eye holes. "Don't you want Moosey in the pic?"

The camera began to beep louder.

"Sure, silly," she said. "That's why his head can go on the empty platter. But I also want the real Vincent McKnight in the first Moosehead Artisan Bakery Christmas photo."

I felt a warmth inside my chest, despite the cold.

The camera beeped louder.

"Quick," she said, "the camera is going to go off."

"Okay." I set the moose mask on the tray and twisted it so that the snout was facing the camera, just in time for a long and final beep.

"Say, *Tannenbaum*," I cheered.

Stefanie laughed. Snap! Snap! Snap!

"There!" she said. "Jordan said if I emailed them the file

before six, they could have cards printed and ready by ten to-morrow morning. That way, you can deliver them with the cook-ies."

"Sure." I walked back to the camera. "And, hey, thanks for having me in the photo."

"Of course." She smiled. "If I can't pay you full-time wages, at least I can offer you fame and glory."

"Trust me," I said. "You've made me infamous."

To my left, I heard the sound of ice skimming pavement. Turning, I saw Raj approaching, kicking a small ball of ice down the sidewalk. He had his hands in his pockets, slouched over, wearing a red face mask and no hat.

"Hey, Raj!" I said, waving a hoof.

Stefanie nodded at him.

"Hey, guys."

He sounded absentminded and depressed. He stopped at least eight feet away from us.

"How's it going?" I asked.

He shrugged. "One thing about these..." He pulled at his mask and let it snap back into place. "They keep your face warm."

"You might also want to try a hat," said Stefanie. "Studies show they are exceptionally good at protecting people's ears from frostbite."

"Yeah, well, you two might want to try a mask yourself." He kicked the ice ball hard, letting it explode against the brick wall of the bakery. "You freakin' anti-maskers are making this freak-in' coronavirus last freakin' forever."

"Actually," said Stefanie, sounding like a storm was coming, "coronaviruses have been around for millions of years. And a mask with openings on either side is not going to extinguish them."

"Only thing that's going to kick this virus in the butt is a vac-cine," said Raj. "Not your armchair philosophizing." He sneered at her.

"Raj," I said. "What the hell's up with you?"

"Ah!" He groaned and looked away from us both. "Craig's shut the arena down."

"What?" I said. "That's nuts! It's open ice. And the lockdown hasn't even started—"

"No hockey until case counts are down. New cop showed up yesterday. Said we can't social distance enough on the ice."

"This is insane!" Stomping my right hoof on the sidewalk, I suddenly felt a real moose's urge to charge. "We had the ice reserved tonight. We have a membership."

"Craig said he'd refund us."

"I don't want a refund," I almost yelled. "I want to play the game."

"Yeah, well, it's not happening."

"Take everything else away but leave me hockey..."

"Freakin' pandemic," said Raj.

"Raj," said Stefanie, in a softer voice, "there is no pandemic. It's just the cold and flu season. Look at the shop window—"

"What the hell do you know?" snapped back Raj. "You think you're some bloody scientist?"

"Hey, Raj!" I cut in, instinctively. "Don't talk to her like that."

Raj's eyes flashed at me. "Got the hots for your boss?"

"Show some respect or you keep on walking," I said firmly. I sounded angry, but probably looked laughable, still holding the cartoonish moose head on the tray in front of me.

"Why doesn't she show some respect?" he continued, glaring at me and ignoring Stefanie. "Damn signs in her window since the summer telling people to spread the disease around."

"Hey—" I began, but Stefanie stepped in.

"Guys! It's minus twenty! I may not be a scientist but I bet the river is frozen solid. Play outside in the fresh air; like real Canadians."

A moment of silence passed.

"Yeah," I finally said. "I'd rather be outside anyway. It's not like they let us use the dressing rooms anymore."

Raj swayed from foot to foot. "It's freezing out here."

"Ah, put on a winter hat," I said, shaking my head. "Once we get moving, we're sweating like whistling pigs in July."

"Hmm," said Raj. "Remember, we used to skate on the lake behind your grandfather's cabin?" Despite his mask, I could tell by the crinkles at the corners of his eyes he was cracking a smile.

"Yeah," I said.

"Hey," said Stefanie, "you can use the bread van to move your nets and gear."

"Thanks, boss," I said.

"And it can serve as a 'dressing room' where you can lace up without getting frostbite."

"Yeah, hey, thanks... boss," Raj said, pulling his mask down below his chin. "Sorry, I have a short temper."

"Have a cookie instead," said Stefanie.

"Oh, I—"

But before he could say another word, she shoved the head of a gingerbread man into his mouth.

"Thanks," he muttered, breaking the gingerbread at the neck.

"Grab the door for us, would you?"

"Sure," he mumbled, chewing.

Stefanie took the tray from me. I donned the moose mask on my freezing head and grabbed the camera and tripod. As we all shuffled into the warmth of the bakery, I immediately heard a familiar ringing sound.

"That must be Josef," said Stefanie, somewhat glumly.

She slid the stacked trays onto the front counter and passed through the beaded doorway in no apparent rush. Normally, whenever she would hear that Skype ring she'd almost lift off the ground like a ballerina being carried away by her Nutcracker Prince.

"Who's Josef?" asked Raj, taking another bite of gingerbread.

"Her fiancé," I said with a sigh.

"*Fiancé?* Bummer, man."

"Come on." I gestured with my hoof and led him through to the bake room.

"Na, alles gut?" Stefanie was saying, leaning back in the swivel chair, hand on mouse.

"Stefanie," said Josef, as his sideburns came into focus.

I walked by the webcam, mask on my head and Raj in tow. "Guten Abend, Josef," I waved a hoof.

"Herr Elch, good to see you, you ol' elk." He leaned forward a little. "Hey, Stef, did you hire someone else?"

"No," said Stefanie. "This is Raj. He and Vincent were just going to borrow the van."

"Merry Christmas," said Raj, waving the remaining legs of

the gingerbread.

"Same to you," said Josef.

Stefanie looked at me. "Don't stay out too late on the ice. An army of gingerbread men will be awaiting you in the morning, ready for deployment."

I held the back door open and Raj passed through. "Tomorrow, at 8:30 a.m. Don't worry. I'll be here." I nodded to the webcam. "Hey, in case I don't see you Josef, Frohe Weihnachten!"

"Merry Christmas, Vince," he said, sincerely, yet softly. "Thanks for all you do for Stefanie. I really appreciate it."

He sounded sad.

Why wouldn't he be?

She was here. He was there. It was Christmastime. They thought they'd be married by now. They must feel so depressed.

"No prob," I said.

"Where on the river will you be playing?" asked Stefanie.

"By Brian Peckford Park, I figure."

"Feel free to use the van's headlights to help you see."

"Thanks."

With that, I stepped out into the back lot, snagging my antlers on the doorframe for the very last time.

52. Where Mamma Hides the Cookies

The headlights of the bread van, parked on the frosty grass of Brian Peckford Park, shone across the frozen French River. In the distance, a quarter moon hung over town hall.

I slapped the puck hard, skating after it on the lumpy ice. AJ swooped in, scooping it up, while coasting the imaginary boards (marked by extra hockey sticks) of our informal rink. I pressed my blades into the ice, skating as fast as I could to retrieve the lost puck.

My goodness, it felt good to play outside—even if the air was frigid. AJ (the dork) still wore his Tragically Hip face mask below the plastic shielding of his fishbowl hockey helmet. I slid past him, my stick tapping the puck away from his jerky blade, as my skates sped in the direction of Mathéo and their net. In the distance, another hundred metres downriver, I could see the railway bridge high above the frozen water.

AJ was upon me in seconds. I evaded his dancing blade by sending a saucer pass up into the air, to land on Raj's blade. Cradling the puck, Raj swerved to the right of Mathéo and then shot the vulcanized rubber into the net, literally skimming the goal's upper crossbar.

"*Gino!*" I yelled, raising my stick over my head.

"Sweet cheddar shot," shouted Léo, who had been waiting at the edge of the bank for a turn on the ice.

"Right where mamma keeps the cookies," mumbled AJ as he banged his stick on the hard ice.

Léo shook his head and began sliding toward AJ. "*Aweille!* You had that *rondelle!*" He looked at AJ but pointed his own stick at the puck. "You sure that mask's not on too tight?"

"Ah," said AJ in a muffled voice. "I'm just warming up."

"Well, I'm freezing," said Léo. "Ref for a bit, you bender."

Léo pulled his helmet down. His long, black hair streamed out to the sides of his helmet whenever he skated—what hockey fans would call a "real salad." But we had neither fans, nor even, really, a team. We were just guys who loved the game and played for fun.

And we were having fun.

As I had heard on the van's radio that morning, Travis Green, coach for the quarantined Vancouver Canucks, said, "Hockey brings back a little bit of normal for a lot of people." Yeah, the *real* normal.

Léo pointed his stick at Mathéo, as he skated to centre. "And, hey, Pylon, the idea is not to let the puck in the net."

Mathéo said nothing, tapped the puck, sending it sliding toward AJ, who picked it up and glided to centre ice.

"Where's Greg and those other benders?" asked Léo.

"I texted them," said Raj. "Too cold for Greg. Marvin and the others think we're breaking the law—even though I told them Bindu says it's not illegal."

"Is, um, she still expected back tonight?"

"Yeah. She left Thunder Bay at eight this morning."

"Long drive," said Léo.

"Eleven hours."

Léo skated to centre. I pushed forward to meet him.

"Nah," said Léo, shooing me aside with his stick. "Let me face off with Raj."

"Sure."

I shrugged and skated back toward the net, as Raj glided into my spot.

"Here's the deal," said Léo, looking at Raj, big smirk across his face. "If I score, then you get your mother to let me have a *real* date with your sister. If you score, then I'll get you a date with my sister."

"But I don't want a date with your sister," exclaimed Raj. "She's a moose."

"Hey!" I cut in. "Whaddya got against moose?"

"Nothing. Just don't want to go out with one."

"Then you better let me win," said Léo.

"Forget it, Léo," said AJ, holding the puck out in the air between the two. "Her mother's never going to let her marry a plumber. Bindu's a lawyer. Her husband *must* be a doctor. It's astrology 101. Time to move on."

"Thanks," said Léo, eyes fixed on centre ice, "but I never take dating advice from a surgeon."

AJ snorted behind his mask.

Then he dropped the puck.

And covered his ears.

Rrrrrrr!

The short wail of a siren blasted across the ice.

Raj froze and Léo took off with the puck.

My head snapped in the direction of the riverbank. A police cruiser, lights flashing red and blue, had just pulled up beside the bread van.

53. Gestapo Time

"*Ayoye!*" exclaimed Léo, letting the puck drift away.

Raj cursed and slouched forward, as if hiding his face.

Mathéo straightened up out of his hunched goalie position and stared at the flashing lights of the police cruiser.

"Frack!" said AJ from behind his black Tragically Hip face mask. "Gestapo time."

All ten of our skates now pointed toward the cop car. After

another short wail, the siren died away and the door opened. A thin silhouette stepped out, pulling a fur cap down over his head.

"Hey, boys!" said a jovial voice.

I immediately recognized Constable Corona.

"Good evening, officer," said Raj, hesitantly.

"Nice barn you boys set up here," said Mackenzie, rubbing his hands together. "You're true Canucks. Must be minus ten out here."

"We don't mind," said Léo. "Gets the blood—"

Mackenzie slammed his door shut and walked toward us, blinding headlights behind him.

"I grew up playing outside," he said. "My dad would make a rink in the backyard."

In the starry sky above, a flock of geese honked, making up for our silent stares.

"Heard you boys yelling," said Mackenzie, walking slowly toward the bank. "All the way on Main Street."

"Sorry, if we were too loud," I said.

Mackenzie waved a gloved hand. "No, no. Just kids having fun."

He stepped closer.

"But all that yellin' spreads the virus around."

Another step.

"And I see none of you are wearing masks, except for Jacques." He pointed to AJ.

"*Jacques?*" said AJ.

"You boys too young to know Jacques Plantes?"

"Edmonton Oilers," I said.

"Actually," added Mathéo, slowly, "Plantes started with the Montreal Canadiens."

"That's right!" said Mackenzie in a voice better suited for a history teacher with a pointer stick, not a cop with a Glock 17M pistol. "Jacques Plantes was the first NHL goalie to wear a mask. Hard to believe, but up until the late seventies, goalies didn't wear masks. Guess they thought they were invincible."

He paused, letting his point sink in.

"But you know today," he added, "if a mask falls off a goalie by accident, the whistle's blown and play is stopped immediately."

Another pause.

"That's how important it is to keep each other safe."

Yeah, I thought, *like full contact hockey's the model for health and safety.* Speaking out loud I said, "Well, it doesn't take an electron microscope to see how a goalie mask would protect a guy from a frozen puck breaking his front teeth. But..."

"Well, then trust those with the microscopes," said Mackenzie, "who say masks will stop you from giving the virus to others."

He was close enough now that we could see he had a black mask covering his lower face. With the fur cap, only his eyes were visible.

"You guys Leaf fans?" he asked, switching back to a chirpy voice. "I'll forgive this little transgression if you're Leaf fans."

Indeed, we were all loyal devotees of the Toronto Maple Leafs—especially Raj.

"Winnipeg Jets," I said.

"Ottawa Senators," said AJ.

"Calgary Flames," said Mathéo.

"*Canadiens de Montreal,*" said Léo.

Raj paused. "Chicago Wolves," he said, voice wavering.

A few seconds of silence passed before Mackenzie said, "That's too bad, fellas."

I cleared my throat. "Well, even though we don't root for the same team, doesn't mean we can't get along."

Mackenzie nodded slowly. "Hmm. But we still have to play by the same rules. And the rules of the game right now are no gatherings of five or more people from outside your bubble." He forced a friendly chuckle. "Unless you're all brothers, I'm going to have to throw you all in the penalty box."

"Why do NHL players get to play on an indoor arena," I asked, "and we can't even play in the open air?"

"I know it's hard for you to understand, son," said Mackenzie. "And I commend you for taking the precaution of playing in the open air. But hockey is a close contact sport."

"Seems then like there's more risk of breaking our back than dying from COVID."

"I'll make this simple for you," said Mackenzie. "You're

breaking the law and putting lives at risk just so you can knock a puck around. It's not quite manslaughter, but...."

Manslaughter? I felt a competing blend of shame and disbelief.

"Manslaughter?" I blurted out, unexpectedly. "I don't know anyone dying from COVID." I looked side to side. "Any of you guys seen anyone die from this pandemic?"

"Not me," said Léo.

"Nope," said Mathéo.

AJ and Raj didn't say a word.

"Well, I have," snapped Mackenzie so loudly it felt like thunder had clapped. "You may be young and healthy, but you need to think of—"

"—of the elderly! The vulnerable!" interrupted an even louder voice from behind him.

Another silhouette appeared in the headlights.

Mackenzie turned toward her.

"All you healthy young men need to stop exercising," she continued, "stop working, stop socializing, stop marrying and having children... because the sick and elderly are dying."

I could just make out Stefanie's face as she passed Mackenzie. The white frill of her Santa hat looked blue with the glow of the cruiser's light bar.

"Where'd you come from?" said Mackenzie.

It sounded like a dumb question, showing she had caught him by surprise.

"The North Pole," she said.

She halted at the edge of the frozen river, winked at me and then spun around to face Mackenzie. Over her shoulders hung a pair of white skates.

"There's more than five of us, now," she said. "So, we are definitely in breach of your unlawful playbook."

54. Ice and Isolation

Now that we had stopped playing, the cold was easily penetrating my Goose Tundra hockey pants. The wind coming along the open river had partially frozen the left side of my face.

Warm vapour escaping from Mackenzie's face mask, turning

red and blue in the swirling lights of his cruiser behind him, drifted up into the starlit sky from his vantage point on the river bank.

"They're not my laws," Mackenzie said, extending his arms. "And I'm the first to admit that limiting gatherings is extreme. But so are hospitals overrun with COVID cases. What's the worst of two evils? A winter spent in isolation or a winter full of body bags?"

"The University of Toronto is expecting over two thousand deaths from suicide as a result of lockdowns." Stefanie sounded mad. Almost as if someone she had known had taken their life. "And that's just those who kill themselves because of unemployment. It's not counting those who can't bear the loneliness, anxiety and depression. You may not want to forget to count those body bags when deciding how evil your laws are."

"It's not for me or you to decide whether a law is just or not," said Mackenzie. "But I'd rather have too much order than chaos."

"You can't swing the pendulum of government all the way to the other extreme and claim you're being just," countered Stefanie, standing erect on the edge of the bank. "You're a police officer. You took an oath to protect our rights, not take them away because some politician told you to."

"I'm protecting people's right to life."

"Like hell you are!"

He was keeping his cool. He sounded calm. Stefanie sounded ready to explode. *What is up with her?*

"How can any sane person think that avoiding normal human interactions will extend the life of an eighty-eight-year old in a nursing home?"

She turned back and reached out with a green-mittened hand toward me. Surprised, I extended my four-roll glove. She slid onto the ice and wrapped her arm around my waist. My face suddenly didn't feel so numb. I realized, of course, she was only putting on a show for Constable Corona.

Turning back to her opponent, she continued, "So why don't you get back to keeping the country safe from bad guys, instead of becoming the poster boy for COVID-1984?"

"Hey," I said, holding up one of her skates, "you play

hockey?"

She smiled. "I figured you'd need a referee."

"That's for sure." And I nodded toward Mackenzie.

Léo chuckled.

Another clap of thunder, as Mackenzie smacked his leather gloves together and pointed a finger at Stefanie.

"All right, I tried being friendly," he bellowed. "Now, if I don't start seeing your anarchist asses moving off that ice, I'm going to start slapping them with $880 fines." He paused. "And I doubt any of you can afford that. So, unless you want to be paying your dues in Sudbury Jail..."

Nobody moved or said a word.

"He can't be serious," I heard Raj mutter. "This is Canada."

"All right, you want to play like that," he said and pulled a ticket pad from a side pocket. "Don't say I didn't warn you." He pointed his pen at AJ. "What's your real name, Jacques?"

AJ just stared back.

"This can get real ugly," said Mackenzie.

"Hey!" AJ held up his arms. "I'm out of here, guys."

"Don't let him get to you," said Stefanie. "Let him write his tickets. Any judge will dismiss—"

"Listen, Joan of Arc," said Mackenzie. "If I hear another word from you, I'll make sure your little bakery never bakes another conspiracy theory in Ontario again." He pointed back to AJ and spoke kindly, "Come on, son. Do the right thing. Get off the ice."

AJ skated to the edge. We could see he was breathing heavily, vapour fuming out the sides of his Tragically Hip face mask. He stepped off the ice and wobbled across the frozen grass on his skates.

"I just need to change into my boots," he said to Mackenzie, pointing to the van.

"So much for the great dragon slayer," I mumbled. "What a dork."

"Of course," said Mackenzie, not turning to face his first re-cruit, but keeping his attention fixed on Stefanie. "Now, if any of you have two brain cells to rub together, you'll follow Jacque's wise example. Once he's done, I want each of you, one at a time, to head to that van, take off your skates, put on your boots and get the hell out of here." He sighed and rubbed his forehead.

"God knows, I don't like slapping fines—"

"Then why don't you get the hell out of here, yourself?" said Stefanie. "Stop turning Moosehead into a Soviet police state."

Mackenzie reached behind his back and removed a pair of handcuffs from his belt.

"I think we better go," said Raj, quickly. "We can play a game of NHL20."

"Yeah," said Léo, grudgingly. "I guess that's what an Xbox is for."

"No!" pleaded Stefanie. "This is how governments take away freedoms. They make up some danger and then—"

Mackenzie set his right boot on the ice. "All right, forget about tickets. If I don't start seeing asses moving off this ice I'm going to start making arrests."

Stefanie squeezed my arm and whispered: "Please, don't be a turtle."

Oh, why me? I suddenly realized how much I loved her. I loved her more than I feared Mackenzie.

"Guys," I said loudly, with obvious anxiety, "like, what's he going to do? Arrest all of us? He's outnumbered. And if he calls this in, you know Yamamoto's going to laugh it off."

"I don't need to arrest all of you." He held out the handcuffs and began sliding in his black boots toward Stefanie. "Your pretty ringleader is clearly the source of—"

"Go ahead, arrest me," she said slowly and held out her wrists.

Mackenzie paused.

"Dig yourself a hole you'll never get out of," she added.

"Was that a threat?" he asked.

"Hey, this guy's nuts," said Léo. "Let's just get out of here before someone gets hurt."

Mackenzie continued to slide toward her, handcuffs dangling in his right hand, while his left hand moved to his holstered taser.

Suddenly he jerked, losing his balance as the bread van's horn sounded in one prolonged blast. Its headlights flickered and AJ stuck his unmasked head out of the driver's seat window.

"Home, guys! I'm going home! Home, you hear me?"

Then the van revved, jolted back in reverse, turned around,

and quickly became a pair of taillights vanishing into the night.

Mackenzie had fallen down hard on his knees, hands forward on the ice, head turned back staring. He cursed at the retreating van.

Maybe AJ's not such a dork, after all, I thought to myself.

"He just stole my van," muttered Stefanie.

"Sorry, boss," I whispered.

"It's not your fault," she said, staring into the dark field.

"That's not what I'm sorry about."

"What then?"

"This!" I dropped my stick and scooped her up into my arms, circled around and aimed my skates downriver.

"What are you—" began Stefanie as her left arm clung tightly around my neck.

"Follow me!" I yelled out as I passed Raj, Mathéo and Léo.

"What the—" was all I heard from Raj, followed by an "Oh la vache!" from Léo and could that have been a laugh from Mathéo?

I didn't look back, but I could hear sticks clattering to the ice, followed by all eight of our blades slicing fast and hard—as if Mackenzie had opened fire. We sped under the railway bridge and down the widening French River, leaving the yells and curses of Constable Corona behind us.

55. Free to Freakin' Freeze

With the weight of both our bodies, the blades below my feet were slicing deeply into the ice. I imagined they might cut through to the rushing waters below. We'd sink to the bottom of the French River and escape the nightmare of 2020.

"When I said don't be a turtle," she protested, "this wasn't what I meant."

Stefanie's back and legs relaxed a little. Her arm around my neck, however, held tight, while my arms burned with lactic acid.

"Thank God you're as light as a dandelion," I lied between heaving frosty breaths.

"I'm flattered, but, really it's not necessary." She lifted up one of the white skates hanging around her neck. "I got these."

"Figure skates?" I said with a raised eyebrow.

"I used to compete."

"Of course you did."

I slowed to a stop and set her on the ice.

"I don't know whether to thank you or slap you," she said.

I dropped down on all fours.

"Here, I'll be a stool."

"You're being silly," she protested.

"Actually, I was looking for an excuse to take a break."

She sat on my back as the others began circling us.

"What the freakin' hell are we doing?" yelled Raj. "We just ditched a cop."

"Relax!" said Léo. "This is awesome!"

"He's got a cruiser, we got skates. Who do you think is faster?"

"He's not going to drive on the ice," argued Stefanie, as she tugged at her laces.

"He can see us from the road."

"Then let's keep going," said Léo. "Once we hit the bush, we'll be out of sight."

"And out of our minds," countered Raj. "What the hell are we going to do in the freakin' bush?"

"Let's find out," said Stefanie, leaping off my back and onto her skates.

We were moving quickly, more to stay warm than anything, but it was making it even harder to see. I was relying on a quarter moon and the Milky Way as our only sources of light, as we sped between the banks lined by the dark silhouettes of denuded trees.

How will I ever see where the river splits? I thought. *Have we already passed it?*

"It's way too cold," Raj called out from behind. "We need to start heading back before—"

That's when I yelled. But not at Raj. Ahead of us, to the right, on the northern bank, stood a man.

Mackenzie?

I bent my knees and shifted to the left as I dug the tip of my right skate into the ice, coming to a scraping halt. Stefanie did the same, but the other guys shot past us in the direction of the figure, who almost seemed to glow on the dark river bank.

"Watch out!" I shouted.

All three pairs of skates began scraping.

And the man on the bank began laughing.

And slapping his thighs.

"Grandad!" I muttered.

"Miskwaadesi!" he called out. "You passed it!"

He pointed back the way we came.

And then he vanished.

"Mon Dieu!" Mathéo exclaimed.

"Vincent?" said Stefanie, staring at me.

Raj and Mathéo skated back, circling to a halt on either side of us.

"I thought I saw..." I didn't finish my sentence. "Did you see him?"

"I didn't see anyone," said Stefanie.

"He's gone completely crazy," concluded Raj, speaking as if he was wearing a lab coat in a mental asylum, rather than a hockey jersey in the bush.

"I think I saw someone," said Mathéo, quietly. "For a second."

"Then you're crazy, too," Raj concluded.

Léo appeared out of the darkness, dragging his left skate at a forty-five degree angle.

"Who did you see, *niijii*?" he asked me.

"Uh," I stuttered. "I, well, I think I saw Mackenzie."

"Don't worry," said Stefanie, putting her hand on my shoulder. "No way he'd find us this far out. Too much bush between the river and the highway."

"Yeah, we're safe," agreed Léo.

"Safe?" said Raj. "We're stuck in skates, on the ice, in the freezing cold, with an armed police officer guarding the only way home. You call that safe?"

"At least we're free," snapped Stefanie.

"Free to freakin' freeze! I'm the one with the East Indian DNA, remember."

Stefanie shrugged. "Better to die free."

"I don't want freedom," exclaimed Raj, his voice almost cracking. "I want my freakin' boots! What the hell is AJ doing? All our stuff was in that van. Even our cells."

Ignoring Raj, Stefanie poked me in the chest with her mittened finger.

"Mackenzie was about to arrest me," she almost barked.

"Yeah," I said, still staring at the bank. "I kind of noticed."

"You should have let him." She sounded angry. "I'm fed up with all of it."

"Ummm..." My voice trailed off. "You want to go to jail?"

"It's like Thoreau said."

"Who?"

I was only half-paying attention. *Did I just see Grandad?* Raj was right, I was losing it.

"Henry David Thoreau," clarified Stefanie.

She poked me again. This time I faced her.

"And what did Henry say?"

"Under an unjust government, the best place for a just man is a prison.'"

Raj was warming his face with his hockey gloves. "You can't be both free and in jail," he said.

"Gandhi spent two years in prison to free India," she countered, sounding a touch calmer.

"But we're free now," I argued. "We outsmarted Mackenzie. We escaped. We resisted. What good are we in jail?"

Raj rubbed his hockey gloves together. "At least we'd be alive in jail. The night's young. And it's only going to get colder."

"Aww!" interrupted Léo. "Don't ruin it! We made that creep look like an idiot."

"Oh, yeah," said Raj, sarcastically. "He's probably sipping hot coffee in his nice warm cruiser, while we are standing on a frozen river, in minus three hundred degrees Celsius, in the dark, without even a freakin' flashlight."

Stefanie pulled a small flashlight out of her coat pocket, flicked it on and shone it in Raj's face.

"How about a cellphone?" he said, covering his eyes now too.

"They give you cancer."

"I'd rather risk leukemia than hypothermia."

She rolled her eyes and turned back to me. "I was thoroughly prepared to get arrested, you know."

I cleared my throat. "Let the record show that Stefanie Müller did not flee in fear."

"I wish I could have seen his face," said Léo, skating backwards in a circle around us. "We made him look like Dudley Do-Right."

"What is wrong with you people?" said Raj, sounding like he was more at risk of hyperventilation than hypothermia. "We're resisting arrest. You can go to prison for that."

"He never said we were under arrest," said Mathéo.

"So no one's resisting," added Stefanie. "He wanted us to stop congregating on the ice and we're still here—albeit a little up-river. I guess we could say we won that battle."

She smiled slightly.

"He still broke up our game," said Mathéo.

Mathéo began spinning his arms side to side, still wearing the large goaltender blocker gloves.

"All right, we didn't cream him," Léo conceded. "But we still won."

"Hooray for us," grumbled Raj. "And as our award we get to stay out here all night in the freakin' freezing cold while he guards the only way home."

"Relax," I said. "We have a better plan."

"We do?" said Stefanie.

I smiled, pulling my helmet off. Despite the freakin' freezing cold, my hair was drenched with sweat.

"You mean, I'm actually ahead of you this time?"

She scrunched her eyes, staring back at me. A couple seconds later her pupils went wide with understanding.

"Of course," she said.

56. Moosehead Pirates

Raj was breathing so heavily now his helmet looked like a smokestack. Stomping a skate on the frozen river, he demanded: "What're you two talking about?"

"Don't worry," I said, only half paying attention. "We have a plan."

"Like what? Spending the entire twenty-eight-days of lockdown breaking holes in the ice, surviving off raw fish we catch with our frozen hands?"

"Now *you're* going crazy," said Léo, raising both his hockey mitts in the air. "But I know what I'm going to do! I'm gonna be a *pirate*... on the River Saskatchewan!"

"Aye, Matey!" said Mathéo, growling like Blackbeard, and elbowing Léo. "Get it? Matey. Métis."

And then the two of them began to hum the melody to "The Last Saskatchewan Pirate."

"Even our phones are in the van," continued Raj, speaking even louder and more anxiously, over the humming pirates. "I might have been able to call Bindu. If anyone would help us it would be her..."

Mathéo and Léo hummed even louder. Reaching a crescendo, Stefanie's mezzo voice began to sing.

Stefanie? I'd never heard her sing in English before, no less something as silly as The Arrogant Worms.

The three of them filled the quiet night with one of the funniest Canadian songs ever composed—about a bankrupt farmer who takes to raiding barges of wheat and barley on the Saskatchewan River. When they got to the part where the Mountie joins the crew Raj couldn't take it anymore.

"Knock it off!" he hollered. "I can't stand those stupid worms."

"*Stupid worms?*" exclaimed Stefanie, her eyes scrunching in offence. "That you even know the band's name and recognize the song suggests you secretly listen to The Arrogant Worms, but are too proud to admit you have a sense of humour."

Léo stopped humming, looked at Stefanie and said with surprise: "So you're a fan of the Worms, too?"

"Of course," she said, a smile creeping onto her face. "But even better than their music is their motto."

"What's their motto?"

"Help us save the world," said Stefanie. "Or at least make fun of it."

They all laughed harder than the joke warranted.

"You're all freakin' nuts!" said Raj.

But even he was laughing now.

The only one not laughing was me. Their banter seemed a world away, as I rotated on the ice looking for... *Grandad?* He had said we missed "it." We'd gone too far. I stared into the darkness from which we had come. Off the south bank, a little downriver, headlights of a car rattled over a metal bridge. A bridge meant water would be underneath. Whomever (or whatever) I saw on the bank was right—we had gone too far.

"We passed the Wingekisinaw." I pointed in the direction of the vanishing headlights.

"What the hell do we need the freakin' Wingekisinaw for?" said Raj.

"The Wingekisinaw River will get us *home*," I said

"The Wingekisinaw doesn't run anywhere near Moosehead," snapped Raj.

"You obviously haven't figured out the master plan," said Stefanie.

Mathéo began spinning his arms in large circles. "Whatever the plan, we need to keep moving," he said, "or we'll have to start amputating fingers."

He was right. Already, numbness had entered my fingertips and was creeping up my arms. The front page of the next *Moosehead Gazette* flashed before my mind's eye: "Five freeze to death evading COVID-19 restrictions."

"All right, mateys," I announced, "the Wingekisinaw River beckons!"

"Onward, brave pirates!" cheered Stefanie.

"Aye, Captain Dandelion!" hollered Léo. And in a deep voice he began to sing:

And it's a heave-ho, hi-ho, no new-normal lies,
Livin' free without a mask, no one's gonna die.
It's a ho-hey, hi-hey be not at all afraid
When ya see the Moosehead Pirates in our open ice parade.

We all (except Raj) repeated the last verse a second time:

When ya see the Moosehead Pirates in our open ice parade.

"You guys are all freakin' nuts," Raj spoke out, the words gurgling in the back of his throat.

"Ah!" I yelled and bodychecked him as I passed, leading the way back downriver.

I sounded confident, but I was full of doubt. What if I was wrong about what awaited us? We could easily die, left to the elements.

A minute or so later, we veered to the right, heading south along the narrower Wingekisinaw River. All the while, my eyes scanned the banks for that laughing man who sounded so much like my grandad.

A half-hour later, our pace had slowed. Staring up at the countless stars above had kept us in a silent awe. The new normal felt millions of miles away, as we glided down that frozen path of unrestricted ice. The Wingekisinaw's banks were flanked by leafless trees, many growing into the water at ninety-degree angles—their trunks and branches half-encased below the ice.

Canada, a nation of rivers. These were the watery highways of my grandad's people—a people who lived here four thousand years before the Colosseum was built. By the end of the eighteenth century, the Ojibwe people held strong the north shores of lakes Huron and Superior—effectively governing over the white newcomers.

Just as the French River divided Southern and Northern Ontario, so the river of my life flowed between the worlds of my Indigenous and European heritage; and now, between the old normal and the new normal of the corona deception.

"Anybody going to tell me where the freakin' hell we're going?" grumbled Raj, from behind.

"You still don't know?" asked Léo, coming up beside him.

"Forgive me, my brain is frozen."

Ignoring Raj, Léo skated up to my right. "Ça alors! I can't even see the riverbank, much less what's on it. How are we ever going to spot his place?"

"Oh, I don't know," I said whimsically.

I pointed ahead.

On the eastern bank were flashing headlights.

"I think AJ's made it rather easy for us."

57. COVID Vigilantes

As we skated closer to the flashing headlights, we could hear the van's radio playing, "Ding Dong! Merrily on High." AJ's silhouette was waving at us, antlers protruding from his head.

Léo yelled, "Ahoy, land lover."

"What took you guys so long?" AJ shouted back in a voice muffled by the moose mask.

"We got lost," said Raj.

Once close enough, we could see that AJ was standing on a dock. Behind him stretched a frozen field, where his father grew corn in the summer. In the middle of the barren field stood his parents' two-storey home. Between the river and the house burned a large bonfire. On either side of the field were tall woods, hopefully providing some protection from the freezing breeze.

"Heat!" I said hungrily. I had almost no feeling left in my fingertips.

We all scraped to a halt around the dock, staring up at my moose mask on AJ's skinny body.

"Moosey!" said Stefanie, sternly. "How many times have I told you not to borrow the van without permission?"

"Moosey?" said AJ, in an offended tone. "Moosey!" He then switched to a deep and dramatic voice. "I'm Mooseman!" He put his hands on his hips and rotated his antlered head back and forth. "I saved the day!"

I chuckled. "You did pretty good. I must admit."

"*Oui, oui!*" said Léo. "That was some stunt you pulled. You're a superhero, in my book."

"More like the freakin' villain," said Raj. "Superheroes aren't at odds with the cops."

"You must only read kiddie comics," said Mooseman.

"Actually, I don't read comics at all."

"Ah, so you're illiterate."

"Whatever," said Raj.

"I'm more like Batman, Zorro or Spiderman," said AJ. "The vigilantes the cops are always trying to catch."

"Vigilantes," muttered Raj, shaking his head. "Just let me get to that fire." He reached out his hand to Mooseman.

"Ah, ah, ah!" said Mooseman, turning to Stefanie and extending his hoof. "Ladies first." She accepted, and he pulled her onto the dock.

A couple minutes later, we'd all clunked across the wooden dock with our skates. At the van, we swapped our helmets for our winter hats and grabbed our boots. Waddling over the frozen field to the fire, we sat on encircling logs, waiting until our fingers had enough circulation to remove the skates from our sore feet. While we thawed, Léo recounted our adventures to AJ, ending with another rendition of the "Moosehead Pirates" song.

"I'd let you guys in the house," said AJ, having now revealed his thin face and oversized glasses, "but even if you were all wearing hazmat suits and promised not to breathe, Mom would freak. And Cindy has a cold, so Mom's doubly scared right now."

I looked over at the house. Most of the lights were on and a car was in the side driveway.

"But she's cool with us being outside," continued AJ. "She even gave me a gallon of her homemade cider." He pointed to a large metal camping kettle, sitting in the fire's embers.

"Ah," said Raj. "I hope that's a strong cider."

"Sorry, guys. It's just cider."

"What I'd do for a—" muttered Raj.

"But I do have—" AJ reached behind his log and pulled out a six-pack of Corona Extra—"*la cerveza mas fina.*"

"Now we're talking!" said Raj.

AJ pulled a can out from the plastic ring and tossed the pack to Raj. Raj snapped off a can and strolled over to Mathéo, who sat on the next log beside AJ.

"*Merci,*" said Mathéo, extracting a can.

AJ then swung around the fire and extended the pack to Stefanie on the next log.

"It's vegan." He grinned.

She shook her head. "I'll stick to the hot cider."

Raj shrugged and moved to my log.

"Ah," I said, hesitating. Between Dad's drunken example and Grandad's warnings about the "wicked waters of the white man," I rarely drank. But after all the stress and exertion we'd been through, I felt like I'd earned a brewski. I reached for one of the cans dangling from Raj's gloved hand. As soon as my mitt touched the icy aluminum, my hand froze.

As if he'd always been there, I suddenly found myself looking at Grandad, standing tall behind Raj. He appeared a decade younger. His face almost glowed, with the fire blazing behind him. Or was he in the fire? He wore a rustic wool top and animal hide leggings decorated with porcupine quills. He frowned at me and in a perfect Shakespearean accent recited:

"O God! that men should put an enemy in their mouths to steal away their brains."

And then he was gone, as if he had spontaneously combusted into the dancing flames.

"I think I'll stick to the cider, too," I almost whispered, pulling back my hand.

Two hallucinations in one night, I thought. *My God, he seemed so real. Am I losing it?*

I must have looked a little spooked, because Raj didn't offer a retort—just walked over to the next log where Léo sat. As he stepped aside, I could see Mathéo on the other side of the fire. He was staring at me, wide-eyed, looking as spooked as I felt.

"Merci beaucoup!" said Léo, pulling out a can. Then speaking to all of us, he added, "Boy, we sure showed that COVID cop, didn't we?"

"Get over it," said Raj sarcastically, "He got our nets and sticks and pylons. I bet they'll end up in some police auction."

"I think that would be called stealing," said Stefanie.

Raj grunted, sat down on the log between Léo and AJ, and popped the tab on his Corona.

AJ filled three metal camping mugs with some of the cider and delivered two of them directly to Stefanie and me.

Stefanie held it to her nose. "Mmm, cinnamon and cloves."

"Smells good," I said. "And hot."

"A toast!" said AJ, holding up a beer can in one hand and a mug of cider in the other. "To the Moosehead Pirates of the Wingekisinaw River!"

We all lifted our drinks and cheered in a way that sounded more like a sigh of relief.

"I don't think beer or apple juice is going to sustain me," Mathéo said.

"Fortunately," said Stefanie, "the getaway vehicle was well stocked."

She drained her cider, stood and walked back to the van. While she was gone, my eyes darted around, looking for Grandad.

You're just stressed, seeing things in the firelight, I told myself. *Forget about it.*

Stefanie returned carrying one of the green bins. Opening the lid revealed a dozen sourdough loaves in clear plastic bags. She handed me one of them. They felt half-frozen.

"Pull off a chunk and pass it around," she instructed. "You can toast it over the fire on the end of a branch."

"Oh, by the way," said AJ, standing up. "Mom told me to remind you all to sit six feet apart."

Stefanie promptly sat down beside me on my log.

"And to wear your masks," added AJ.

He unzipped the front of the moose costume and pulled out a blue medical mask from his pants pocket.

"You're not going to revert to your secret identity as a dork, are you?" said Léo.

Instead, AJ stretched the mask like a slingshot, and let it snap forward into the fire. We all looked at him in surprise.

"What?" he said. "Doesn't everybody incinerate their face mask after a day of collecting the most dangerous virus known to man?"

"Nah!" said Stefanie. "They just hang them by their bedsides."

"Or on their rear-view mirror," added Mathéo. He pulled a white mask out, crumpled it into a ball and tossed it into the flames.

"Ah," said Raj, hesitantly pulling a mask from his own pocket and committing it to the flames. "It's so freakin' cold out here, how could a virus survive?"

"Actually," piped up Léo, "it's a myth that the freezing cold can stop a coronavirus, according to the World Health Organization."

"You mean the World *Hoax* Organization," said Stefanie

"The only thing that's going to stop this virus," repeated Raj, hovering his bread chunk over the fire, "is the rollout of the vaccine."

I glanced at Stefanie. She grimaced and took a bite of the crunchy toast from the end of her stick.

58. A Flaming Dandelion

"Are you getting the jab?" AJ asked Raj, as he jabbed another chunk of bread with a branch.

"Yeah, of course, I'll get it." Raj started shaking his stick, as his bread caught fire.

"Aren't you at all concerned about the side effects?" said Stefanie, without looking at him.

"Yada, yada," said Raj. "You anti-maskers say we shouldn't be concerned about the virus' side effects, so why should we be concerned about the vaccine's?"

"Actually, that's not what we say."

Raj shrugged. "Like, yeah, I mean not everybody should get the shot. The immune-compromised, kids with cancer, peanut allergies, et cetera. Which is why I'm getting it. Because they can't."

"You sound like a PSA," said Mathéo.

AJ laughed. "Hey, I heard these mRNA vaccines alter your DNA. Maybe we'll all become like the X-Men. Get superpowers!"

"Sorry to disappoint you," said Stefanie, "but there isn't any real evidence it'll interact with your genetic code. It doesn't penetrate the cell nucleus."

"How do you know so much?" asked Léo.

"I was on a Zoom meeting last night with Professor Denis Rancourt. He's a physicist in Ottawa."

"You have Zoom meetings with physicists?"

"Well," she conceded, "there were hundreds of us. It was with Vaccine Choice Canada."

"Never heard of it," grumbled Raj. "Anyway, what's a physicist know about viruses?"

"So, this professor," I interrupted, "what's he saying about the COVID shots?"

"He's saying there are a lot of dangers with mRNA vaccines that we have not even begun to understand," she replied, pulling back her toasting chunk of rye to check its crispness. "Horrible things can happen. And if you want proof, just look at all the dead ferrets from earlier mRNA experiments."

"Ah," said Raj, "it's still safer than getting the wild virus itself."

"Tell Tiffany Dover that."

"Who?"

"That's that nurse in Tennessee, isn't it?" said Mathéo. "The one who lost consciousness after getting the shot."

"Yeah," said Stefanie. "And she's disappeared ever since. Stopped coming to work. Stopped posting on Facebook."

"Stopped posting on Facebook," said Léo, with mock surprise. "She must be dead, then."

"Freakin' anti-vaxxers," said Raj. "Last Monday the hospital posted a video of her back at work."

Stefanie let out a curt laugh and said, "You mean that silent video with another nurse with darker, curlier hair, a broader face, different eye colour, darker skin and an extra twenty pounds, wearing Dover's name tag?"

"It was bad lighting." Raj shook his head. "People like you wouldn't believe she was alive even if they posted a video of her running a marathon with Robert F. Kennedy, Jr."

Stefanie snorted. "Unless the vaccine really does mutate people, you tell me how her appearance could have changed so much in five days? And why the hospital wouldn't let her talk?" She paused and thrust her bread into the fire. "She's dead or so badly injured she can't even show up for an interview."

"Even if that is true," said Raj, dismissively, "one in a million may die from it. But that's better than one in a hundred dying from freakin' COVID."

"You mean one in a thousand," she corrected. "And that's only if you count people over the age of seventy-five. Otherwise, one in five thousand."

"Whatever," said Raj, pulling off the chunk of burnt bread from his stick. "Still worse than one in a million."

"How do you know it's going to be just one in a million?" said Stefanie sharply. "They've just started testing this thing—*on us*. The COVID-19 injection is not even approved. They've just 'authorized' it for emergency use."

"And," I added, "tell them how you were saying that three percent of people can't even perform normal daily activities after getting the vax."

"Three percent," said Léo. "That's like one in every thirty-three people."

"I don't believe it," said Raj. "Which conspiracy website did you get that fake stat from?"

"The Centers for Disease Control and Prevention," countered Stefanie.

"Well, it's probably just temporary. When people get COVID they can't perform daily activities either."

"Then I'd rather stick to getting a cold," retorted Stefanie, "if it's all the same."

An icy wind hit us from off the river, chilling the heated debate for a second. When it had passed, the soft voice of Mathéo began to speak.

"One mouse says to another: Are you going to get the COVID vaccine? The other mouse says, No way! I'll wait until they're done the human trials."

We laughed so hard Constable Corona would have fined us for excessive breathing.

"Well, hey, guys, let's look on the bright side," said AJ in a cheerful voice. "At least I don't have to go to another family gathering this Christmas. You know, sitting in the living room listening to old people talk about what they did before they were old."

Je suis du même avis." Léo hooted in agreement. "If I hear *Oncle* Jean tell that story again about the day he caught that twenty-pound perch at Manitou Island, I'll turn Jewish just to avoid Christmas."

Mathéo shook his head. "I don't know. I take *Tante* Sofia to her brother's in Sudbury for a big Christmas gathering every year. I'd see my nephew and nieces. I love those guys."

"It's up to us," said Stefanie, "not a politician, how we celebrate Christmas." She removed her well-toasted chunk of bread from the end of her stick and looked at AJ. "Just because you'd rather stay home and read your comic books, doesn't mean it's right to stop other people from getting together."

I could tell she was getting irritated again. I sensed there was something else wrong. I looked at her face flickering orange before the fire. *It must be hard for her having Christmas without Josef,* I thought. Likewise, her father, sister and half her family were back in Bavaria. Here in Canada, it was just her, and her mother in the big city, where they were discouraging family gatherings.

"The whole thing feels wrong to me," I admitted, suddenly feeling devoid of emotion. "Calling off Christmas, I mean. But,

I guess it's just one year. Once they've distributed their vaccines and made a bunch of money, they'll give it a rest. Next year'll be better."

"Yeah, right!" said Stefanie, peeling away the burnt edges from her toast. "You really think they'll back off on this? They're testing us. And we're failing the test."

She tossed her entire piece of bread into the fire.

"Take some freedom away," she continued. "Say it's only for a little while. Let you get used to it. Then say they need to do it just a little longer. Then give it back, but not really. You can go to the store but must wear a mask. Or you can visit Grandma if you keep the visit to thirty minutes and six feet apart."

"Well," said Léo, stretching his arms, "what are we supposed to do? It's not like we can skate away from this."

Raj piped up. "Ah, just take the vax and forget about it. My parents didn't immigrate to Canada so we could lose the family business."

"Yeah," said AJ, "and how long can we live without hockey?"

"You're both freakin' nuts," said Stefanie, and stabbed another chunk of bread with her stick. "They've never managed to make a safe mRNA vaccine. They've been trying for three decades. You think they suddenly figured it out? Even if I was into vaccines, I wouldn't line up to be their guinea pig."

"Easy for you to say," said Raj. "They didn't close down your bakery. You're still working."

She stared at Raj, as she thrust the stick and bread into the fire. "I had a Help Wanted sign up in the window for two months. You never applied."

"Yeah, well, I guess I thought you were looking for psychiatric help. Anyway, I knew I'd be going back to work with Baba's moving company. I'm a mover, not a baker."

"Hey, Raj," I cut in, "that's all I really do. Move bread around."

"Stefanie," said AJ, sympathetically, "it's not that we don't agree with you—more or less. Government does lots of dumbass stuff and this one sure takes the cake. But we gotta survive even if that means paying a vax tax."

Stefanie rose from the log with a flaming stub of bread at the end of her stick.

"Do you really believe that's all they want?" she said, letting her bread burn. "If they wanted more money, they could just start a war in the Middle East or fake a landing on Mars. This is much more diabolical. They want to see if you will obey orders. They want to see how many are compliant enough to wear a dirty mask, go bankrupt hiding from the common cold, and then get injected with a genetic experiment."

"Ah!" hollered Raj, waving his beer can in the air. "You're just blogging out loud, now. It's not 'diabolical.' At worst, it's just a bunch of capitalists turning a crisis into a money-maker."

Stefanie laughed. "Maybe that's where they're coming from. But history shows us that's not where they'll end. It will end when we're all slaves. When everything you do is tracked and approved. When you serve the state until you became too old, sick or obsolete to be of any use—and then they euthanize you."

She paused to fill her lungs. Her body shuddered. Everybody was staring at her. A log in the fire split and crackled.

"Good grief!" she suddenly erupted. "You guys love these superheroes fighting the bad guys. Well, look at our prime minister—a comic book villain come to life. And what about the creep running the World Economic Forum? He looks and sounds like some ghoulish Sith from *Star Wars*. You spend hours watching action movies and playing video games; but you let bureaucrats and rich old geezers scare you into complacency. I'd understand if you were a bunch of seventy-year-old women in a quilting circle—not healthy young men with way too much free time on your hands."

She let out a small groan of frustration, threw her flaming bread into the fire and sat down on the log. In the distance, the ice on the river cracked.

Mathéo cleared his throat and said slowly: "I think she just called us a bunch of wusses."

"And she's probably right," I said.

Silence fell over us. Even Raj was gazing downward, hands folded. Léo was nodding. AJ had crossed his arms and sighed.

And I wore a faint smile of admiration.

I knew Stefanie was right.

We all knew it.

So right.

And yet I was so scared. Not just for me. But for her. I was no history buff, but I knew enough to know what tyrannical governments have done in the past with outspoken voices like hers. I looked at her. The light of the campfire danced in her eyes as she took a sip of cider.

I didn't want anything to happen to her.

59. French Revelations

After the Dandelion's Joan of Arc speech, only the crackling fire made a sound. AJ took off his glasses and rubbed his eyes. Raj grabbed the last can of beer. Mathéo chewed quietly. As for Stefanie, she simply stared into the flames.

Ten minutes of reflection later, suddenly all our heads turned toward the sound of a vehicle pulling into the driveway. I pursed my lips and glanced at Stefanie.

"Mackenzie?" she said, staring at the bright headlights.

AJ took a deep breath, before speaking in cowboy drawl, "Well, pretty lady, we boys might get that chance to redeem our manliness after all."

"Whatever he says or does," I said, "don't back down. Hold your ground."

"If he arrests us," said Stefanie, "it doesn't mean we have to do what he says. You won't get charged with resisting arrest if you simply don't cooperate. Let him carry us if he—"

"Forget that," said Léo. "I'm so sick of this guy, I'll citizen arrest him and call the police myself."

The headlights blinked off. The door opened. A figure stepped out into the dark. The door slammed shut.

We all stood, except Raj.

"Forget it, vigilantes!" he said, crushing his beer can loudly. "It's just my sister. I texted her."

As she approached, we immediately recognized Bindu's East Indian countenance, peering between a scarf and wool hat. Reading from her cellphone, she said, "I got your message, little brother. Breaking rules, evading cops, fleeing on ice. I'm jealous. Yet so proud of you."

"I didn't mean to get involved in this," he countered. "I, just, um... When the cop started, I—"

"Hey, Bindu," said Léo, stepping forward. "Great to see you

back."

It had been nearly four months since she left for school in Thunder Bay.

"Hey, you band of unmasked bandits," she said to us all, granting Léo no special attention. "Couldn't you have waited for me another day before executing an act of civil disobedience?"

Stefanie laughed as she walked over to Bindu and gave her a hug. "Sorry, this was all improv, I swear."

"It was great!" boasted Léo. "Cop shot me in the leg as I was skating away. Boy, that hurt! But thank God, Mathéo's an excellent surgeon."

Mathéo, who was piercing half a loaf of bread with a pointy stick, glanced up and shook his head. "Don't believe a word he says."

"All right. There were no bullets," admitted Léo. "But he fired a few shots with his stun gun. Melted a hole right through the ice."

"He had a taser, not a phaser," said AJ, shaking his head.

"But, yes, Léo's been very brave," I added. "I think Mata will let you marry him now."

"Oh, for goodness' sake," said Raj, knocking Léo aside as he approached his sister.

"You hungry?" Stefanie asked Bindu. "We got bread and cider and... sticks."

"There ain't time," cut in Raj. "If I don't get inside soon, Mathéo really will be amputating my freakin' toes."

"I'll go sterilize the butcher knife," said AJ. He leapt over his log and began sprinting toward the house.

"Screw you!" yelled Raj.

AJ turned, walking backwards. "Just joking. I gotta use the can."

Bindu outstretched her gloved hands toward the heat of the fire. "Looks like Raj has had all he can take of being a free man on the land."

"If the cell's warm, I'll take it," he said, turning toward the van. "And I'd rather get out of here before that cop finds your little anarchist meet-up group."

"Anybody else want a lift home?" said Bindu, sneaking a half-second glance at Léo.

"Count me in!" said Léo, and then turned to Mathéo. "Hey, big guy, you wanna roll with us?"

His stick was now rotating another chunk of sourdough over the fire. "I'm still eating."

"He can get a ride with us," I said. "Right, Stef?"

"Sure."

"All right, I'll grab my gear," said Léo, and he began jogging toward the van.

"How do you open this back door?" shouted Raj, already at the van.

"One sec," I shouted back. "I'll show you."

Five minutes later, I was standing on the country road in front of AJ's, watching the taillights of Bindu's car head back toward Moosehead.

When I returned to the fire, I found Stefanie on Mathéo's log, both speaking in French. After barely passing Mademoiselle Gauthier's grade nine class, I stopped taking *français*. So most of what they were saying was incomprehensible to me. I sat down on the opposite side of the fire.

Mathéo pulled his stick in and felt the toast for crispness. "Bon pain," he said.

Ah, two words I know. Good bread.

Stefanie put her mittened hand on Mathéo's shoulder and said softly, "Vous avez dit avoir vu quelque chose sur la rive du fleuve."

Something about the river. Mathéo nodded and extended the stick back over the fire.

"Qu'as-tu vu?" What did you see?

There was a long silence, before he spoke. "*Je l'ai vu.*" And he looked up at me. Stefanie's head followed. "*Son grand-père.*"

My grandfather?

60. Fourteen Years to Flatten The Human Race

Both Mathéo and Stefanie were staring across the fire at me, silently spooked as if they were looking at a ghost.

"You guys talking about me?" I called out, jokingly.

Stefanie rose and walked toward me. "Don't flatter yourself."

She sat down beside me and stared into the fire.

"You mad at me?" I asked.

"No, but Josef might be." She forced a smile. "Usually, turtles hide at the bottom of a frozen river, waiting for the cold and darkness to pass."

I stretched my neck and rotated it in a circle. "Not hightailing it over the ice, fleeing from cops, carrying their boss in their arms?"

"No," she replied. "Turtles can't skate that fast."

"Sorry, if I, um—"

"It's okay. It was fun. And I think he'll forgive you."

"Ah, yes," I said somewhat anxiously. "Your six-foot-three fiancé."

Not looking at me, she said, "Actually, I've lied about Josef."

"Hmm?"

A pause.

"He's only six foot one."

"Oh. Well, that's a relief," I said. "Then he only has four inches on me."

"Yeah," she said, distantly.

"You miss him?"

She didn't answer.

"Sorry. Stupid question."

She nodded. Even in her bright red Santa hat, she looked pretty sad.

"Well," I said, "maybe once they vax enough of the sheeple, they'll open up the country—"

She started to cry. I immediately wished I had kept my mouth shut.

"Hey," I said, reaching my hand out, but not touching her. "I'm sorry. I can't imagine how it must feel, living separate from the person you love."

"I try to love everyone," she said. Then she looked me in the eye. "Even turtles and *meese*."

I wasn't sure how to take that.

"I think it's time to go," she said and stood up.

"Hey, Mathéo," I said, as I rose up. "We're going to get the van warmed up. Whenever you're done eating, come and find us."

A minute later, Stef and I were sitting on chilled upholstery, in the front seats of the van. I turned the ignition and jacked up the heater; but the vent only blew freezing air at our faces. I slid its shutters downward until it warmed up.

"If you want, I can drop you off first. Then I'll drive Mathéo home, and then..."

She suddenly buried her head in her green mitts. I couldn't hear her crying, but I sensed that she was.

"Is there something else wrong?" I asked, softly.

"We've called it off."

"Called what off?"

"The engagement," she said, sitting back up, her face wet with tears. "The marriage. They're never going to give Josef permission to come to Canada if he isn't vaxxed."

"Well, maybe you could go back to Germany—"

"No," she said.

"Not permanently," I was speaking quickly. "Just to get married, before they start some kind of vaxport. You have German citizenship. They can't turn you away. Once you're married you just bring him to the Canadian consulate. He'll have to learn the anthem, bow to the queen and get dunked in maple syrup and covered with goose feathers; but then, before your pig even learns to whistle, he'll be a full-fledged Canuck. Mathéo and I could run the bakery while you're gone. At least, I think we can."

Stefanie stared up through the windshield at the frozen Wingekisinaw River. "That's sweet of you to offer."

"Yeah," I continued, trying to sound upbeat. "Have a European wedding. I wish I could attend. See you in a big white dress."

She spit out a laugh.

"I'm joking," I said. "I'm sure you'll have a very unconventional wedding—probably in a field dressed as a dandelion."

She leaned forward against the dashboard. This time there was no doubt she was crying.

"Hey," I put a hand on her back. "It'll work out. Most people would kill to be married in Europe."

She sat back up and wiped her eyes with her green scarf. "No, it's not going to work."

"Oh, come on, Captain D. You're the last person this side of the French River to balk at a little government bureaucracy."

"No." She sniffed, holding back more tears. "Josef. He, he's already got the jab."

"*What?* How do you know?"

"After you left, this afternoon. When he Skyped. He really trusts Trump. Says the vax is just 'optics' so we can go back to normal."

"Optics?"

"He says the pandemic is fake. The vax is fake. Big Pharma gets its money, we get our freedom. All hail Donald J. Trump."

I pulled off my winter toque, starting to feel hot, even though the heater had barely made a difference yet.

"But," I said, "how'd Josef get the shot so soon?"

"Remember, he's a paramedic," she said. "Frontline worker."

"Oh yeah," I said. "But, I mean, so what? He got the jab. He seemed fine today, on Skype. Wasn't having a stroke or anything. He'll probably be okay."

"Who knows?" she said. "And who knows how he'll be after the third, fourth, fifth... or eighth shot?"

"Eight shots? I thought it was just one, maybe two."

"Ha!" she said rather than laughed. "It'll be endless. Eventually he'll get sick. I know it. How could he not?"

"I guess that's the 'for better or worse, sickness or health,' part of the marriage vow."

"And it might make him infertile," she continued. "The spike protein is similar to sperm. His immune system could attack his testes. Chemical castration."

I removed my gloves and unzipped my jacket. It was getting way too hot in that little van.

"Bill Gates already uses vaccines in Africa as a form of birth control. We might not be able to have any children. Or if we do, they could be deformed, or sick, or..."

She popped open the glove compartment and pulled out some tissue paper.

"Oh," I said, stunned more by her motherly ambitions than her revelations about Gates' eugenics hobby. "You didn't strike me as the child-bearing type."

"I am a woman, if you haven't noticed."

"Sure..." I stumbled. "I mean, of course, I've noticed. I mean, I thought, you'd be more, um, liberated."

She snorted. "Phooey! I don't buy into any of that women's lib, human depopulation nonsense."

"But how can you run a bakery and have a child?"

She shrugged. "Baby sling. Women have been making food and raising children for thousands of years."

"Yeah," I said. "Um, and, I.... I'm sure you'd make a great mom. The best, really."

She closed her eyes. "Well, it doesn't look like it's going to happen."

Slowly, as if she was disarming a bomb, she slid the green emerald ring from her finger, set it in the glove compartment and then closed its door with a click.

"He's right," she said. "We are literally a world apart. He and his QAnon buddies think by getting the clot shot they're flattening the curve. All they are really doing is flattening the human race."

"You really think the vaccine is that dangerous?"

"It's not a vaccine!" she exclaimed, pulling off her Santa hat and slapping it down on the dashboard. "It's a bioweapon! He'll see. I'm not crazy! He's the crazy one. He knows it. A quarter of the healthy young subjects in the Pfizer–Moderna trial ended up in the hospital. That was only after two shots and six weeks. What about after eight shots and fourteen years? And who knows, really, whether they are even using the same concoction as they did in the trial?"

"I don't get why he's doing it then," I said. "Josef's no dummy."

"He wants to keep his job. He wants life to go back to normal. He said it's the only way they'll let him on a plane so he can come and marry me. But I don't want to marry him if..."

She shuddered.

"He says he still loves me. And I know I love him. But... love isn't always enough, is it?" She chuckled softly, almost maniacally, then shook her head, tears flowing quietly. "I thought he was the one I'd be spending the rest of my life with."

What could I say? Life was unpredictable? Uncertain? Grandad always said, if all you have to say is a cliché, best not say anything at all.

"Last December," she continued, "we spent Christmas together at his parents' place in the mountains in Bavaria. If you had told me that by this Christmas we'd have been separated for twelve months because the world was scared of the common cold, I would have laughed. It's too hard to believe."

"Yeah," I said.

"I just blow him kisses over a Skype connection. It's all..." She trailed off and laughed softly. "I'm sorry. I'm just babbling."

"No, no," I said. "It's good to talk. And to have someone to listen. If it wasn't for Grandad's ear I'd be a total basket case by now." I paused, feeling how much I missed him. "You gotta be easy on yourself. You're in shock. It's almost like Josef is—"

I stopped myself, but she finished for me.

"Dead," she said. "Yes. Like he dissolved into the internet. I don't know him anymore. Or maybe I never did. I can't believe he would cave so easily..."

New tears ran down her eyes.

The side door of the van rattled opened. I looked back.

"Hey, Mathéo," I said, as he lumbered in.

Stefanie inhaled deeply and forced a cheerful tone, saying, "You can use any of the sacks of grain for a seat, if you like. Make a couch if you like."

"Merci," he said.

"De rien," she replied.

The door rattled closed.

"Time to go?" I asked.

She nodded as she looked ahead into the night.

I felt really sad for her.

And, I'm ashamed to say, happy for me.

61. A Tree Laughing in the Frozen Dark

"Sorry, big guy, there's not much for comfort back there," I said, over my shoulder, as I drove down Queen Street back into town.

Mathéo didn't say anything. I glanced back to see he had made a shallow sofa for himself out of the sacks of wheat and rye in the back of the van.

"We'll drop you off first," I continued.

No response.

In the passenger seat, Stefanie twisted her upper body around so she could face the silent one.

"Mathéo?" she said.

"Oui?" he responded, softly.

"Do you have any Indigenous blood?"

If I was a cat, my ears would have perked up.

"Non." He replied immediately. "Je suis français."

"But French settlers married among the First Nations. Are you sure you don't have even a little Indigenous DNA?"

"Je suis sûr."

"How can you be so sure you're not a bit mixed?" I asked, sounding unintentionally offended. "Sudbury's like the Métis capital of Ontario."

"My mother had one of those ancestry DNA tests," replied Mathéo. "It said she was 100 percent European. Mainly French and Belgian."

"What about your dad?" I asked.

"He was born in France."

"Oh, yeah," I said.

Stefanie turned back in her seat. "Hmm."

Ten minutes later, I brought the van to a halt in front of Mathéo's apartment building. He lived alone in a bachelor flat.

"Here you go," I said. "I'll bet you'll sleep well tonight."

"I'm not sure," said Mathéo, as he reached over and opened the sliding van door.

"Joy-ex No-well!" I tried to pronounce.

After all, I did remember what 'Merry Christmas' was in French.

"Pardon?" asked Mathéo.

Just not how to pronounce it.

"He said Joyeux Noël," repeated Stefanie.

"Pareillement," said Mathéo and he dropped out onto the parking lot.

Stefanie powered down her window and stuck out her head. "You seeing your folks for Christmas?"

"No," I barely heard him say.

I cleared my throat and spoke softly. "Mathéo's parents died a while back."

Stefanie glanced at me, shock in her face. "Oh." She turned back to the window, but Mathéo had already walked around the van, moving toward the front doors of the low-rise unit. I powered down my window and shouted, "Come by the bakery tomorrow. I have access to an all-you-can-eat supply of ginger-bread men."

He turned and smiled. "Maybe I will."

"Okay!" And then pumping my fist in the air, I cheered: "Moosehead Pirates of the Wingekisinaw!"

He shook his fist in the air and turned back toward the building.

I powered up the window and pressed down on the acceler-ator.

"He acts like a calm old Indian chief," said Stefanie.

"Is that why you were asking him if he had Indian DNA? Be-cause he acts like the reincarnation of Sitting Bull?"

"No."

I turned onto Main St.

"Why were you asking, then?"

"You know why."

I laughed. "I do?" Did I?

"He saw your grandad on the bank of the river. Just like you did."

"Grandad? I didn't see Grandad."

"You called out 'Grandad' just before stopping on the ice."

"Oh, that!" I tried to sound nonchalant. "That's just an ex-pression I have when I get startled. You know, like some people say, 'Christ!' or 'Gadzooks!'"

"Or jeepers," she added.

"Yeah, exactly."

"You're a bad liar, Vince."

I glanced over at her.

"You've never called me Vince before." *Always Vincent.*

"I figure, if I'm going to call you a liar, I should be informal about it."

"That's sweet of you."

"I specialize in sourdough."

We were passing into the downtown strip. Only a day and a half before Christmas. All the stores would normally be flicker-ing with coloured lights. This year, only a few.

"Okay, yeah," I admitted. "I thought I saw him. But it was just a trick of the mind. I saw this movie once about this guy, Aaron

Ralston. Got trapped in a canyon in Utah. Three-hundred-pound boulder pinned his arm down. After five days, with only his own urine to drink, he was dehydrated, famished and sleepless. Started seeing visions of people who weren't there."

"I don't remember any of us drinking our own urine."

"No, but... but stress. You know. Constable Corona chasing us out into the bush. I was so sure he would appear on the bank and taser us all. I was freakin'."

"Maybe," she conceded.

"Yeah," I said.

"But probably not."

I let out a sigh of exasperation and hit the brakes, having almost passed the bakery.

"It was just a tree, then," I said, as I backed up a little.

"A tree?"

I forced a laugh. "A tree is more believable than my eighty-eight-year-old grandfather standing in the bush, in the dark, in twenty below zero, laughing at me."

"So he was laughing, too?"

"The tree was, yes."

I felt my nostrils flare out as I gripped the steering wheel, even though we were stationary.

Stefanie put her hand on my shoulder. "If he hadn't told you that you'd missed the Wingekisinaw, we'd still be out there in minus twenty."

I glanced at the time on the dashboard. "Yeah, we'd probably have reached the urine-drinking stage by now."

I chuckled, nervously.

She didn't laugh.

"Let's get real," I said. "How could it be Grandad?"

"Keep driving, and I'll tell you."

"But we're at the bakery. I can walk home."

"You're going to be sore enough in the morning. Let's go to your place. I'll drive the van back."

I really didn't want to get back out in the cold, so I continued down Main Street, hoping we could change the subject.

"It must have been a vision," she said.

I sighed.

"Okay, listen," I began. "I know people think anyone with

some Indigenous DNA are having visions all over the place—while checking emails, brushing our teeth, walking to work—but trust me, it's not happening. Maybe other natives are on a perpetual vision quest. I don't know. But it's not happening with my sliver of Ojibwe DNA."

"You're a quarter Ojibwe," she corrected. "Hardly a sliver. That's one-and-a-half slices of pie."

"Well, all I'm saying is that it was probably just my subconscious finding a clever way to tell me we'd missed the turnoff."

"Then why did Mathéo also see him?"

"Ah, he just heard me yell 'Grandad.' Jumped to the same conclusion."

"Mathéo doesn't strike me as the kind of guy who jumps to conclusions."

I grinned at her. "It's hard to read those silent types."

I turned onto Magder Road.

"Did your grandad ever have visions?" she asked.

I extended my fingers outward, still gripping the steering wheel with my thumbs. "Sure. Yeah, I mean, he's mentioned seeing his ancestors. Usually after dehydrating himself in his sweat lodge." I shrugged and glanced at her. "You really buy into all that Indigenous spiritual mumbo-jumbo, don't you?"

She didn't respond.

"Anyway, it's always *dead* ancestors. I guess they're seeing their ghosts. But not living people. At least, I've never heard of that."

"Ahem," she uttered softly.

"Therefore," I continued with emphasis, "I *couldn't* have seen Grandad, because he's still alive. And Mathéo couldn't have either, because he's as white as a French baguette."

I laughed. She stared silently ahead.

"Maybe you need to check on him," she said.

"Yeah," I said putting my hand to my head. "I'm a little worried about the big guy being all alone over Christmas."

"Not Mathéo. Grandad. Make sure he's okay."

My chest seized. I suddenly felt sourdough and apple cider creeping back up my esophagus. I gulped back the burning stomach acid. "I talked to Grandad last night. He was fine." I coughed. "Just a little cough. Nothing."

"Why not find out for sure?"

I looked at the time on the dashboard: 8:52 p.m. "It's too late. I'd just be waking him up. They serve dinner there at five. By eight he's a goner."

"Can't you call the nursing station? Front desk?"

"Yeah, I can do that."

I pulled into my parent's driveway, halting almost bumper to bumper with Dad's Buick. "All right, the getaway vehicle's all yours."

"Please call Claudia," she said.

"I will."

"I have an uneasy feeling," she added, eyes blinking rapidly.

"He's fine."

"Can you call now? You have your cell."

"You said cellphones give you cancer."

"I'll take the risk. Please call."

I inhaled audibly. "All right." I pulled out my phone and began scrolling through the contact list until I came to Moosehead Long Term Care. It rang five times before a Latino accent answered.

"Claudia! Hi, it's Vince."

"Oh, hi," she said, sounding distracted.

"Yeah, hi. I was just wanting to check on Grandad. He had a cough yesterday. I had to work late today. Been on the run all evening—" I shot Stefanie a grin. "—and couldn't call earlier."

"Yeah." Claudia spoke hesitantly, not in her usual abrupt tone. "Yeah, it's crazy here, too. So many people sick."

"What about Grandad?"

"He's sleeping. I was just in there."

"Is he okay?"

A long pause.

"He's asleep. Not much more I can say."

"He's not coughing."

"No, he's sound asleep."

"Yeah, I was just wondering how—"

There was another voice speaking to Claudia from a distance.

"Hey, Vince, I gotta go. We're short-staffed. Two attendants are in quarantine."

"I need help with Sofia," said the voice in the background. "She's had diarrhea again."

"Okay, I understand," I said quickly. "Good luck."

"Yeah. Chao."

The call ended. I slipped the phone back into my jacket and let out a sigh. "Sounds like he's doing better than Mathéo's aunt. I don't think he'd take it well if she—"

Stefanie pursed her lips.

"But, there we go," I said in a more upbeat tone. "Grandad's still alive. Mathéo's not Métis. And I don't take magic mushrooms. It was just a tree laughing in the dark."

"I'm glad he's okay," she said. "It's a relief."

Silence fell. She was frowning, eyes cast down.

"What about you?" I asked. "Are you going to be okay?"

"Hmm?" she responded, without looking at me.

"I mean, with, um, Josef and you calling off the—"

"Yeah," she said quickly. "At least I can stop waiting. That's a relief."

I stared at her, not sure what to do. *Hug her?*

"I'll see you tomorrow," she said. "Eight thirty sharp! We have an army of gingerbread men to deploy."

I glanced into the back of the van, where the moose mask stared at me from the darkness. "You hear that, Moosey? We got work to do!"

I nodded at Stefanie and quickly opened the door. As I stepped out, she shuffled over to the driver's seat.

"See ya tomorrow," I said.

"Thank you, Vincent."

"Sure."

She pulled the door closed. I backed away toward the lawn. She pulled in reverse a foot or two, then stopped, and powered down the window.

"Vince!"

"Yeah?"

"It was an unforgettable first date," she said quickly, almost giggling.

My mouth opened, but nothing came out. Which is probably what she preferred. She immediately backed the van out of the driveway. I stood, watching the headlights zoom past the five hundred blinking Christmas lights around the McLean's house.

All fatigue had left me. My heart felt open and radiating heat. The freezing night had lost its bite. I couldn't wait to return to work the next morning and see her again. Little did I suspect that when I did see her again, I wouldn't even recognize her.

62. Hats, Mitts and Sanity

As I unlaced my boots in the front hallway, I heard Dad's voice from the living room.

"Hey, Vince."

He spoke slowly, devoid of energy. Was he drunk? Probably getting there. I walked to the living room threshold.

"Hey, Dad." I spoke as nonchalantly as I could after a night of fleeing from a cop.

Dad sat in the chair by the fireplace. A flaming log licked at the brickwork. A stubby Christmas tree, covered with white lights, glowed beside him. The warm room and the aroma of pine felt comforting. Not often did Dad stoke the fire or even sit in the living room. He usually didn't stray far from the minibar in the basement. Nonetheless, he had a bottle of red wine at his side. Red wine was usually saved for special occasions.

"Everything okay, Dad?" I asked, remaining in the hallway.

He had bags under his eyes and a cloth mask hanging loose under his chin.

"Vince," he said, gravely, "your grandad. He's sick."

"Sick?" My heart skipped a beat as I walked to the centre of the room. "Yeah, I know. He has a cough."

"Fever," said Dad. "They tested him for COVID." He paused. "He's positive."

"Uh-huh," I said. "That test is so sensitive it doesn't mean much." I pulled out my phone. "I literally just called the home. Claudia said he was sleeping fine."

"That's because that's what I told her to tell you."

"What?"

"We thought it better you hear it from us," said Mom, coming out of the kitchen and putting her hands on my shoulders from behind.

"Hear what? That he's sick?"

"Vince," Dad said, almost in a whisper. "He's dying."

I immediately felt pressure against my tear ducts. Pulling away from Mom, I exclaimed, "That's nuts. He's sleeping. He has a fever."

Dad sighed. "He's eighty-seven years old."

"Eighty-eight," I corrected. "His birthday was in November."

Dad nodded. "Doctor was in today. Said his oxygen was very low. Nothing he could do. Too old for a ventilator."

"Dad," I said. "We gotta get him out of there. He's locked up all day in a dirty room. Eating frozen dinners. No fresh air. Of course, he's going to get sick."

"They're giving him morphine so he'll feel no pain."

I sat down on the couch, letting my hands rest on my knees. "Morphine? That's like freakin' heroin. That'll kill him."

Mom put her hands together. "There's nothing we can really do at this point. Just pray."

I stood up. "This is insane." My eyes scanned the wall, stopping on the photo of Dad as a boy with Grandad, fishing. "How can you leave him in there? He can move into my room. It's big enough for two beds."

"Absolutely not," exclaimed Mom.

She stepped into the living room and faced me head on. Her hands were shaking until she clenched them tight. "We love your Grandad, but we can't have him bringing COVID into this home. Not until we are all vaccinated, at least."

"Vaccinated?" My mouth hung open. "I'm not submitting to no medical experiments."

Dad swigged back his wineglass and set it on the table beside him. "If you want to live under my roof, you sure as hell are goin' to get jabbed."

It felt like Dad had just stabbed me with a bayonet. Suddenly, I wasn't good enough if I didn't have some pharmaceutical injection.

"Until everybody's vaccinated, no one is safe," recited Dad. "Especially your grandad."

"My grandad?" I clenched my teeth. "Why do you always call him *my* grandad? He's your father!"

"I don't appreciate your tone."

I glared at him.

Dad's head swayed to the side, his eyes glazed over, and he reached for the wine bottle to refill his glass. Mom stepped forward and returned her hands to my shoulders, looking me in the eye. "We all know you love Paul as much as any grandchild could."

"Yeah," said Dad. "I can't imagine how hard this is for you. And, hell, that ol' Ojibwe may pull through. He survived TB back in the res school. He just as well could live through COVID. Either way, until we're all vaccinated the virus is going to keep wiping out the elderly."

"The virus?" I said. "Neglect is wiping out the elderly. Remember what the Armed Forces found in the spring? Nursing homes with cockroaches, clogged feeding tubes, rotting food..."

"They're doing the best they can," said Dad.

"They don't even give them baths each week. How healthy is that?"

"Healthier than having infected staff breathing on them."

"It's the common cold, not the bubonic plague."

Mom stepped back beside Dad, who was grinning.

"Whatever you say, Dr. Vince," he said with a chuckle.

I wanted to slap him. Instead, I clenched my fist tight and slid it into my pants pocket like a concealed weapon.

"Either way," continued Dad, swirling his wine glass in a circle, "the lockdowns aren't going away until everybody has been immunized. Right or wrong. Like it or not. That's the reality."

I looked at them both. They gazed back with concerned eyes.

Maybe Dad's right. Maybe Josef was right. I closed my eyes and breathed slowly through my nose. *If we just take their damn vaccine, then they'll leave us and Grandad alone. Let the government print more money and give it to the pharma giants for their placebo. Then we can burn our face masks, end the lockdowns, and put to rest this Monty Python act.*

Suddenly, relieved, my mind settled into that quiet space we all have in our hearts. Except this time the heart had something to say. And it spoke with the voice of a dandelion.

"Yeah, right," I found myself saying aloud. "This won't end with a vaccine. That would only be the beginning."

"Holy guacamole," exclaimed Dad, with exasperation. "I think it would be good if you could talk to someone other than that German baker."

I opened my eyes.

"Maybe Father Lacombe?" said Mom.

"I'm not talking to Lacombe." I said it slowly, shaking my head. "I can't stand that arrogant bas—"

"Vince!" gasped Mom, making the sign of the cross. "He's a priest."

I shrugged. The calmness I'd briefly experienced was now breaking apart like ice on the river in spring, revealing the rushing water underneath.

"God knows," said Dad with a snicker, "we're not sending you to Father Shostakovich. He makes your girlfriend look sane." He set his near-empty wine glass on the side table and pulled out his iPhone. "Hey, there's this number you can call. It's free." He tapped on the screen and handed his phone to me:

ConnexOntario: Ontario's mental health, addictions and problem gambling help line, which can provide contact information for local mental health and addictions services and supports, including crisis lines. 1-866-531-2600

I exhaled, shaking my head. Here Dad's getting pissed drunk every night of the week and he wants me to call an addiction hotline.

"You're kidding?"

I handed the phone back. Dad tossed it on the side table, picked up the wine glass and drained it.

"Vince," said Mom. She stepped toward me. I stepped back. "Vince, we know how devastating it must be for you to know Grandad is..." Her voice trailed off.

"I'm outta here." I sidestepped back into the hallway, pulled my chilled jacket off the rack and slipped my arms in.

"Dear, where are you going?" pleaded Mom, following me. "It's freezing out there."

I slipped into my boots, not bothering to tie them.

"Let him go," said Dad. "He needs to clear his head."

I grabbed my hat, mitts and sanity.

"I'm not coming back," I declared. "This isn't my home

anymore."

I didn't mean it. Or did I? Either way, it proved to be rather prophetic.

I opened the door and stepped out into the frozen dark.

63. The Facts and the Fury

I ran down Magder Road, past the glow of the McLean's five million kilowatt Christmas lit home. At Main Street I made a left. I ran past the Green Dragon, banging into Mr. Chung's CURB SIDE TAKE OUT sign. I ran through an empty town square, where light streamed out of Mayor Hill's office window. I ran up Queen Street, passing Brian Peckford Park, scanning the empty field for a police cruiser. I crossed the Louis Riel Bridge over the French River, glimpsing our abandoned hockey nets tipped over on the ice. I ran past St. Jerome's, wondering if Father Shostakovich was praying for us sinners.

I continued running until I reached the front steps of Moosehead Long Term Care. Those very steps were the last place I had seen Grandad when I wheeled him back on that last Sunday in October—before the premier renewed his second prison sentence. The red and golden leaves that once covered the lawn had been since raked up, bagged and hauled away for compost. The frozen brown grass that persisted looked all the more grim in the dark night. Above, the wind had carried in cloud cover which now blocked the moon and stars.

The world felt cold, dark and deathly.

I climbed the front steps, two at a time, and slammed my mitt on the buzzer. No answer. I kept on pressing the plastic button with my right hand as my left yanked at the front door. Locked! I banged on the glass and peered inside. I saw no one at the reception desk.

Letting go of the door handle, I pulled off a sweaty mitt. My fingers hovered in front of the keypad beside the door. What was the code? I hadn't been inside in nearly a year.

My index finger punched four numbers, 4891. The small LED flashed red.

I tried 6771. Another red light.

"Come on!"

I pounded the buzzer again.

And then I remembered, 5121.

Green flashing light. Click!

I pulled the door open and burst into the empty lobby. It felt like I walked into a sauna—it was so hot and dry. I unzipped my jacket and let my eyes adjust to the bright lights.

Framed prints of Algonquin Park—landscape paintings by the Group of Seven—covered the walls. The place looked more like an art gallery than a medical penitentiary. Hallways extended to the right and left. I turned left, heading for the stairwell. Railings flanked each side of the hallway. Behind closed doors, TVs blared with a cacophony of commercials, news reports, and the voice of Jimmy Stewart confronting the miserly Mr. Potter.

In past years, at Christmastime, these hallways were hanging with multicoloured Christmas ball ornaments, the railings decorated with glitter and the lobby framed with blinking lights. Other than a limp and semi-leafless poinsettia at reception, nothing suggested that St. Nicholas soon would be there.

Before I made much progress down the cheerless hallway, one of the doors opened. A gown, mask, visor and pair of gloves walked out. As the figure turned to me, I saw Claudia's black hair stretched back in a tight ponytail and her eyes popping out of her head. She froze. I think she thought I was an intruder. And, I guess, I was.

I pulled off my black wool hat. "It's me, Vince,"

"What you doing here?" she said under her breath.

"Why did you lie to me?" I retorted with unexpected fury.

"What?"

"You said Grandad was sleeping."

"Your father thought—"

I cut in. "Did you give him a sedative, as well as the morphine?"

"You can't be in here."

"Being drugged isn't the same as sleeping. And sedatives can kill. Just like morphine. Lungs get so relaxed they can't breathe."

The short Latino took a few steps toward me. "You don't even have a mask."

"Phooey!" I cried, flailing out my arms, suddenly feeling

possessed by a dandelion. "Stop pretending all that muzzling is doing anything."

She stopped about twelve feet away and bowed her head slightly. "I'm sorry. I wanted to tell you. But... privacy rules. Your father—"

"Doesn't care about him," I interrupted. "He doesn't care if Grandad dies."

Claudia inhaled and exhaled, causing her mask to drop below her nose. "No one lives forever, you know."

"I know that! It's you people who've forgotten. Locking him up like a POW to protect him from the inevitable."

Her eyes narrowed. "Hey," she said weakly, pulling her mask back up over her nose. "I don't make the rules."

"No, you just execute them. Like you execute your patients."

She jerked, crossed her arms as if she was hugging herself, and whimpered slightly.

"Did you give him the morphine injection?" I asked.

"I, I was—"

"Just obeying orders."

"He has COVID. The doctor didn't want him to suffer."

"COVID! COVID! COVID!" I exclaimed, louder than the TVs. "I'm so sick of hearing about COVID. What is COVID, anyway? Some code word for euthanizing the sick and elderly?"

She pulled out her phone. Her hand was shaking.

"How do you even know if he has COVID?" I took a step toward her.

She stepped back. "They did a PCR test."

I rolled my eyes. "Tarot cards would have been cheaper." My heart was now beating faster than when I was running.

"He couldn't sleep," pleaded Claudia. "Coughing a lot. I know COVID when I see it."

"Yeah, and how is it any different from the flu?"

Her mask stretched down, showing that her mouth had opened but no words escaped.

"What other symptoms does he have?"

She paused. "Like I said. Coughing a lot. Fever. Low oxygen."

"How low?"

"I'm not sure."

"Below ninety?"

She didn't respond.

"Yeah, that's what I thought." I raised my index finger. "I just ran here. And I'm furious. You put an oximeter on my finger and I bet you it's lower than Grandad's. Maybe you should give me a morphine injection too?"

I didn't sound like myself. Six months with the Dandelion had made me bolder, smarter. Most of the time I only half understood what she was telling me. How blood oxygen saturations around ninety is hardly life-threatening. How the PCR tests were run at too high a threshold. How the vaccine was never tested for safety. How suicides are counted as COVID deaths. How lockdowns are killing ten people for every one person they *might* be helping. The facts and the fury had all been fermenting in my brain like a super slow batch of sourdough. Now the sour truth was bubbling with outrage.

"What about his blood sugar?" I demanded. "What was his last reading?"

"Uhh, a little high," she said, followed by a deep inhale.

"How high?"

"I can't remember every blood sugar."

"Did you give him insulin?"

"The doctor didn't think—"

"No, hey, why waste insulin on a diabetic with COVID? Just let him die."

"Vince." She reached a hand out to the railing, looking like she was going to faint. Instead, she started to cry. Her other hand dropped her phone back into her uniform's oversized pocket and then covered her eyes, knocking her visor to the ground. "I'm... I'm so tired."

I stepped closer.

"No entiendo nada. Yo... Yo..." Her voice trailed off. She looked at me. Cheeks wet. "I love taking care of all of them. *Son mis abuelos*. They're all my grandmas and my grandpas. I didn't sign up to be their jailer. I'm not a bad person." She continued to cry. "I don't know what to do. If I don't do what Andrew says, then he'll fire me. Who will take care of them, then? If they are going to die, I can at least—"

I stepped closer, inhaled, put a hand on her shoulder. She was as much a prisoner as the residents. "Claudia," I said softly.

"I'm sorry. I just want to see Grandad."

A few paces behind Claudia a door swung open. A tall female attendant with blonde hair stepped out. Claudia immediately pushed herself away from the wall and picked up her visor. The attendant glared at me with disgust. She looked about thirty, wore white running shoes and had irises so black it was impossible to make out her pupils.

"What the hell is going on?"

"Hey, relax," said Claudia. "He's here to help."

"Like hell he is," she shot back and she began stomping toward us.

64. Turtle Albino

The blonde attendant abruptly ended her stampede toward Claudia and me at about six feet's distance, as if she had hit an invisible barrier.

"You!" she barked at me. "Out of here. Now!"

I'd never seen this attendant before; but I had the eerie impression she knew who I was.

"He's here to help with Paul," said Claudia.

"We don't need his help."

"I'm family," I said.

"I don't care if you're the premier." She pulled out her iPhone and aimed its lens at me, followed by the sound of a camera shutter. "It's against the rules. We could get fired. No visitors allowed. And for God's sake," she said to Claudia, "he doesn't even have a mask."

"He's not a visitor," said Claudia. "He's staff. I just hired him."

"Andrew didn't say anything about—"

Claudia pointed to me. "Minimum wage to start. Twelve-hour shift. You're already three hours late. Come with me. We'll get you suited up."

She turned and began walking back toward the lobby. I nodded at the masked attendant and followed Claudia.

"We need to clear this with Andrew," called out the blonde maniac, her squishy running shoes keeping step with us.

"Andrew's on a plane to Tahiti," said Claudia, without stopping.

"Tahiti?" said the attendant. "Andrew's in Tahiti?'

"No lockdown or outbreak is gonna stop his Christmas vacation."

"But... we can't just let anybody in here. Has he even had a COVID test? Andrew will—"

"Screw Andrew! Screw the test!" Claudia swung around to face the attendant, who was a foot taller than her but suddenly seemed smaller. "I'm in charge! We can't keep up. People are *dying*. The place is a mess. Sofia will probably need an IV. George, Melinda and Grace all need diapers changed. Rosa still has to be fed. Alice needs help with Zoom so she can see her grandkids. We still haven't got dinner trays out of all the rooms. We need help, not stupid protocols."

The attendant's forehead creased.

"Please," said Claudia, in a calmer voice. "Vince is here to help Paul. Palliative care. Do you want Paul to be alone right now?"

The attendant looked at me.

"I'm his grandson."

"I know who you are," she said, as if my real name was Adolf Hitler, Jr. She turned back to Claudia and said nervously, "But what if he has COVID?"

Claudia threw her arms up. "Ha! Who cares? Half the residents have COVID."

The attendant's phone buzzed. She answered it.

"Yes, Sofia. I'm coming. Just hold on." She hung up and muttered something under her breath before looking at me. "Just stay away from the other patients." She turned and marched off.

Claudia took a deep breath and said, "This way."

I followed the five-foot-two nurse past the lobby to the opposing hallway. On the right, we passed the dining area. Plastic trays with dirty dishes and half-eaten meals, brought back from people's rooms, covered the unused tables. A drop cloth hid the piano.

We turned left into the nursing station. Boxes of masks, gloves and hand sanitizers, intermixed with empty boxes of Trozzi's pizza, covered the large desk and three chairs. Shelves were strewn with gowns, bandages, and PCR kits. A transparent garbage bag, full of empty cans of diet Coke, sat atop two large cardboard boxes. On the sides of the unopened boxes, in black marker, was written "xmas decorations."

Claudia grabbed a small box of surgical masks and extended it to me, at arm's length. I stared at the 3M box as if she was offering me street drugs.

"You know," I said, hesitantly, "not one randomized control trial has found these masks do anything to protect anybody."

"Humour me," she said, tossing the box at me. "I'm trying to not get fired."

I slowly pulled a mask out by the string and stretched it around my face. I hadn't worn a mask (without antlers) since I started working at the bakery. I gazed into a mirror hanging on the wall. The mask was white, not green; nonetheless, it made me feel like a turtle—an albino turtle.

I pinched it tight around my nose, smelling the synthetic material, wondering whether they were really made with graphene oxide.

Is the Corona Goddess of Death now appeased? I thought. *May I now enter her sanctum?*

"Put these on, too," said Claudia, extending a box of gloves.

Apparently, the ritual was not over. I stretched the blue latex around my toxic hands. Holding them out, I said to Claudia, "Mis manos."

My Spanish was on par with my French.

She squinted and said questioningly: "Si, manos."

"Manos," I repeated. "Manos. Man. Hu-man. Hands are what make us different from animals. Our hands. Our face."

She handed me a visor.

"Our eyes," I said, pulling the visor over my head. "The window to our souls."

Next she held out a long blue plastic robe. I slipped my arms through the opening and tied it at the back.

I breathed out and didn't breathe back in for a few seconds. I now looked like her. Like all of them. I had been... assimilated.

Claudia sighed, blowing out the edges of her mask. "*Listo?*"

I raised an eyebrow.

"*Listo,*" she repeated. "It means ready."

I nodded. "Si, señorita."

But I wasn't *listo.*

I wasn't ready to say *adios*.

65. A Hellhole Before Paradise

Claudia stepped out of the elevator and turned right. I followed her onto the second floor, passing down its hallway. As on the first floor, there was no sign of Christmas, other than the odd carol playing on the other side of a resident's door. Before COVID, I remembered, most residents kept their doors open day and night. It made it easier for them to get out and the attendants to check in on them. Now, every single door was shut.

I shook my head as we passed, seeing light escaping underneath each door. The gap was so wide, a baby mouse, not to mention an airborne particle, could easily enter. The only thing the old folks were being protected from was human contact.

We stopped at Grandad's room. His door was labelled 206 Paul McKnight. Claudia opened the door.

"Keep your mask on," she said. "And don't forget—"

"Claudia!"

I turned to see the attendant with the short blonde hair marching toward us from the end of the hall.

"Sofia threw up again. More diarrhea."

Claudia sighed, as her hands dropped, hitting the sides of her thighs. "*Dios ayúdame*," she whispered, and then moved briskly toward the attendant. "Get an IV pole."

"We've used the last one."

"Get the one out of Bill's room. God knows he don't need it now."

"But Bill," she stuttered, "he's still there, isn't he?"

"Just get it!"

Claudia sped toward Sofia's room and vanished through its door, as the attendant rushed past me toward the elevator, muttering obscenities.

In a few seconds, I was alone in the hallway before Grandad's open door. I stepped inside, passing the two-piece restroom on my right and an open closet on the left. Stepping into his actual living space, I gasped. I'd forgotten how small his cell was. It barely allowed for the single bed, nightstand, bookshelf, table and chair. Before COVID it was just a place he came to sleep. A literal bedroom. Now it was his world. His small world. A world that smelt of mold and urine.

"God," I whispered, "let him live and I'll get him out of here. Somehow."

A reading lamp beside the bed cast a dim light on his pale face. Grandad lay in the bed on his back. Before I saw his face, I saw his shoes, still on his feet, sticking out from under the blanket.

I moved to the window and opened it slightly. Cold air seeped in. But at least it was fresh air. Either way, the room was so hot I doubted Grandad would freeze to death. That's when I noticed the tray on the nightstand: an untouched plate of peas, mashed potatoes, two slices of roast beef, a slice of sourdough from the bakery, and three insects (which I could not identify) swimming in a melted bowl of ice cream.

"So much for sanitization."

I immediately took the tray, stepped back out into the hallway, and set it on the floor.

Returning, I pulled the chair up beside his bed, adjusted the lamp and looked down at him. His long white hair was splayed out over the pillow, as he sucked air in and out noisily through an open mouth.

"Close your mouth and save your life!" he'd say anytime he caught me walking around with an open mouth. "Breathing with your mouth is like eating with your nose."

"Grandad," I whispered.

His mouth closed and he stopped breathing completely. A calm fell on the room. Seconds passed. Then his nostrils flared. His mouth opened again. The snoring resumed.

To my right, on the wall, hung a large-screen TV. Every room came with one. Grandad probably didn't even know how to turn it on. Pictures of me, Dad, Mom, Grandma, Uncle Thomas and Aunt Linda flanked either side of the screen. Uncle Thomas was still a teenager in the photo, dressed in an Elizabethan tunic, on stage at the Stratford Festival. Aunt Linda looked even younger, wearing a dress, standing in front of St. Jerome's with Grandma. A layer of dust rested on the frames, as well as the TV and the bookshelf. And even in the dim light, I could see scuff marks and grit on the old wood floor.

"Grandad," I said, "just hold on another night. The room over Mr. Chung's is still vacant. And I get free food from the bakery. We can live off rye bread and nut butter. Breakfast, lunch and dinner. You know, the bread you like so much? At first, I found it tasted too sharp, too sour. But now, I love her. It. I love it. The bread."

Grandad's mouth moved a little. He groaned.

Then his eyes opened.

"Grandad!" He stared back without recognition. I hastily pulled down my mask with my blue hands. "It's Vince."

He smiled.

Then he closed his eyes.

And began snoring again.

"Why have you pulled down your mask?"

I looked toward the doorway to see the silhouette of the blonde attendant. I snapped the mask back up over my nose.

"He didn't seem to recognize me, with the mask—"

"Of course not." She put her hands on her hips. "He's dying."

"You don't know that." I said it sheepishly and regretted how weak I sounded.

"People move in here. They don't move out. This is the last stop before paradise."

She snickered a little.

I looked around at her hellhole before paradise.

"If you love him," she said, condescendingly, "then let him go."

"He'll make it," I said.

"He has pneumonia."

"Pneumonia?"

"It's a disease of the lungs."

"I know what pneumonia is."

"It's the final stage of COVID-19," she continued. "You know what COVID-19 is, don't you?"

Is she enjoying this?

"I know you and Stefanie don't believe in COVID-19."

My heart rate accelerated.

"You think it's just a hoax."

I sat straighter, my body tensing as if preparing for an attack.

"Now you're going to see it's not a hoax. You're going to see what happens to old people when you don't wear a mask. When you don't social distance. When you don't shelter in place. When you think you're smarter than the experts."

I inhaled deeply, the scent of old urine filling my nostrils.

"Maybe," I said slowly, "he wouldn't be dying if he wasn't locked up in this filthy crypt. When's the last time you cleaned this place?"

"I already put in enough overtime changing diapers."

I shook my head, heart beating faster.

"I'm sorry you have to learn the hard way," she said. "But, for God's sake, smarten up before you have any more deaths on your hands."

A cellphone in her pocket beeped. She pulled it out and appeared to be reading a text message.

"Excuse me," she said, with mock politeness. "I need to make a very important phone call."

She walked away from the doorway. A few seconds later, I heard a ding, the elevator sliding open. "Hi, Andrew," was all I heard her say before the doors closed.

66. Dumping Ground

Grandad slept on, oblivious to my confrontation with the psycho nurse. I pushed myself up out of the chair. The latex gloves already felt wet with sweat on the inside. I yanked them off and tossed them into an overflowing trashcan in Grandad's washroom. The washroom looked like it hadn't been cleaned in weeks either, revealing the source of the nauseating ammonia smells. A dusty room was one thing; a dirty bathroom was inexcusable. I knew Grandad would have cleaned it himself, if he wasn't so frail now.

"Time to clean this dump up," I said aloud, standing at the foot of Grandad's bed. "I'll be right back. Don't go anywhere."

He responded with a wheezing snore.

I reached down, removed his shoes and pulled the sheet over his socked feet. Spinning around, I marched into the hallway, scooped the dinner tray up off the floor and made a left toward the stairwell.

Downstairs, I pushed the door to the kitchen open with my

foot. After dumping the dishes in the sink, I washed the sugar-intoxicated insectoids down the drain. I hope they enjoyed their last meal. I didn't bother to turn on the lights; enough streamed through the windows from the street lamps along Jackson Road. To the left of the sink was a full dishwasher. I swung it open and unloaded its contents into the cupboard, before placing Grandad's dishes on the rack.

Remembering the mess Claudia and I had passed earlier, I rolled a cart through the swinging double-acting door into the adjoining dining room and began gathering stacks of dirty trays and dishes from the unused tables. I remembered the days when the dining area resounded with residents talking and laughing. Most Saturdays Bindu would play Beatles songs on the piano at lunch, with Léo accompanying on his guitar. Now the social centre of the home was a dumping ground for half-eaten meals.

I wheeled the cart back into the kitchen, scraped the leftovers into a trash can and filled the dishwasher. All the plates and utensils were caked with dried potato.

While the machine hummed, I dropped a bucket in the sink. As it filled, I pulled out my cell and tapped on Moosehead Bakery. After four rings, Stefanie's voice answered:

"Hello. You've reached Moosehead Artisan Bakery. Fresh-baked bread. 24-hour ferment. No yeast. One hundred percent organic. Distilled water. Sorry, no one is available—"

I could have hit the star button and skipped the message, but I wanted to hear her voice.

"Please leave a short message and someone will get back to you." *Beep!*

"Hey, Dandelion," I said, nonchalantly. "Turns out your shamanic hunch was right. Grandad's very sick. They've given him morphine and who knows what else. Claudia let me in. I'm cleaning up his room. It's a mess." My voice started to waver. "I don't know if he's going to—"

I sniffed back a sob. The bucket was running over. I turned off the faucet.

"I can't leave him. I can't let him be alone. Not if he's..." I started to cry. "Ah!" I yelled and whacked the bucket, spilling it over, soaking my shirt and mask. "Damn!" I set it upright and turned the tap on again.

Grandad was more my dad than my dad was. Weekends were always when Dad drank the most. But Grandad, he'd pick me up right after school on Friday. And Grandma always had warm bannock wrapped in a towel and a big pot of stew waiting for me. In the summer, Mathéo would come and we'd camp out in a tent. Grandad would take us fishing on the river, skating in the winter. Without him, I'd probably be more messed up than my dad.

I turned off the water. Silence filled the room. I pulled the wet face mask down. I looked at the cellphone, mutely, watching the call duration count upward. I felt confused, lost, standing there in a dark kitchen I've never been in before.

"I'll do my best to be there tomorrow morning at eight thirty. I don't know. I—."

Beep! "You have exceeded the maximum length for your message," said a robotic female voice. "If you are happy with your message, press one. If you want to—"

I pressed one. "Thank you!" Beep! The screen displayed: "Call ended: 10:28 p.m." I started tapping and swiping until I brought up a photo I snuck of the Dandelion kneading bread: one fist in the air, flour dusting her green apron, two long blonde braids wound around each other, snaking down her back.

Why do I love her so much? I thought to myself. *She's way too idealistic. The bakery is losing sales every day. And she's making it worse by posting those "It's A Hoax, Folks" signs. And, these days, who can afford to pay for organic artisan bread at eight dollars a loaf?* Already, I knew she was relying on donations from her Coronacircus YouTube channel. But how long until she was banned from YouTube? How were we going to survive?

I stirred a squirt of lemon-scented soap into the bucket of water, until bubbles crept over its rim. The soap was probably meant for dishes, not floors. Dropping a scrub brush and some rags into the bucket, I hauled it out of the sink and back into the hallway.

At the fire door leading to the stairwell, I reached out to key in the access code. My hand froze, as I squinted at a large art print hanging on the wall beside the keypad.

I knew that painting.

Brown wood framed a white canoe, resting on the shore of a still lake. Before the canoe, bare branches stood erect. In the distance, dense evergreen forests covered the lake's farther shores. An empty canoe waited to take a traveller to greener lands. I leaned forward to read the placard.

Tom Thomson's "The Canoe" (1912)

Thomson. That's what I thought. It had been a while since grade nine art class with Mr. Hammer. I took the course because I thought it would be easy. No studying. Boy, had I been wrong. We spent half the class memorizing the names, births and deaths of more Canadian artists than I would have thought existed.

I put down the bucket and glanced behind me. The hallway was clear. I tapped 0391 into the stairwell's keypad. Click! Holding the door open with my foot, I carefully lifted the picture frame off its hook and tucked it under my right arm. With my left hand, I picked up the bucket and slipped into the stairwell.

The print was surrounded by double matting, glass glazing and decorative molding within a three-by-five-foot frame. Not cheap. And I had just stolen it.

Add it to my growing list of new-normal crimes, I thought. *Make me wear a mask, like some common thief, and you deserve what you get.*

67. An Empty Canoe

The wind the night before had blown maple leaves onto the surface of Nepahwin Lake. Our aluminum canoe cut through the buildup of bright red foliage on the water.

"Grandad," my six-year-old self had asked, sitting backwards in the bow of the canoe, "why are some leaves bright red, and others dull brown?"

He grinned, as he brought the oar up and laid it across the stern. He wore a bright orange life jacket and a white wide-brimmed hat. He reached into the water and retrieved a wet maple leaf.

"The red leaves are the happy leaves," he said.

"Happy to die?" asked Mathéo.

He nodded to Mathéo, who was sitting on an extra life jacket, in the centre of the canoe, leaning against the yoke. Even at six, he looked stocky.

"Why are they happy to die?" Mathéo asked again.

Grandad smiled but didn't answer. I squirmed in my life jacket. During such pauses, I wondered if he was recalling ancient Indigenous wisdom or simply making something up.

"It depends how the leaf lived its life," said Grandad, finally. "If it lived a good life, it dies full of joy."

I opened my eyes, finding myself slumped forward in the chair by Grandad's side. Raising my head sent a spasm of pain down my stiff neck and spine.

I pulled out my cell: 4:30 a.m. Christmas Eve.

I rubbed my eyes, yawned, and looked around. The open window had sucked out the stuffiness and filled the room with the crisp air of winter. It still wasn't paradise, but the place didn't feel or look like hell's showroom anymore. It had taken another trip to the kitchen for a second bucket, a broom and a mop. The floor wasn't big, but the water got dirty so fast. I had even washed down the shelving, before placing his complete collection of Shakespeare plays back in alphabetical order.

And where the dusty TV had hung on the wall, I had replaced it with the Tom Thomson painting—its empty canoe still waiting to take its passenger to a farther shore.

Many assume Thomson was part of the Group of Seven. I remember my grade nine art teacher telling us that Thomson actually died three years before the group of painters formed in 1920. Mr. Hammer told us Thomson would spend his summers portaging the 7,000 square kilometres of Ontario's Algonquin Park, even sleeping in his canoe in the middle of lakes to avoid mosquitos. Then, one afternoon in 1917, a camper spotted his upturned canoe on Canoe Lake. I guess he was a restless sleeper. Eight days later, his body was found at the bottom of the lake. He was only thirty-nine, yet had completed over 450 paintings. I think it's safe to say he died like one of Grandad's bright red maple leaves.

I twisted my sore neck toward Grandad. His mouth still hung open, and he was breathing rapidly. His face was so pale he looked as white as my three-quarters Irish skin.

Standing, I stretched my arms out, and walked to the washroom to empty my bladder. The toilet had been the grossest to clean—stains older than Grandad. Washing my hands in the white-again sink, I stared into the mirror. I still had the mask on my face. I'd slept with it on. Hardly noticed it until now.

Maybe the mask wasn't such a big deal?

I walked back into the room and admired the transformation of his cell. Maybe I could get a job here after all? According to Claudia, I already had one. But a full-time, official job. Custodian? They sure could use one.

If they won't let Grandad out, maybe they'd let me in?

"Miskwaadesi," Grandad suddenly called out.

I shot to his side and squatted down. "Grandad!"

He smiled at me. Our eyes locked. I felt a burst of hope and happiness.

His dry mouth opened. "Remember... the whole world... rests on the back... of a turtle."

His eyes closed.

His mouth closed.

Through his nostrils, I heard a rush of air emptying his lungs.

And I knew instantly that another maple leaf had fallen from the tree of earthly life.

I reached out and held his hand. It felt warm.

I put my ear to his heart. Silence.

I rested there, head on his chest, holding his hand tight.

The whole world rests on the back of a turtle.

But he would no longer be there to help me carry the weight of it.

Tears flowed.

Raising my head, I whispered, "Why did they do this to you? Why can't they leave us alone?"

I didn't know who "they" were. The government? The vaccine companies? The shadowy billionaire elites? Power-hungry monsters willing to sacrifice the vulnerable to stage a pandemic, so they could justify tyrannical control?

"One more Christmas together," I said, running my hands through his long grey hair. "One more year. We had more time."

I suddenly felt completely alone—like that great turtle

swimming solo in the vast, empty ocean. Why couldn't I just wear the mask and be one of them? Back in June, I hadn't questioned any of it. Not consciously, at least. Not until that Dandelion held a mirror up to my face.

I rose and fell back into the chair, my masked face hanging forward, like a marionette whose strings had been cut.

68. Every Snowflake

Five minutes later? Ten minutes? A half-hour? I don't know. All I know is, a hand suddenly touched my shoulder. I looked up. Claudia stood there, holding a white, folded sheet. Her eyes glistened as she spoke softly:

"Paul's at peace now. And he didn't die alone."

I rose, pulled out some tissue paper from a box on the nightstand, yanked off the tear-soaked mask and blew my nose. She didn't back away.

"I can't believe he's gone," I muttered.

Claudia nodded. She laid the white sheet at Grandad's feet and slowly unfolded it to cover his entire body.

"The funeral home's already coming for Bill Cooper at nine o'clock. I'll let them know about Paul."

This was happening too fast.

"What... what are they going to do with the body?"

The body. I didn't like the way that sounded. But that's all it felt like, now. A silent, inanimate corpse. A piece of meat that would begin to rot.

"It will be cremated immediately," she said.

"Immediately? Like today?"

"It's the law with a COVID death. No funeral. No delay. No spread."

"No autopsy?" I asked.

"No."

"What about a funeral?"

She shook her head. "You can, of course, hold a memorial service for Paul's ashes."

"What?" I blurted. "On Zoom?"

An awkward silence followed.

"But, but," I stuttered, remembering when Grandma died.

"Ojibwe don't cremate. They bury."

"I'm sorry, Vince. Your father has already given the go-ahead."

I gritted my teeth and stared at his covered body. At least they weren't delaying.

"Her spirit needs to start her journey right away," Grandad had said to me as we stood, so many years ago, at Grandma's grave. "It takes four days to get to *Gaagige Minawaanigozigiwin-ing*—the land of happiness and joy."

Grandad set a bowl of mashed squash drizzled in maple syrup and a piece of dried deer meat at her grave. "The food will sustain her on her journey."

"Won't the animals just eat it?"

He didn't say anything. He then put tobacco in another bowl and lit it. "The smoke will guide her upward."

But Grandad would get none of that. No food to sustain him on his journey to the place of happiness and joy. No smoke to show him the way.

Looking at Claudia, I said, "I'll wait until they come for his body. I won't leave him alone."

"You're a good grandson."

She stepped away and closed the door. Immediately, on the other side, I could hear the blonde, short-haired attendant speaking sternly, but could not make out the words. Claudia responded with muffled profanity.

I stared at the shroud.

Waiting.

I half expected Grandad to bolt up, swing his legs out of bed, slap his thighs, laugh out loud and yell, "Run!"

That's how he escaped the residential school.

But this time he wasn't escaping.

Or had he already escaped?

I pulled the shroud back and gazed at the face of my Ojibwe ancestor for the last time. Kidnapped by the government as a child, starved and beaten in a residential school, bombarded with racist bigotry for most of his life, to finally die a widower, a diabetic, a prisoner in a germophobic society, forgotten by his sons and daughter, euthanized by a nurse, sent to the crematory fires without a funeral—did he fall a bright maple leaf before the winter of death?

That day on the canoe, I had proclaimed: "Grandad! I hope you never die."

"Never's a long time," said Grandad, raising an eyebrow. "Why would you condemn me to forever in this old body?"

"Not forever," I said. "Just not before me. I would miss you too much if you died first."

He put his oar back in the water and paddled our canoe away from the shore.

"Our people say that when we leave the body we join the Great Spirit," he said. "Then I'll look down upon you from the stars. I'll pitter-patter as rain falling on your umbrella. I'll wave to you in the grass. I'll sing to you in the trill of the pine warbler."

"What about in the winter? Will you be in the snow?"

"In every snowflake."

Lifting the shroud back over his face, I said, "I hope you were right, Grandad."

That's when my phone's latest ringtone (courtesy of Franz Schubert) began to play:

Und Lenz wird kommen,
Und Winter wird gehn,
Und Blümlein werden
Im Grase stehn.[*]

I pulled out the cell. "Incoming Call. Mathéo Côté."

I hit the green telephone icon.

"Mathéo?" I said.

"Vince," he responded, almost in a whisper.

"It's 5 a.m.," I said.

He didn't respond.

"Mathéo, what's wrong?"

"Votre grand-père." He paused. "You grandfather, I saw him again."

I stopped breathing for a few seconds.

---

* And spring will come,
And winter will go,
And flowers will
Grow in the grass again.

"He told me to tell you..." Mathéo paused again.

"What?" I asked.

"He said... to tell you that... he's not there anymore."

Glancing at his shroud-covered corpse, I held my breath. Still holding the phone to my ear, I turned and stared out the window. Snow had begun to fall. Snowflakes glowed in the streetlights as they zig-zagged to the ground.

In every snowflake, he had said.

More tears flowed, unabated. Happy tears.

Only half believing this was really happening, I asked. "Did... Did Grandad say anything else?"

"Yes."

"What?"

Another pause.

"What, Mathéo?"

"He said, now's not a good time to be a turtle."

"What?"

"He said run as fast as you can."

"What?"

"Run!"

It was the first time I ever heard Mathéo sound urgent.

"Run, run where?"

But I didn't wait for a response. Adrenaline began flowing to my fingertips. I felt my mind fall silent in a strange swirl of transcendental survivalism. I ended the call and dropped the cell back into my pants pocket. I pulled my jacket off the chair and moved toward the rectangular outline of light marking the cracks around the closed door.

Once in the hallway, I ran for the stairwell, where I descended two at a time. Exiting the door at the bottom, I burst into the first floor hallway, passing the TV from Grandad's room that now hung on the wall where I'd lifted the painting.

I pounded past the nursing station where I heard raised voices.

"Andrew told me to," barked the blonde attendant.

"Andrew's a heartless bully," retorted Claudia. "He only—"

I made a left into the lobby. Tapping the 5121 into the keypad, I yanked open the front door and ran out onto the wheelchair ramp. Halfway down, I froze. Waiting at the bottom stood a man with a black winter hat and black mask. His black jacket had OPP patches on each arm.

"Hey there, son," said Constable Corona, raising his right hand. "Not so fast."

69. Prison Planet

Even if it hadn't been snowing, I would have been frozen in place. I stood at the bottom of the ramp, a mere six feet from Constable Corona, railings flanking me on either side.

"They told me what you did," said Mackenzie, gently.

I took a step back.

"I'm proud of you, son."

I glanced over the railing. It wasn't a far drop. I could—

"You sat by the bedside of a dying loved one," continued Mackenzie. "You risked catching the virus. You've entered the ranks of the frontline heroes."

Did he not recognize me?

"Don't worry," he said, shaking his gloved hands in the air, palms outward. "I've forgotten all about that, um, little incident on the ice. Like you said, just because we don't root for the same team, doesn't mean we can't be friends."

"Friends?" I said slowly, carefully.

"And, I'm sure," he nodded toward the nursing home, "after seeing what you just saw, you'll be sticking to the rules from here on."

"My grandfather was eighty-eight-years old," I protested. "The place is a death trap."

He continued, as if he hadn't heard me. "I know what you've been through. I've seen firsthand what this disease does to people. Once it takes over the lungs. Nothing you can do to stop it. That's why—"

He stopped and gazed over my shoulder. I turned to see Claudia, wearing only her thin blue uniform, standing at the top of the ramp, the door slowly closing behind her.

"Vince!" she said loudly. "I'm sorry. I didn't know she called the police. I didn't have anything to do with it."

Mackenzie raised his hand again. "Don't worry. No one's in trouble here. This lad's done a good thing. But, like all good things, they come with a price."

"Price?" I said, turning back toward him.

"You've been in close contact with a confirmed case. Fourteen days quarantine. Last thing we need is you spreading the virus through all of Moosehead. I'm sure you don't want this happening to anyone else's grandfather."

"Fourteen days? I need to go to work. My boss. She needs me in—" I pulled out my cell: 5:30 a.m. "—three hours."

"I'm afraid she'll have to make do without you." Mackenzie snickered. "She's mighty self-reliant, that one. I wouldn't worry." He then nodded toward Claudia. "Get back inside, dear. It's freezing. I'll make sure he gets home safely."

Claudia looked wearily at me, saying, "Take care of yourself, Vince." She then retreated back into the warm lobby.

"All right!" said Mackenzie, almost cheerfully. "You can ride in front with me." He gestured to his cop car.

"Aren't you afraid of getting the virus?" I spoke hesitantly; but not out of concern for Mackenzie.

"No worries, mate. I've already had it." He waved his hand in the air as if swatting a corona. "I reckon that makes me immune, eh?"

"Oh."

"Anyways, it's got to incubate before you're contagious."

He walked over to his cruiser and opened the passenger door. I didn't follow. He put a hand on his utility belt and said, "I trust you won't be giving me any trouble."

Run! Grandad had said. But, I felt too tired to run. *Where would I run? How far would I get?*

"I'm just taking you home. There's nothing to fear. Where do you live?"

"Magder Road."

Why did I say that?

"All right, hop in. Before we both freeze to death."

"You swear you're just taking me home?"

"On my oath," he said loudly, almost laughing, brushing snow off the windshield with his glove. "I'm with the Ontario Provincial Police, not the Moosehead Mafia. Come on! It's nice and warm inside the cruiser." And he ducked down into the driver's seat.

I walked slowly to the open door and almost fell inside. It was warm and smelt of strong coffee and hot chocolate.

"Buckle up," he said as he slammed the door, causing snow to topple off the roof.

Quarantine? I thought. *That means Mom and Dad'll be in quarantine, too. They're gonna freak.* Then I realized... *Fourteen days stuck with Dad and his minibar. I'm gonna freak.* Spring lockdown was bad enough—back when Dad was exercising some moderation.

I pulled the seatbelt out and across my chest. Mackenzie turned the ignition. The radio lit up. Bing Crosby began singing "I'll Be Home For Christmas."

Mackenzie reached into his pocket and pulled out a small plastic bottle. Dumping two white pills in the palm of his hand, he looked at me.

"Haven't needed these in a while," he said.

He closed the lid and set the red-and-white bottle on the dashboard. Its label read, "Tylenol No. 3 with 40 mg of codeine."

"That little fall on the ice..."

He rubbed his knee with the hand clutching the pills, as if he could massage the opiates directly into the inflamed joint. Taking a sip from a coffee mug, he downed the two pills and, reclining back in his seat, let out a deep sigh. "If it wasn't for the constipation, I'd be tempted to take this dope 24/7."

Above the bottle, dangling from the rear-view mirror, hung a black mask. It was intertwined with a paper snowflake hanging from a red string.

"My grandson made that," said Mackenzie, pointing.

"The snowflake or the mask?" I grumbled.

"Ha!" he laughed, pulling the mask off the mirror. "No, this is OPP issue. Collector's item! Try it on."

I stared at the black mask. "Rather not."

He threw the mask on my lap.

"I'll keep this simple: We're not moving till you're masked."

"I thought you said you were immune?"

"Optics," he said. "We need to be a good example."

I just wanted to get home, so I picked it up and pulled the thing around my face. Immediately, Mackenzie began pulling out of the lot.

"Folks say your grandfather was a good man," said Mackenzie.

I didn't respond. Did anyone really tell him that or was he just talking?

"His middle name..." said Mackenzie, his voice trailing off. "Nig-a? Nee-ga?"

"Niigaanii," I corrected. "It's Ojibwe for 'he leads.'"

"Hmm. Indian. That's what I thought." He turned onto Queen Street. "That's right, you told me you were Métis. That was you, wasn't it? Back in the summer at the bakery."

I started to sweat.

"I'm not really Métis. They are their own people. I'm just a touch Ojibwe."

"Either way, I guess that explains it."

"Explains what?"

"Natives, they don't think the rules apply to them."

"I don't think the COVID rules apply to anyone," I said. "Especially forcing people to self-isolate."

"Don't worry," he said, crossing Louis Riel Bridge. "Two weeks will fly by. Shortest, darkest, coldest days of the year. Timing couldn't be better."

I swallowed hard.

"And you're young. If an old fart like me could survive COVID, you'll do fine."

"Then why imprison us?"

"Prison?" He sounded genuinely surprised.

"Quarantine. Lockdowns. Isolation. You're turning the world into a prison planet."

"Huh." He shook his head. "This ain't nothing like prison." His voice became ominous. "Trust me, son, you don't ever want to know what being locked up for real is like."

I gritted my teeth and stared ahead. We turned left onto Main Street, passing town hall. On the radio, Bing Crosby died away. Mackenzie reached out and shut off the radio.

"Nope," continued Mackenzie. "Sheltering in the comfort of your home ain't nothing like doing time, son. In fact, last night, I was telling the very same thing to Joan of Arc."

My body jolted and my head spun to face him. "Stefanie!?"

He sighed. I suspected he wore a grin under his mask. "After you guys gave me the slip, I figured eventually the van would end up back at the bakery. When she pulled into the back alley, I was waiting for her."

"What, what did you do to her?"

He groaned. "What do you think? Tried to talk some sense into her pretty little head. All braids, no brains, that one. She means well. I can tell. But so did Hitler, some say." He glanced at me. "German, isn't she?"

I didn't respond.

"Did you know Hitler was a vegetarian, too?"

The cruiser passed Magder Road.

"You," I stuttered, suddenly short of breath, "you passed Magder."

"Damn! Sorry," he said nonchalantly, glancing into his rear-view mirror. He then turned right onto the next street. "We'll circle back. No worries. Like I said, you have a few days incubation. There's no rush."

My fists clenched, heart pounded.

"You didn't hurt her?"

"Hurt her?" He let out a mix of a sigh and a laugh. "I'm the good guy, son. She's the one who slammed the door in my face."

My fists unclenched.

"I even left her a Christmas gift."

And then tensed again.

"Gift?" I exclaimed. "What kind of gift?"

"Ah, that would ruin the surprise."

70. I'll Be Quarantined for Christmas

Mackenzie clucked his tongue and made a right onto Qureshi Road, another right onto Thomas, and then a left onto Magder. Seeing the McLeans' five hundred Christmas lights, he exclaimed:

"My God, I'd hate to see that guy's electrical bill. That's not your house, is it?"

"No, it's the one beside it."

"My wife," he said, distractedly, "My wife, Patty. Crazy Christmas light fanatic, that one. Every year, she'd drag me on a tour. We'd drive past almost every blinking light in Greater Sudbury."

We pulled in behind Dad's Buick.

"You didn't do it this year?" I asked, feeling relieved to see the front door of my home.

"Not many lights this year," he muttered, pulling the key out of the ignition. He opened his door. "You live with your folks?"

"Yeah."

Walking up to the porch, Mackenzie rang the doorbell.

"I do have a key," I said, reaching into my pocket.

He held up his hand. "I need to talk to your parents, first. Make sure they understand the situation."

We stood there, silently, for a minute, seeming to admire the homemade wreath Mom had hanging on the door. The hallway light turned on and, through the narrow window beside the door, Mom's face peeked out. I waved. Immediately, she pulled open the front door, dressed in a light blue night robe.

"Vincent, what's going on? What are—"

Her mouth opened wide as she realized who was standing beside me.

"It's okay, Mom. Grandad and I just robbed a bank. Cop here says they'd let us off easy since we were wearing masks and all."

"What?" she said, with a mix of disbelief and anxiety.

"Ma'am," said Mackenzie, in a formal tone, "your son is not in any trouble. At least, not with the law."

"Richard!" shouted Mom back over her shoulder. "Richard!" Then looking back at me she said: "Vince, I've hardly slept at all, worrying about you."

Dad staggered down the hall, hair disheveled, dark pouches under his eyes, wearing a white T-shirt and boxer shorts.

"What the hell's goin' on?"

Mackenzie pulled out his notebook and addressed Dad. "Richard McKnight?"

"Yes."

"I am sorry to inform you that your father, Paul Niigaanii McKnight, passed away early this morning from COVID-19."

Dad nodded, lips pursed. "I understand."

"Your son spent the night at his bedside."

Mom and Dad gazed at me as if Mackenzie had told them I'd opened fire on a schoolyard. Mom put her hand to her mouth, turned and retreated down the hallway.

Dad glanced back at her, and then to me. "You did what?"

"Grandad was alone," I felt my heart rate increase. "You should have seen his room. Took me an hour to clean."

Mom rushed back wearing a brown facemask with a red ball sewn to the front. She handed a duplicate to Dad.

"Vince," said Dad, strapping the Rudolph the red-nosed reindeer snout over his mouth and nose. "Why in God's name would you do such a thing?"

"Do what?" I said with exasperation. "Sit with Grandad as he lay dying?"

Dad nodded, the red ball flopping. "I'm sure your Grandad would not have wanted to put anyone else at risk—"

"You have no idea what Grandad would want!" I shouted.

Dad didn't respond or even blink.

"Let's all just calm down," said Mackenzie, patting the air with his hands. Silence fell for a few seconds. Mackenzie slipped his notebook back in his pants pocket and sighed. "We need to assume your son is infected."

"Assume?" said Mom. "He can be tested. Can't he?"

Mackenzie nodded. "Yes, in three days, he could have a test. If he tests negative, then—"

"Forget it!" I said, my voice almost cracking. "I'm not letting anyone stick God-knows-what up my sinus cavity."

"But, dear," began Mom. "If you—"

I cut her off, "PCR tests are as reliable as a fortune teller."

Dad rolled his eyes. But Mackenzie nodded.

"I couldn't agree more," he said. "The test is not perfect. Despite how sensitive it is, it could still miss a case. Best you just stay home for fourteen days. Play it safe. Assume you're infected. There's too much at risk. Especially this time of the year."

Both my parents' eyes grew wider than the red noses on their masks—gazing at me as though I'd just been diagnosed with end-stage cancer.

"Fourteen days?" said Mom, putting her hand to her forehead.

"Longer, of course, if symptoms persist," said Mackenzie.

"Symptoms?" said Dad.

Then he took a step back.

"I'm sorry," he said, avoiding any eye contact. "He can't stay here. There's no way."

71. A Four-Star COVID Hotel

I suddenly felt like I was going to throw up. And not from COVID.

"He needs to go into isolation," said Mackenzie. "Either here or at a quarantine facility."

Dad nodded quickly. "Maybe a facility would be better."

"Dad!" I exclaimed. "What are you saying?"

My bladder suddenly felt full. I clenched my buttocks together.

"My wife, she, uh, has a bit of a breathing problem," Dad blathered to Mackenzie. "And, my, uh, liver, hasn't been doing all that well. Doctor, he says I'm high risk. We both are. Especially without being vaccinated. And, of course, we need to think of the neighbours."

"I see," said Mackenzie, sounding as shocked as I felt. "I can understand your concerns."

"I don't!" I almost yelled. "It has a 99.8 percent survival rate. Only one in every five hundred die. And almost all of them over eighty."

"Almost," said Mackenzie, with a melancholy edge. "*Almost* isn't good enough if it ends up being someone you care about."

"I'm not going to no COVID concentration camp," I said. "I know my rights."

Actually, I didn't. The Dandelion kept on telling me to read the Canadian Bill of Rights. I'd thought we had a Charter of Rights. No, she told me, that was just a decoy created by Pierre Trudeau (our fifteenth prime minister). The Charter of Rights and Freedoms had an easy opt-out clause for the government. The Bill of Rights, she said, that's what they don't teach us in school. I laughed at her when she told me to keep a copy of both on me at all times. I wasn't laughing now.

"A facility, though, is meant as a last resort," said Mackenzie. "Is there not somewhere else he can stay?"

"Hey!" Dad chuckled. "Maybe with that German girlfriend of his?"

Mom elbowed him in the ribs. "He's not staying with a girl," she scolded. "What would Father Shostakovich think?"

Dad shrugged his shoulders. "Beats me. He's as much a nut-case as her."

"It's up to them," said Mackenzie, nodding in my direction.

"If I go to the bakery, does that mean it has to close down?"

"Absolutely," said Mackenzie, almost cheerfully.

"Forget it, then," I instantly responded.

"What's the COVID hotel like, officer?" asked Dad.

Where will I go? My mind started racing.

"Well," said Mackenzie, "these COVID facilities are top-notch."

The Chatterjees'? Not a freakin' chance. Mata would kill me, wait until I reincarnate, then kill me again.

"It's like a four-star hotel with medical staff on site," continued Constable Corona.

AJ's? His mother would die of COVID instantly, then haunt me for the rest of my life.

"Netflix. Wi-Fi. Room service."

Léo's? He lives with his five siblings, grandparents and parents in a four-bedroom house. I'd no idea how they already managed.

"Vince," said Dad. "The hotel sounds nice. Think of it as a Christmas vacation paid for by the federal government."

Mathéo's? He lives in a one-room bachelor flat. Rolls out of bed onto his stovetop.

Mom crossed her arms and spoke hesitantly, "Well, it doesn't sound too bad. It's not like a jail."

My mouth opened, but no words came out.

"No, ma'am," said Mackenzie. "Nothing like a jail."

Fingertips to my temples, I exclaimed, "Wall-to-wall carpeting doesn't stop it from being a prison. You're talking about locking me up! For what? Not letting Grandad die alone in that gulag?"

Dad cast his eyes toward the ground and mumbled through his mask: "No, son. That's not it. What you did, it was good. I'm glad Paul didn't... I'm glad you were there."

"Yes," said Mom, folding her hands together, as if praying. "We are very proud of you. And we just want to make sure no one else gets—"

"Ah, whatever!" I said and stepped across the threshold. Mom and Dad backed down the hall with surprising speed. "I've had enough. I need to get cleaned up, take a nap, eat something and get to work."

Suddenly a hand seized my right shoulder, squeezing hard.

"Son," said Mackenzie. "Your parents have not consented to you staying here. While I don't necessarily agree with their decisions, I'm sworn to defend their property rights."

"This is my home, too," I yelled, twisting my shoulder out of his grip. "I've lived here my whole life."

"I understand," said Mackenzie. "And, I'm sure you'll be welcome back in two weeks' time."

"Vince," said Mom, starting to cry. "You're sick. You have the virus. You need to be taken care of."

"Sick?" I yelled. "Sick! I'm not sick. Do I look sick? It's you people who look like the sickos." I pointed at my reflection in the hallway mirror, yanking the black police mask off my face. "You're all walking around like you're living through the Black Death. You look like freakin' morons." I tossed the mask at the mirror.

Mom cupped both her hands over her mask and let out a tiny scream. Dad wrapped his arms around her and backed them both into the living room.

"Son," said Mackenzie, as if he was talking to a five-year-old, "you're getting out of hand."

"Stop calling me *son!*" I yelled. "You make the Gestapo look like the Jehovah's Witnesses."

Mackenzie stepped closer. "We can sort something out. Maybe if you confine yourself to your room, your parents might let you stay."

I shook my head and began walking down the hall toward the stairwell. Instantly, Mackenzie's left hand was gripping my wrist, twisting it up and over toward my forearm as he yanked my arm up behind my back. I cried out as he pinned me against the wall. I couldn't move without an intolerable level of pain threatening to snap the small bones in my wrist.

Saturday morning martial arts classes at the Green Dragon surfaced in my mind.

"Don't fight back at the place of struggle," Mr. Chung often said.

Instinctively, my left leg rose and slammed down on top of Mackenzie's right foot. Instantly, he let go, allowing my right leg to kick back against his kneecap. He stumbled backwards, tipping over the threshold of the open door and onto his back. I spun around, shocked at what I'd just done.

Mom screamed louder. Dad ushered her out of view.

"Call Yamamoto," I heard him say to her.

I now stood facing Mackenzie, fists out, knees bent, as he pushed his lanky body up into a sitting position. Rubbing his knee, he cursed. I'm not sure what I would have done next, if Dad hadn't stepped in between us.

"Vince, have you lost your mind?" he hollered. "What the hell have you done?" He squatted down to Mackenzie's side, speaking directly to him: "It's that girl. She's confused him with her conspiracy theories."

"I understand," said Mackenzie, sympathetically. He rose to his feet with a groan. His hat had fallen off, revealing his balding head. "But he's just assaulted a peace officer."

"I'm so sorry," pleaded Dad. "He—"

"Yeah!" I cut in. "So sorry, my son won't let you abduct him without a fight."

"Son, I know you're scared," said Mackenzie.

"Damn right, I'm scared," I said. "I'd be a fool otherwise."

Mom spoke up from the end of the hallway. "Maybe he can stay." She choked on the words. "I don't want him to miss Christmas. His Grandad just died. We're supposed to all be in this together."

Dad raised his hand. "He's not a little boy anymore. He made a choice. He has to take responsibility for his decisions."

I laughed. "Oh, you're one to talk, Dad."

He didn't respond—just squinted at me with those dark circles under his eyes.

After another awkward silence, Mom began to sob. "Why couldn't you have waited for the vaccine?" she murmured.

"Grandad was dying!" I yelled, throwing up my arms. "Sorry we couldn't reschedule his death."

Mom sniffed back another sob.

"What would you like me to pack for you?"

I stared back at her, too shocked to even breathe. They were really kicking me out, because I *might* have the common cold.

"You're sure it's a nice hotel?" said Dad to Mackenzie.

"I've never been there myself."

He picked up his fallen hat, brushed off the snow and then looked at me.

"Son, while I don't—"

"Stop calling me *son.*"

"While your mother packs your bag," he continued calmly, "I'm going to have to ask you wait out here with me."

"Ask all you want." I didn't move.

He sighed, noisily. "If you comply, I'm willing to forget you assaulted a police officer."

"You assaulted me first. I was defending myself."

"My patience and generosity only go so far." I saw his hand moving toward his taser. "Your parents have asked you to leave. I need you to respect their wishes and cease trespassing on their property."

"I'm a tenant. I pay rent. Three hundred per month. They can't just kick me out."

I looked at Dad. He looked away. I could hear Mom's footsteps moving up the stairwell.

"I didn't know you were a paying tenant," said Mackenzie. "That changes matters. But I'll need to see your rental contract."

I gritted my teeth.

"You do have a rental contract?"

I didn't respond.

"Then, I'm sorry, you have no right to be here."

I inhaled and exhaled.

"If you don't immediately exit the building, I will have no choice but to arrest you for trespassing."

I suspected such an arrest wouldn't hold up in a court of law. Assuming laws still mattered.

Mackenzie took a deep breath and said, "Would you rather spend Christmas in a jail cell with some wino, or a hotel suite with Wi-Fi?"

Stefanie would make him drag her off to jail.

She was the lion.

I was the turtle.

So I turtled past Dad with his stupid red-nose reindeer mask and onto the cold porch.

Mackenzie reached out, grabbed the handle and pulled the front door shut.

Now everybody was safe.

72. Christdorn

The snow was still falling. We waited silently on the porch, as Mom readied my bags for my two-week stay at Camp COVID.

Mackenzie rubbed his left knee—not the same one that hit the ice, but the other, which I had back-kicked—and then pulled out a second bottle of painkillers. I knew it wasn't the same bottle as before. This one said Tylenol No. 4. He'd left No. 3 on the dashboard. Cursing, he quickly downed two more codeine-enhanced tablets without any fluid. After a euphoric pause he looked at me and laughed.

"Don't worry," he said. He slid the bottle back into his jacket's breast pocket. Before zipping back up, he patted a pouch on his police vest. "If I overdose, just spray a little naloxone up the nose. Works like magic. I've had to use it enough times this year, I should know."

Did he mean he'd used it on himself, or on 911 calls? I'd heard that opioid-related deaths so far had killed an extra two hundred more people in Ontario than before the lockdowns.

Mackenzie laughed again, pulled out his smartphone and began thumbing. His hands were bare, as if they were oblivious to the freezing bite of the night air. While he scrolled, he was singing softly to himself, "You better watch out, you better not shout..."

I tried my best to ignore his opiate-induced jingle as I pretended to admire Mom's wreath on the front door.

"This is interesting," my abductor said, matter-of-factly, reading his screen. "Says here, those aren't berries." He pointed to the bright red balls of holly decorating the wreath. "They're actually a stone fruit. Like an apricot, I guess." He clicked his tongue. "I never knew that."

He was acting like we were waiting for a bus. I didn't acknowledge his Christmas trivia.

"Also says, druids believed hanging holly twigs brought eternal life; because the leaves stay so green and the fruit so red throughout the dead of winter."

I rolled my eyes. "When I was six, I ate a handful of holly berries. Ended up in the ER with diarrhea."

"Hmm," said Mackenzie, slipping his phone into his pants pocket. "Maybe that's why there's no druids anymore."

He laughed again, as if his joke was far funnier than it was.

I made sure he laughed alone.

His laugh quickly morphed into a big yawn. Covering his masked mouth, he said, "Hardly slept a wink in two nights. Had the last three night shifts, with court cases all day yesterday."

Part of me wanted to like the guy. He was obviously overworked and in physical pain. And I could not imagine the mental stress he must be under, being ordered to trample on the rights and freedoms of those he'd sworn to protect. But I would not assuage my kidnapper's conscience with any familiarity or sympathy.

Pulling out my cell, I glanced at the time: 6:02 a.m.

"*Christdorn!*" I muttered to myself, much to my own surprise.

Christdorn is a rather archaic way of saying holly in German (so Stefanie had told me when I had given her one of Mom's wreaths); not to be confused with the *Christusdorn* plant (which looks nothing like holly). Both botanical names, however, mean the "thorn of Christ"—referring to the crown of thorns the Roman soldiers wedged into Jesus' head. His crime? Healing the sick and dying while opposing the high priests of the Sanhedrin. I stared at the wreath, with its pointy leaves spotted with the blood red fruit, realizing that I too was being hauled away like a criminal by a tyrannical government. My crime? Caring for the sick and dying while opposing the high priests of sanitization.

But instead of the wreath being placed on my head, it suddenly retreated, as Mom pulled open the front door. At least, I assumed it was her. She had replaced her red-nosed face mask with a N95 respirator. I didn't even know she had an N95. And as if that wasn't enough protection from her leper-son, she also wore a face shield. Staying at arm's length, she extended a brown leather suitcase across the threshold.

"Vince, dear, I packed a whole tin of my shortbread cookies." Her eyes were glistening. "Just baked them yesterday."

"Keep them," I said. "I don't want 'em."

"But you love my shortbread."

"I've gone vegan."

Starting that very moment. Stefanie had finally convinced me.

Ignoring the suitcase, I turned and stared out at the front yard. The slow glow of dawn, which takes so long at these, the darkest days of the year, tinged the eastern sky on my left. The maple tree in the middle of the lawn, bereft of leaves for two months, now had a light coating of snow.

Camouflaged in its branches, I could hear the rippling whistle—*per-r-r-ri*—of a snow bunting.

I think I hear my snow bunting whistling. The thought made me smile for a second. When I was little, I'd wondered why snow buntings never escaped to the south for the winter. But Grandad had told me that the tiny bird had indeed already travelled south—from their home in the Arctic. Ontario was their Florida.

I heard Mackenzie step forward and grasp the suitcase from my mother. "Let me get that for you," he said, amiably. "Mmm. My wife, every Christmas she bakes up a storm. Every year." His voice trailed off.

Dad hadn't returned. I figured he was already popping corks and bottle caps.

"Lucky guy," Mackenzie said, as he walked past me, and down the porch steps. "Fresh-baked Christmas goodies." He popped open the trunk of his cruiser and set the suitcase inside.

What do you think, I'm some kid? I thought to myself. *Give me a cookie and everything's okay?*

"Vince," said Dad's voice. I turned back toward the front door where he was now standing, holding a box wrapped in red and green paper. "You can have this now if you promise not to open it until Christmas morn.'"

I felt abashed. Instead of fixing himself a scorpion, he'd been wrapping me a present. Still, I remained silent and did not extend my arms.

Mackenzie returned and took the gift, saying, "A bit light. I wonder what it is?"

"Be careful," said Dad. "It's fragile. Don't shake it."

Disbelief filled me toe to scalp. *I'm being abducted by the government and they are playing Kris Kovid Kringle.* I hated the new normal so much.

"We'll call," said Mom. Then, turning to Mackenzie, "We *can* call him?"

"Of course!" said Mackenzie. "It's four-star. I'm sure they have a telephone." He tucked the gift under his armpit. "Time to go."

Mom put her fingers to her face shield and blew me a kiss. "Goodbye, dear. We'll be back together soon."

I stared at her and her black N95 mask. *Who was this person?*

Dad nodded at me, mutely, eyes cast down at the red ball sticking out of his facemask.

I turned around to see Mackenzie opening the back door of the black-and-white cruiser.

"Sorry, son," he called out. "Won't look good when we arrive if you're riding shotgun. Optics."

I started down the porch steps but couldn't help glancing back at Mom and Dad as they stood in the entrance to what I had called home for the previous twenty-four years.

At least I'll be welcome at the COVID concentration camp.

When I reached the cruiser, I peeked inside. The back seats had no cushions, no upholstery—nothing but hard plastic.

"Sorry," said Mackenzie, still holding the door. "Not too comfy back there. Easier to clean up after the drunks throw up."

I no longer felt like throwing up. Instead, my bladder felt ready to burst. I clenched my teeth. No chance of Mom and Dad permitting their only son use of their bathroom.

"Where exactly are we going?" I asked.

He took a deep breath. "Not allowed to say."

"How long will it take to get there?"

He paused before answering, "Hour or so."

I sighed and took another glance at the hard seats, wondering if I could hold it that long.

"Don't worry," said Mackenzie. "The limo may lack lustre but the destination doesn't. Breakfast in bed. They do your laundry.

I bet they can even get you an Xbox, or whatever it is you kids play these days."

They'd take care of me. Amuse me. All I had to do was withdraw into the turtle shell of that warm cruiser. I turned to face Mackenzie.

"If anyone should be arrested it's the director of that nursing home. Instead, he's enjoying a real hotel in Florida."

Sounding exasperated, Mackenzie replied, "No one's under arrest. We're just keeping everybody safe."

Safe? I thought. *Like they kept Grandad safe in the nursing home? Like they kept him safe in the residential school? Like they keep kids safely masked up in numbered cohorts in schools today? Like they keep families safe in food bank lines after taking away their income? Like they plan to keep people safe with an experimental vaccine against a virus they haven't even isolated?*

I found myself, turtle that I may be, finally, fully understanding that wild dandelion: If that's what they call safety, I'd rather risk freedom.

Lifting my right foot, I slowly set it on the bottom rim of the cruiser's back door frame. Then, quickly, I pressed down, propelling myself backwards. As soon as my boots hit the ground, I spun around and made a dash across the front lawn. Once again—this time without ice or skates—I found myself fleeing from the law.

This time, however, I didn't make it far.

Before even reaching the maple tree, I heard a popping sound, followed by a sharp pain in the back of my right thigh. The chirping of the snow bunting was instantly replaced by what sounded like the clicking of an electric cricket. My back muscles contracted in a tight spasm. Paralysis ripped along my spine, hijacking my central nervous system. The muscles in my arms and legs locked. My fingers and toes clenched tight. I crashed face first, sliding forward into the snow like a wooden sled at the end of its run.

73. Screaming Sheeple

Mom screamed like I never heard a human being scream before. Footsteps raced toward me as I lay face first in the snow, unable to move or even breathe.

They say a taser charge only lasts five seconds. It felt like eternity. But when it ended, it ended instantly. The paralysis vanished like lightning, leaving only a tingling sensation throughout my body.

I turned my head to the left, out of the smothering snow. I saw Constable Corona kneeling at my side, with what looked like a plastic toy gun in his hand. Wires ran from the square barrel to my back and leg. I began to gasp for air.

"Vince!" cried Mom. "What has he done to you?"

She ran to my other side.

"My God, officer! You didn't have to shoot him," shouted Dad from somewhere behind my boots.

"I didn't. I stunned him," said Mackenzie, his voice turning nasty. "He's putting all of Moosehead at risk."

Mom kneeled and began to stroke my hair. "Oh, dear! He can stay with us. Vince, I'm sorry. Of course, you can stay."

I was still dazed. I couldn't believe how much it had... *hurt?* What I had just endured was so outside of anything I had ever experienced I didn't know if it even fell into the category of pain. It had felt awful, that was certain—my entire nervous system blinking out while a million ants crawled over my skin.

My heart was pounding hard and fast against the ground, as I panted heavily. I tried to push myself up, but my arms were like jelly. Directly ahead of me, two black boots planted themselves in the snow. I tilted my head to see another man in a black uniform with the word POLICE across his chest. He knelt down. I squinted at his face.

Grandad!

He looked years younger. Dark black hair. Totem pole frown. Was I dying? Had he come to usher me into the world he had only so recently entered? I gazed at him, still gasping for more air.

"Shut your mouth and save your life," he said, sternly. "The turtle lives so long because it breathes so slow."

He put a hand on my back, where the barb to one of the taser's darts clung to my jacket. Immediately my breathing began to slow. I closed my mouth and felt my chest relax. I dropped back down into the snow, head to the side.

"You monster!" exploded Mom. She leapt at Mackenzie and began pounding his bulletproof vest. Dad's snow-covered slippers then appeared, as he took hold of Mom.

"Calm down!" he yelled at her. "It was just a taser."

"He didn't do anything wrong," she cried.

I closed my eyes. *At least she still cared.* I wasn't sure.

"My baby! He needs help. Someone call an ambulance."

I opened my eyes, yelping in pain, as I felt Mackenzie yank the barb of the second dart out of my thigh.

"That winter jacket would have absorbed most of the shock," he said, pulling the other dart out of my jacket. "I didn't want to do this. But I don't want to see anyone else die in Moosehead. One death was enough."

Slowly, I rolled over on my back. Turning my head side to side, I could no longer see Constable Grandad—if I had really seen him at all.

"It's okay, Mom," I managed to say. "It's like *Star Trek.* You know, phasers on stun."

Mom kneeled back down in the cold snow. She was no longer wearing the N95 mask. I pushed myself up into a sitting position. She wrapped her arms around me, still sobbing. Grandad had once told me that mother turtles never care for their young. They lay their eggs on land and head back to the water. I was glad my mother was more a sheeple than a turtle.

Dad tried pulling Mom up onto her feet.

"Carol, it's too cold," he said.

I glanced up at Mackenzie. His face mask hung from his left ear. A bloody scratch streaked his right cheek, which smeared when he wiped it with the back of his hand. He tossed the mask to the ground and stared at me.

"He can stay with us!" repeated Mom, rising and grasping Dad's shoulder. "He can stay with us. We're all infected now. He can stay with us. He can stay with us. Tell him, Richard!"

Dad's eyes darted from my raging mother to the smouldering cop, as if trying to decide who posed more danger.

"Yes, yes, of course," he finally blurted out. "This has gotten out of hand. I overreacted. He should be home for Christmas."

"I'm afraid your offer's a little late," said Mackenzie. He pulled out his cuffs and walked toward me. "You are under arrest for evading quarantine, assaulting a police officer, violating the Reopening of Ontario Act and interfering with an officer of the peace. You have the right to retain and instruct counsel without delay."

"We said he can stay!" yelled Mom.

She looked ready to pounce again but Dad held her back.

Mackenzie sneered. "Like I can trust him to quarantine at home. Do you think I'm stupid?" He shook his head. "I've played Mr. Rogers long enough with this self-centred punk. Doesn't give a damn if his freedom ends up killing the entire town. Can't bear the inconvenience of a mask or two weeks in a four-star hotel."

I started backing away on all fours, bum down.

"God knows none of this seems fair," continued Mackenzie, stepping toward me. "Life's not fair. Time to grow up."

I shot up out of the crab walk and turned to bolt again. But the old guy was quick or maybe I was still half-stunned. In two seconds, he had my left and right wrists cuffed in hard, cold metal.

"Let's add resisting arrest to the list." He tightened the cuffs around my mitts, cutting off circulation. "You have the right to remain silent. Anything you do or say may be used as evidence. Do you understand?"

I didn't reply.

"Do you understand?"

And he yanked at both my arms so hard I thought they'd pop their sockets.

"How could I possibly understand?" I growled.

Just as he had done in the bakery, the Dungeon Room and at Brian Peckford Park, Constable Corona was abandoning reason for fury. Except, this time, something felt different—as though a dragon, which he usually kept deep in his own subconscious dungeon room, was waking.

"I'm sorry, Vince," said Dad, shaking his head. "I tried to stop you—"

"What's going on?" cried Mom, beginning to shiver. "Oh! What's happening?"

"Get her inside!" barked Mackenzie.

Dad put his arms around her shivering shoulders.

Whispering in my ear, Mackenzie said, "Give me any more crap and I'm charging your mother for assault, too."

I don't know if Mom heard him, but she suddenly let out a wail.

Dad looked at me, as if he didn't know what to do.

"Don't worry about me, Dad," I said, without making eye contact. "Get Mom inside. Take care of her. Can I count on you to do that much?"

"No!" cried Mom. She tried to resist, as Dad led her up the porch. He opened the front door and pushed her inside. Even when the door closed behind them, I could still hear her screaming.

74. Five Seconds

Mackenzie slapped me on the back with surprising strength for such a slim man.

"If you had just done what you were told..." he muttered. "Your poor parents."

I didn't respond.

"On Christmas Eve, too."

He was shoving me toward the cruiser.

"For crying out loud," I exclaimed. "I haven't hurt anyone."

Suddenly, I found my face pressed down on top of the frost-covered roof of the cop car. I heard something crack. *Was that my nose?* Mackenzie's one hand held the back of my head, while the other rummaged through the pockets of my jacket and pants. He tossed my cellphone and wallet on the roof in front of me. He then pulled me upright. My nose might have been bleeding, it was too cold and numb to tell.

"Get in, this time."

I squatted, hands cuffed behind my back, and slid into the back seat. Mackenzie leaned down and pulled a face mask out of the large side pocket of his black pants and extended it toward me.

"Put this on!"

Without looking at him, I muttered back, "The back seat's sealed off."

He threw the mask at me.

"Put it on!"

I felt trapped. Plexiglass and a metal mesh separated the front seat from the back. The opposing door had no handle.

"Put it on!"

"I can't put it on!" I pleaded, terror in my voice.

"Put it on!"

He didn't speak loudly, but the command was direct and forceful like an awl being driven through a leather belt.

"I can't!"

This time he withdrew his taser and aimed it at me.

"Are you insane!" I cried out. "I'm in handcuffs! I can't pick up your freakin' mask."

"Put it on!" he growled.

I backed away across the plastic seat, pressing myself against the other door. He placed one knee down and began to crawl in like a puma entering a cave.

"What the hell is wrong with you?" I cried.

He froze. "Patty begged me to wear a mask." His face melted of expression as if he was suddenly possessed. "Please, dear, wear the mask, she would say."

In the distance I heard a police siren.

God, not more of them.

"Please, Justin, wear the mask," he said in a louder voice.

"Get away from me," I yelled.

"She was always asking me to wear a mask," he now yelled.

He extended his taser at me.

"But I was too proud to wear a mask," said Mackenzie. "I thought they were stupid. But *I* was the one who was stupid."

He let out a ferocious blend of a groan, wail and scream, like an injured mountain lion preparing to attack. I raised my knees up to my chest. I was about to kick out, but I wasn't quick enough. He thrust the electrodes of his taser deep into my left calf, piercing my jeans and long johns. A crackle echoed in the confined space as 50,000 volts discharged throughout my body.

This time it definitely hurt.

One second.

Excruciating pain rattled my brain like a peanut in a jar.

Two seconds.

My arms and legs extended outward, my body a rigid plank.

Three seconds.

My fists were squeezed in tight fists, yet unable to throw a single punch.

Four seconds.

My cells screamed, as my throat uttered a deep moan. I was helpless, absorbing the pain that would never end.

Five seconds.

Like a light switch the pain switched off instantly.

I fell limp.

And, for some reason, I started to laugh—until he rammed the butt of the taser against my forehead. I felt blackness overtaking my mind.

"She asked me to wear a mask," he stuttered as I heard him toss away the spent cartridge in his stun gun. "She told me I needed to stay home." A new cartridge snapped into the barrel. "I didn't listen. I thought the rules were stupid. I thought—"

He growled and plunged the taser into my calf again, piercing more skin, releasing more volts of pain. This time I cried out immediately; but only for a second, before a third wave of paralysis spilled over my body.

Two seconds.

"If only I had listened," Mackenzie said, pressing so hard the electrodes broke the skin.

Three seconds.

"If only someone had made me listen."

My heart pounded so hard it hurt more even than the current of pain.

Four seconds.

Suddenly, black gloved hands appeared, reaching under Mackenzie's armpits, pulling him and the pain away.

Another uniform. Another police officer.

"Grandad?" I gasped. *No. No. It's, it's—*

Narrow Asian eyes peered out from between a black mask and a mouton fur aviator hat with the OPP insignia.

"My God," he said. "Are you all right?"

I just curled up into a ball. Teeth chattering. Body shaking.

"Can you tell me your name?" said the cop.

I knew him. He wasn't Grandad. But I knew him.

"Yamamoto," I said.

"Vince," he gasped. "You're leg, it's bleeding."

Constable Yamamoto backed away, pulling out his radio from his vest, calling somebody for something. Behind him, I could see Mackenzie slumped forward on the frozen lawn, face in hands, his bald crown bereft of hat, maple tree towering up behind him.

"She told me to wear a mask," he was muttering. "She told me to sanitize my hands."

She?

"To stay away from people not in our bubble. I didn't listen." He looked up at Yamamoto, eyes holding back tears in the same way a dam holds back a flood. "I thought it was silly. Now she's..."

Yamamoto knelt down beside him, tucking his radio back into his vest, and putting a hand on Mackenzie's shoulder.

The snow had stopped falling. The sun was casting a pink glow behind the maple tree, where the whistle of the snow bunting had changed to an eerie warble: *hudidi-feet-feet-feew-hudidi.*

"I didn't keep her safe. I wouldn't listen," he began to holler. "No one listens. They think it's a joke. It's not. She's dead! The virus killed her. I killed her."

My eyelids slowly fell as I curled up into a tighter fetal position. I felt my pants get warm and wet. I didn't care. My mind and body couldn't take any more. I felt so weak. My head hurt from the blow. My broken nose felt like it would explode with pain. My heart was breaking speed limits.

Was I really dying this time? I almost hoped so. I wanted to join Grandad—under a maple tree in *Gaagige Minawaanigozigiwining*—the land of happiness and joy. The place where leaves remain forever red and never fall—like the *christdorn* on Mom's wreath on the door of the house that was no longer my home.

PART FOUR
The Dandelion Tempest

"In true love, you attain freedom."
—*Thích Nhất Hạnh,*
Thiền Buddhist monk, peace activist and author

75. The Cross of St. George

Beep... Beep... Beep...

My eyes didn't want to open; but I was awake. Barely. My left calf stung. My nose ached. My head felt swollen and drunken. I felt like a snowplow had mashed me up against a wall.

Beep. Beep. Beep...

Unbelievable memories surfaced... Paramedics wearing respirators with large exhaust valves. Mom crying. The smell of urine. Dad threatening to sue. A warm ambulance. Sirens.

Beep... Beep... Beep...

Doctors with goggles. Nurses with visors. Needles. X-rays. At the time, it all seemed so far away. I had been so tired, physically and mentally, I didn't resist. I barely spoke. I was embarrassed, dejected, exhausted. Unconsciousness offered sweet escape whenever they would allow it.

Beep... Beep... Beep...

I was now lying in a bed, waking from sleep. Stiff, warm blankets covered me up to the neck. The smell of cleaning alcohol stung my nostrils.

Beep... Beep... Beep...

Both my arms were pulled out of the blanket and to either side of me. I forced my eyes open to see a needle taped to the left forearm. A thin tube ran from the needle to a plastic bag, hanging from a pole, half full of dripping fluid. My right wrist was still trapped in a metal cuff, the other handcuff fastened to the bed's railing. An oximeter, clamped to my left middle finger, had a wire leading to a display which produced the rhythmic amplification of my pulse—proof that death had not found me yet.

Beep... Beep... Beep...

My eyes shut again. The lights were too bright. I wanted to go back into the shell of unconsciousness.

"Ahem," said a familiar voice at my feet.

My eyes opened wide. Grandad sat upright at the foot of the bed in a grey metal chair. This time he looked as young as me. The sides of his head were shaven to the skin. The strip of dark black hair that remained was braided and pierced with a small length of antler. The antler held a fistful of coarse moose hair which stuck straight up and fanned outward. He smiled at me, red warrior paint around his eyes.

"You've been brave," he said.

Then his lips collapsed into a frown.

"Rest now. But remember, government is still winning."

I blinked. The brown moose hair fell over his painted face and morphed into a plastic visor.

"Grandad!" I leaned forward, trying to reach out, but the handcuffs snagged me back against the elevated bed.

"Hey, amigo!" said Yamamoto.

Like a channel being changed on a TV, Grandad had blinked away. Only the visor remained. And behind the visor, in the same chair, now sat Constable Yamamoto, gazing at me over an open copy of an *Outlander* novel.

"I thought you'd sleep the day away," he said.

He set the book down, revealing a white medical mask below the visor. He had removed his police vest. On the sleeve of his black shirt, I could see the Ontario coat of arms: three yellow maple leaves and the red Cross of St. George. St. George, so Father Shostakovich had told us one Sunday, was a third-century Roman soldier, put to death for not recanting his Christian faith.

"How ya feeling?" Yamamoto asked, standing.

He had short black hair, which made his big ears appear only bigger. He looked 100 percent Japanese, even though, if I recalled correctly, he was a third-generation Canadian. He certainly didn't have a Japanese accent.

"Where..." I began to say, but my mouth was too dry to talk. I wanted to ask where Grandad had gone.

"Where are you?" said Yamamoto, walking to the side of the bed. "Sudbury General."

I lifted up the handcuffed wrist and stared at it, wondering if it was made of dream stuff or solid metal. My eyes moved toward the taser hanging from Yamamoto's duty belt.

"Don't worry," he said. "You're safe with me." Reaching up, he pulled off the visor and tossed it on a mobile table. "I'm on your side." Then he yanked his face mask down around his neck and smiled.

I stared at his clean-shaven face and then back at the

handcuffs. "I'd hate to see how you handle your enemies."

Yamamoto gave me a lopsided grin. "Come on, amigo. You'd prefer Constable Mackenzie?"

An image of Mackenzie reaching out with his snapping taser, as I cowered in the back of the cruiser, flashed before my mind, sending a shudder down my spine. I shook my head slightly, almost nervously.

"No," I said slowly. "You stopped him. You saved my life."

"Ah," he waved his hand in the air. "Let's not over exaggerate. 'Nough of that happening these days."

He then stood more erect, looked at me with unblinking eyes, and switched to a formal tone.

"I just want to apologize on behalf of the Ontario Provincial Police for Constable Justin T. Mackenzie's conduct. Please be assured we are launching a thorough investigation."

Not sure how to respond, I nodded slightly.

I felt relieved to be with Yamamoto, even if I hardly knew him. A few years back, I'd seen his photo in *The Sudbury Star*, announcing his graduation from the Provincial Police Academy in Orillia. He was born in Toronto but was assigned to Sudbury region for his first year of probational duty. He'd never left. Moosehead didn't suffer much crime, so I'd only seen him about town sporadically.

Dad said he was a good guy. I think Dad preferred cops who were a minority, like us. And, of course, AJ had said Yamamoto was the dungeon master for The Little Shop of Heroes' secret gaming sessions on Friday nights. *And* he had also been tipping Stefanie off on which days she could hold her soup kitchens without Mackenzie busting down the door. Those were usually the days he was working, so I'd never really interacted with him much—only saw him passing on the street on rare occasions. But Stefanie trusted him, so I guess I was in safe hands.

That's when I remembered.

"Stefanie!"

"She your girlfriend?" asked Yamamoto.

"No, my boss! I'm late for work. We have a ton of orders—" I sat up and yanked at the cuff. "What time is it?"

"Settle down, amigo," said Yamamoto. "I think you're going to have to call in sick today. Mackenzie roughed you up pretty bad."

I inhaled and exhaled deeply, feeling exhausted to the bone.

"But it's Christmas Eve," I protested.

"Where do you work?" he asked.

"The bakery on Main Street. I deliver the bread."

"Hey!" he said, breaking out in a smile and pointing his finger at me. "Are you the moose?"

I didn't know whether to feel flattered or embarrassed.

"Yeah," I said. "That's me."

"Wow! You're like Moosehead's unofficial mascot. Double shame on Mackenzie. I hope they throw the book at him." Flattening his smile, he added, "I'm so sorry. I've heard cops flip out like that sometimes. The stress, the hours, and now, with these damn new rules." He brushed his hand through his short hair. "I'm just glad I was able to stop him. For both your sakes."

"How did you know to come for me?" I asked. "How did you get there so fast?"

"I was actually the one assigned to pick you up at the old folks' home. Mackenzie just beat me to it. So, when your mother called in an altercation, it was easy to put two and two together." He chuckled. "Dispatcher wasn't too sure who was more in danger, you or Mackenzie."

I took a deep breath. "I wasn't the one with the weapon."

Yamamoto held up his arms and stared at his own hands, disbelievingly. "'Always doing the right thing for the right reasons,'" he quoted. "That's the OPP motto. But it seems we're doing the wrong things for the wrong reasons, these days."

"So, you don't buy into the COVID hype?"

He shrugged. "All I know is, ticketing people for going to church, running their business, or shopping without a mask, isn't what I signed up for."

"Where..." I attempted to say, but my throat had turned dry again and I coughed.

Yamamoto grabbed a Styrofoam cup from the table and held it out for me. I sucked up ice water through the straw.

"Where is he now?" I finally asked. "Constable Corona."

"Constable Corona!" exclaimed Yamamoto with a laugh. "God, he'd probably like that."

"Is he under arrest?"

With a tilt of his head, Yamamoto replied, "Not yet. But he is suspended without pay. I assume he's observing stay-at-home orders."

"You assume?" I replied, feeling my adrenaline rise. "You mean you think he might get out and—"

He shook his head. "No, nothing like that. He's the last one to disobey lockdown orders. I'm more concerned about him being alone for Xmas day. He's a good cop, just a bit unstable. He's been through hell."

"His wife," I said, "she died, didn't she? I heard him. What he was saying after you came. She's dead isn't she?"

Yamamoto nodded.

"When?" I asked.

"Last spring," he said.

"From COVID?"

Yamamoto shrugged. "So they say."

"You don't believe 'em?"

"Don't trust 'em." He shrugged. "Come on, amigo, you know as well as me that half these people don't even have pneumonia when they die. His wife was overweight, diabetic, with high blood pressure. She had a fever and a cough and a positive PCR test. They rushed her into ICU. Next thing you know they have her on dialysis. They said the virus killed her kidneys. Seems this virus can do just about anything. I rather suspect the drugs they gave her shot her kidneys and the ventilator finished her off. But what do I know?"

Remdesivir, I thought, thinking back to what Stefanie and Josef had told me about the drug in the summer.

Yamamoto took the cup from me and set it back on the mobile table before continuing.

"But as far as Mackenzie's concerned, COVID killed her, and all those who spread it. It's almost like he's on a mission now." He crossed his arms. "At least it keeps him away from the bottle."

"Hearing him freaking out like that," I said. "It shocked me almost as much as his taser."

"He's a crab. Hard on the outside, soft on the inside."

"My boss says I'm a turtle," I said, suddenly feeling a strange connection with the man who, only a few hours earlier, had been torturing me. "Turtles and crabs. Sort of the same."

Yamamoto crossed his arms. "I think Mars was in Cancer when he was born."

My forehead scrunched up, questioningly.

"My girlfriend was really into astrology." Yamamoto shrugged. "Anyway, he blames himself for his wife's death, ultimately. His penance? Making sure we all stand six feet apart." He grinned. "At least, that's how I see it. Keep in mind, I'm a cop, not a psychoanalyst."

I yawned and rubbed my eyes with my unshackled hand. I wasn't sure if I was waking up or falling back asleep. Scanning my new surroundings, I saw a curtain draped behind Yamamoto, blocking off the rest of the small room. I couldn't see any windows. On my left, where the hanging monitor beeped, was a sink, trashcan and two doors. One door was ajar and appeared to be for a restroom. The other was closed. I wondered if it was locked.

Clang! Almost in response to the mental query, a bolt on the other side of the door slid open. Yamamoto snapped his mask back into place, a soldier-like stare coming over his eyes. A grey-haired man with red-framed glasses entered. He was a bit pudgy, wearing black dress pants, a light blue dress shirt with a paisley tie and a white lab coat.

"Ah! The troublemaker's awake," he said behind his N95 mask.

76. The Premier Who Stole Christmas

I was the victim of assault, attempted kidnapping, and possibly even attempted murder, yet I was the one handcuffed to a bed under armed guard. I'd expected the doctor, who had just entered the hospital room, to be outraged. Instead, he seemed tentatively amused. Pulling out a swivel chair from under the sink, he set his right shoe in the centre of the seat, propping a data pad on his elevated knee. With downcast eyes, he scanned its screen.

"Three tasings," he read. "Two of them drive stuns. Man, that must smart. But, hey, it's sort of like free shock therapy." He put a hand to his temple. "We use it in the psych ward. Balances both hemispheres of the brain."

I stared back, gripping the side of the bedrail. The doctor was lucky my wrist was handcuffed. I was tempted to grab Yamamoto's taser and give him a sample of the shock therapy he was praising. The monitor began to beep faster.

"Sorry," he said. "Bad joke."

He sighed through his mask, steaming up his glasses. My fist loosened.

"My name's Dr. Roberts," he continued, in a more serious tone. "We ran some bloodwork and you're as fit as a horse. Your cholesterol levels are the lowest I've ever seen. You're not on a statin, are you?"

"I went vegan," I replied.

"Oh?" His eyebrow raised. "How long ago?"

"Since this morning."

"Hmm."

"So can I go, now?"

The doc took his shoe off the stool, leaving a footprint. "Well, you're stuck here for at least fourteen days."

"Fourteen days!" I turned to Yamamoto. "Here? What about that four-star COVID hotel?"

Yamamoto shrugged. "Come on, amigo. That was before Mackenzie arrested you."

"Plus," said Dr. Roberts, "you have a small fracture to your nose, and we need to keep an eye on your leg."

I kicked my left leg loose from the bottom of the blanket and stared at a white bandage around my calf.

"That's just a flesh wound," I protested. With my left hand I touched my aching nose. "And my nose..." It did feel bigger than usual.

"Don't worry, both should heal up fine," said the doc. "Just let the nurse know if you want some pain meds."

"Fine!" I blurted out angrily. "Give me some Tylenol No. 4 and discharge me."

"Lad," said the doc, "now that you are contained, we don't want to risk moving you and exposing more people. Says here—" he looked at his data pad "—that you were present for the death of a confirmed COVID case."

I could almost hear Stefanie prompting me in my one ear, as I said, "The Bill of Rights requires—"

"You mean the Charter of Rights?" interrupted the doctor.

"No, the Bill of Rights."

"Isn't that an American thing?" he said.

"Look it up. We have one, too. And it says without an act of Parliament you can't just go and lock me up in a room that doesn't even have a damn window."

"What do you mean?" said the doc, with a nervous joviality. He pointed up over my head to a two-by-four-foot glass pane that was flush with the ceiling and covered with snow.

Yamamoto looked at me with sympathetic eyes and said, "I know it's not Caesar's Palace."

"Easy for you to say." I pulled the oximeter off my middle finger. The monitor broke out in a long squeal. "It's not like you're stuck here for the next two weeks."

"Actually..." Yamamoto pulled back the curtain behind him, revealing another bed, a TV and a set of lockers. "We're all in this together." He raised his eyebrows. "Well, at least me and you."

"What?"

"Listen amigo," he said. "They wanted to throw you in the slammer. But, since the correctional officers didn't want to get COVID, and I offered to use my vacation days, they were willing to compromise and let me bunk with you here." He slapped his hands together. "Anyway, I am a certified dungeon master, as you might have heard."

Was he seriously going to stay in this medical dungeon with me? On his bedside chair sat a duffel bag. On the mobile table an iPad, two more *Outlander* novels, and a photo of a girl and boy. Yamamoto's OPP jacket lay on the bed.

"But you'll miss Christmas," I said, a bit shocked at the sacrifice he was making.

Yamamoto shrugged. "After the first six weeks of lockdown, Zoom wasn't cutting it with my girlfriend. She ended up in bed with the Amazon delivery guy." He smirked and rolled his eyes from left to right.

The doctor pointed toward the photo of the boy and girl. "What about the young 'uns?"

"They're my brother's," he said. "Niece and nephew, back in Toronto. Haven't seen them since the second wave. Their paranoid parents are too scared of the virus. Thought it best I didn't visit this year."

"Bummer," I said. "What about your parents?"

"Ah," said Yamamoto, dismissively. "They moved back out to Manitoba five years ago. So I figure, might as well hang with you. We can watch *The Premier Who Stole Christmas*."

I tried to raise my right hand. The handcuff clanged against the railing. "Am I going to be shackled to the bed the whole time? You know, I might need the bathroom."

"As long as you behave," said Yamamoto, waving his index finger in the air with a mocking edge to his voice. "Once Dr. Roberts is done, I can uncuff you." Then his voice turned dead serious. "But if you make any attempt, any attempt, to escape, I can assure you that you'll end up somewhere that'll make this place feel like Caesar's Palace. And your cellmates will make Constable Mackenzie seem like Mahatma Gandhi."

I gulped but didn't say anything.

"Mackenzie's pressing five charges. But considering how he handled the situation, I think they'll all be dropped. You just need to sit tight until a judge sorts out the mess."

I inhaled deeply.

The doctor, who'd been tapping away at his data pad, chuckled. "The snow's falling nonstop," he said. "And it's so bloody cold out there. No way you're going to be running anywhere."

"Not dressed like this," I admitted.

I glanced down at the hospital gown and assumed it had the customary split in the back. I shook my head. Stefanie would be disappointed in me, but I had had enough.

"Don't worry, I won't give you any trouble," I promised. "Three tasings. That's enough."

My legs jerked at the memory of Constable Corona reaching into the back of the cruiser and pressing the electrodes to my left leg. That's when I realized there was something on the other leg. I kicked at the sheet, revealing a small black device strapped around the right ankle, with a flashing red light.

I began to shake the leg, trying to knock it off as fiercely as I would have kicked away a snake.

77. The Den of the New Normal Dragon

I tried to reach for my right leg with my left arm, but the IV line had as much give as the handcuff on my other wrist. The bed rattled as I shook the leg, trying to knock away the flashing device. They must have fastened it around my ankle when I was sleeping.

"What is it?" I yelled.

"Whoa, settle down, amigo," said Yamamoto. "It's just a tracking anklet."

"What's it do?"

I stilled my leg, but the rest of my body began to shake.

"It'll sound an alarm if you try to leave the building."

"Will it zap me?"

"No," assured the doctor. "Nothing like that. Same kind we use to stop people from kidnapping babies from the NIC unit."

"Zapping you is my job," said Yamamoto, wryly.

I glared at him, still shuddering.

"Sorry," he said with a sigh. "Another bad joke."

He got up and walked toward the two lockers. A key hung from a padlock on the left door. He slid off his duty belt, unloading the taser, gun, baton and pepper spray. "I don't think we'll be needing these," he said, as he slid the weapons onto the top shelf. Shutting the door and clamping the padlock, he added the key to his overloaded keyring.

The doctor looked at Yamamoto. With the N95 mask it was hard to discern his expression, but the unblinking eyes and furrowed brow signalled that he did not approve of Yamamoto disarming himself.

"He's harmless," said Yamamoto. "I'd trust him with my niece and nephew."

The doc tapped his data pad. "Says here he's charged with assaulting a police officer."

"Ah, yes. I forgot about that." Yamamoto inhaled deeply. "The officer attacked him first. It was purely self-defence."

"Well, that's some comfort," said the doc.

"Don't worry, Vince and I go way back," Yamamoto deadpanned. "He's a good guy. I know his whole family."

"Native?" asked the doctor.

Yamamoto shrugged.

"Quarter," I said.

The doc nodded, typed something into his data pad.

"First Nations people are much more susceptible to COVID," he said. "Too bad we don't have a separate hospital for your people anymore. Like we did with TB."

I couldn't believe he had just said that.

"Well," he continued, looking at Yamamoto. "As long as he's cuffed when staff's in the room, I'll leave the rest to your discretion."

"Yes, sir," said Yamamoto, respectfully.

The doctor let the data pad hang at his side. "Well, I think I'm done. You seem more than stable. If you need a nurse, just pull that cord there." He took a last glance at the monitor. "Your oxygen saturation is at 98 percent. So you'll need to start wearing a mask. At least, when staff's in the room. Especially considering your, uh, contact history."

"Handcuffs, mask," repeated Yamamoto, amiably. "Got it!"

"Well," said the doctor, taking off his steamed up glasses and rubbing them on his white coat, "a guy who risks his life to sit by his dying grandfather can't be all that bad."

"I couldn't agree more," said Yamamoto.

The doctor adjusted his N95 mask and slid his glasses back into place. "Well, a safe Christmas to you both. Remember, we're all in this together."

"Yes, sir," said Yamamoto. "Thank you, sir." I thought he was going to salute.

I just nodded at the doc as he sauntered toward the door. Reaching out for the handle, he froze, and twisted his head back.

"I'm sorry it's like this," he said. "I guess that's war. We're at war with a virus." He was almost mumbling, as if he didn't believe what he was saying, but wanted to. "And the enemy doesn't take Christmas off. But it sounds like Santa's elves are going to have enough vaccines ready for all of us soon. By the time you are both out of here we'll be on our way back to normal."

Without waiting for a response, he opened the door and passed through, pulling it closed behind him. I heard the bolt slide into place.

"Hey," I said, turning to Yamamoto. "Are you able to open

that door from the inside?"

"Nope." He pulled down his mask and grinned. "At least, not easily."

He turned to his duffel bag and rubbed his hands together. "Better unpack," he said to himself.

Again, I noticed the red cross on his shoulder patch and remembered the legend of St. George from Sunday school when I was really young; how a dragon had descended upon a city in Libya and demanded two sheep per day for lunch or the beast would burn the city to ashes. Eventually, sheep failed to satisfy its hunger. The dragon wanted human sacrifice. When the king's daughter was to become one of those daily offerings, St. George arrived. He pierced the dragon with the lance of Ascalon and saved both princess and city.

Now, there I lay, shackled to a sacrificial stretcher, the very altar of this new medical tyranny that had descended upon the world. While I was glad to have Yamamoto on my side, he bore no almighty lance that could slay this emerging medical monstrosity. He was as much a prisoner as I, trapped in the den of the new-normal dragon which was sacrificing society, one day at a time, in its lockdown jaws and sanitizing fires.

78. Inoculation or Incarceration

Ten minutes after Dr. Roberts had left, I was still propped up in the hospital bed, tied to an IV and handcuffed to the railing, trying my best to relax. The monitor showed my heart rate was in the eighties. It usually rested in around sixty beats per minute. Remembering Granddad's posthumous advice, I tried to slow the breath as it entered and left my nostrils, while my mind played an intense game of tennis with a thousand doomsday fireball thoughts.

Yamamoto was calling in a report to the Greater Sudbury Police Department on his cell phone. As soon as he finished, I spoke up.

"Constable, do you—"

"Hey!" he interrupted, "We're roomies! You don't have to call me Constable. The name's Dave."

"Dave?" I replied. "*Dave? But everyone in Moosehead calls

you Yamamoto."

"Ha!" he laughed. "You don't think cops have first names?"

"Actually, I kind of thought your first name was Yama, and your last Moto."

"All right, amigo. You can call me Yama," he said. "But I just want you to know, you won't be the first."

"How about George?" I said, looking at the Cross of St. George on his uniform. "Anyone called you George before?"

"George? Why George?"

"Long story," I replied, shaking my head. "Yama it is."

"That's what my girlfriend used to call me. She was really into yoga. Said *yama* was Sanskrit for self-restraint and conjugal chastity."

"The same girlfriend who ended up in bed with the Amazon delivery guy?"

"Yeah." Yamamoto scratched his head. "You were going to ask me something?"

"Do you think he was right?" I asked.

"Who, the Amazon delivery guy?"

"No, the doctor. About things going back to normal now that Santa's bringing the vaccine?"

Yamamoto laughed, halfheartedly. "Bill Gates doesn't look a thing like Old Saint Nick." A sigh. "Still, that's what my brother Brad's telling Cindy and Michael." He pointed to the picture of his niece and nephew. "For Christmas the world gets a vaccine so they can go back to school and play with their friends."

"Are you getting the shot?" I asked.

"Probably," he said, glumly.

"But you don't look too scared of the virus," I nodded toward his discarded mask on his bed.

"Ah, those things are only good for stopping dust balls." He picked up the mask and dropped it into a plastic Ziplock bag he'd pulled out of his pocket. "If I'm going to get SARS-CoV-2, I'm going to get it. Anyway, I think we both know a coronavirus ain't much to fear. COVID's just the common cold with a great PR team."

"Then why are you getting vaxxed?"

He stretched out his arms. "Hey, trust me, amigo, if I can get out of it, I will. You know the joke, don't you? One mouse says to the other, 'Are you getting the COVID vaccine?' And the other mouse says—"

"'I'm waiting for the human trials to be over,'" I finished for him.

"Hmm," he said, looking disappointed I stole the punchline. "Well, anyway, so far, everyone in the human trials fell sick or had some mild side effect. Every single one. Some were even hospitalized. Some died. It's insane! But I'm a cop. It'll probably be required. Heck, won't surprise me if they try to force this on everyone."

"Like bust down doors and jab the needle into people's arms?"

He shook his head.

"I don't think they'd go that far. Instead, they'd just herd the unvaccinated into work camps."

"Work camps? This is Canada, not Communist China."

"Come on, amigo," said Yamamoto, as he pulled out his massive key ring, "you ever read your World War II history? My grandpa owned a fleet of fishing boats on the West Coast. When the Japanese attacked Pearl Harbor, the War Measures Act took away his boats, his home, and all the money in his bank account. Sure, they didn't imprison them. They just made it so that if any of the twenty-one thousand Japanese-Canadians living in British Columbia wanted food, shelter or heat, they had limited options."

He fumbled through the key ring, as if he was having trouble recognizing which key was for the cuffs.

"First they came for the able-bodied men," he continued. "*Sofu*, my grandfather, was packed onto a train and hauled off to Alberta to work a sugar beet farm for the rest of the war. He bunked in a chicken coop with twenty other men."

Of course, I knew about the camps. Just as most people know about the residential schools for the Indigenous. And, as with most people, it had been nothing more to me than an embarrassing footnote in a grade ten textbook. Nothing that would ever have any bearing on my life.

"A few months later, they came for the women and children," he continued, with resentment. "*Sobo,* my grandmother, was given twenty-four hours' notice before she and her sisters were herded onto dusty trains."

"Trains?" I said. "Sounds like Hitler."

"Well, these one's probably had seats. Not cattle cars. Have to keep the standards a notch above the Nazis."

"What happened to your mother's family?"

"They were deposited in overcrowded internment camps in the BC mountains. No running water. No electricity."

"It's hard to believe," I said.

"And *Sobo,* Grandma, was born in Canada. *Sofu,* he served in the Canadian Corps in France in World War I. He lost his middle finger to shrapnel. But he lost everything when he came back home to the supposed true north strong and free. Even after Hiroshima, they never returned his money, his boats or even bought him a train ticket back to the coast. Instead, they shipped the family out to Manitoba to fend for a living in the bush. Somehow they all survived."

"I'm sorry, Yama," I said.

Yamamoto grinned. "Hell, they even detained David Suzuki."

"He's that *Nature of Things* guy, isn't he?" I asked.

Yamamoto nodded. "He was only six when the government seized his parents' dry cleaning shop. They sold the biz to pay for his family's detention. His sister, Dawn, was born in the camp. And—" he paused— "Suzuki and his siblings were only Japanese *sansei.*"

"What's *sansei* mean?" I asked.

"Third generation," said Yamamoto. "Like me. They were born in Canada. Their parents were born in Canada. But that didn't stop the Canadian government from herding them into detention centres and work camps."

"Didn't anyone refuse?" I asked.

"Sure," he replied. "They were the ones hauled off to official POW camps. You know, with the German prisoners in Manitoba."

I shook my head.

"Not a single Japanese-Canadian was ever charged with an offence," continued Yamamoto as he singled out a key on his keyring. "So it won't much surprise me if they do the same to people they claim are not immunized from a virus they've never even proven exists. Just like my grandparents, they suddenly become 'the enemy' because some politicians said so and enough people cry, 'Crucify them!'"

"Even though," I added, "they haven't even proven the vaccine works."

"Just like they couldn't prove that a five-year-old Japanese-Canadian girl was a threat to national security." He held up the key and said, "Sorry, amigo. I forgot what I was doing."

He slid the key into the handcuff attached to the bed rail. It clicked and opened. I rubbed my sore wrist. He took a deep breath before changing the subject.

"Doc wants to leave the IV in until tomorrow. So, for Christmas you'll get your other arm back. But, the IV pole's on wheels, so you can move around. Need the bathroom?"

I shook my head. "I'm actually really thirsty." I pointed to the Styrofoam cup he'd left on the mobile table. He passed me the ice water. I took a sip before saying, "It's unthinkable what happened to your grandparents. But that was seventy-five years ago."

"Long enough for people to forget," said Yamamoto, slipping the keys back into his pocket with a pat. "So, yeah, come on, I'm going to get the vaccine. Not what I want to do. Might make me ill, but I doubt it'll kill me. I'm more worried about my parents. They're getting on."

"The very people they claim to be protecting," I said.

"Yeah, right," said Yamamoto. "If these politicians really cared about old people, they'd put the money into making old-age homes livable, not pumping billions into drug companies."

My mind flashed back to the unidentified floating insectoids in Grandad's bowl of ice cream.

"Even if the vax doesn't kill you," I said, "it could maim you."

"Yeah," admitted Yamamoto, walking toward the bathroom carrying some rolled-up clothes. "Better odds for turning out paralyzed than winning the lottery. Still, chances are I'll be fine. But If I don't take it, I might be digging mines in the Yukon."

"Inoculation or incarceration," I said softly.

"On the subject of incarceration," said Yamamoto. "You still get your one phone call. You wanna call your parents? Lawyer? Girlfriend?"

"Boss," I said.

"Go for it!"

He pulled out his cell and handed it to me.

"Where's my phone?" I asked.

"Forensics," said Yamamoto. "Sorry, amigo. I couldn't stop them. I was pushing it enough keeping you out of jail."

I nodded.

"I really appreciate all you've done for me. You've practically made yourself a prisoner, too."

"Prisoner?" he said. "Remember, I'm the Dungeon Master!"

And then he launched into a poetry recital:

Stone walls do not a prison make,
Nor iron bars a cage;
Minds innocent and quiet take
That for an hermitage;
If I have freedom in my love
And in my soul am free,
Angels alone, that soar above,
Enjoy such liberty.

"Is that from Dungeons and Dragons?" I asked him.

"Oh, no," he said with a laugh. "That was Richard Lovelace."

I considered pretending I knew who Lovelace was, but decided best to be honest and silent.

"I had to memorize it in high school English. Lovelace wrote it when he was locked up in London's Gatehouse Prison in sixteen-something."

"Why was he in prison?"

"He disagreed with something the government did."

"Oh," I said.

He pursed his lips. "Well, hey, you call your, um, boss and I'll take a shower."

And he stepped into the bathroom and closed the door.

79. To Scare a Dandelion

I stared at the dial pad on Yamamoto's cell. Fortunately, I'd seen the bakery's phone number enough times—on the van, in the store window and on flyers—that I had it memorized.

The phone rang only once before she picked up.

"Hello?"

"Hey, Captain Dandelion," I said.

"Where are you?" she blurted out. "I called the nursing home. They told me you were sent home." She was talking fast. "I went to your place. Your Mom said that cop tasered you. She started crying on my shoulder. Then she said she contaminated me. Then she started crying more, saying now I had to go into quarantine. I called your cell. Been calling hospitals. I, I—"

She paused to take a deep breath. Her usual calm demeanour had been shattered. She sounded frightened, outraged, and aghast, all packed together into one high-speed snowball.

I didn't know how to respond.

"Vince, are you okay?" she pressed.

"Well," I said slowly. "I think I qualify as okay. I mean, I'm alive. Doc says there's nothing serious. Just a gash in my leg and a fractured nose."

"He broke your nose?"

"No, Dr. Roberts is nice enough. Constable Corona did it."

"Don't joke! You're not okay."

"Ah," I said. "Had worse happen to me on the rink last year." I was still feeling pretty shaken up, but was trying to keep my cool (or, at least, seem to). "I just feel super tired. I'm on an IV."

"An IV?"

"It's just salt water, I think. Maybe some glucose, too. I'm certainly not hungry."

"This is nuts!" exclaimed Stefanie. "The police have gone Gestapo!"

I could hear Yamamoto singing "I Wish You a Merry Christmas" over the sound of the shower.

"Well, not all cops," I said. "Yamamoto wouldn't hurt me." At least, I didn't think he would. "He's here with me."

"Is he going to get you out of there?"

"No, um, he's the Dungeon Master."

"The what?"

I explained to her the situation.

"So you're his prisoner?" she asked.

"Yeah," I conceded. "Makes me realize how Grandad must have felt."

"Oh, your Grandad! I'm so sorry, Vince." Her voiced slowed. "But I'm so glad you were there for his passing. That you didn't let them keep you away."

Two tears emerged spontaneously and dropped down onto the hospital gown.

There were a few seconds of silence before Stefanie asked, "Which hospital are you at?"

"Sudbury General."

"I called them first," she said. "They told me you weren't there."

Strange, I thought. Then I remembered.

"Hey, doesn't your mom work here?"

"Yeah," she said, distractedly.

"Maybe I'll finally meet her."

"Not likely. She's a neonatal nurse," Stefanie replied. "Besides, she's off for Christmas break."

"Surprising they can spare a nurse in the middle of a pandemic."

She ignored my comment and asked, "Which room are you in?"

"The one with the skull and bones painted on the front door, I suspect."

"No, seriously, what's the room number?"

"No clue," I said. "I suspect we're in the basement, though."

I glanced up at the small window near the ceiling.

"The basement!" she said, disgustingly. "That's the psych ward."

"Well, it is a bit crazy around here."

"I'll be there as fast as I can. You can stay at my place until this blows over."

"Oh," I said, in surprise. I was just getting used to the prospect of quarantining with St. George Yamamoto, and here she's tempting me with fourteen days locked up with her. "I'd really like to accept... But, I'm Catholic, you know."

"That doesn't bother me."

"No, I mean, it wouldn't be proper for me to be staying with you. You know, you being female. A rather beautiful one, at that. Father Shostakovich would handcuff me to the confessional for an additional fourteen days as penance."

"Hey!" said Stefanie, quickly becoming defensive. "I wasn't going to share a bed with you. You can sleep on the futon in the bake room."

"They'd shut the whole bakery down."

"I don't care. You're not safe there. I want you here."

I looked around the room. If there wasn't an IV in my arm, a bolted door and a cop in the bathroom, I might have made a run for it.

"It's just not possible," I said.

"What do you mean?" she argued. "It's not like you're under arrest. They can't—"

"Actually, I am."

"What?"

"Five charges."

"Five?"

"Yeah. Let's see. Assaulting a police officer. Evading quarantine. Um, it's hard to remember them all. Violating the Reopening of Ontario Act."

"Reopening of Ontario Act," she grumbled. "What the hell does that mean?"

"I think that was for the illicit skating."

"Ich glaub mein—" she began to say.

"Elch pfeift," I finished.

I think I hear my elk whistling. Elk. I thought it was clever.

"That's not funny."

She was obviously not in the mood for clever.

"You can't stay there," she said, shakily.

"The door's bolted shut from the outside."

"When a nurse comes in, just run," she ordered. "Don't be a turtle!"

"Yama has to handcuff me every time staff comes in," I explained.

"Handcuff you?" She let out a scream. Boy, I'd never heard her act like this.

"Dandelion," I said, trying to sound calm and confident. "Right now, things aren't all that bad. It's only fourteen days."

"You're locked up in a hospital, with a tube running into your arm, a broken nose, a gash in your leg, assumed to have the twenty-first-century bubonic plague, with an armed guard watching over you, and you're saying things aren't that bad?"

"Actually, he put the gun in the locker." My voice sounded as tired as the rest of me felt. "Listen, Dandelion, if you'd been through what I've been through you'd say I was in paradise."

"Exactly!" she exclaimed. "They torture you and then make you feel grateful when they simply lock you up."

"What am I supposed to do?" I said, feeling another rise of indignation. "I've stuck my neck out enough, and nearly got it hacked off. We gotta get real here."

She didn't say a word; but I could hear her breathing. Finally, she said, "I'll call a lawyer and raise hell."

"You don't have the money or the time," I said. "What about the deliveries? It's past ten. You gotta get them—"

"I don't care about the orders," she said. "People can live without cookies."

"You need the money."

"My Bitcoin investment is soaring," she replied.

"The cookies will go to waste."

"I'll freeze them. We can live off gingerbread for the rest of the year."

"Call AJ," I urged. "He'll deliver them. We know he can handle the van."

A pause. "That's a good idea."

I felt a twang of jealousy at the thought of AJ the Brave taking my place at the wheel.

"I'm sorry I'm not more daring."

"No," she countered. "You've been amazing."

"Oh," I said, a bit shocked at the unexpected appraisal.

"I'm just angry," she said.

"An angry dandy-lion?"

"Don't turtles get angry?"

"A little. Don't dandelions ever get scared?"

"I'm scared right now."

I actually didn't think she was capable of fear. I figured she had a recessive gene.

"What are you scared of?" I asked, tentatively.

"That you're going to die in there."

"What, from COVID?"

"No, from a ventilator or something they slip in your IV."

"Hey, this isn't New York. It's Sudbury, Ontario. I'll be fine. They'll probably just ignore me. They're just trying to make the place look full."

The bathroom door opened and Yamamoto stepped out with wet hair, wearing nothing but a towel around his waist, carrying his folded uniform.

"Is anything else bothering you?" I said into the phone.

"This letter."

"What letter?"

80. When Love Frees Itself From Pain

I heard the flap of paper on the other end of the phone.

"Mailman just dropped it off," said Stefanie. "Local public health unit, wishing me a merry Christmas and letting me know that I and my staff—namely you—qualify as essential workers who will be moved near the front of the COVID-19 vaccination line. They say getting vaxxed is critical in order to continue operating a retail outlet in 2021."

Yamamoto, still wearing nothing more than a towel, put his folded uniform on the top shelf of his locker.

"Listen, Captain," I said. "We have enough to worry about right now without fretting over what might happen next year."

"Yeah," she admitted, sullenly.

"Being stuck here for Christmas stinks enough."

"Hey!" said Yamamoto. "I just took a shower."

"Yama, do you mind?" I spoke out, holding my hand over the phone. "I'm in a confidential business meeting."

He saluted, walked over to his bed and pulled across the curtain separating his side of the room from mine.

Suddenly, I remembered.

"Mackenzie!" I said. "He told me he saw you last night."

"Yeah," she said. "Pretty creepy. He was waiting for me when I got back."

My body tensed. "He didn't hurt you, did he?"

"No," she said. "I got inside as quickly as I could."

"Good." I said, feeling relief. "He said he left a gift for you."

"Huh? I didn't see anything."

"Maybe a ticket?" I asked.

"If he left one, it's blown away. There's nothing out there."

"Hmm." Rather than relief, I felt more unease. "It's probably best you don't stay there alone."

"No kidding," she said. "Why don't you join me?"

"Promise to call AJ, get him to help out."

"I will."

"Offer him my salary."

"That won't be too tempting."

"Well, there's always Mathéo. You can pay him with cookies. Maybe see if Bindu will hang with you. Have a Christmas Eve party or something."

"I don't like parties."

"A soup kitchen then. Just don't stay alone. If Bindu's there, then it'll be easy to get Léo there, too."

"Good ideas," she said. "Maybe Sandy, too."

I was surprised that the self-reliant Dandelion was willing to reach out for help. *She must really be scared.*

"Are you going to visit your mom for Christmas, tomorrow? You said she's off work."

"What? Oh. Yes, right. Mom. Yeah. Good idea."

There was an awkward silence. I kind of felt like we were having two different conversations. A rather loud yawn escaped my mouth before I even felt it coming. My eyelids slowly dropped for a second. "Boy, I feel so tired. I hardly slept last night, watching Grandad sleep."

"Do you miss him?"

I swallowed. "Part of me doesn't believe he's dead."

"I'm sure he's still with you," she said.

Boy, that's an understatement, I thought, as I glanced over at the empty seat at the end of the bed, where'd I'd last seen his ever-morphing apparition.

Stefanie continued, "There has to be more to life than just our time here in this insane asylum."

"Grandad would agree. Today, I thought I was going to find out."

"I'm glad you didn't," she said. Then she shyly added, "Do you know why?"

I laughed. "Yeah! I'm the only guy in town willing to dress up as an ungulate to deliver your sour bread."

She didn't laugh. There were a few seconds of silence before she bluntly said, "Yeah, that's it."

"I'll call you tomorrow, if Yama lets me," I said.

"Two phone calls?" said Yamamoto from the other side of the curtain. "Why not? It's Christmas, after all! Ho! Ho! Ho!"

"Hey!" I hollered. "Private conversation!"

And then I coughed.

"Are you okay?" said Stefanie, anxiously.

Yamamoto poked his head out from behind the curtain.

"Relax!" I said hoarsely, sucking up more water through the straw. "My throat's just dry."

"Yeah," agreed Yamamoto, hesitantly. "This place could use a humidifier."

His head retreated back behind the divider.

"You sure you're okay?" said Stefanie.

"Yeah," I insisted. "Hey, I have a gift for you. It's in my room. Maybe Mom can—"

"Don't worry about it," interrupted Stefanie. "I have one for you, too. We'll exchange gifts soon." And then, almost in a whisper, she added, "Maybe under some mistletoe."

Mistletoe? I glanced at the bag hanging from the IV pole. What was in that drip? Psychedelics?

"When your mom told me what happened to you," she continued, quietly, yet quickly, "I was so afraid you may have died."

She paused, sounding like she was both crying and laughing.

"And that made me realize... Made me admit to myself how much..." She paused again. "How much I love you."

My mouth fell open. I raised my left hand, dangling the tube running from the IV pole. Whatever was in that drip, I wanted more of it.

"Bye," she said.

The phone beeped and the display changed to: CALL ENDED.

My heart was pounding. Despite my tasered and exhausted body, I felt a soothing current running up and down my spine. Words from Schubert's *Lied* sang out in my weary mind:

Und wenn sich die Liebe
Dem Schmerz entringt,
Ein Sternlein, ein neues,

Am Himmel erblinkt;*

I let my hand with the phone fall to the bed. I leaned back on the pillow. Any pain in my battered body meant nothing to me. My eyelids slowly descended over my watery eyeballs.

Da springen drei Rosen,
Halb rot und halb weiß,
Die welken nicht wieder,
Aus Dornenreis.†

As absurd as it may sound, everything felt perfect. What more did I need? I had the protection of St. George, the guidance of an Ojibwe ghost and the love of a dandelion.

81. The North Pole's Pharmaceuticals Department

"Sorry, I have to do this," said Yamamoto, the next morning. Christmas morning. He snapped the handcuff around my right wrist again. "But I'm sure you want to be free of that IV."

"At least I'll be able to take a shower."

Honestly, though, I didn't mind being fastened to the railing once again. I didn't mind the lumpy bed, which, after a long night's rest, had made my sore back even sorer. I didn't mind waking up a prisoner in a quasi-windowless, medical dungeon. I didn't even mind that all the dry air was seriously inflaming my throat. I didn't mind anything.

Stefanie and I were in love, and that's all I needed for Christmas. I just hoped I hadn't imagined her last words in some post-traumatic delirium.

---

* And when love frees
Itself from pain,
A little star, a new one,
Twinkles in the sky;

† And three roses spring,
Half red and half white,
That never wither,
From the thorny stem.

The door unbolted and opened enough to allow a bulky male nurse to stick his head in. He had dark skin, a white medical mask and a plastic face shield.

"Ho, ho, ho!" He spoke French with an African accent. "*Est-il sécuritaire d'entrer?*"

"*Oui, oui,*" affirmed Yamamoto, dropping the key in his pocket. "*Il n'y a aucun danger.*"

"Okie-dokie," said the nurse. He opened the door all the way and entered. Pulling out the stool (which still had Dr. Roberts' footprint from the day before), he slid up beside me and spoke cheerfully, yet incomprehensibly:

"*Le Père Noël dit que vous avez été un bon garçon, alors pour Noël, vous récupérez votre bras.*"

I responded with the one complete sentence I could say flawlessly in French, "*Désolé, je ne comprends pas le français.*"

"Oh, sorry," he said, reverting to English with even thicker African intonations and rhythms. "I was saying that Santa told me you have been a good boy, so for Christmas you get the arm back."

"Ah," I said.

Instead of punching him, I reached for a mask and covered up. I felt too good to care one way or another about their stupid rules and corny bedside manner. Besides, I needed him to tell me something.

"Hey, what exactly's in that IV?" I asked.

"*Voyons voir.*" He stood up and held the bag close to his face shield, reading the fine print. "Le sel. Le dextrose. L'eau. Just salt, sugar, water."

"No hallucinogenics?" I asked.

"Hallucinogènes?" The nurse laughed. "No, no, nothing like that."

Good, I thought. But, of course, I may have misunderstood Stefanie. I was tired. She might have been feeling sorry for me, having been tasered and all. And she might just have meant she loved me as a friend. Maybe as a brother. Or a pet. A pet moose. Though, Grandad had said *meese* make lousy pets.

The nurse quickly slid the plastic cannula out of my vein, while pressing a cotton ball in its place. "Hold that, *s'il vous plaît*," he said, after taping the cotton to my forearm. "Keep pressure for *dix minutes*." He held up ten digits. He then stood, tossing the IV bag and line into a yellow biowaste container on the wall. "And, no weightlifting with that arm today."

"Not on Christmas," I said, amiably, but made a point of not thanking him.

"*Un Noël en toute sécurité*," he said, as he opened the door. Then in slower English, "A very safe Christmas to you both."

"I'd rather have a merry one," said Yamamoto, looking up from his *Outlander* novel, as he leaned his chair back against the wall.

"Well," said the nurse, "it can be hopeful. Did you hear the news?"

"Nouvelles?" said Yamamoto, tossing the book on the foot of his bed.

The nurse pointed toward the two TVs hanging over our beds. "Activez CBC."

And with that he scooted out the door. As soon as the bolt had locked into place, we both pulled off our masks.

"You speak French pretty good," I said, "for a cop from Toronto."

"Forty-one thousand francophones in Greater Sudbury," he answered. "Made me learn quickly."

"What do you think he's on about?" I asked. "What news?"

Yamamoto sighed, dropping his mask into his Ziplock bag, before saying, "Probably some rich guy's donating a million masks to all the homeless people who've lost their jobs to lockdowns."

I rolled my eyes and laid back on the elevated bed. Yamamoto grabbed a remote control from the side table and aimed it at the TV over my bed.

"*Voyons!*" he said in French. "Let's see."

He began flipping through channels, stopping at an anchorwoman's talking head. "The prime minister announced from Rideau Cottage, early this morning, that Santa had left a surprise last night."

The screen switched to the prime minister wearing a red Santa hat and a green mask bearing the words "'Tis the Season to Be Safe." He sat in an elegantly carved wooden chair that looked like it had time-travelled out of a Dickens novel. To his right a fire crackled, staged dangerously close to a pine tree full of red blinking lights.

Speaking to the camera, the PM said, "The elves in the North Pole's pharmaceuticals department have been working over-time. Last night, Rudolph and his gang dropped off a million COVID-19 vaccines with the Canadian Armed Forces."

The camera panned back to reveal a white-clad nurse with a red face mask sitting beside the prime minister.

He stood up, removed his black blazer and said, "I'd rather not be the first to benefit, but I also want to lead by example."

Sitting back in the chair, he rolled up his left sleeve. The nurse rubbed an alcohol swab on his upper arm.

"I must confess," he said, "the only needles I like are pine needles."

The nurse giggled as she ceremoniously held up the COVID-19 mRNA elixir and wiped its surface with another alcohol swab. With wide-eyed wonderment, the PM gazed at the vial as if he were a child seeing his first snowflake.

"Here's our ticket back to normality," he said.

The nurse jabbed a needle into the vial, tipped both upside down, and pulled back the plunger. Almost on cue, a blond-haired boy, wearing a black mask emblazoned with a yellow Bat-man symbol, sauntered on screen.

"Daddy, what're you doin'?" he said in a rehearsed voice.

The prime minister wrapped his free arm around his son's shoulder. "I'm doing my part to help keep all Canadians safe this coming year."

"Are you ready, Mr. Prime Minister?" asked the nurse.

In a mock Scottish drawl he said enthusiastically, "You better believe it!"

With one hand she pinched his deltoid muscle, while the other quickly jabbed the needle into his shoulder and then slowly pressed the plunger.

Yamamoto muttered, "I bet you dessert it's just saline solu-tion."

Considering how bad the food had been so far, it wasn't much of a wager.

"No way they'll risk another scene on camera," he continued, "like with that nurse who fainted in Tennessee. What was her name?"

"*Shhh!*" I said.

The prime minister had begun to sing through his green mask to the tune of "We Wish You a Merry Christmas":

We wish you a sa-afe Christmas
We wish you a sa-afe Christmas
We wish you a sa-afe Christmas and a COVID vaccine.
True freedom it brings to you and your kin
We wish you a sa-afe Christmas and a COVID vaccine.
Oh, bring us herd immunity
Oh, bring us herd immunity
Oh, bring us herd immunity
Corona's obscene.

"Sing along, son!" he cried, and the blond boy piped in:

True freedom it brings to you and your kin
We wish you a sa-afe Christmas and a COVID vaccine.

With increasing fervour and volume they continued together:

We all want those antibodies,
We all want those antibodies,
We all want those antibodies,
No more nee-eed to screen.

The Prime Minister then signalled to the nurse, who stood up and unleashed an operatic soprano:

True freedom it brings to you and your kin
We wish you a sa-afe Christmas and a COVID vaccine.

Then he pointed back to his son, who bellowed out the finale, solo:

I won't go until you jab me,
I won't go until you jab me,
I won't go until you jab me,
So inject me right here.

And the boy pointed to his shoulder as his father applauded him.

"Did it hurt, Daddy?" asked the boy.

The PM smiled and shook his head. "Nah! Just a prick, all it was."

"I can't wait to get mine," said his son, robotically.

"Atta boy!" said his father, ruffling his hair. "But kids will have to wait."

The screen switched back to the anchorwoman who was laughing.

"I can't wait for my turn, either," she said in a cheerful tone she could only sustain for about two sentences. "But I'll have to wait, too. The military is deploying the one million doses across the country to those who need it most. Starting with seniors and health care workers; followed by those working directly with the public, such as hospitals, clinics, school staff, hair salons and re-tail businesses, especially those providing essential goods like grocery stores, restaurants, bakeries—"

Yamamoto aimed the remote at the screen and muted it.

"Boy," he said with a sigh, "I haven't drunk a drop of eggnog this Christmas, yet I feel like I'm going to puke."

82. COVID on 1984th Street

I sighed as I continued to stare at the muted TV screen—where I'd witnessed our prime minister, Canada's top pharmaceutical salesman, hijack the Christmas spirit to push an untested and unnecessary drug on the masses.

My chest suddenly felt heavy.

"You know," Yamamoto said, clapping his hands together si-lently, "they get an A for presentation. I mean—"

His phone began to ring. Pulling it out, he glanced at the display and tapped it with his thumb.

"Hey, Brad!" said Yamamoto; then, after a pause, "Merry Christmas to you, too! Are Annie and Michael up yet?... Already under the tree?... No breakfast! Come on, bro, you gotta make them eat their Wheaties first. Remember, that was the rule when we were little."

Yamamoto began pacing the length of the small room. Still shackled to the bed, I let the handcuffs slide along the rail, as I slid to the foot of the bed where the suitcase Mom had put together was waiting.

"What?" continued Yamamoto. "Oh yeah, we just saw it. It's crazy! I thought with testing, and all that, it would be another year.... I mean, it's not even really a vaccine. It makes your cells produce a protein that looks like a coronavirus spike. But it also looks like protein found in human heart tissue, brain tissue, even sperm and.... Yeah, yeah, I guess I'm a bit of a conspiracy theorist." He shot me a wink. "But it seems a little crazy to test this on a billion people all at once.... Oh, come on, we aren't in that critical of a state...."

With my free hand I opened the suitcase. I grinned when I saw a brand new pair of red plaid pajamas, rolled up with a green ribbon around them. Every year, Mom made me a new pair. This year she had put a V on the breast pocket. *V for Vincent.* Folding them back into the suitcase, I unpacked jeans and a T-shirt. I ignored the tin of shortbread that I had vowed I would not eat.

"You got them *what* for Christmas?" said Yamamoto in surprise. "How did you pull that off? Come on, bro, that's impossible.... You did what? Don't you think they're too young?... They don't need that crap." Yamamoto's voice had shifted from festive to frantic.

I stared up at the silent TV screen and saw an image of a patient in a hospital bed connected to a ventilator. Three seconds later, the scene switched to footage of masked seniors slouching in chairs, needles being plunged into their pale arms.

"Okay, Brad," said Yamamoto. "Sorry, I'm just concerned. I guess I'm old-fashioned. I got Michael a model airplane kit and Annie a doll."

Canada's chief public health officer was now on screen, talking at a podium. Even though she wasn't wearing a mask, her face was expressionless as always. Using my free hand, I stretched toward Yamamoto's table for the remote but couldn't quite reach it.

Yamamoto looked over at me. "Hey, sorry, amigo." One hand holding the cell, the other fished in his pocket for the keys. "Hey, Brad, I gotta go. The prisoner's getting restless.... When Annie and Michael are done tearing open their gifts, can you have them call me?" He pulled out his keys. "Yeah, a safe and merry Christmas to you, too. Love to Laura."

He ended his call, slid the key into the cuffs and freed my right arm, singing: "All I want for Christmas is my two forearms." But this time his carolling rang about as jovial as a Gregorian chant.

"Sounded like your call got a little tense," I said, as I rubbed my wrist.

"Oh," he said, "I just disagreed with my numbskull brother about one of the gifts he got the munchkins."

"BB guns?" I asked.

"Yeah, something like that," he said, begrudgingly. "It's kind of like the year he got them that Xbox, when what they really needed was a basketball hoop, not another reason to sit on the couch."

"Has their school been in lockdown?" I asked.

"No, not since the spring," said Yamamoto. "But Brad and Laura don't let them attend. Laura has asthma. She's afraid her kids are going to kill her or something. So it's all virtual classes. And even if they did get to go, the schools have cancelled phys ed." He leaned back on the edge of his bed. "I suspect the real reason Brad didn't want me over this year was because he doesn't want me to see how much weight they've gained."

"Almost sounds like child abuse," I said, unthinkingly.

"No!" exclaimed Yamamoto with a sudden edge of anger. "They love them! They're just trying to keep Laura safe. It won't be for much longer." He paused, took a deep breath, and closed his eyes. "Easter. It'll be a year since all this began. A year is all even my brother can probably take of this COVID BS."

"Sorry," I said. "Didn't mean it like that. What's he do for work?"

"City planning department in Toronto. Not really all that sure exactly what he does. They keep changing his title. Lots of paper pushing. He's about halfway up the food chain, though he sometimes acts like he's the bloody mayor."

I stood and began walking around the bed, holding the railing.

"You need a hand, amigo?" said Yamamoto.

"No. I'm okay," I replied. "They bringing breakfast soon? Unlike your munchkins, I'm ready to eat."

"Ah, you finally feel hungry. That's a good sign."

I hadn't eaten anything the day before. Any food they brought I turned away, which wasn't hard, considering it was hospital food. Yama's dinner, served on a disposable plastic plate, had been dry and cold—reminiscent of my first solo attempt at bannock back in the summer. But there was another reason I went without.

As I moved my stiff legs, I remembered the morning Grandma died. I had been only eleven. My parents and I took Grandad back to his cabin, where he refused to eat any dinner even though he made some for us.

"Grandad," I had said. "Why have you stopped eating?"

He put his arm around my shoulder and said, "When the spirit of someone I love departs, I stop eating for the rest of that day to mourn them."

"Boy, Grandad," I replied. "I hope that you die after dinner, so I won't miss a meal."

Grandad chuckled. "I'll do my best."

"You okay?" said Yamamoto, gently shaking my shoulder with an extended hand.

"Yeah," I answered with a sad smile. "Hey, can I borrow the phone again?"

Yamamoto pulled it out and extended it to me. "Merry Christmas. Fourteen days of unlimited phone calls anywhere in Canada or the United States. Borrow it whenever you want. I'll leave it on the nightstand."

"Thanks."

I took the phone and plopped down in the chair. It rang four times before I heard her voice:

"Hello."

I immediately replied: "Hey, Dand—"

"You've reached Moosehead Artisan Bakery," the voicemail message continued. "Fresh-baked bread. Two-day ferment. No yeast..."

My heart sank in the same way yeast does not, as I listened to the rest of the message followed by an abrupt beep.

"Hey," I said with disappointment. "Sorry I missed you. Maybe you're sleeping. Or you're at your mom's already? If you want—" I paused and looked at Yamamoto. "Is it okay if my boss calls me back at this number?"

"Sure," said Yamamoto in a baffled tone. "But my boss would be the last person I'd want calling me on Christmas day."

"Yeah," I said into the phone, "if you want, you can call back at this number. Anytime. I wasn't planning on heading out today." I rolled my eyes at my own bad joke. "But if you get too busy I understand. That's fine. I'll be fine. In fact, I've been fined five times." I paused, hoping this time I was giving her space to laugh. "Yama said we'd watch some Christmas movies on Netflix. Maybe *COVID on 1984*th *Street*." Another pause. "Well, I better hit the shower."

Yamamoto pinched his nose and nodded vigorously.

"I hope you have a... nice Christmas." Wishing her a merry Christmas felt stupid. "I'll talk to you later. I..."

I wanted to say, "I love you." Like she had said the day before. But Yamamoto was in earshot. Besides, doubts were mounting about what my "boss" had really said and meant. Perhaps she regretted it and was purposely avoiding picking up, now that—

Beep! "You've exceeded the maximum length for a message," said the voicemail's abrupt robotic voice. "If you're happy with your message, press one."

I hit one.

"Goodbye."

The cell's display read: Moosehead Artisan Bakery. Call ended at 8:58 a.m.

I sighed. Something didn't feel right. "I hope she's okay..."

"Your boss?" said Yamamoto, with a slight smirk.

"Yeah. I'm just a little worried. Some people don't like her much."

"Why, does she smell, too?"

I sniffed my armpits. *Oh, that was me.*" No, it's not that. She smells great." My tongue stumbled into my next words. "It's just, well, she's been pretty outspoken about the corona measures."

Yamamoto scratched his head and spoke in a whisper, "She's the one with that soup kitchen thing, isn't she?"

"Yeah."

"I've been letting her and Roger—you know Roger, right?"

"Oh, yeah."

"I send them emails letting them know when Mackenzie's

off duty."

I nodded. "I know."

He whistled and returned to a normal speaking voice. "Mackenzie absolutely hates her."

"He doesn't seem too fond of her," I admitted.

"Well, don't worry about him," said Yamamoto. "Constable Corona won't be giving you or her any more trouble. I got an email today saying he'll probably be transferred up North. Only tickets he'll be handing out are to grizzly bears who won't mask up."

"That's good to hear," I said, staring at the silent phone in my hand. "You don't think he'd give her any trouble before he leaves?"

"Nah!" said Yamamoto. "Like I said, he's a by-the-book kind of guy."

I raised an eyebrow.

"Well, until lately, that is."

"He said he left Stefanie a gift." I could hear anxiety in my voice. "But she said there were no tickets or anything at her door. I'm a little worried—"

"What, that he left a bomb? Gonna blow up the bakery?" Yamamoto laughed. "He may have a few screws loose, but he's no psychopath."

"You think he's on any psychiatric drugs?"

Yamamoto shrugged. "Wouldn't surprise me. He's been through a lot. He definitely likes his painkillers. Probably takes some anti-depressants."

"Dad tried those once," I said, with a shiver. "He got violent. Had to go back to booze, which keeps him sedate. Only time I ever saw him hit anybody."

I was glad it had been me and not Mom.

"Well," said Yamamoto, sounding at a loss for words, "Mackenzie's never shown much aggression. I mean, until yesterday."

I moved back to the bed, knowing I really should have been heading to the shower. I just didn't have the energy at that moment.

"Hey! That reminds me," said Yamamoto, as he strolled over to the lockers, waving his arms loosely.

"Uh," I said. "You're not getting your gun?"

"No, amigo." He opened my locker, reached for the top shelf and pulled down the gift-wrapped box Dad had given me. "Merry Christmas!" He smiled, carrying the present over and setting it carefully on the mobile table.

Inside was a gift that I would forever associate with two of the worst days in my life. The first being the day Grandad died, my parents disowned me and Mackenzie tasered me; the second day was yet to come—the day the contents of that box would help someone save my life at their own expense.

83. The Stare of the Wooden Amik

It looked like a three-year-old had wrapped the gift, with jagged cuts and white masking tape sealing it at the ends.

"Hmm," I said, frowning. "That's the gift my parents..."

My stomach clenched. I leaned back on the hospital bed and closed my eyes. Suddenly the room seemed too bright.

"Ah, darn!" said Yamamoto. "I thought all that shock treatment would make you forget, and you'd think it came from me." He extended his empty hands. "Because I'm afraid, I really didn't get you anything."

"Don't worry, I don't want anything."

I pushed away the table and the gift.

"You not going to open it?" said Yamamoto.

I shrugged. "Why don't you open it?"

Yamamoto cocked his head. "*No problema*." He tore off the paper, revealing what looked like an old-fashioned hat box. Lifting the lid, he gazed inside. "Wow!" He reached in. "'Tis the season for masking." He pulled out a full head mask.

It was carved out of wood. Two stubby ears protruded from the top. White and green eyes were painted around two holes in the wood. Below the eye sockets was painted a large black nose, with two more holes in the nostrils, and fat red lips around two long, white, buck teeth.

It didn't look quite scary. That wasn't the right word, but, rather ominous. Its stare was trying to tell me something, warn me of something that was coming—something horrific that must come to pass, like all this corona insanity must come to pass, so that us dense, lazy and apathetic human beings could evolve and grow.

Yamamoto whistled. "Your dad make this?"

I shook my head.

"No way. Mom's the costume maker; but that's not her style. She works with felt, wool, polyester. Not wood and paint."

Yamamoto stared at it. "It's superb." He lifted the mask up toward his head. "You mind if I?"

"Go ahead."

I reached out with my right hand and tipped the box toward me. A note lay at the bottom. I pulled it out, recognizing Dad's barely legible handwriting:

Son, being the mask rebel that you are, we thought you'd appreciate this. It's been in the attic ever since Grandad moved into the nursing home. He made it for one of those Ojibwe plays they'd put on at the community centre. I'm sure he would want you to have it. It's the *amik*. Love, Mom and Dad.

I looked up at Yamamoto, now wearing the mask.

"It's an *amik*," I said. "A beaver."

"Why a beaver?" he asked.

"It's a long story."

"I got time," he said.

"The Ojibwe have this legend about water spirits flooding the earth."

"Kind of like the Noah's ark story?"

"Sort of, but it was before any of the first humans were born. Actually, that's why the water spirits flooded the earth—to stop Geezhigo-Quae's children from surviving and ruling over the land."

"Geezhigo-who?" asked Yamamoto.

"She was the mother of the first humans."

"Sort of like Eve?"

"Yes, but Geezhigo-Quae lived in the moon, not on a garden on earth. And I don't really think she was human herself. More like a Goddess."

"Ahem." Yamamoto nodded respectfully. "But I thought your people believed we lived on the back of a turtle, not a beaver."

I nodded back. "She asked the beaver to dive down into the

ocean to retrieve soil from the flooded earth to cover the turtle's shell."

"Ah," said Yamamoto, in a muffled voice, "it would have been a hard life living on a hard shell."

He lifted off the mask and carefully set it upright on the medical table.

"So, what happened next?"

"Well," I continued, "the beaver dove for as long and far as he could. But he couldn't make it to the bottom without running out of air."

"So he never got the dirt?"

"No," I said, distantly. "He tried his best."

I sighed and closed my eyes.

"So how did Turtle Island end up with all this topsoil?" asked Yamamoto. "Did the Moon lady ask an octopus for help?"

"No, I think the octopus is considered evil," I replied. "Instead, Geezhigo-Quae called on the muskrat."

"Oh. I thought rats were considered evil."

I shrugged.

"The muskrat was gone for a long time," I continued, almost sounding like Grandad was talking through me. "When evening came, the muskrat's body floated to the surface. In his claws, stiff with death, he was holding a lump of dirt. Geezhigo-Quae took the dirt and rubbed it on the back of a turtle. The dirt multiplied, covering the entire shell, and super-sized the turtle, forming the North American continent. And, so the myth goes, Geezhigo-Quae's children, my Grandad's ancestors, survived."

Yamamoto crossed his arms, sat back on the edge of his bed and said, "The rat succeeded because he was willing to sacrifice his own life for the greater good."

"Either way, he would have died," I said. "He wasn't a fish. He couldn't swim forever. So death wasn't much of a sacrifice."

"But another animal could have made the sacrifice in his place," said Yamamoto. "And he could have lived on Turtle Island."

"For how long?" I said flatly. "How long does a muskrat live, anyway? Death would find him, Yama. Every leaf falls from the tree, one day. No exceptions."

My mind flashed back to that day in the canoe on the lake.

"It all depends how the leaf lived its life," Grandad had said. "If it lived a good life, it dies full of joy."

I hoped the muskrat died full of joy. Maybe even the beaver, when its day came, knowing it had tried its best. I reached out my hand and felt the roughly carved cedar mask.

And then I coughed from deep down in my chest.

Yamamoto squinted at me. "That doesn't sound like a dry throat."

"Ah," I said, getting up to refill my cup with water. "It's nothing."

But it wasn't. I knew it wasn't. My throat felt sore. My lungs felt heavy. Drinking some water, I stared back at the beaver mask. The beaver had tried to be brave, and failed. It was only the muskrat, who was willing to be a martyr, who saved the day.

The intercom on the wall buzzed.

"Constable," said a female voice. "The breakfast trays are coming 'round. Please secure the pris—" She caught herself. "The patient."

"Roger that," said Yamamoto, pulling out a mask with one hand and his keyring with the other.

I squeezed my upper lip, suppressing another cough.

"Bet you're hungry," said Yamamoto.

"Actually," I said, laying back on the bed. "I've lost my appetite."

I looked at the phone on the mobile table. Deep down, I knew the Dandelion wouldn't be calling back. Not today. Not ever.

"Wrist?" said Yamamoto.

Was she regretting what she said to me?

I lifted up my right arm as he snapped the cuff into place.

Had something happened to her?

With my left arm I covered my mouth as I coughed again. Yamamoto pulled out my mask, looking concerned.

"With that cough, they're really going to want you to mask up."

The bolt slid open and an older woman with two trays entered.

"Safe Christmas!" she said, cheerily.

"But not a merry one," I muttered, as I singlehandedly

looped the mask around both my ears.

84. Double Masking Crazy Horse

That same evening, I stabbed at a dry, processed turkey slice, with the dull points of the plastic fork. Instead of piercing the luncheon meat, the disposable utensil bent to the point of snapping.

Maybe I'll be sticking with that vegan diet a little longer, I thought to myself, as I directed the disfigured fork to the dry mashed potatoes on the other side of the plastic plate that held my Christmas dinner.

"Tomorrow, Daddy says he has one more gift for us," said Yamamoto's niece over his cell's speakerphone, resting on the nightstand between our two beds. "But Daddy couldn't wrap it."

I glanced at the framed photo on Yamamoto's nightstand of his niece and nephew. Annie's black, braided hair trailed down the front of her, reminding me of Stefanie's equally long blonde hair. Michael's hair was buzzed short like his *Oji* Yamamoto's. (*Oji*, I had so far gathered, meant "uncle" in Japanese.)

"Well, aren't you lucky, Princess." Yamamoto spoke with his usual cheerful tone, yet I could detect a hint of reserve.

While they chatted, I managed to scoop a few hard peas into my mouth. Most of them, however, rolled off the fork, falling to the mobile table. They would have rolled to the floor if they hadn't collided with the beaver mask. Its giant buck teeth grinned back at me.

"And, *Oji* Dave," said Michael, "Mom measured me. I've grown one-and-half centimetres since the summer."

"Like a boss!" said Yamamoto. "If this second wave doesn't end soon, next time I see you, I'll be looking up to you."

"Yeah!" said Michael, "that would be way cool."

Discarding his flimsy fork and using his fingers, Yamamoto rolled up a turkey slice around peas and potatoes and slid it into his mouth.

Not even finishing the potatoes, I pushed the tray away. There was some mushy pink concoction oozing out of a pie crust that I didn't dare eat. Everything was cold. The attendant who brought us our holiday meal had apologized, explaining that

COVID patients were always served last.

"Well, call me tomorrow, munchkins," said Yamamoto. "After you get your last Christmas gift, you can tell me all about it."

"Okay!" said Annie.

"Bye, Oji Dave," said Michael.

"We love you!" said Annie.

Their carefree voices helped lighten the heavy feeling in my chest. Indeed, I hadn't coughed since they called. Still the room was feeling as stuffy as a hazmat suit.

"Oh!" said Michael, "Mom just told us we should thank you for the gifts."

"But we're not sure why," said Annie, "because we already said thank you. I think Mom thinks you're getting old-timers."

Stefanie hadn't called back, I realized. *Should I try again? Of course I should. Is she all right? Is she embarrassed over what she had said? Regretting it, probably. She just got carried away in the drama of the moment. I should just pretend it never happened.*

Yamamoto laughed, as his eyes rolled around, gazing at our small room. "Sometimes I wish I was getting Alzheimer's. Merry Christmas, Munchkins!"

"Merry Christmas, *Oji* Dave!" both kids yelled back.

"Enjoy your dinner!" replied Yamamoto.

"You too, Uncle Dave!"

Yamamoto stabbed his last two peas with his plastic fork. I took a sip of the apple juice they had included in our Christmas banquet. My mouth always felt dry now. I was pretty sure dry mouth was one of the hundred symptoms blamed on COVID-19.

"Love you guys!" said Yamamoto. He reached over and tapped the phone with a grin on his face.

"They seem happy," I said.

"It's Christmas Day," said Yamamoto, picking up his dessert plate, "if you haven't noticed."

"All I'm noticing is how many days and hours I have left in this cell."

"Bored of my company, already?"

I didn't respond and swigged back the last of the juice. As I tilted my head I gazed up at the ceiling, which appeared to be getting lower with every passing hour.

"You gonna eat that?" said Yamamoto, pointing to my dessert.

"It's all yours," I said, sending the mobile table rolling toward his bed.

"Thanks!" he said. "The portion sizes are pretty small here." He slid the pie-like substance onto his tray and began devouring it while he mumbled, "You want to call your parents?"

I crushed the plastic cup and tossed it into the trash can. "Not really."

"They're probably worried about you."

"I'll call them tomorrow."

"You want to try your friends again?"

Earlier, I had called 411 and managed to get numbers for AJ and Mathéo. Oddly, both their phones went straight to voicemail, as if they had been deactivated. *Did they have them off so they could focus on family?* I wondered. Maybe AJ. But what about Mathéo? I still worried about him, all alone in his apartment on Christmas day. *Why wasn't he answering?*

"I don't want to bother them on Christmas Day," I said, hiding my concern. "I'll try them again. Tomorrow."

"Okay." Yamamoto shrugged. "What about your *boss*?" And, when he said "boss" he drew the word out in an insinuating way. "Want to give her another go?"

"Yeah," I said, trying to sound like the idea hadn't occurred to me a hundred times already. "I should check in with the captain. See how the ship's doing without its first mate."

"Mate?" he mumbled.

"Well, not mate, pilot."

"Pilot?"

"I do deliver the bread."

"Why do you never deliver me any bread?" said Yamamoto, poutingly.

"You never ordered."

"Oh! So that's how you do it. Can I order some now?"

"You're nuts."

Yamamoto laughed. So did I. A little. I was glad he was here.

"Give her a call!" he encouraged, gesturing toward the phone.

"All right," I said, with mock disinterest.

I stretched my hand out, picked it up and dialled the bakery, wishing she owned a cellphone. As I expected, voicemail picked up again.

"Hey, Dandelion," I said after the beep. "I'm a little worried. Can you call me? Let me know you're okay. I don't want to bug you. I'm just concerned."

I swallowed hard, but it was no use, and I ended up coughing again.

"Excuse me. It's so dry in here. Water tastes like it has sand in it. You spoiled me with your ultra-purified, distilled water." I cleared my throat and started to speak faster, as if I could out-race the next cough coming on. "Anyway, call when you can. As soon as you can." I didn't make it. My lungs sounded like they were snapping open and shut. "Damn!" I said and hit the End Call button.

I'm not getting sick, am I?

I stared up at the closed window. Even if it was designed to open, the other side was barricaded with snow.

I need fresh air.

I took a deep breath, triggering another spasm of coughs.

Yamamoto pushed his empty tray away, stood up and looked at me with a furrowed brow. "You sure you're all right, amigo?"

I nodded. "Just need more sleep. I'll be fine."

I handed him the cellphone and laid back on the elevated bed.

Buzz! The intercom sounded.

"Constable," said a male voice.

"Yes?" said Yamamoto.

"This is Dr. Roberts. I'll be coming in in a minute to complete my rounds. Please make sure Crazy Horse is secure and has a mask on."

My mouth dropped open at the Crazy Horse slur. Crazy Horse was hardly a near relative of mine. Nonetheless, Grandad had told me about his life. And his death. At thirty-seven, the Lakota war chief, after years of fighting for his people's land and freedom, surrendered to the US Army. While escorting Crazy Horse to his cell at Fort Robinson, Nebraska, the guard stabbed him in the back with a bayonet. That was nearly a century and a half ago; nevertheless, the image triggered another loud and fluid cough.

"Actually," added Dr. Roberts, surely hearing my hacking lungs, "make sure he has two masks on. And a visor."

85. Not on St. George's Watch

Eleven hours later, I opened my eyes for the hundredth time that night. Swallowing off-tasting saliva, I was able to fend off another cough. My sinus cavity hurt, my throat burned and my chest ached.

The lights were off, except for what slipped through the crack under the bathroom door. Yamamoto was in the bathroom, humming along to the buzz of his electric razor. My coughing must have kept him up all night.

I turned my head. The screen on the vitals monitor showed 6:38 a.m. *Christmas was finally over,* I thought. *Boxing Day has begun. I doubt I'll be doing any shopping.*

And then my body tensed. Even though I was no longer connected to the oximeter, I could tell my heart had skipped a beat. Someone was standing at the bedside. I could just make out his shadowy outline. But, almost immediately, I relaxed and smiled.

I was starting to get used to this.

"Grandad," I whispered, happily.

His face smiled back, dimly visible under the glow of the monitor's LCD. For this visitation, my Ojibwe elder wore a white lab coat with a stethoscope around his neck. His grey hair was pulled back in a tidy ponytail.

"Did I die from COVID-19?" I asked, hoarsely.

He looked at the data pad in his hands.

"It says here that you're not getting off so easily."

And he began to laugh softly.

Yamamoto opened the bathroom door, casting light into the dark room and an abrupt end to Grandad's mirth. I shielded my eyes with my hands.

"You call me, amigo?" he said.

Yamamoto flicked on the light switch. I put down my hands. Grandad was gone. I coughed again.

"I think I'm sick," I said.

"No guff," said Yamamoto, as he filled Grandad's position at the bedside.

"You better stand back," I warned.

Yamamoto snickered. "You kidding me? We're both in this little room with that one vent and no open window. If I'm going to get it, I'm going to get it." He patted his chest. "Rather get my antibodies from nature than a vaccine."

"We all want those antibodies..." I sang softly. And then I swallowed and squeezed my throat in a futile effort to stop another pulmonary eruption. When my coughing died away, I mumbled, "A vaccine sounds pretty good about now."

"Ah, come on! You've been tasered three times. What's a cold? You'll be fine! Just rest! Drink lots of water. You know a coronavirus is nothing to worry about."

"I'm more worried they'll put me on a ventilator."

Yamamoto swatted the air with his hand and rolled his eyes. "Come on," he said. "A healthy young guy like you?"

"They did it in New York," I replied. "Hospitals collected 30K for venting healthy young blacks and Hispanics who were having anxiety attacks."

"Then don't have an anxiety attack."

I suddenly wished I had never watched that YouTube interview with the undercover nurse from Elmhurst Hospital—the one Stefanie had emailed me back in the summer.

"Anyway, this ain't the States," said Yamamoto, dismissively. "And you're not a minority."

"I'm a quarter Ojibwe," I protested. "Haven't you noticed how much of the COVID propaganda is targeted at the natives, saying how vulnerable they are?"

"Ah, you look white enough to me," replied Yamamoto.

"To them I'm an Indian in a white man's hospital, coughing up a lung in the middle of a pandemic. Who knows what they'll do? I could be sedated and intubated and never wake up."

He just shook his head slowly.

"No way. Not on my watch. Just relax, amigo."

I took a slow, deep breath. This time without coughing.

"All right," I said. "Thanks."

He nodded, smiled and said, "No one's coming for you."

Rat-a-tat-tat. My head jerked toward the door. Someone had just knocked, followed by the familiar sound of the bolt sliding away.

"Buongiorno!" said a female nurse, in a thick Italian accent, as she opened the door.

We both looked at her, without saying a word.

"That's a good morning in *italiano*," she said, with a hint of arrogance.

It was more her appearance, rather than her bilingualism, that had left us tongue-tied. Strapped to her face was a heavy-duty respirator with two pink valves protruding on either side. The dual filters made her voice reverberate in an inhuman way, reminiscent of an Italian Darth Vader.

Even more perturbing than her appearance was that she was backing a wheelchair into the room.

"X-rays!" she announced.

86. Nurse Vader

Yamamoto wasn't wearing a mask, and he didn't bother to put one on. His eyes were fixated on the heavyset nurse who had just barged into our dungeon room. He pulled out his cell to check the time.

"It's kind of early," he said.

"Tell me about it," said Nurse Vader, looking at her wristwatch. "Dr. Roberts is a very concerned about our patient here. Sounds, uh, kind of serious."

She also looked pretty serious. One step down from a haz-mat suit. Besides the black and pink respirator, she was covered head to foot in blue plastic coverings. With her goggles and visor blurring her eyes, the only hint of a human under the PPE getup was her curly, reddish-black hair, cut off at the shoulders, that snuck out from under her plastic hood. She pushed the wheelchair beside my bed and stared at the vitals monitor, tapping a few buttons with her blue gloves.

"How's the patient a doing?" she said, without even looking at me.

"I'm coughing a lot," I grumbled.

"Mamma mia, yes you are." She nodded slowly. "They can a hear you all 'em way to Buckingham Palace."

"He'll be okay," said Yamamoto.

"We'll see to that," said the nurse. "Doc wants a chest X-ray. Make sure there's no COVID a growing, you know?"

"You do X-rays this early in the morning?" questioned Yamamoto.

"What do you think this is? A bank?" she said, facing him, hands on bulging hips. "Of course, we do! 24/7."

She was short, but well padded. Plump would probably be the polite word. Either way, it only added to her intimidating bedside manner. Yet, in some strange way, I almost found it attractive. Not her fault she was raised by bulldogs.

"And doc much rather the COVID poster boy go early when the halls are clear of people," she continued. "Last thing we need is a bloody outbreak."

Yamamoto suddenly straightened his posture and said, "Understood."

I thought he was going to salute her, too.

"Can you stand?" she said to me, as she positioned the wheelchair flush with my bed.

"Sure," I said. "But I'm not really sure I want an X-ray."

She picked up two disposable hospital slippers that had been resting on the wheelchair's seat.

"I think you'll need these," she said.

I slowly swung my legs out of bed.

"Shouldn't I change my clothes?" I asked.

"What you got on is fine," she said. "Looks like brand new pajamas."

I rolled my eyes. "Christmas gift. My mom made them."

"Sweet," said the nurse.

She squatted down and hastily slipped on the footwear.

"I really think I'm better off staying here," I argued. "For everyone's safety."

"We can talk about it on the way to radiology," she responded, patting the wheelchair.

I felt too tired to argue. And getting out of that stuffy room had its appeal. But would they bring me back? Or would the next stop be the ICU?

Pulling me up, she swung me into the wheelchair with the same grace I'd toss a bag of wheat into the back of the delivery van.

"I really understood that he was not to leave this room," said Yamamoto, formally.

The nurse fiddled with her respirator valve.

"Well, we can't exactly bring the X-ray room to him," she said. "And it's not like we're going on a tour of the neonatal intensive care unit."

She reached into the back of the wheelchair and pulled out a mask, cap and visor.

"Put these on."

She dropped them in my lap.

"Stop the spread. We don't want no more dead."

I picked up the mask with a sigh.

"All right," said Yamamoto, "I'll escort you."

"No need for that, cowboy," said the nurse, resting her Italian accent so she could imitate a Texan—a Texan with a respirator. "I think he's sounding way too rough to give a nice lady like me any trouble."

I coughed as I pinched the mask into place.

"Not like he killed a man, has he?" she said.

I coughed, again.

"All the same, it's my duty," said Yamamoto. "If he goes, I go."

I felt he was stepping in more for my protection than hers. Honestly, the thought of being anywhere in this den of the new-normal dragon without St. George Yamamoto was unthinkable. Hospitals across the province had been running below capacity. In the middle of a second wave, an ICU with only five patients doesn't look too good. A vulnerable native with a real chest infection—just what they needed to help justify stockpiling all those expensive ventilators.

"All right then, pardner," said the nurse to Yamamoto, in her Southern twang. "If it's your duty, you'd better come 'long. But you'll need a mask."

"Of course," said Yamamoto.

I felt my shoulders relax.

Back to her native Italian accent, she pointed to my Christmas gift on the mobile table. "Mamma mia, what is that?"

"It's a beaver mask," I said, softly. "Native Indian."

Yamamoto picked it up and slid it over his head. "What do

you think?" he said, with a slight echo. "Can I wear this to radi-ology?"

"I doubt it meets PPE standards," she said, sternly.

"Ah, come on," said Yamamoto. "You ever heard of a beaver getting COVID?"

I almost chuckled, but just ended up coughing into the face mask I was now wearing. Immediately, Nurse Vader began pull-ing my wheelchair back out through the open door.

"Better put on an N95," she ordered Yamamoto. Parking us in the hallway, she leaned back into the room and pointed to-ward the sink area. "Should be one in one of those 'em drawers. I'll just check us out at the nursing station."

"Better if you wait," said Yamamoto.

His beaver mask still on, I saw him jut around the beds and out of view.

I glanced up and down the empty hallway lined with ham-pers, disposal bins, racks full of supplies, and a beige handrail covered with white tinsel. Unlike the nursing home, which had been devoid of Christmas decorations, hundreds of coloured balls hung from the ceiling and a blizzard of hand-made paper snowflakes covered the pink walls.

Inside the room, I could hear Yamamoto opening and clos-ing drawers, looking for the N95.

"I just need a second," he hollered.

"Take your time," said the nurse.

Then she reached out, pulled the door shut and slid the bolt lock into place.

I could feel blood flowing out to my hands and feet, as my heart rate doubled. Looking up at Nurse Vader, she stared down at me with her goggles, respirator and visor—a frightful zombie of walking PPE.

The door to the room rattled as Yamamoto yanked at the handle.

"What the hell's going on?" he cried. "Open up!"

I pushed myself up, to get out of the wheelchair; but her hands came down firmly on my shoulders, pushing me back into the seat.

"Sit still and be quiet," she ordered, no longer in that fake Italian accent.

Then she leaned down to my ear and whispered, "This is not the time to come out of your shell."

Turning the wheelchair, she pointed it down the empty hallway.

"Dandelion!" I exclaimed, gripping the armrests. "My God, what are you doing?"

Immediately, Stefanie began pushing the wheelchair forward, away from Yamamoto's banging and hollering.

"I'm breaking you out of here."

87. Code Yellow

Briskly pushing the wheelchair down the hallway, I could hear Stefanie breathing heavily through her respirator.

Leaning forward, she whispered, "Act sick. Pretend to cough. That'll get 'em to keep their distance."

Instantly, I did cough, but I wasn't faking.

We made a sharp right around a Christmas tree at the nursing station, where two masked nurses stared at handheld devices, sipping coffee, taking no notice of their escaping patient. Picking up speed, Stefanie continued down another hallway until we reached an elevator lobby, stopping at a fire door. Above the door, painted on the cement wall, were the words UNDERGROUND PARKING.

"I borrowed my mom's car," she said quickly.

"Looks like you borrowed her identity, too," I replied.

"You did suggest I visit her for Christmas."

She pushed on the long metal crash handle, but the door didn't budge. I gulped, looking over my shoulder. Extending her arms, Stefanie reached into her left sleeve and pulled out a pass card. It displayed a photo of her mother's smiling face and curly black hair. She ran it through the card reader beside the door. It beeped, the door clicked, and she slapped the wheelchair button and pushed me through. A long hallway, with flickering florescent lights, stretched out before us. It was colder and had a damp, musty smell. The right wall was uninterrupted cement, the left had three doors.

Stefanie started running down the corridor, pushing the wheelchair at a speed for which it was surely not designed. The left wheel rattled like it would pop off at any moment. Her respirator valves hissed with the sound of her breathing. The first room we passed said BOILER on its door, the next SUPPLIES and the third ELECTRICAL.

At the end of the long hall was another fire door with the words PARKING GARAGE. As we slowed to a halt, a frantic female voice announced over the intercom: "Code Yellow. Code Yellow. Section Zero-B."

Stefanie slammed her side against the crash bar of the door to the parking garage. The handle pushed in but the door did not. She swiped the pass card along the door's reader and tried pressing the handle again. This time, however, the card had no effect.

"*Mist!*" she exclaimed.

That was German for "phooey"—if I wasn't mistaken.

She slapped the metal door with her palm, sending an echo down the narrow hallway.

"They've locked the doors. Yamamoto has already blown our cover."

"What do you expect him to do," I exclaimed, "after a crazy nurse just ran away with his prisoner?"

"I'm not crazy," she said, ripping off the respirator and tossing it to the ground. "And I'm not a nurse."

Pulling back the plastic hood, she revealed an explosion of short, reddish-black, curly hair, where once her long blonde hair had been.

"Please, tell me that's a wig," I said, looking up from the chair.

"It's a wig," she said, scanning the hallway.

"Code yellow," repeated the voice over the intercom. "Possible code purple, code white. Section Zero-B."

"You're unbelievable," I said.

I wasn't sure if I meant it as a compliment or not.

88. Second Dates

"We need to hide," she said.

Spinning the wheelchair around, she pushed me to the first door, now on our right, marked ELECTRICAL. She ran the card along its reader. It had no effect.

"*Mist!*" I exclaimed, this time.

She pushed me to the next door, SUPPLIES. This time the card worked. She backed me in, shut the door and hit the lights. Deep wooden shelves and tall metal wire racks crammed the large room. Each shelf was packed with toolboxes, gauges, sockets, pipes, wires, and unidentifiable replacement parts. Masks and protective eyewear stared down at us from above the closets lining one of the walls. Stefanie began running up and down each aisle.

"What're you doing?" I gasped, as the reality of what was happening overtook me.

"Taking inventory," she said.

"If they catch you..." I didn't want to go there. "You don't need to do this."

"Consider it payback," she replied, from the other side of the shelves.

"Payback? For what?"

"Wednesday night on the ice," she said. "Whisking me away from Constable Corona on your ice skates."

"I really don't think this is comparable," I said, folding my hands on my lap. "I mean, you weren't under arrest and being held captive."

"I admit," she said, mirthfully, "this is a bit of an overpayment. But I wanted to make sure our second date was even more memorable. You know how second dates can be a bit of a letdown. Gotta keep the magic alive."

How could she sound so light-hearted? My heart was pounding. I was breathing heavy, but not coughing—for the moment. Too much cortisol running through my veins, I figured.

"It's too risky," I pleaded. "I mean, they were going to let me out in two weeks."

"With that cough?" she said, pulling off her visor and goggles. "Who knows what they would have done to you. You could be on a ventilator by New Year's." She rolled her eyes and began pulling a mess of cables and wires out of a trash bin. "They are making up new rules every day. We can't trust them. I couldn't leave you here."

She may have been right. This was my one and only chance

to escape. But as scared as I was to stay, I felt even more fear in leaving. If we failed...

"Even if we can get out of here," I said, "which seems very unlikely, where will we go? Where can we run? The bakery? That'll be the first place they look."

Ignoring my question, Stefanie dropped the bundle of wires and cables from the trash can onto the floor.

"Out of the chair!" she ordered.

"I'm sick!"

"You're not that sick."

She grabbed my hands and hoisted me to my feet. Opening the door, she stuck her head out. Seeing no one, she pushed the wheelchair out into the hallway, letting it roll toward the door to the parking garage. In a second, she was back inside, just as I started to cough.

"Best if you don't cough," she said.

"No guff."

She squatted to the floor and began pulling toolboxes out from the bottom of one of the shelving units. Passing them up to me, and pointing to the trash, she said, "Dump these in there." Once cleared, she pointed to the empty shelf and said, "Get down here."

I shrugged. All I felt like doing was lying down, anyway. I tossed my mask, visor and cap into the trash can, dropped to my knees and slid into the bottom shelf. Stefanie flicked the light off and, in the pitch dark, I felt her sliding into the space in front of me, pressing her back against my chest.

Despite being sick and hunted down like a rabid dog, I must admit I found it an absolutely delightful predicament to be in. I heard her pulling the tangled wires and cables in front of us. Once in place, and us hopefully well hidden, I felt her body relax, and a sigh of relief follow.

I reached out, running my hand along her upper arm, and whispered, "Remember, you promised me an X-ray."

"Knock it off," she said, with an elbow to the chest.

Her jab triggered another coughing attack.

"Try pinching your upper lip," she ordered.

I did and the coughing stopped. Just in time. In the distance I could hear footsteps slapping the cement floor, out in the hallway.

"Look!" barked a husky, male voice. "There's the chair."

A younger male voice swore and said, "They must have got into the garage before the doors locked."

There was a pause, the sound of static over a walkie-talkie, and then the husky voice speaking loudly: "Bill! They're in the parking garage. We're going in from corridor C."

"Search in and under every goddamn vehicle," said a high-pitched voice, barely audible over the speaker. "I'll send Roy and Art in through the street entrance."

"We're on it," said the husky voice. "Over." The walkie-talkie beeped and returned to static. "Let's go!"

"Wait," said the younger voice. "Let's check these rooms first. They might not've had time to get into the garage before the door locked."

My heart began to pound so hard I feared they could hear its telltale drumming.

"They aren't there!" said the older voice.

Suddenly the door to our room opened, casting in light from the hallway. A spasm of fear rippled through me. I felt an urge to reveal myself, raise my hands and surrender. But I didn't. Instead, I held my hands tight over my mouth and nose, suppressing another cough, commanding my body to relax.

The light turned on as the guard stepped in. I could hear his feet rotating in a circle and then walking up and down the aisles. He even sniffed, as if he could track us down like a bloodhound. Fortunately, the room stunk of plastic, rubber and chemicals. In the distance, I could hear the other guard checking the next room.

A minute later, I heard the footsteps of the older guard back out in the corridor, saying, "Come on! told you they're not here. They're in the garage."

"All right," said the younger voice, reluctantly. He stepped out and closed the door without turning off the light. I heard a card reader beep, and the fire door open.

Before the door slammed closed behind them, the older guard said, "We need to get these sickos before they infect anyone."

89. When Angels Cut Their Wings

Releasing my nose and mouth, I broke out in a cough that seemed to propel Stefanie, along with the camouflaging cables and wires, out of the shelf in front of me.

"This is getting exciting," she said.

I wearily wiggled out and stood, using the shelf as support.

"This isn't a game," I said, taking a deep breath. "You hear what he said? We're in so much freakin' trouble."

"The whole world's in so much freakin' trouble," she replied, stripping off the plastic coveralls. Underneath, she was wearing a nursing uniform. A well-padded uniform.

"You're fat," I said, matter-of-factly.

"Four layers." She lifted up her top to reveal a sweater underneath. "My Mom and I don't share the same waistline."

"Your hair," I continued. "I thought it was a wig." But it wasn't. Her blonde hair, which once hung down to her waist, had been sheared to her shoulders and curled. "It's short."

"You like it?" she said, fluffing it. "Turned out Bindu's quite the hair stylist."

"It's not blonde," I added, slowly, disbelievingly.

"Black henna," she said. "All natural dye from the mignonette tree. It'll start to fade in fourteen to twenty-eight days."

I shook my head. "You said our getaway vehicle's in the garage?"

"Afraid so," she said. "Mom's car."

I nodded slowly. "So, we can add old-fashioned crimes like grand auto theft and impersonating a registered nurse to our list of new-normal offences."

She just stared at me, eyes barely blinking. I stared back into her green irises—which seemed to be dancing with both fear and laughter.

Green?

"Your eyes are blue," I blurted.

"Contacts," she said. "I'm flattered you noticed."

I didn't know whether to be impressed with her or terrified of her. Was she brave or bonkers?

"That garage is going to be crawling with guards," I said. "And once they realize we're not there, they'll be coming back here."

She nodded.

"So," I continued, "I suppose you have a backup plan, Jane Bond?

"Of course."

Reaching down into a sub-layer of clothes beneath the uniform's blue pants, she pulled out a black walkie-talkie. Holding it to her mouth, she pressed its large grey button and spoke loudly:

"Moosey, this is Captain Dandelion. Come in, Moosey."

She released the button and held the speaker to her ear. All I could hear was static.

"Phooey!" she said, looking at the room around us. "We may be too far underground. Too much cement."

"No," I said, slowly, as if talking to a crazy five-year-old. "It's because Moosey can't talk. He's made of felt."

Ignoring my comment, she grabbed one of the long wires from off the floor, held it to the stubby antenna and tried again: "Moosey? Moosey, can you read me?"

More static. I rolled my eyes. *Of course, who am I to criticize? I'm the one seeing visions of my dead grandfather.*

"Moosey!" she repeated, speaking even louder. "We're moving to plan B. I repeat, Plan B."

She released the button. More static.

"I don't know who's more crazy," I said. "You or the government."

Ignoring me, she began to strip off her nursing uniform, followed by two sweaters and two pairs of sweat pants, until she was down to one layer of jeans and a purple "Fear is the Virus" T-shirt. My eyebrows were raised for the entire shedding of layers. She then walked past me and opened one of the closet doors.

"*Gefunden!*" she said softly, as if uttering a prayer of thanks.

A dozen grey coveralls hung from hangers in the closet, covered with dust, oil and grime. She pulled out two and handed the larger and dirtier one to me.

"Put this on. Quick!"

As I stepped into the coveralls and my leg came out the other end, I suddenly froze, aghast. There, wrapped around my ankle, with a blinking red light, was the tracking device.

"*Oh boy,*" I said with a sigh.

"What's wrong?" she asked.

I finished zipping up and then pulled at the right legging exposing the anklet. Stefanie took a deep breath.

"All right," she said, calmly. "I know."

"Of course, you do," I muttered.

Recklessly, she began searching through the shelves lined with tools, some falling noisily to the floor. Finally, she returned with a pair of wire cutters. It took three tries before she managed to snap the tracking anklet off, bruising my ankle in the process. Wielding a hammer, she was about to smash the blinking device.

"No!" I said, plucking up the anklet. "I've a better idea. For once."

"What?" she asked, hammer still raised high.

"Trust me," I said. I dropped the device into the large right pocket of my new pair of coveralls. "It's a little more daring, but that seems to be the theme, today."

She pursed her lips and dropped the hammer. Moving to the closet, she pulled out a plastic hard hat and handed it to me. She then pulled her hair up and under a black winter hat and covered it with another of the yellow hats.

"Now..." she said. Her voice trailed off, as her eyes scanned the room, stopping at the shelf above the closets where rows of N95 masks, in clear plastic bags, called out to us with their warning labels. We both fastened one around our face and then stared at each other, as if looking in a mirror.

"You know," I said, in a mask-muffled voice, "the chances of breaking out of a big city hospital in the middle of a pandemic are pretty slim."

She shrugged and sang a line from *The Beautiful Maid of the Mill*:

Und die Engelein schneiden
Die Flügel sich ab
Und gehn alle Morgen
Zur Erde herab.

I rubbed my feverish face. "Forgive me, but I'm going to need a translation."

"And the angels cut off their wings and every morning go

down to earth."

"I don't see the relevance."

She shrugged. "Our job is to do our best. To do the right thing. Then trust that unseen forces of good will take care of the results."

As insane as that sounded, it actually made me feel a touch better.

"Well," I said, yielding to a spark of hope, "it seems a wingless angel saved us on the ice out in the bush."

"Maybe he'll help us again."

Despite the mask I could tell she was smiling. Months ago, I had seen some sign at the post office, paid for by Public Health Ontario, reminding us to "Smile with your eyes." At the time, I thought it sounded stupid. But, staring at her mischievous green eyes, I realized the government got something right.

I reached up to the top of the closet and pulled down two pairs of old-fashioned safety glasses. "This should complete our disguise," I said, handing her a pair.

After slipping on the eye protection, she returned to the trash can and pulled out two of the toolkits I had tossed, handing one to me. My hand began to shake with the weight of it and a sudden attack of fear. My eyes darted at the door.

"Your hands look girly," I said, noticing her small palms, thin fingers and well-manicured nails.

Reaching back into the closet, she pulled out two pairs of work gloves.

"We have no idea what they might do," I said, stretching the gloves around my hands. "They see us as lepers on the run; spreading a killer virus. They've gone psycho."

"Yeah, I've noticed," said Stefanie.

"They could taser us," I said.

A shiver shot from the centre of my back, up to my head, and down to the soles of my feet.

"Or kill us," she added.

"I'm not sure which is worse."

"Both are better than living in a cage," she retorted without hesitation.

I looked back at her through the plexiglass frames. I didn't want to be caged. But did I prefer pain and death?

"We could just end up in a worse cage," I protested. "And the bakery—you don't want them taking it away from you."

"Ha!" she blurted. "The way things are going, we'll be eating lab-grown food, delivered to us by drones, in communist apartment blocks."

"It won't get that bad," I said, shaking my head.

"Only if we put up a fight," she said, in her newfound Southern drawl. She hoisted her toolkit as if it was a rifle. "You comin' or are you stayin' in your shell?"

I stared at her.

I was hardly even willing to risk an $880 corona ticket to retain my own freedom. But the freedom to be with her? I was willing to risk death. And, boy, that feeling scared me more than all the guards, cops, and tasers in Ontario. She scared me. This dandelion—standing tall on the battlefield of life, basking in the open sun, unafraid that at any minute her beautiful henna-dyed head could be hacked off by a *law*-mower—was calling this turtle to extend its limbs and come with her.

"You know," I said, "my life was a lot simpler before I met you."

"You can thank me later," she said and turned toward the door.

I sighed and slowly reached out—as if I were truly a turtle stretching a leg out, tentatively, from the safety of its shell. Wrapping my gloved hand around the door handle, I gingerly pulled it open. Glancing outside, I could only see the discarded wheelchair at the garage door, a fluorescent bulb flickering above it.

With a slight bow, I said, "Ladies first."

"I'm not a lady," she replied in a deep voice. "I'm a maintenance man."

With the oversized N95 mask, she almost sounded like one. In the grimy coveralls, she almost looked like one—if you didn't look too closely.

Good grief, I thought, *there's a 99.8 percent chance we are going to get caught.*

She stepped out into the hallway, and I followed. Heart pounding.

90. She Must Be Mad

"Maintenance men don't swing their hips like that," I said, as I caught up to Stefanie.

"Hmph!" she replied and straightened her gait.

Side by side, we continued toward the elevator lobby, toolboxes clunking together. I tried to reassure myself that our disguises hid not only our identity but also our humanity: just two moving pairs of grey coveralls, white masks, dusty safety glasses, yellow hard hats, grey gloves and... a pair of slippers.

Slippers!

Looking down at our feet, Stefanie wore black, rubber snow boots, which would barely pass as steel-toed work boots; but I was still sporting the light green, hospital-issued slippers Nurse Vader had given me.

I sighed and said in a hushed voice, "The only way we'll get away with this is because they'd assume no one was crazy enough to attempt it."

Stefanie chuckled, replying, "That strategy seems to be working well for the COVID criminal enterprise. Isn't that the reason they're getting away with turning the flu season into a pandemic? With rolling out an untested vaccine? Quarantining people with no symptoms? People assume no one would ever attempt such a deception."

I pulled my hard hat down. I agreed with the logic, but still feared another tasing.

"Just remember," she whispered, as if she could read my mind. "If they identify us, we run."

"And where do we run?"

"Just follow me," she said, stopping at the fire door to the elevator lobby.

Pulling out her mom's pass card, she swiped it through the reader. I didn't breathe, fearing the door would not open. But either the "lockdown" only worked one way, only applied to the outermost doors, or it had been ended now that they thought us to be cornered in the garage. With a sigh of relief, I watched Stefanie pull the door open.

Following her into the elevator lobby, my heart rate doubled. I squeezed my upper lip with the lower to suppress another cough. The French African nurse who had removed my IV the day before was waiting before two elevator doors on our left. The elevator doors were bordered with red and green tinsel. The African nurse was chatting with a young female nurse who had an explosion of freckles covering the unmasked portion of her face. And her curly hair, pulled back in a ponytail, was the brightest red I'd ever seen.

To our right, in front of two other opposing elevator doors, stood an elderly woman dressed in a yellow uniform. Her mask had slipped down below her nose. She was leaning on a cart full of cleaning supplies and appeared to be chewing gum—its spearmint fragrance managing to penetrate my supposedly impenetrable N95 mask.

We walked in between the nurses and the cleaning lady, just as an elevator on the right dinged open. The cleaning lady began to back her cart inside.

"Hey," I said, stepping toward her. "Mind if I toss a broken thingamado in your trash?"

"Go ahead," she said with a shrug.

I pulled the tracking device from my pocket and dropped it into the black bag hanging at the end of her cart.

"Thanks!"

As soon as I withdrew my arm, the doors closed.

Stefanie nodded her head in seeming approval. I felt glad I had finally done something clever enough to complement her scheming.

"Yeah, she ran off with the guy," I overheard the redhead nurse say to the male nurse.

"You think she was really a nurse?" he replied, in his deep French African accent.

She shrugged. "All I know is she managed to outsmart a cop."

"She must be mad," muttered the male nurse.

"Madly in love, I bet," said the female nurse. "Breaking her beloved out of quarantine."

I smiled under my mask. Stefanie reached out and pressed the elevator button on our right.

"You read way too many romance novels," said the male nurse.

"They're historical fictions," she snapped back.

"Bien-sûr," he replied, disbelievingly.

"Anyway, who can blame them?" continued the female nurse. "This whole coronavirus thing is so overblown. Leave it to the ministry not to admit when they've made a mistake."

"No, no, no," replied the male nurse, condescendingly. "There were two hundred and fifty new cases in Toronto on Christmas Day alone. I saw it on CBC."

"The CBC," she said with a snort. "The Coronavirus Broadcasting Corporation. Cases! Cases! Cases! Big deal. Happens every year. Deaths make a pandemic, not super-sensitive lab tests."

"You know better than to talk like that," scolded the male nurse, in a hushed voice, glancing back at us.

"Hey, you guys," said the redhead, turning to us. "You see any body bags piling up?"

"Uh," I stuttered. "No."

The male nurse shifted his weight from side to side. One of the elevators on our left dinged, saving him from a rebuttal. Both nurses entered and turned around to face us. The redhead held the door and called out, "Hey, come on, there's room."

"Ah," said the male nurse, holding up a hand. "We all have an obligation *de pratiquer la distanciation sociale.*"

The redhead laughed. "Ha! I'll admit, saying it in French does make it sound a little less absurd." She stood there, inside the spacious elevator, holding the door open. "Any airborne virus anybody might exhale is just going to collect in this unventilated elevator, whether we're packed like sardines or not. God, am I the only one who didn't sleep through virology 101?"

"We'll wait," I said holding up my hands. "Thanks."

"*Un homme bien,*" said the male nurse, giving me a thumbs-up.

The doors closed on their masked faces.

Stefanie immediately hit the button on the wall to summon another lift. Almost on cue, I heard a high-pitched voice from the direction of the nursing station. It sounded like the man named Bill the guards had called on their walkie-talkies. Turning my head slightly, I saw him approaching at the end of the hallway from the psych ward I had so recently escaped.

"Don't move," whispered Stefanie. "Just act like you own the place."

As Bill approached, I saw he had a greyish-blond crewcut, wore a white surgical mask, and was holding something in his hand. At first, I thought it was a taser. I almost bolted, but a few steps closer, and I could see it was only a smartphone.

"Goddamn app's still downloading the update," he said to another figure approaching from behind.

The second man wore jeans, a white T-shirt, and my buck-toothed beaver mask.

"Don't worry, we'll find them," said Yamamoto, as he came up alongside Bill.

"You sure you've got no symptoms?" said Bill, veering away from Yamamoto.

"I'm fine!" replied Yamamoto. "I don't feel sick at all."

"Then how did you let a goddamn girl steal him from right under your nose?" demanded Bill, waving the smartphone in the air.

"Come on, she was disguised as a nurse," replied Yamamoto, through the wooden mask.

"And what in God's name are you supposed to be? A chipmunk?"

They both halted in the elevator lobby, Bill staring at his smartphone. Stefanie and I rigidly faced the two elevators on their right, keeping our backs to them. I couldn't help notice that Yamamoto had his duty belt on, complete with pepper spray, taser and a loaded gun.

"You give me goddamn COVID and I die..." Bill muttered to Yamamoto, sounding out of breath. "Stand farther away. Twelve feet."

I heard Yamamoto's feet shuffling.

"No problem, amigo."

Bill's smartphone beeped.

"Yes! Install the goddamn update," he said angrily, tapping the screen.

"If you'd feel safer, I can go back to the room," offered Yamamoto.

"You're the only one who knows what they look like," muttered Bill.

The smartphone beeped.

"Is it done?" asked Yamamoto.

"Ninety percent."

I strained my ears, trying to hear if an elevator was descending to our rescue.

"You two!" barked Bill.

We didn't turn around—just twisted to look over our shoulders.

"Hey," said Stefanie through the N95 mask in her fake male voice.

"You see anything strange?"

We both looked at each other and didn't say a word.

"I said, you see anything?"

"Like what?" I said, trying to mimic a French accent.

"Nurse with a COVID patient making a run for it."

"No, no," I replied. "Nothing like that."

Yamamoto immediately walked around so that he was now standing in front of us. Despite the beaver mask hiding his expression, I instantly knew he had seen through my fake accent and dusty safety glasses.

"Amigo..." Yamamoto said slowly, his voice trailing off.

I gulped.

"Amigo!" repeated Yamamoto quickly, turning to Bill. "We need to get to the garage and stop those two."

Suddenly the smartphone began to make a steady beeping sound.

"It's working!" announced Bill.

He aimed the phone in the direction of the garage and stomped over to the fire door. But the beeping became weaker.

"It's saying they aren't that way," flared Bill.

"But your men said they—" began Yamamoto.

"What do those yahoos know? It's saying he's—" he aimed the phone back in our direction and the beeping increased in volume and frequency. And then he tipped the phone upward, pointing it toward the ceiling. It beeped even louder.

"They must have doubled back and taken an elevator," Bill said.

"Okay," said Yamamoto, slapping his hands together. "Let's take the stairs, the elevator's too slow."

"Goddamn it!" grumbled Bill, dropping the beeping phone in his pocket.

Yamamoto sprinted to a glass fire door marked STAIRS and pulled out a pass card. Opening it, he ushered Bill through, beaver mask glancing back at us for a second, before disappearing.

Ding! Before they had finished opening, Stefanie and I squeezed through the elevator doors. We turned around and she hit the button marked G. The doors stayed open for a long moment, but then, finally, slowly began to close.

Every muscle in my body felt tense. I could hear my heart pounding.

Just as the doors were about to seal shut, they began opening again, revealing Bill, one hand outstretched on the elevator button. His eyes went wide as he stared at my feet.

"Where're your goddamn shoes!?" he yelled.

I looked down, innocently, at my two slippers and then hoisted my toolbox up into both my hands.

"I think they're in my toolbox," I said and thrust it at his chest.

Instinctively, Bill let go of the button to grab the heavy projectile, causing him to stagger backwards. I hit the "DOOR CLOSE" button. As they slowly came together, Stefanie flung her toolbox through the opening, hitting Bill in the chin.

We heard him yell as the doors sealed shut.

We both took a slow, deep breath.

The elevator jerked and began to ascend.

91. COVID Breakout

"When the doors open, we need to make a left," said Stefanie with a hint of nervousness to her otherwise even tone, "and walk calmly but swiftly to the front lobby."

I tensed my fists.

The elevator creaked upward.

"What about the running part you promised me?" I asked, already sounding out of breath.

"It's coming."

I inhaled deeply, coughed, and then said, "In case we don't make it, could you let me know something?"

"Sure."

"How did you find me? I mean, you knew I was on the

basement floor. But how did you know which room?"

She paused for a half second and then said: "Mathéo told me."

"*Mathéo?*" I said. "How would he know?"

Another pause.

"Your Grandad told him."

I inhaled and exhaled slowly.

When angels cut their wings.

The elevator dinged.

The door opened to an empty lobby. We quickly made a left, marching through open fire doors into a long hallway. An extra tall (and extra wide) nurse walked far ahead of us. A few metres in front of her, at the end of the hallway, where it opened up into the front lobby, a grey-haired man with a white medical mask sat back on a bench against the wall, hands folded atop his cane. Halfway there, we heard another elevator ding behind us, followed by "Goddamn it!" from Blasphemous Bill.

"*Run!*" announced Stefanie.

Her N95 fell to the floor as she bolted forward. The sound of footsteps pursuing us propelled me on her heels. Hearing the commotion, and seeing us approaching, the old man rose from the bench, using the assistance of his cane. I looked over my shoulder to see Bill's crewcut head and Yamamoto's buck-toothed mask not far behind.

Looking forward, I saw Stefanie scoot around the old man, who now faced me head on. Silver-framed glasses were sliding down his nose. And his massive grey beard spilled out from behind his puffed up mask—its extreme length tucked under the white collar of his black cassock.

"Father Shostakovich!" I exclaimed, coming to a sudden stop.

"Keep going, man!" he urged under his breath, and tapped my ankle with his cane.

I nodded, stunned, and shot around him.

"Goddamn it!" yelled Bill. "Someone stop them!"

I ran after Stefanie, who was already crossing the lobby. Without stopping, I took in the scene of a dozen or so people sitting at socially distanced tables, eating and drinking. A Tim Horton's kiosk was built into the wall on my right. The space smelt of Timmy's fresh-brewed coffee and fresh-baked sugar. A fake Christmas tree stood in the centre of the tables. One man sitting alone at a table stood out. He was dressed in a white dress shirt with a black tie and wore big black glasses. His grey hair was neatly combed, gelled and parted at the side.

"Goddamn it!" I heard Bill shout from behind me. "Out of my way—" And then he yelped.

Looking back, I saw Father Shostakovich, with his cane extended, toppling Bill forward onto the hard floor.

"Thou shalt not," bellowed Father, in the voice of a Southern Baptist, "take the name of the Lord thy God... *in vain!*"

Yamamoto appeared, a half second later, and clumsily tripped over Bill's face-first body. I didn't wait to see what happened next as I crashed through the tables and chairs. Ahead of me, like a wild deer, I saw Stefanie gracefully leap over a knee-high line of backless benches at the edge of the eating area. She had almost reached the two large glass sliding doors at the front of the lobby leading to our freedom. On either side of the doors, beside hand sanitizer dispensers, stood two tall and broad shouldered sentries—staring at us through their face shields.

"Everybody hit the floor!" yelled Yamamoto from behind.

People screamed, rising from their seats. Some scattered, others dropped. Was Yamamoto pointing his taser at my back? Or maybe his gun? The two bulky sentries hesitated, for a second, but even they fell prone on the floor. Oddly enough, the man with the black tie and glasses didn't budge from his table, calmly tipping back his coffee cup as if everything was perfectly normal.

Staring ahead, I realized that even without the sentries blocking our escape, the automated doors would take time to open, once Stefanie reached them—first the interior door, then the exterior door. Together that could take six or ten seconds. By then, Beaver Cop and Blasphemous Bill would surely overtake us. As I leapt over the hurdle of benches, I was half expecting Stefanie to crash through the front window, seeing it as our only hope of escape.

But before Stefanie even reached the sensor, the doors slid apart, revealing a woman with a thick wool scarf wrapped tight around her face. The exterior doors behind her remained open, as a boy about half her height tagged behind. He also wore a scarf around his face, a quiver full of arrows strapped to his back and a bow in his hand.

I almost smiled as I realized, *So Santa got him a real archery set like he wanted.*

Without a pause, Stefanie leapt over the prone sentries, flew around Sandy and Josh, and out through the second pair of sliding doors.

Following, I tore off my mask and hung it on the hand sanitizer dispenser, toppling it over, its contents exploding when it hit the ground in a sudden waft of alcohol.

"Stop them, G— gad-dang it!" yelled Bill at the two sentries, as he closed in on us. "Get the hell up!"

As I passed Sandy, she winked at me and then began to fall to the ground. Instinctively, I halted to catch her. Josh shook his head at me. Pointing both his thumbs up, and forefingers out to his right toward the exit. He was making the sign for "Run!"

Instead, I froze, crouching down, holding Sandy's limp body, as her deaf son continued to sign me away. I was overwhelmed, confused. What the hell was going on? What was happening to my world?

As if in response to my inward call for normalcy, my world got even stranger.

"I'll stop them!" yelled a new voice.

I turned to see not only Bill and Yamamoto running across the last stretch of the lobby, but also the man with the suit and tie. As he cut in front of Bill—tossing his oversized glasses to the ground—I recognized him at once.

"Stand aside," yelled Roger as he ripped open his white dress shirt, revealing a red and yellow S symbol on the chest of his blue Superman costume.

I can't believe this is happening to me.

Josh threw both his index fingers at me—the sign for "Go!"— just as Super Roger snagged his foot on one of the prone sentries, flew forward as if he would take off like a bird (or a plane) but then crashed to the floor, further barricading the entryway.

"Fly!" he whispered to me.

Setting Sandy, who still feigned unconsciousness, beside Roger, I leapt through the open exterior doors into the cold morning air.

"Mommy's fainted!" cried Joshua.

I halted at the outer threshold, turning back to see the doors slide close. A hand grabbed my shoulder. It was Stefanie.

"They're fine!" she said. "Don't stop!"

Of course they are, I thought.

Stealing a final glance, I could now see Bill and Yamamoto blocked by the rising figure of Super Roger—a red cape now hanging down his back—with his sidekick aiming a bow and arrow directly at me.

"Come on!" yelled Stefanie, as an arrow hit the other side of the glass door.

She grabbed my hand and yanked me. The sky was only half-lit with what sunlight could pierce the canopy of grey clouds and falling snowflakes. I couldn't help smiling when I turned toward the drop-off area. Bright yellow, and impossible to miss, hummed the bread van like a ray of sunlight. Vapour rose from its tailpipe. Its sliding door, at the passenger's side, was open and flush with the walkway. Stefanie leapt through the opening, I followed a second later, both of us crashing into sacks of rye and wheat, stacked high.

In the driver's seat, the moose costume sat erect. His snout and droopy nostrils turned to face us. In a muffled, cartoonish voice he sang:

"On Prancer, on Comet, on Turtle and Dandelion..."

"Get us out of here, Moosey!" shouted Stefanie.

"Aye, Captain," he responded in a Scottish accent.

Two hands shot out from under the hooves of the costume and gripped the steering wheel. As the van lurched forward, the antlers flapped back.

I reached for the handle to the sliding door.

Suddenly, a beaver was looking me straight in the eyes. Yamamoto had leapt up and was holding onto the top rim.

"Hey, amigo!" he said through the wooden mask.

I hesitated to push St. George out of a moving vehicle. He'd helped me out. He'd—

As the van swung around the roundabout, Yamamoto tumbled forward into the sacks of grain beside Stefanie. Leaning back for a moment, he pulled off the beaver mask, smiled at us and said, "Sure nice to get out of that stuffy room for a little exercise."

We both stared back, mouths open.

"Don't worry," he said, whimsically. "I'm just trying to make it look like I'm doing my damn job."

He handed Stefanie, who finally looked genuinely stunned, the beaver mask. "Merry Christmas, *boss!*" And with that, he crawled to the open door and leapt out.

I stumbled to the rear of the van and stared out one of its windows. Yamamoto had landed in a massive snowbank and was already on his feet. Bill was rushing to his side. I couldn't hear what Bill was saying, but his swinging arms suggested that he was already back to breaking the second commandment.

Stefanie rolled the sliding door shut. We stared at each other, both breathing heavily. She handed me the beaver mask. I accepted it and said, stunned, "You guys just broke me out of COVID jail."

"Yahoo!" cheered Moosey. "And here I thought COVID would make this the boring-est Christmas ever."

"You better take that mask off," ordered Stefanie, climbing into the passenger seat. "We don't want to attract any attention."

She reached over and lifted away the felt mask revealing AJ's grinning face. Usually clean shaven, he now had two days' worth of stubble.

"Where are your glasses?" asked Stefanie.

"I leant them to Roger. Don't worry, there's hardly any cars on the road. I can do this."

I reclined, exhausted, onto the sacks of grain, hugging the beaver mask. All of a sudden, all I wanted to do was go to sleep. *Was this shock?*

I heard Stefanie buckle a seatbelt.

"Anyway," said AJ. "The city's in lockdown. The roads are empty. No one to hit."

"Then go faster," urged Stefanie.

"Already hitting the speed limit," responded AJ, as I heard the engine accelerate. "Don't want to break the law, you know?"

I have to be dreaming, I thought. *Or I have the bravest, craziest and best friends in the entire freakin' world.*

Within minutes we were racing out of the Nickel City, down

a highway between treeless expanses left lifeless from decades of mining ore out of the Sudbury Basin. Normally, this apocalyptic landscape looked a dark and pitted black. But on that wintery Boxing Day, those rising mounds of Precambrian rock—charred from decades of smelting and acid rain—were pristine white. Fast falling snow had covered up a century of reckless mining practices.

"Where are we going?" I asked wearily.

"Beats me!" confessed AJ. "I'm just the getaway driver. Captain D keeps us foot soldiers on a need-to-know, when-we-need-to-know-it basis."

"Well," I said, still trying to catch my breath, "I think I need to know."

Captain Dandelion looked back at me and smiled.

"Somewhere safe," she said. "Safe from them."

PART FIVE
Beaver's Labour Lost

"Greater love hath no man than this,
that a man lay down his life for his friends."
— *Jesus of Nazareth, John 15:13*

92. Mr. Whiteout

The cessation of the van's engine gently roused me. I must have dozed off, reclining back on the bags of grain, still hugging the beaver mask like a teddy bear. The hardhat I had stolen (yet another offence on my growing list) had fallen off. The pyjamas Mom had sewn me for Christmas clung to my skin, damp with sweat, trapped under the maintenance coveralls I had also stolen. My broken nose throbbed with pain and was probably as red as Rudolph's.

"Did I sleep the whole day away?" I asked wearily.

"No," said AJ. "We've barely been on the road a half-hour."

I gazed out the front window into a dimly lit garage. Glancing back out the rear window, I saw a overhead door come rumbling down, blocking out grey sky and falling snow. That's when I noticed four suitcases stacked at the back of the van. I had a feeling I wouldn't be seeing Moosehead again, anytime soon.

Stefanie opened her passenger door and leaned out.

"You get him?" said a muffled, male voice.

"He's in the back," she replied.

I heard a hand grab the handle of the side door and roll it open. I jolted back. A double valve gas mask stared at me. The black respirator covered not only the man's mouth and nose, but included large goggles over his eyes.

"Freakin' fugitive," he said, through the respirator. "Come on, get out before I change my mind."

"Raj!" I exclaimed.

"Codenames, codenames," he said. "It's Mr. Whiteout."

I wearily scuffled forward to the edge, letting my legs drop out. Raj extended a thick work glove. I held out my right hand, clutching the beaver mask in the other, and let him yank me to the ground.

"Why Mr. Whiteout?" I asked.

"You'll see."

Instead of white, he wore dark blue coveralls. Across the chest was a logo of a truck and trailer above the words "Chatterjee Moving."

I coughed. Raj backed away.

"Sorry," I said, looking at his heavy-duty respirator. "Good thing you have that mask on."

"This ain't to protect me from your freakin' COVID."

Stefanie dropped out of the passenger seat and came to my side.

"Captain D," said Raj with a nod.

"Mr. Whiteout." She nodded back. "Everything ready?"

"As ready as we could be with such short notice, the day after Christmas and with supply chains moving slower than frozen molasses."

I looked around. We were in a massive, two-storey garage. Two white trucks were parked behind Raj on a cracking cement floor. Along the walls were workbenches, shelves and metal pegboards loaded with accessories. The space felt only a few degrees above zero.

AJ stretched across the front seats of the van, powered down the passenger window and called out, "Do you want me to leave the van here?"

"Yeah," said Raj. "Actually, a little closer to the wall." He pointed toward a long workbench covered with power tools and metal cans.

The van slowly rolled forward.

"Can I help?" Stefanie asked.

Raj shook his head. "My assistant will be here in a minute."

Immediately, we heard a door open behind us. Stefanie and I turned around. Now that the van had moved forward, we could see a series of office windows and doors along the far wall. Out walked Raj's father, his black hair slicked back, white teeth smiling, dark skin glistening, wearing blue coveralls identical to Raj's.

"Oh, so very good to see you!"

His thick East Indian accent echoed in the small space. He came right up to me and extended his bare hand.

"Mr. Chatterjee," I said, reaching out.

He clasped my hand tightly with both of his, and spoke softly, "I'm so very sorry about your grandfather. Moosehead has suffered a great loss."

He paused. I nodded.

"But I'm so proud of what you kids are doing," he added,

glancing at Stefanie.

"You are?" I said, shocked.

"Yes, yes," he replied, head drooping a little, as if heavy with unwanted memories. "I left India because my local government was so corrupt. When I lived in Bihar, just to run my shop, I had to pay the police one hundred rupees every week, even though I paid the city four hundred rupees a month for license already. The police tell me, 'You doing good, why not buy us tea, eh?' Once I didn't pay, and they took my motorbike. I had to bribe a judge five hundred rupees to get it back. And then still pay the police. I came to Canada for freedom, for fairness, for dignity. This is my home. This is where Raj and Bindu were born. I will not see it be taken over by crooked politicians and their army of masked zombies."

"But, Mr. Chatterjee," I said, hesitantly. "You always wear a mask at church."

"No more!" he announced, letting go of my hand and spreading his arms out like a magician before the rabbit pokes its head out of the hat. "My wife may divorce me, but I will not betray my conscience any longer."

"Mom won't divorce you," said Raj, walking over to the workbench. "She'll just burn the chapatis."

"I can handle that," said Mr. Chatterjee. "We all have to make sacrifices." Then he stood back and looked at me and Stefanie. "Some of us more than others."

Stefanie nodded and took off her yellow hardhat, letting loose what was left of her hair.

"My, my," he said, putting his hands on her shoulders.

"Your daughter may be missing her calling with that law degree," said Stefanie. "Bindu's quite the hair stylist."

He tilted his head back and forth. "Yes, yes," he replied, "she may need a backup career, anyway, with the way things are going."

Raj returned with a roll of masking tape, several large garbage bags and a second gas mask. His father took the respirator and looked at us.

"Forgive me. I know I just said I wouldn't wear a mask but..."

Stefanie chuckled. "Baba, some masks have their place."

He tied the strap around the back of his head and breathed

heavily through the valves. Raising his arms up like a zombie, he started walking toward us, speaking in a robotic voice: "Resistance is useless. You will be sanitized! Sanitized! *Sanitized!*"

Stefanie and I backed away, feigning fear, banging into Raj, who had begun wrapping a garbage bag around the front tire of the van.

"Cut it out, you guys," he said, swatting us away. "We have, what, three hours to get a twelve-hour job done. And that's if we don't get caught first."

"Yes, yes, quite right," said Mr. Chatterjee, dropping his arms and turning toward the workbench.

On the other side of the van, I heard the driver's door open. Two antlers appeared over the rooftop.

"I can tape the window frames," said AJ, as he came around the hood, wearing the moose mask again.

Raj threw him the roll of tape.

"After that, you'll need to clear out, felt face," said Raj, moving to the next tire. "That snout ain't exactly up to OSHA standards."

AJ peeled off a strip of masking tape, and began stretching it across the edge of the windshield.

Feeling a bit unnerved, I said, "You guys aren't doing what I think you're doing?"

Before they had time to answer, I began to cough.

"It's too cold in here," said Mr. Chatterjee, patting me on the back. "Take him into the office." He pointed to the door he had just exited. "I have the heater going. There's a couch. Make yourself at home. I left a thermos full of chai."

"All right," I said, already feeling like lying down again.

Stefanie led me toward the office, holding the door while I walked through. The room smelled of cardamom.

Behind me, Mr. Chatterjee was saying to Raj, "Let's start with 180-grit."

I glanced back to see him plugging in a large power tool with a square, flat base. Stefanie lingered at the door, staring at her yellow van, in the same way one would watch a loved one being led into surgery.

93. Nuremberg 2.0

Ten minutes later, I was lying in Mr. Chatterjee's office on a prickly wool couch. Stefanie sat behind a massive, solid wood desk, in an ergonomic office chair, her head leaning against an adjustable headrest. As she sipped chai tea, I watched her. She looked so different. Grey coveralls, short hair, tired blue eyes. At least she had removed the green contacts.

"I can't believe you pulled this off," I said. "You're unbelievable."

"Thank you," she replied, as if too tired to utter any more syllables.

Behind her, snow fell steadily on the other side of a double-pane window, revealing a flat panorama of white farm fields, interspersed by clumps of evergreen woodlots. Chatterjee's Moving was located down a country road off Highway 69, halfway between Moosehead and Sudbury, if I remembered correctly. I'd only been here once before, but not inside.

Eleven years ago, the Chatterjees had purchased a life-size statue of St. Joseph. Looking out the window now, I could see the backside of the replica of Jesus' Middle Eastern father. Joseph probably never saw a flake of snow in his entire life. Now he was covered in it. I was only thirteen when Baba had invited everybody from St. Jerome's to the unveiling of the statue.

"Almighty everlasting God," had prayed the late Father Chittick at the gathering, "who does not forbid us to carve or paint likenesses of your saints, in order that whenever we look at them with our bodily eyes we may call to mind their holy lives, and resolve to follow in their footsteps..."

The Chatterjees had indeed followed St. Joseph's entrepreneurial footsteps. The statue clutched a carpenter's square—reflecting Joseph's status as the patron saint of hard-working people. And, most fittingly, he was also the patron saint of house sellers and buyers, making St. Joseph an apt guardian for Chatterjee Moving.

I think it was Baba's way of trying hard to fit in. I'm not sure it worked. Lay people owning such large and expensive statues, let alone displaying them on their lawn, was unheard of even among the most devout in twenty-first-century Moosehead. I rather suspect such practices were more common in his mother country of Hindu gods and goddesses.

Another reason they chose the statue was that St. Joseph was also the patron saint of immigrants. St. Joseph, after all, had had to escape to Egypt when the local government was hunting down the baby Jesus.

Now that I was being hunted down by my own government, I closed my eyes and said a silent prayer to St. Joseph, also considered the patron saint of Canada—a country certainly in need of all the prayers it could get. My silent appeal for intercession made me remember...

"Father Shostakovich!" I blurted. "Do you think he'll be all right? Do you think they'll arrest him?"

"Arrest a Catholic priest?" said Stefanie, whimsically. "Seems priests can get away with just about anything."

I took a deep breath and said, "I'm serious."

"I warned him we all might end up in jail," she replied. "He just shrugged and said if prison was good enough for Paul, John and Jesus, it was good enough for him."

"But Sandy and Josh," I said. "You shouldn't have got them involved. They could have got hurt."

She put down her tea so forcefully it spilt over the side of her mug. "Sandy was only supposed to *drive* Father and Roger there. And then drive them back afterwards. That's it! Not become part of their human obstacle course. Her and Josh were both disobeying direct orders."

Disobeying direct orders? My eyebrows raised as I countered, "Well, good thing they did come through when they did."

"It was hardly a coincidence," she replied. "When I hit the front lobby, I saw them standing outside, looking through the window. They were waiting."

"At least, they won't be charged," I said. "I mean, it's not like they did anything wrong. Just walked in and fainted."

"Josh might get a ticket for bad acting," said Stefanie. "But Sandy deserves an Emmy."

"And Roger?"

"He was trying to help catch the bad guys," she said, with a shrug. "Quite frankly, I think hospital security will be too embarrassed to admit they were outwitted by an elderly priest with a cane, a comic book collector wearing a red cape, a fainting woman with a medical degree, and her deaf boy with a bow and arrow. I doubt they'll press any charges."

I chuckled. "Good point." I hoped she was right.

The office door swung open. AJ Moosey stepped in, carrying one of the green plastic bins from the van, plus a suitcase.

"No meese allowed!" yelled out Raj from the garage.

AJ kicked the door shut and set the bin down in the middle of the floor.

"Howdy, pardner," said Stefanie, reviving her Texan accent for a fleeting moment.

"Hey," he said reluctantly through the moose mask, sounding a bit nervous.

I didn't say anything. Just stared at him from the couch. There he was, wearing my furry uniform, carrying the bread bins and driving the van—he'd practically replaced me.

"Tea?" said Stefanie.

"If it's hot," said AJ, falling back into the swivel chair between the desk and the couch. Instantly rebounding forward, he leaned down and opened the bin. "Breakfast, anybody?" He pulled out a white cardboard box and opened its lid, releasing the explosive aroma of gingerbread. "A high-caloric meal for a high-stress emergency."

"No, thanks," I said, slouching back on the couch with a hand to my gut. "I'm still recovering from the barely edible matter the hospital served me. I can't stomach even the smell of food."

Stefanie poured AJ a cup of tea and he immediately dunked the head of a gingerbread man into the steaming liquid.

"I always eat the head first," he said. "Seems the most merciful." He inserted the cookie into his moose snout, and then pulled it back, decapitated. "Mmm. That's how I'd want to go. Not losing my legs and my arms first."

Stefanie reached for the box and pulled out another gingerbread man.

"Thanks, AJ," she said, sarcastically. "I've never felt guilty about eating a gingerbread man before."

She snapped its neck.

"Here you thought leaving out the lard and the eggs made them vegan," I said. "But you're actually being a cannibal."

She popped the head into her mouth. "Add it to my list of crimes."

"*Crimes?*" said AJ, holding the cup of tea up to the mask's snout. "I'd like to think we're the good guys." He put the tea down without attempting to take an impossible sip.

"We are the good guys," said Stefanie. "It's the politicians, the public health officers, the WHO who are committing the crimes against humanity. One day they'll be before Nuremberg 2.0."

"A Nuremberg trial?" I questioned.

She nodded. "Nazi doctors were hung for far less. The lockdowns alone could kill millions. The masks are nothing short of child abuse. The vaccine is untested and experimental. The neglect of seniors in nursing homes is torture. Make no mistake about it, we're up against the most dangerous men in the world. As the German Coronavirus Investigative Committee has stated, we are witnessing the greatest crime in the history of humanity."

"Yeah," said AJ standing and speaking shakily. "That reminds me. You know, I've been having second thoughts about driving."

94. New Normal Nazguls

AJ suddenly didn't sound like much of a hero anymore. He was slouching, moose mask drooping, looking worse than I felt.

Stefanie leaned forward over Mr. Chatterjee's desk, broke the back of her gingerbread man and asked, "What kind of second thoughts are you having?"

"I mean," continued AJ, "you don't really need me from here on out. There's only two seats in the van. And, well..."

He fell silent, standing there, hiding inside the moose mask.

"I wouldn't ask anything more of you," said Stefanie. "I can't thank you enough. We couldn't have saved Vince without you."

He sat down and picked up his gingerbread torso.

"Yeah," he said. "I mean. If you need me, I'm there for you. But..."

"Well, we sure could still use the help," replied Stefanie. "There's a long drive ahead. Vince is too sick to be doing any of it. And I've hardly had any sleep. Seat space isn't an issue. I could sleep the whole way there on a bed of rye."

AJ broke the arm off his gingerbread man.

"I guess," he said, staring at Stefanie. "I'm just getting cold hooves. I mean, right now they don't know I had anything to do with this. I'm not like you two. They know who you are. But if they catch us together..."

He dropped the remaining gingerbread torso into his tea, stood up and started pacing the small space.

"I don't mean to sound like a coward," he continued. "I mean, it's just, all these new laws. It's like, it's like—"

"The Scouring of the Shire," finished Stefanie, in a British accent.

AJ stopped pacing and looked straight at her, as if she just said something of profound importance.

"The Scouring of the *what*?" I asked.

"You know," said AJ, slapping his hooves together, "the second to last chapter of the *Lord of the Rings*."

"I only saw the movies," I confessed.

"It's after the war," said AJ, with sudden fervour in his voice. "Frodo, Sam, Merry and Pippin return to Hobbiton to find it's been taken over by Saruman's ruffians. Hobbits are living like slaves in their own country, rules posted everywhere telling them what they can and cannot do. Businesses shut down. Food shortages. No one's even allowed to sing."

He began pacing the room again, his antlers bobbing back and forth.

"But Frodo and company," he continued, "they just got back from battling trolls and orcs and Nazguls—"

"Nazguls?" I said.

"Yeah, Nazguls!" said AJ.

And then, from his cartoonish moose mask, he let out a terrifying screech that sounded like metal scraping metal mixed with the squeal of a dying pig. After allowing a moment for a shiver to run down our spines, he continued excitedly.

"So Frodo and Sam aren't scared. They rouse the town of hobbits, tear down the rules, lift up their pitchforks and drive away the ruffians."

Stefanie took a sip of her tea, nodded and said, "That's what we're like."

"Hobbits?" I asked.

"No! Vigilantes!" said AJ, extending his bare hands out of the costume, and slapping them together. "Fighting the New Normal Nazguls."

What a nerd, I thought.

"We're superheroes!" he exclaimed.

A super-nerd.

Stefanie laughed. "That's our brave Super Moosey."

He stopped his pacing with a stamp of his feet, put his hands on his hips and grumbled, "Do I look like a Moosey to you?" His snout, antlers and bulging white eyes rotated to look at each of us.

"Okay," replied Stefanie. "Mooseman it is!"

"No, not even Mooseman," he said.

"How about Moose Lee?" I offered.

"Listen," he said, "if I'm going to remain a part of your Corona Justice League of Ontario, I need a cool name like Captain Dandelion or Mr. Whiteout. I don't want to be a moose."

He sat back down and took off the moose mask. Opening the suitcase he had brought in, he pulled out a pair of glasses with red frames—apparently backups to replace the pair he had lent to Roger Kent.

"Hey!" I said. "A big strong moose is better than being a tiny box turtle."

"What do you mean, man?" said AJ. "Teenage Mutant Ninja Turtles! Cowabunga! You're a hero in a half shell!"

"Hmph!" I replied, dejectedly. "I can't say I've been even a quarter of a ninja."

"We may not be ninjas," said AJ, "but we can still be heroes." He closed his eyes for a second, took a deep breath and then continued being a nerd. "It was the same with the Ninja Turtles. When the show got sent to the UK, they renamed it Teenage Mutant *Hero* Turtles."

"Why did they do that?" I asked.

"Ah," replied AJ shaking his head, "they said that ninjas were too violent for a kid show. The British government even made them take it out of the theme song. They changed 'Splinter taught them to be ninja teens' to 'Splinter taught them to be *fighting* teens.'"

"Fighting teens was less violent than ninja teens?" I asked.

"That's a politician for you," said Stefanie. "They just have to look like they're doing something. Doesn't have to make any real difference."

"It must be all the tasing," I said, rubbing my head. "But who was Splinter, again?"

AJ pushed his glasses up his nose and explained, "Splinter was the turtles' anthropomorphic rat sensei who taught them martial arts in the New York sewers."

"Ah, yeah, that's right," I replied, staring over at the beaver mask sitting on the desk, remembering the story of the muskrat who saved Turtle Island.

"Anyway," said AJ excitedly, "give me a better superhero name and I might agree to your crazy caper. Mooseman's too corny."

"Corny?" I said, dumbfounded. "How is it any more corny than Batman or Spiderman?"

"I don't want to be named after an animal. Give me a unique name like Zorro."

"Actually," said Stefanie, "zorro is Spanish for fox."

"What, really?"

"Yeah," I said, my eyes closing again for a second. "She's right."

A comforting memory flashed before my mind, of Grandad sitting beside a roaring fireplace on a dark winter night, reading a six-year-old Vince McKnight *The Mark of the Zorro*.

"Oh, yeah," said AJ reflectively. "And I guess there's also Robin, Hawkman and Wolverine."

"Wolverine?" asked Stefanie, with a cock of her head. "Who's that?"

"He's Canadian," said AJ.

"So's a moose," I reminded him.

"And... a beaver," he shot back, pointing to my Christmas gift on the desk. "If I'm going to be an animal, I'd rather be a beaver."

"Okay," said Stefanie. "We can call you Beaverman."

"Or, maybe..." AJ paused, before continuing in the deep voice of a 1940s radio drama. "The Green Beaver! You know, like the Green Hornet."

"Green Beaver's the name of an organic deodorant company," replied Stefanie.

"Oh."

"How about The Red Beaver?" she suggested. "Same colour

as the maple leaf."

"Now that's corny," I said.

"No," said AJ. "I like it!"

I let out a sigh of exasperation, stood up and picked up the beaver mask, which conveniently had more red than brown paint composing its wooden stare. Turning to AJ, I held it above his head. "I christen you The Red Beaver." He removed his glasses, bowed his head forward and allowed me to slip on the mask.

"You can keep it," I said, flopping back down on the couch. "Merry Christmas!"

"You serious, bro?" said AJ, feeling the mask with his fingertips.

"You took a big risk for me," I said. "It's the least I can do."

It was hard to let go of it, knowing Grandad had made it.

"Thanks!" he said. "I mean it."

I grimaced. I didn't want him to feel like I was bribing him to risk his neck on our behalf.

He stood up and examined his reflection in the glass window between us and the dimly lit garage. In the garage we could see Raj applying a sandblaster against the rear of the van.

Turning back to us, The Red Beaver said, "You know why I like the beaver so much?"

"No idea," I responded.

He put his hands back on his hips, and said rather gallantly, "Because the beaver, he gives a dam!"

That made me laugh. Hard. Despite the fear, the fatigue, and the chill creeping up my arms and legs, I couldn't help myself. But laughter brought coughing. And coughing brought a spasm of shivering. At that moment, I wished that AJ was a real beaver, snug in his lodge in the middle of a frozen lake. And that I was really a turtle, safe in my half shell, at the bottom of that same lake—both of us waiting for this dark winter to pass.

"Hey," said Stefanie, looking over at me. "Are you warm enough?"

"Not really," I said.

She stood up. I was kind of hoping she'd come over and cuddle. Instead, she began unzipping the hospital coveralls, revealing her purple "Fear is the Virus" T-shirt and black jeans. She handed the coveralls to me.

"Put these on. Double up. You need to keep warm. I'll turn up the heater."

In a matter of minutes I was sleeping soundly on Mr. Chatterjee's couch, somehow hoping, when I woke up, everything would have righted itself.

95. The Altar of Freedom

"Hey, time to go."

I heard her voice as if she were speaking from a faraway land. Slowly my eyes opened. A black-haired Dandelion blinked back at me. I had fallen asleep on the couch, to the sound of power tools blasting the van. Two red winter jackets blanketed my body. I sat up and looked at her, bundled up in her green winter jacket, red hat and yellow mitts. Behind her, through the office window, the snow was still falling, burying St. Joseph up to his ankles.

"Where're we going?" I asked, almost in a whisper. "Egypt?"

She shook her head. "We're heading north."

"Egypt would be warmer," I argued.

"Here," she said, handing me a jacket.

I pushed myself into a sitting position. My chest felt a bit better but the rest of me could have lain there forever. I slipped into the jacket and stood up, noticing that the garage was now quiet. A moment later, the door swung open, and Mr. Chatterjee strutted in, smiling, his blue coveralls speckled with white paint.

"The surgery was a success!" he announced in his thick East Indian accent.

Raj followed, shaking his head. "But don't expect the patient to live long. It's the freakin' worst job we've ever done."

"That doesn't matter," said Stefanie. "We just need it to last the day."

"What have you done?" I asked, dreading I already knew the answer.

"Come and see," said Mr. Chatterjee, eagerly.

He put his hand on my shoulder and guided me out into the garage. All three garage doors were wide open now. Nonetheless, the smell of acrylic paint lingered heavy in the air. Parked in the middle of the floor was a *white* bread van. The words "Moose-head Artisan Bakery," the phone number and the bright yellow paint of the van I had been driving for six months... all gone.

The horn beeped.

The Red Beaver stuck his head out the driver's window and hollered, "Cowabunga! Awesome job, Mr. Whiteout!"

"Careful not to touch the paint," cautioned Raj. "It's far from dry."

Mr. Chatterjee pointed to the rear. "We swapped your plates with one of the moving trucks'."

I walked over to the rear license plate. No longer did it say GRTBREAD but merely random numbers and letters between the words ONTARIO and YOURS TO DISCOVER.

"And take a look at this," called out AJ.

Stefanie and I walked around to his open driver's side door, where he was pointing to the dashboard near the windshield. "Raj even replaced the vehicle identification number. He's like a criminal mastermind."

"I'm no such thing," countered Raj, tossing a wrench loudly into a bucket.

I'd no idea what the original ID number was, but screwed into the holder was FMHK6C85KBWQ4527 beside a QR code.

"You guys are amazing," said Stefanie.

She sounded happy—or at least grateful—but I could sense a touch of mourning at sacrificing her van (and, possibly, the bakery) on the altar of freedom.

"It's the least we can do," Mr. Chatterjee replied.

"No kidding," grumbled Raj. "We applied a rust inhibitor, but we didn't have time to cut out and weld the bad patches. So the paint will probably bubble. Give it a week and it'll look like crap."

"It just has to last until nightfall," said Stefanie. "Thank you so much." She wrapped her arms around Mr. Chatterjee's neck and squeezed.

"Hey, don't I get a hug?" asked Raj.

Stefanie reached out and embraced him. "Thanks a million, Mr. Whiteout."

Raj and Baba both get hugs? I thought. Not like she'd ever hugged me.

"The cops are looking for a yellow van," said AJ, his voice

echoing a bit before it found its way out of the wooden beaver mask. "Now we got a white van in a white snow storm. They'll never spot us."

"Does that mean The Red Beaver is coming with us?" I said.

"You can count on me, Ninja Turtle!" And then, pumping his fist in the air, he cheered: "Corona Justice League of Ontario!"

Raj rolled his eyes and whispered to us, "He's such a nerd."

"I just need to know where the heck we're going," added AJ.

Stefanie walked over to the van and whispered a destination into one of his pointy beaver ears.

"Really?" he exclaimed, like a child just told he'd be going to the moon. "*Really?*"

She nodded.

"Count me in!" he hooted. "Why didn't you tell me in the first place?"

Stefanie shrugged. "If you had decided not to come, I was concerned they might use torture to extract the information out of you."

She said it so deadpan, I didn't know whether she was joking or not. And, maybe, neither did she.

"I'd never tell," he promised. "Let's just hope we can make it that far without stopping for gas."

"We siphoned fuel into the van," said Mr. Chatterjee. He pointed to a gas can, air pump and about twelve feet of plastic tubing resting on the cement floor near one of the moving trucks. "Should be full now."

"And that baby's running a Duramax Diesel V8," I said. "A full tank can push over a thousand klicks."

"Well, we only have 540 kilometres ahead of us," said Stefanie. She glanced at her wristwatch. "It's going on noon now. At ninety, it'll take us about five or six hours. If we leave now, we might get there before nightfall."

96. Moonbeam

My four legs were pressed tight against my scaly sides. Below me was nothing but empty space. No ground. No surface. Not even air. A vacuum of blackness. Above, I bore the opposite extreme: a hard shell growing out of my ribs and backbones. Atop the dome of fused calcium plates I could feel billions of tiny people bustling about, unaware that I supported them all.

"The turtle carries the world on its back." I heard Grandad's voice ahead of me. I pushed my head out of the shell. Two large brown eyes stared back at me out of the blackness—a blackness broken only by spiky white coronaviruses, twinkling like stars. I extended my four legs from the safety of the shell. Serving as paddles, my green limbs propelled me forward into the nothingness, hoping to reach those unblinking eyes.

"Grandad!" I called out.

Immediately, dark lids fell over his brown eyes, melting them into the blackness. After a moment of cold silence, the corona stars began to vibrate in synch to a singing male tenor:

Gute Ruh', gute Ruh'!
Tu' die Augen zu!
Wandrer, du müder, du bist zu Haus.[*]

I opened my eyes, finding myself, as I had spent most of the trip, lying on a mattress of paper sacks full of wheat and rye. Over the speakers was playing (for the third or fifth time) the only CD we had in the van. Ian Bostridge was belting out the "The Brook's Lullaby" from the end of Schubert's *Die schöne Müllerin*:

Die Treu' ist hier,
Sollst liegen bei mir,
Bis das Meer will trinken die Bächlein aus.[†]

After hours of near ceaseless motion, the van had finally stopped; otherwise we'd only paused once at a roadside ravine to relieve ourselves.

Pulling at the plastic tarp that I used as a bedsheet, I glanced

---

[*] Rest well, rest well!
Close your eyes.
Wanderer, you weary one, you are at home.

[†] Fidelity is here,
You'll lie with me
Until the sea drains the brook dry.

to my left where Stefanie had spent most of our journey on a separate bed of grain. She had slept more than me—as if she hadn't slept in days. AJ had insisted on doing all the driving. He even wore a mask when behind the wheel. Sadly, even in that first year of COVID-19, nothing would make you look less conspicuous than wearing a face diaper while you were driving (even if you were the only one in the vehicle).

"My mug shot isn't being plastered all over post offices from Bona Vista to Vancouver Island," AJ had told us. "I'm just some white dude with a Tragically Hip face mask driving a white van."

I couldn't say I'd ever seen a wanted poster in a post office in Canada. AJ probably was reading too many American comic books. Still, Stefanie and me lying low seemed like the safest move for all three of us.

As my eyes came into focus, I could see that Stefanie was no longer in the back of the van, resting on her bed of grain. I sat up slowly and looked back over my shoulder. There she sat in the passenger seat, gazing at something in her hand before an open glove compartment box. Through the windshield, I could see that twilight was almost upon us, that the snow had stopped falling, and that the driver's seat was empty.

In a groggy voice I asked, "Hey, where's AJ?"

Stefanie's hand jerked as if I startled her. Dropping whatever was in her hand, she leaned forward to retrieve it from the floor carpet.

"What?" she asked, sitting back up. "Sorry, what did you say?"

I saw it plainly for a second before she quickly returned Josef's engagement ring to the glove compartment and shut the door. My mind flashed back to Wednesday night, after the campfire, when she told me about their breakup, removed her emerald ring and put it in the glove compartment—discarded but, so it seems, not forgotten. I wondered if she would mail it back to him.

Pretending I hadn't seen the ring, I repeated, "Where's AJ?"

"Oh," she said in a distant voice. She gazed at me for a second, forced a smile, then turned her head one-eighty so she was looking out her passenger side window. "AJ's making first contact."

This time it was my turn to ask, "What?"

Slouching a bit to avoid banging my head, I walked forward and fell into the driver's seat. I fell into the seat not out of exhaustion; but out of shock. Less than ten metres to the right of the van stood AJ. He was bundled up in matching black ski pants and a thick winter jacket, with a hood encapsulating his head. His hand was outstretched as he felt the rim of a... *flying saucer*—except it wasn't flying.

Three metallic legs, no taller than AJ, extended from its bottom and disappeared into a foot of snow. Atop the legs, two white saucers were sandwiched together (like two cymbals frozen in a cosmic clang). The saucers were capped by two domes on the top and bottom. Round, black windows spotted the lower dome; while a layer of snow covered the top dome. An antenna pierced the mound of snow on the upper dome, sticking straight up toward the darkening sky. Behind the spacecraft, in the small clearing, towered a two-storey wooden building painted bright red.

At first I didn't know what to think or say.

Stefanie calmly clarified, "On Christmas morning, the extraterrestrials visited me in a dream." She held up a piece of paper with handwritten notes. "They told me to meet them at exactly 49.3432 degrees north and 82.1541 degrees west. They are going to take us to their home planet where there are no lockdowns, face masks, or pharmaceutical salesmen pretending to be altruistic politicians."

Outside, I could hear AJ calling out to the UFO. "Take us to your leader. Earth has gone to hell in a hand sanitizer."

That's when I noticed a wooden sign hanging from the red building: INFORMATION.

"Ich glaub, mein Schwein pfeift," I joked.

Stefanie smiled and nodded. "Of course you do. We've been listening to pigs whistle all year long."

I sighed. "All right then, what's really going on? Where are we?"

"Welcome to the township of Moonbeam, Ontario," she replied, grinning and sounding like her melancholy was beginning to thaw.

"Moonbeam?" I repeated, reflectively. "Why does that name

sound so familiar?"

"It's on Highway 11 halfway between Timmins and Thunder Bay." She began reading from her piece of paper. "Settled 1912. Incorporated 1922. Population 1,231."

I shook my head. "How did it get a name like Moonbeam?"

"Wiki says the first settlers—mainly miners and farmers from Quebec—often saw flashing lights dropping from the sky," she explained. "Probably northern lights mixing with the moonlight." She shrugged. "Or aliens."

AJ ran over and knocked on Stefanie's passenger side door.

"Isn't this great?" he exclaimed, as Stefanie powered down the window. "Can one of you snap a picture of me in front of the craft?" He lifted up his iPhone.

"That better be in airplane mode," snapped Stefanie, "or you'll have every cop in Northern Ontario upon us. We'll really need Scotty to beam us out of here."

"No worries," said AJ. "I just want a keepsake. I'm not going to upload it anywhere."

Stefanie grumbled to herself.

"Anyway, we need to look like tourists," continued AJ. "I mean it would be weird to not stop when confronted with such a work of art."

"Work of art?" I retorted, disbelievingly. "It looks like a leftover from a 1950s B-movie."

"And I doubt this place gets many tourists in December," added Stefanie. "Especially when the province has been put into lockdown."

AJ's head suddenly snapped to the left.

"Frack!" he blurted out.

The back of the van filled with white light, as two approaching headlights shone through the rear door windows.

Without turning to face us, AJ uttered one word: "Cops!"

97. Tragically COVID

We could hear the police cruiser veering off the road, scrunching the fresh fallen snow with its winter tires before coming to a halt beside the flying saucer. Petrification flashed across AJ's face, as he stood on the other side of the passenger side window.

"I told you we shouldn't have stopped," scolded Stefanie.

"Get in the back, both of you," he ordered. "I'll take care of this."

"Are you sure?"

He opened the door and shooed her away. "Get under cover." Then with one hand he reached for his Tragically Hip face mask, which he'd left dangling from the rear-view mirror, and with the other he powered up the window.

Stefanie and I scurried back onto our grain sack beds, covering ourselves with the tarps, like vampires being sought out by torch-yielding villagers. Outside, I could hear the sound of the police car's door opening and shutting.

"Hey, pal," said a male voice, which sounded mask-muffled.

"Perfect timing, officer," said AJ, cheerfully, as he shut the van's door. "I hate selfies. You think you can take a shot of me in front of the mothership?"

"Oh," said the cop, with a chuckle. "That ain't the mothership. Mayor keeps that in orbit. That thing's just a shuttlecraft."

AJ laughed.

The cop's voice came closer. "Sure thing, pal, give me the phone."

"Thanks!"

"A little to the left," directed the cop. "All right. Say, Moonbeam!"

We heard the sound of digital shutter clicks.

"I have to hand it to him," I whispered to Stefanie. "He's really going from super-nerd to Super Beaver."

She shushed me.

"Where're you coming from?" asked the cop.

"Kingston," AJ lied.

"Kingston, eh?" he said. "Long trip to be making with stay-at-home orders, don't you think?"

"Yeah, well," said AJ, "the guidelines said we could go for a spin by ourselves."

"Kingston's over 900 kilometres away. Quite a spin."

"Tell me about it," said AJ with a sigh. "I've been on the road since eight." His hand thudded against the side of the van. "Duramax V8 diesel engine. Can handle 1K without a refuel. Borrowed it from a pal of mine."

"Where you headed?" asked the cop.

"Uh," said AJ. "Nowhere now. I've reached my destination. Just, just wanted to get a shot with the spacecraft. Then I'll be heading back home, officer."

"You came all this way just to see Moonbeam's novelty road-side saucer?"

"Yeah," said AJ, with failing confidence. "I, um, I'm really into UFOs. Project Blue Book. Area 51."

"Uh-huh," said the cop. "You think you're fooling me?"

I heard Stefanie groan.

"I can explain," said AJ, his voice quavering.

"Don't bother," said the cop. "I know who you are."

AJ fell silent.

"It's written all over your face."

I held my breath.

"You're a Tragically Hip fan."

My lungs relaxed and sucked in air.

"Uh... you, you caught me," confessed AJ. "Guilty as charged."

"No guilt in honouring Gord," said the cop.

"Gord Downie," said AJ reverently.

Gord Downie, the Hip's deceased lead singer. Another angel may have just cut his wings.

"Yeah," continued AJ. "Well, in the *World Container* album, as you must know, he said there were two places he always wanted to visit.'"

"Yep!" confirmed the cop. "Track four. 'The Fly.' Two places he'd never been and always wanted to see: Mistaken Point, Newfoundland and—"

"Moonbeam, Ontario," finished AJ. "I don't know if he got to either one before he died. But I thought I'd make sure I did."

"You're a little young to be worrying about dying," said the cop. And then, with hesitation, "You don't got COVID or something?"

"No, no, had a PCR test the other day. My nasal cavity is as clean as a whistle. But, you know, with the triple mutant variants on their way, we really don't know what the future's going to be like. I figured, if I didn't make this expedition now, I might never get the chance. Like, I mean, who would have thought Gord would have left us when he did?"

"You see his last concert before the tumour got him?" asked the cop, solemnly. "I was there in Kingston for the end of the Man Machine Poem tour."

"I couldn't get a ticket," said AJ. "Had to watch it on CBC. Which kind of sucked, living in Kingston and all."

"Well, at least they didn't air any commercials. I'll give 'em that."

Another pause.

"Hey," said AJ, "meeting a fellow fan sure makes the pilgrimage feel complete."

"Oh, I'm not a fan," said the cop. "I'm a devotee! Gord's albums have been the soundtrack of my life since age nineteen. We played 'The Heart of the Melt' at our wedding, 'Fiddler's Green' at my dog's funeral."

"That's awesome," said AJ. A moment of meditative silence passed, before he asked, "Hey, I don't know if it's against OPP rules, but you think I can get a shot of you in front of the saucer?"

"Of course!" the cop replied. "Just let me take this muzzle off." His voice suddenly became clearer. "After all, this is sacred."

More footsteps and the sound of a shutter.

"The Hip weren't just the ultimate Canadian band," mused the cop. "They were Canada itself."

"Amen!" agreed AJ.

I sighed. I had never understood why people liked the Tragically Hip so much; but at that moment, I had been converted into one of their most grateful fans.

"You got a long drive back," said the cop. "It's pretty late. Don't want you falling asleep at the wheel."

"Ah," said AJ. "I got a blow-up mattress and a thirty-below sleeping bag in the back. When I get tired, I'll pull over and crash."

"Sweet," said the cop. "I wish I was young and free again."

"And I'm in no rush to get back to my flat," added AJ. "Being trapped in that apartment with my roommate and his girlfriend's yapping chihuahua. And, God help me, all they listen to is Justin Bieber."

"My God! Bieber!' said the cop. "That violates the UN's convention against torture."

"It's lockdown hell," said AJ.

I coughed a few times while the two of them continued to swap Tragically Hip trivia. Fortunately, I was feeling better and the coughs were quiet enough that I doubted the cop could have heard them.

Especially when he and AJ started singing.

They sang all of "The Fly," concluding, tearfully, with lyrics about how people die trying to learn to love. I even heard Stefanie sniffle back a sob. I wasn't sure whether Gordon Downie's poetry moved her heart or whether the cop and AJ's off-key a cappella was grating her nerves.

"Hey, pal," said the cop. "I'll probably have to write myself a ticket for this, but you mind if I shake your hand?"

"Sure thing," said AJ. "We can split the fine."

They both laughed.

"Well," said the cop, reluctantly, "I better hit the road. You take care of yourself. And, maybe, when all this pandemic is over, we'll both meet up at Mistaken Point, Newfoundland and sing another one for Gord."

"That'd be awesome, bro."

Next came the sound of shoulders being slapped, boots in squishy snow and the cop car opening, but not closing...

"Sheesh!" said the cop. "I almost forgot the reason I stopped. Need to check that van out."

98. Love is a Curse

I heard Stefanie grumble one of her signature phooeys. Like me, I'm sure she found our position, hiding under tarps on twin beds of grain, rather vulnerable and ridiculous. My heartbeat was pounding as I listened.

"You need to check the van out?" asked AJ.

"Yeah," replied the cop, "the entire province is on the lookout for a yellow van with a plate that says Great Bread."

We heard his boots approaching the back of the van, where the Chatterjees had affixed a license plate from one of their moving vans.

"Nope," said the cop.

His footsteps then moved around to the driver's side.

"Just need to check the VIN, too."

"VIN?" asked AJ.

"Vehicle Identification Number. Can you open the driver's side door, please?"

The cop's tone had gone from warm and chummy to as cold as the night air.

"Yeah, sure."

Seconds later the door opened, letting in a cool draft. I pinched my upper lip, fending off an encroaching cough. A handheld device beeped. I assumed it was the cop scanning the QR code on the dashboard.

"Looks good," said the cop. "The VIN matches the plate. And neither is what they're after."

The urge to cough subsided, but I held tight on the nerve running through my upper lip.

"Can I just see the vehicle registration papers?"

I doubted the Chatterjees had swapped the vehicle registration papers. Even if they did, their papers would describe a moving truck in Sudbury District, not a van from Kingston.

"Yeah... yeah, sure," stuttered AJ. "Like, like I said, this is my buddy's van. I guess they'd be in the glove compartment. If you let me..."

"You sound a little nervous."

"Just my, my lips freezing."

We heard AJ pulling himself up into the driver's seat.

"But, oh, hey, officer," said AJ. "I was—"

"Call me Gord."

A pause.

"Your name's Gord?"

"I had it changed when I was twenty-one. For obvious reasons."

"Whoa!" said AJ. "You *are* a devotee."

"You better believe it," said Constable Gord. "Here hold this flashlight, I wanna show you something."

There was the sound of the cop's jacket unzipping, followed by a pause.

"Sorry, so damn cold, hard to undo the buttons."

After another pause, AJ whistled, then sounded as if he was reading something, "In... Gord... we... trust."

"I got it inked the day I had my name changed." We heard

MUCH ADO ABOUT CORONA – 419

him pound his chest. "Right over the heart, buddy."

"I'm not worthy to be in your presence," said AJ.

"Cost me half a grand. You may think I'm crazy but—"

"Actually..." said AJ.

We could now hear AJ unzipping his jacket. All of us from the arena's dressing room knew about AJ's shoulder tattoo. It probably cost him more than half a grand—a detailed inking of Gord Downie, wearing one of his signature Lilliput hats, pouring his heart into a microphone,

"Incredible!" said the cop in awe, possibly with palms folded together in adoration. "What are the chances of us two running into each other like this? It's like Gord said—music is what brings people together."

We heard the cop shiver and zip his jacket back up.

"Hey, buddy, better show me those papers before I freeze to death."

"Uh, yeah," said AJ, "sure."

AJ fumbled with the glove compartment, as if he was stalling for time. When it did pop open, I heard Stefanie's engagement ring hit the floor mat.

"What's that?" said Constable Gord.

"Uh, this," said AJ, sounding like he was really going to cry. "This, this is the ring I..." And then he did cry—an explosion of sobs, which sounded both authentic and pathetic. "I asked my girlfriend to marry me on Christmas Day. In front of her parents and everything. We'd been going steady for a year before the lockdown. But, you know, the restrictions, we didn't get that much time together. I thought, you know, if we were married, then we'd be together...."

He really started to cry. Which was a good thing because I think Stefanie was too.

"Anyway, she said no. Said she, well, she..."

The sound of a nose being blown.

"This is so embarrassing. This is why I hit the road, bro. It wasn't just for the saucer. It was to get as far away from her as I could. If the borders weren't closed I would have gone to Mistaken Point, Newfoundland. Because that sums up my life right now. One big, freakin' mistake."

He continued to sob. It was actually heart-wrenching to

listen to—like he was really in love with someone who wasn't in love with him.

"Hey, buddy," said the cop, pounding his jacket again, sounding like he was going to break down also. "Why do you think I got this tattoo burned into my heart? What do you think happened to me at twenty-one? Love is a curse, man. Love is a curse."

Then he started to sing the Tragically Hip's "Love is a First." AJ slowly started to join him for another duet. By the time they finished serenading the flying saucer, AJ sounded better.

"Remember, buddy," said Constable Gord. "In Gord we gotta trust. Love may be a curse, but it's worth it."

"Thanks," said AJ. "I hear you."

"You going to be okay?"

"Yeah," said AJ. "Just running into you, I mean, it's like I ran into Gord himself."

"You'll find another girl. A better girl. I did. Married thirty years now."

"Yeah, I hear you, bro."

"Listen, my shift's ending soon, heading home for a belated Christmas dinner with my folks. You know, my daughter, she's about your age, pretty as a snowflake and a raving Hip fan. You wanna come? My wife makes the best stuffing this side of Sioux Lookout."

"That's really nice of you to offer," said AJ. "But I already ate. I'm just drained now. Exhausted. I really, you know, just want to be by myself now."

"Not good to be by yourself at Christmastime."

"Well, not by myself," said AJ. "Gord's with me. I got my playlist."

We heard AJ's iPhone beep, followed by the sound of Gord Downie's unshackled voice singing his final solo, "Away is Mine."

After a moment of attentive silence, Constable Gord said, "Listen, here's my card. You need me, you just call, email, IM, whatever, you hear? Anytime, for anything."

"Thanks, Gord."

"No prob," he replied. "Hey, buddy, what's your name?"

"Jacque," AJ lied.

"All right, Jacque, maybe next time we meet, it will be at

Mistaken Point, Newfoundland. But it won't be a mistake."

They slapped hands together.

"Stay warm!" said the cop, as he retreated.

AJ actually did it.

We heard Constable Gord get into his cruiser and pull away.

I will never call him a dork, nerd or geek again.

AJ shut the driver's side door and sighed.

I sat up on the sacks of grain and said, "That was close."

"In Gord we trust," whispered AJ as he pulled out his seat-belt. "Boy, that was one Hip cop."

Stefanie shot into the passenger seat and ordered: "No more stops!"

"Fine by me," said AJ. "Which way to the bat cave?"

"Bat cave?" I replied. "I thought you were a beaver?"

"*Dam* right!" He pressed down on the accelerator.

"The turnoff for highway 158 is just up ahead," said Stefanie, consulting the paper in her hand. "We don't have far to go."

The van swerved right. I stood up between the two bucket seats looking into the darkness ahead. We passed a liquor store and a convenience store (the only places open), before leaving Moonbeam's 1,231 inhabitants and their tragically hip, extraterrestrial tourist attraction behind us.

99. Nightfall at the Beaver Lodge

Ten minutes later, we were passing an old church. Its sign—lit by a single spotlight on the white lawn—read Notre-Dame-du-Lac. Our Lady of the Lake.

"We should be coming up to Remi Lake," announced Stefanie, as if we were on a fun road trip and not fugitives of new-normal tyranny. "Just stay on this road. It wraps around the shore."

"Remi?" I asked. "You know where they got that name from?"

"When they were building the Grand Trunk Railway," said Stefanie, a bit absentmindedly, "one of the workers drowned in the lake... so they named it after him."

"How do you know this stuff?" asked AJ.

"Mathéo told me," she said.

"And who told him?" I asked. "Remi's ghost?"

"No, he probably heard it from the locals."

"Ah!" I said, suddenly remembering. "That's where I've heard of Moonbeam before. Mathéo's parents' cabin was up here, wasn't it?"

"Still is," said Stefanie. "Here we go." She pointed to a narrow road vanishing into woods on the side of the highway. "Make a right here." She turned back to me and nodded. "Mathéo's brother inherited it. Rents it out in the warm weather, but it's vacant from November till May."

The van lurched right onto a side road that was due for another round with the snow plough. Through the front windshield, I saw the headlights reflect off white mounds weighing down evergreen branches.

We finally came to a halt and the engine died, giving way to the sound of metal scraping pavement. The scraping abruptly stopped and the side door slid open, revealing a grinning Léo. His face was covered with days-old stubble under a thick fur cap with plaid flaps covering his ears. In his right hand was a snow shovel, held out to the side like a staff.

"They're here!" yelled Léo over his shoulder.

Behind him was a two-storey cabin, all its bottom windows flickering with firelight, casting an orange glow over the white yard. A barely perceptible soft hue remained in the western sky. Night had almost fallen.

Stefanie opened her passenger door and scolded Léo, "Could you yell any louder? Are you trying to let every cop in Ontario know we're here?"

"Sorry, Captain," said Léo, bringing a black glove to his forehead in salute.

"You shovelled the whole driveway?" I asked, stepping out and looking down the winding strip.

"No, way!" he replied. "Mathéo's brother came by with a truck. I've just been clearing the walkway, chopping wood and doing whatever else the Lady Bindu asks of me."

"Bindu's here, too?" I said.

"*Oui, oui, monsieur,*" said Léo, pointing to her maroon car on the other side of the van. "No way she'd miss out on this grand act of civil disobedience."

"You guys are incredible," I said.

"And the hideout's not too bad either," said Léo. "There's two wood stoves, a fireplace, plus a gas stove, fridge and, yes, even a washer and dryer. I think you'll survive."

I gently stamped my feet, now snug inside an old pair of work boots Mr. Chatterjee had gifted me for Christmas. Solid ground for the first time in over five hours. And, despite the bitter cold, the fresh air I was breathing in felt like a salve for my sore lungs.

AJ came around the hood, wearing the beaver mask, with his backup red glasses propped up on the stubby wooden nose. He raised his hand and gave Léo a high-five.

"We did it, bro!" said the Red Beaver.

"Hey, when did you get so handsome," jibed Léo.

Stefanie slipped out of the passenger seat and stood beside me.

"Captain D," said Léo, with surprise. "I love the new hairdo. Short. A little crazy. Darker. Gives you more the criminal mastermind look you probably never wanted."

She tilted her head to the side and, in a British accent, said, "If it be a crime to liberate the innocent, then may I be the most offending soul alive."

"Is that Shakespeare?" asked Léo.

"*Henry V*. Sort of."

I chuckled, but the chuckle immediately morphed into a cough and shivers. Léo took a step back.

"Sorry," I said.

"Nah, no worries," said Léo. "Don't know what it is. A year ago, someone coughing would hardly have made a blip on my radar."

"The only thing on my radar is a hot bath," I said.

"You got it!" said Léo, as he leapt up the porch steps and opened the door to the cabin. "We may have to do it the old-fashioned way, though."

"What does that mean?" I asked.

"Boiling water and dumping it in the tub," he replied. "Unless Bindu's got the water heater working."

"I don't want to put anyone to any trouble," I said.

"Too late for that!" piped AJ, as he took the door from Léo and held it open. "Right this way, Mr. Trouble."

We passed into the warm interior. On the right was a kitchen with a round wooden table and chairs. On the left were two brown leather couches before a large hearth of grey stones. The side wall was flanked with bookshelves. A log, smelling like oak, crackled inside the fireplace. Above the flames hung a flatscreen TV.

"Perfect!" declared AJ, closing the door behind us. "A comfortable, warm beaver lodge rather than a cold, smelly bat cave."

All the walls, and even the ceiling, had knotty pine wood panelling. In the centre of the space, a spiral staircase led up to a loft space. Along the edge ran a balustrade, behind which I could see two doors to what I assumed were bedrooms.

The air was thick with the familiar smell of parsley and peas and... *Could my nose be deceiving me?* My eyes followed the smell over to the kitchen where Mathéo wore a big red apron. He was stirring two cast iron pots over the gas flame on an old black stove.

"Hey, what's cookin', big guy?" I said.

I walked over to my childhood friend and gave him a hug with a slap on the back.

"Aunt Sofia's French Canadian pea soup," he said, slowly, calmly, as if it was just another secret gathering of the Moosehead Soup Kitchen.

"*Odeur délicieuse,*" called out Léo, from the bathroom.

"*Oui, oui!*" agreed Mathéo.

He sounded chirpy. Mathéo rarely sounded anything beyond mildly sedated. I looked in the pot he was stirring and saw large chunks of...

"Ham?" I asked.

Was I hallucinating? The forbidden ingredient of Stefanie's vegan kitchen was now bubbling in the pot on the right.

Mathéo smiled widely, something he never did much, as he said, "My kitchen! No tasteless, bland, low-fat, plant-based dishes devoid of flesh."

Behind me, I heard Stefanie grumble. "I'm going to get the bags. Try not to kill anything while I'm gone."

Turning, I saw her heading back outside.

"Don't worry," Mathéo said, pointing to the other pot, "I made her and Bindu a porkless version."

"That was nice of you."

"More ham for the rest of us."

I rubbed my chin, shook my head and chuckled.

"How is your aunt doing?" I asked, fearing the answer.

"She's better," he said, his smile diminishing. "No more IV. Claudia thinks she'll be fine."

"Good."

The meatless pea soup sputtered. Using the same spoon, Mathéo gave it a stir and reduced the flame.

"Vince," he said, in a near whisper.

"Yeah?" I replied.

"Why can I see your Grandad?"

My head shot to my left and right.

"You see him now?"

"No," he replied. "Not now. But he keeps on coming back. Ever since that night on the river."

"I know," I said.

"But he's not my *grand-père*," said Mathéo. "Why can I see him and no one else? I don't have any native ancestors."

"I don't think it has anything to do with your genes," I said. "Otherwise, Léo—he's a true Métis, more native DNA than me—he would be seeing him too."

"So why can you and I?"

"I was hoping you could tell me," I replied. "He hasn't told you anything?"

Mathéo changed the direction he was stirring the bubbling soup. "All I know," he whispered, "is what he said to you that day at the nursing home."

I raised an eyebrow.

"Back in the summer," he clarified. "About me."

"You mean when he was quarantined in his room and we were talking to him from his window?"

Mathéo nodded.

"I don't remember," I said. "What did he say?"

Before Mathéo could respond, Léo's voice rang out:

"Check it out!"

I turned around to see Léo emerging from the bathroom holding a yellow toy duck.

"A real rubber duckie," he said, handing it to me.

"All I want is hot water up to my neck," I replied, staring the bird in the eyes. "If the duck wants to come that's fine. He doesn't even have to wear a mask." I looked back at the stovetop. "Is there a pot I can use to start boiling some water?"

"No need," replied Léo. "Looks like Bindu got the propane heater going."

Stefanie returned through the front door, carrying two suitcases. She put her hand on my shoulder and said softly, "Take a long, hot bath. Sweat whatever you got out of you."

"It'll be good to go in a few minutes," said Léo. "Looks like the captain might like to join you."

Ignoring the comment, Stefanie marched over to the freezer. "I'm going to start thawing some bread to go with the soup."

"Aye, Captain, I'm starving," said AJ. He was scanning the spines of books on the shelves across the room, still wearing his big red glasses on the outside of his beaver mask. "I'm so hungry I could eat tree bark. All I've had today are a few gingerbread men. And that was..."

He pulled out his cellphone.

Stefanie suddenly slammed the freezer shut. "No cellphones!" she scolded.

"It's in airplane mode," said AJ, holding it up for us to see. "I'm just checking the time."

"I don't care if it's in a coma and you're checking its serial number," shouted Stefanie. "Turn it off! Otherwise, you might as well just call 911 and turn us all in."

100. The Coronavirus Brainwashing Corporation

With pursed lips, AJ powered down his iPhone. Léo and Mathéo both pulled out their phones and began doing the same. Mine, of course, was with the Sudbury Police. I didn't expect to ever see it again.

"Those things are tracking devices, plain and simple," said Stefanie. "I'm tempted to confiscate all of them and throw them in Remi Lake." She began sliding open drawers in the kitchen, until she found a long, thin box. "After you shut them down, wrap them in aluminum foil. Who knows if those things are ever really off."

AJ clucked his tongue. "I know you're the criminal mastermind and all, but I really doubt they'd send out a cavalry of Mounties to hunt down one guy with the flu."

"Isn't the RCMP's motto that they 'always get their man'?'" shot back Stefanie.

"Actually," said Léo, "their motto is, 'Maintiens le droit.' Defend the law. Anyway, the OPP runs the show in Ontario, not the RCMP."

"Plus," said AJ, "it would consume way too much resources and manpower to track us down."

"Yeah," countered Stefanie, "the government would never waste time or money."

AJ shrugged. "Well, even if they did call in CSIS, a guy like me is probably the last person they'd suspect."

Stefanie put her hands on her hips. "All the cops need do is go to Vince's parents and get a list of his friends or go to the arena and get a team roster. From there, a Justice of the Peace will sign away your right to privacy. Your phones will be tapped. Your emails read."

"Read my emails?" said Mathéo. He dropped the spoon in the pot of soup. "*Bon chagrin.*"

"What?" said Stefanie, walking back toward the kitchen. "I told you to only coordinate in person. No email. No WhatsApp. Not even Telegram."

"No, no," said Mathéo. "Nothing like that. Just had some private emails I didn't want no police officer seeing—"

"He subscribes to porn sites," Léo said with a laugh.

"Well..." said AJ, "maybe that'll slow the cops down." He placed his aluminum-covered cellphone on the bookshelf and pulled out a thick volume.

Mathéo's face was turning red as he ruffled his black hair. "I was going to quit. For New Year's."

"Yeah, right, bro," said AJ, handing Léo the package of tin foil. "You should always start your resolutions *before* the new year. That way you're rocking and rolling by January first."

Léo took the tinfoil and pulled out a sheet. "Then what was your New Year's resolution?" he asked. "To metamorphosize into a fat, semi-aquatic rodent with a fetish for wood?"

"*Dam* right," said AJ.

And with that he opened the book he had selected and raised it in front of his bespectacled mask. The cover contained a photo of a beaver with the title *Ontario Wildlife*.

Léo tossed his Faraday phone on the bookshelf and turned to Stefanie. "Here, I'll wrap yours."

"I don't have one," said Stefanie. "They cause cancer."

"Oh yeah," said Léo. "I forgot. Can I make you a tin foil hat instead?"

He snickered, as the door beside the bathroom opened, revealing the room with the laundry machines.

"Laugh all you want," said Stefanie. "But Wuhan was one of the first smart cities in the world to be equipped with 5G. And Sweden didn't see a single COVID case until *after* they installed their first 5G tower."

"Hmm," said Léo, taking on a sophisticated tone. "Correlation isn't causation."

Bindu stepped out of the laundry room, carrying a toolbox in her right hand. "And the Diamond Princess cruise ship advertised 'the best Wi-Fi at sea,'" she added.

"Bindu!" exclaimed Stefanie, rushing over to give her a hug.

"You guys made it," said Bindu, sounding ready to cry. "Mathéo said you got out. But I was so afraid you'd get caught on the way."

"Thanks to your dad and brother's prowess with a paint gun, we got here without incident."

"Ahem," said AJ.

"Well, almost," said Stefanie. "A little run in with a cop in Moonbeam, but AJ took care of him." She walked over to AJ and scratched him behind one of his stiff beaver ears. "Or should I say, The Red Beaver saved the day."

"That's right," he said, pulling off the mask and slipping his glasses back on. "AJ's just my secret identity."

"What'd you do?" asked Léo. "Slap him silly with your beaver tail?"

"No," I answered, "he sang to him, instead."

Ignoring us, Bindu moved toward the TV hanging on the wall over the fireplace and asked, "Léo, did you clear the snow off the satellite dish?"

"Yes, my lady," he responded. He reached for the remote and aimed it at the flatscreen.

"Battery's dead," said Bindu. She pushed a button on the bottom right corner of the screen and began flipping through channels. "With no internet and no phone, this is our only connection with the outside world."

"Hey!" said AJ. "Do you think we can get *Rebel News* on this thing?"

"Not a chance," replied Bindu.

"Rebel News," I said, turning to Stefanie, "that's that site with the funny reporter in the suit, isn't it? What's his name, David 'The Menzoid' Menzies?"

"Yeah," said AJ. "The Menzoid's outrageous! Dares to ask tough questions without breaking a sweat."

"Tamara Ugolini's my role model," said Stefanie. "A journalist *and* a mother fighting for individual freedom."

"Ezra's not bad either," said Bindu. "He would make a good lawyer."

"Well," said AJ. "He sure spends enough time suing the government."

"Someone has to," Bindu responded. "Anyway, I'm afraid we'll have to settle for either the CBC—The Coronavirus Brainwashing Corporation—or CTV."

"What about Fox News?" asked Léo. "They tell the truth some of the time."

Bindu and Stefanie glared back at him.

"Well, once in a while. Just a little. Tucker Carlson."

"Can't get Fox on this dish," said Bindu. "Let's go with CTV. At least it's not as blatantly enslaved to the dictates of Health Canada."

I plopped down on the couch, the heat of the fire warming the left side of my body. A blonde anchorwoman with brown skin appeared on screen, talking quickly:

"Health officials in Ontario are reporting more than 2,400 new COVID-19 infections as hospitalizations related to the disease reach their highest level since early December."

Bindu immediately hit the mute button, making an exasperated sigh. "Remember the days when the news meant they actually told us something new?"

"Hey," said Léo, landing on the couch beside me, "that cop in Moonbeam, was he actually looking for you guys?"

AJ nodded. "Yeah, he checked out the plate and VIN, but Raj had swapped them."

"But was he actually looking for Vince?"

AJ shrugged. "He didn't name anybody. He was told to keep an eye out for our van and plate. He didn't seem to know much else."

On the silent screen, I saw footage of an ambulance pulling into a hospital parking lot. Immediately its rear doors flapped open and a stretcher was hoisted out by paramedics wearing respirators. It seemed they used that same stock footage over and over again across all their local stations. Nonetheless, it sent a shiver down my spine to think, only a few days ago, that had been me being wheeled into the ER.

"What d'you think they'd do if they found us?" asked Léo. "You think we could go to jail? After all, they did arrest that restaurant owner in Toronto just for keeping his shop open."

Stefanie shrugged. "And then they let Skelly go. You heard of anyone actually being convicted? It's all empty intimidation."

Still staring at the TV, my mouth fell open. A reporter was now holding a microphone up to a grey-haired man with a mask. At the bottom of the screen it said: "Dr. Alan Roberts, Sudbury General."

Her back to the TV, Stefanie continued, "All those corona tickets are getting dismissed or dropped before they even see a judge. It's only those who don't file a court case who end up—"

"Guys!" exclaimed Léo, pointing toward the newscast.

Stefanie turned around.

"*Mon dieu!*" I heard Mathéo say from the kitchen.

"*Frack!*" said AJ.

Bindu put her hand to her mouth.

On screen, Dr. Roberts had been replaced by three photos: The first was of me taken from my Facebook page. The second was of Stefanie, from the bakery's website. And the third was a blurry black-and-white photo of Moosey, sitting behind the steering wheel of the van.

For a second I thought I might throw up the pea soup we hadn't eaten yet.

Below the photo were the words: "Up next: Man escapes quarantine, at large, presumed infectious."

101. Canada's Most Wanted

After a commercial break, the anchorwoman with the blonde hair, brown skin, and grim stare appeared again on the TV screen, speaking quickly.

"Very concerning news has reached us today. A twenty-four-year-old man, named Vincent McKnight, has escaped quarantine at Sudbury General hospital, where he was being held in custody by police."

A framed photo appeared, of me up to my neck in Moosey's costume, mask in hand. Mom had taken that photo. It was hanging on her wall in her sewing room. *Did she give it to them? Did they raid the house and confiscate it?*

"On Christmas Eve, after an altercation with police, and suffering injuries, Vince McKnight was placed into hospital quarantine under armed guard. He has been charged with five offences, including assaulting a police officer."

The scene switched to Dr. Roberts speaking in a subdued voice through a blue medical mask:

"The patient refused to be tested. But we know he was showing definite symptoms of the disease. He was also in prolonged contact with an elderly man who died from COVID-19."

Dr. Roberts paused and pulled up his mask.

"Also, it bears mentioning, he is part First Nations, which makes him particularly vulnerable. For his own safety, as well as others, we need to get him back under medical care."

The scene changed to Ontario's heavyset premier. His neck bulged out of his white dress shirt as he stood before a podium. Flanking him from behind, twelve feet in the distance, were four members of his staff, all wearing black masks. They looked like some shadow government come to life, their shifty eyes controlling the mind of the premier.

"Folks, I've just got the news," he said in a dire tone. "This yahoo's considered sick and extremely contagious. Despite being under constant surveillance by an armed officer, he managed to escape with the help of some right wing conspiracy theorist."

His bloated, maskless face held an expression that was difficult to interpret. On the surface, he appeared petrified; yet, at the same time, as if he was trying to hold back a laugh.

"Guys, I don't know what to say," he continued, shaking his head. "We are at war! Not just with a virus, but with these nut-jobs. When we catch this bozo, and especially his ditzy girlfriend, the first thing I want the docs to do is give them an MRI and see if there are any brains in their heads."

On the screen appeared a muted video of Stefanie from her YouTube channel. Her former blonde hair flowed down the front of the green dandelion stem dress—the same dress she was wearing that day we first met in the bakery. Behind her, I could see the bake room, with its kneading table. The anchorwoman's voice commentated the footage:

"Stefanie Müller, an outspoken voice against the public health mandates, has been identified as the one who assisted Vincent McKnight in his escape from custody. Multiple charges have been filed against her; including impersonating a nurse—a felony offence in Ontario."

Stefanie's voice was unmuted, and we could hear her saying in the YouTube clip, "You do not have to obey these so-called public health measures. They are not laws. And they certainly aren't about science or a virus. Masks do not work. Hand sanitizers are poison. Lockdowns are murder."

The anchorwoman reappeared on screen, her eyes rolling. "On the scene we have CTV reporter Joe Polish, with a special report."

A title screen with the words COVID-19 PANDEMIC flashed across the screen accompanied by a violin melody best suited for a horror film; followed by a reporter standing on the Louis Riel Bridge. He wasn't wearing a hat, and his black hair was blown crazy and turning white with snow as he spoke into the camera.

"Both offenders," said the reporter, holding a microphone in shivering hands, "are from here, the small town of Moosehead about an hour south of Sudbury."

I couldn't believe what I was seeing. It was rare Moosehead ever made it on the local news. I looked over at Stefanie who was staring at the screen. When the image switched to the front of the bakery, I saw her put her hand to her mouth. The camera was panning over the newspaper clippings she had taped to the window.

"Vincent McKnight works at this tiny bakery," continued the reporter, "owned by Stefanie Müller. Town folks have been complaining about literature she posts in her window spreading misinformation about the pandemic. I asked the mayor of Moosehead for his thoughts on the situation."

Mayor Hill, sitting in his office in town hall, before a large desk, was now in front of the camera, his bald head shinier than ever. "Both of them are some of the most selfish people I know. I mean, I understand the pandemic has been stressful, and some can't take it as well as others. But, oh, I just don't know what to say. I hope the police do their job and lock them up before they hurt anyone else."

The scene switched to the reporter standing in front of the Green Dragon. "Across the street from town hall, I got a very different perspective on Vincent McKnight's character from the owner of the town's sole Chinese restaurant."

Mr. Chung appeared on screen, standing in front of his buffet with his green mask around his neck, below his white goatee. "No. Vince is good boy. Always cared for his grandfather. Best grandson. They had no right to lock him up. I left China to get away from bad government. Now it's come to Canada."

Next a picture of my parent's home appeared on screen, with the McLean's blinking lights just off to the right. "Vincent McKnight's mother and father were unwilling to speak to us."

A shiver ran down my spine, as I watched the footage of Dad slamming the front door of 211 Magder Road on the reporter standing on their front porch.

A half-second flash of white filled the screen, and now the reporter was standing on the front steps of St. Jerome's, saying, "Despite his recent criminal activity, Vincent McKnight attended religious services regularly, virtually or in person, at the town's only Catholic Church. I'm here with his pastor, Father Lacombe."

Léo, still sitting beside me, groaned.

The camera panned back, and Father Lacombe was now

visible about six feet to the reporter's right. He was wearing a black winter jacket and a black mask, while gripping a black Bible.

"Father Lacombe, how do you feel about one of your flock being led astray, so to speak?"

The reporter held the mic out for Father Lacombe, who leaned into it, speaking slowly. "In the Book of Proverbs, the Bible warns about the power of 'the strange woman' over a young man's mind and heart. Until Vince met Ms. Müller he was a shining example of Christian virtues. Sadly, she seems to have seduced him onto a very ungodly path. We are all praying that he realizes his mistake, turn himself in and ask his Father in Heaven for forgiveness." He looked at the camera. "God will forgive you, Vince."

I could feel my face burning; but not with fever.

The image on screen returned to the reporter standing on the Louis Riel Bridge, his black hair covered with even more of the falling snow. "We have not been able to contact any of Vince's close friends. We hope to follow up soon with their comments. This is Joe Polish for CTV News."

The brown skinned anchorwoman appeared back on screen, squinting a bit as she read from her teleprompter.

"Whether Vince repents or not, the authorities are not waiting for him to voluntarily turn himself in."

The image changed to a woman with short black hair, wearing a white dress shirt and tie. A subtitle read: Inspector Margaret Diefenbaker, RCMP, Ottawa. She was sitting in a chair, apparently looking into a webcam, in what appeared to be an office. She cleared her throat and said:

"Stefanie Müller was already put on our watch list four months ago under suspicion of inciting illegal activity. The RCMP's Emergency Response Team will be assisting the Ontario Provincial Police, with additional resources and manpower, to apprehend all those involved and ensure everybody is kept safe."

The newscast switched to a grainy, black-and-white recording of the front lobby café of the hospital.

"In this footage taken by security cameras," continued the anchorwoman, "you can see first Müller, then McKnight, evading security and escaping through the front entrance, threatening the safety of all those in the lobby."

Stefanie and I appeared on screen, knocking over chairs as we ran to the front door. People were scattering and dropping to the ground, while Roger Gygax could be seen sipping his coffee.

"Absolutely awesome," said AJ with a whistle.

In the video, with Stefanie in the lead, we leapt over the bench on the edge of the eating area. Yamamoto followed, taser extended.

"*Mon Dieu!*" muttered Mathéo.

The footage changed to Stefanie running past the sentries, as Sandy and Joshua Henderson entered. I saw my arm reach out, knocking over the hand sanitizer dispenser, before I caught Sandy as she feigned fainting.

The anchorwoman continued, as the scene switched to an exterior shot:

"A masked driver in a yellow bakery van was waiting in the drop-off circle. While escaping, an OPP officer made a heroic attempt to overtake the vehicle."

We watched as Stefanie and I leaped into the van, followed by Yamamoto grabbing onto the rim of the side door. As the van whipped around the roundabout, the black-and-white video zoomed in on the cartoonish moose mask in the driver's side window. The final moment, with Yamamoto flying out the side door, and landing in the snowbank, was magnified and replayed in slow motion as the anchorwoman commented, "The officer was thrown from the moving vehicle and suffered minor injuries."

Photos of Stefanie, Moosey and me reappeared, side by side, on screen.

"Vincent McKnight is five foot nine, medium build, with black, short hair and of moderate complexion. Stefanie Müller was last seen with shoulder-length, curly, black hair. She is about five foot two, slim and of fair complexion. The unidentified driver of the getaway vehicle was disguised as a moose. Anyone who has any information is encouraged to contact the Greater Sudbury Police Service or Crime Stoppers."

The screen switched to a little boy sitting on his bed, in front of an iPad propped up against his pillow.

"Next," continued the anchorwoman, "we have a story about

how one little boy celebrated Christmas with his self-isolating grandmother over Zoom—"

Bindu turned the screen off and looked at us with a raise of her eyebrows. "*Well...* I guess they are taking this rather seriously."

"They've gone insane!" said Stefanie, starting to pace back and forth between the couches. "SARS-CoV-2—if it really exists at all—has an official infection-to-fatality rate of about 0.2 percent."

"English, please," said Léo. "AJ needs it dumbed down."

"She's saying," said AJ with his eyes cast down as if he was reading notes, "that only one in five hundred who are infected by the virus have died from it—or at least, with it. The other 499 survive."

"Same as the flu," said Bindu. "Flu was even worse in 2017/18. But now they're making it illegal to have a cold." She looked at the blank screen. "Bioterrorists! That's what they're treating you like."

"Phooey!" said Stefanie. "This is obviously not about controlling a virus; it's about controlling our minds."

"And what you've done is shown people that they don't have to put up with it," said Bindu, proudly. "And CTV is providing the advertising for your civil disobedience."

AJ sighed. "More like a warning than advertising—a warning to anybody else who dares resist this mass psychosis."

"The more they make a big deal out of this," said Bindu, "the bigger fools they'll look like."

"It may make them bigger liars, but I doubt they are fools," said Stefanie. "Hitler said that 'broad masses' were always more easily corrupted by 'the big lie.' That because of the 'primitive simplicity' of most people's minds and emotions, they fall victim to the big lie more readily than a small lie. They just can't believe politicians, doctors and nurses would resort to such large scale falsehoods."

"So," said AJ, "what you're saying is, they'll dig their hole as deep as they can, because to back off now would mean admitting they were lying."

"Ha!" said Léo. "These idiots are digging their own grave."

"Or ours," countered Stefanie. "Let's just hope humanity isn't as 'primitive' as it was in the days of the Nazis."

Silence fell over us like a smothering blanket of trepidation.

Finally, Léo lifted it by saying, "Hey, Vince. Your bath's going to get cold."

102. A Great Reset

An hour later, my chest felt lighter and my head less groggy. The hot bath had warmed me to the marrow. I returned to the kitchen dressed in a pair of Mathéo's wide jeans, scrunched up with a belt and an undersized T-shirt that Bindu had gifted me for Christmas. The white shirt had a black-and-white photo of George Orwell with his thin moustache. Above his visage were the words COVID-19(84). Below his chin, in quotes, it read: "Boy, did I call it or what?"

AJ the beaver, Stefanie the dandelion, and Mathéo the bear were gathered around the kitchen table, with Léo the bard and Bindu the princess sitting on the couch. Mathéo was ladling out bowls of soup.

"Feel better?" asked Stefanie, sawing away at a loaf of rye. I could smell the sourdough, and see the singe marks on the hard crust, suggesting she had thawed it near the fire.

"Yeah," I said. "A lot better. That bath was a great reset." I sat down on one of the hard wood chairs. "I even feel a bit hungry."

We were soon all dipping warm bread into steaming pea soup. Well, all of us except Mathéo. Even though chunks of his juicy ham now floated in the yellow soup, he just stared at his bowl silently.

Léo and Bindu were of the opposite extreme, bombarding AJ and Stefanie with questions about our great escape from Sudbury General. AJ described the chase with so many hand movements, I would have thought he was retelling the story to Josh.

"I thought we were done for when that cop jumped on the side of the van," he said. "I mean, it was like out of a freakin' movie."

"Good thing he didn't recognize you in the elevator lobby," commented Léo. "You were so lucky."

Stefanie neglected to mention how Yamamoto had indeed recognized us. I'm sure she knew; but, like me, she was trying to protect him.

AJ lifted a spoonful of the soup, with a thick slice of celery, up to eye level. "Hey," he said, "this pea soup's not all that bad without the ham."

Along with the ladies he had opted for the ham-free version.

"Vous ne parlez pas sérieusement," exclaimed Léo in disbelief. "*Soupe aux pois* without the ham is like a hamburger without the beef."

"Tastes great to me," said Bindu, with a slurp. "It's kind of like the split moong dhal my mother makes. She raised us vegetarians."

"We men were raised eating vegetarians," I said. "Kind of hard to imagine life any other way."

"Actually," said AJ, "I've been thinking I should give a meatless diet a try. After all, if I'm going to be The Red Beaver, I should start eating like one."

He lifted up the *Ontario Wildlife* book he had been reading earlier.

"According to this, beavers are herbivores. I don't think I could live off bark or wood pulp, but it says here they also eat leaves, shoots and roots. That sounds doable."

"What's it say about turtles?" I asked, rolling my eyes.

"Let's see..." AJ flipped pages. "Here we go. Says turtles are omnivores... 'enjoying a balanced diet of algae, insects, snails, and worms.'"

"I'll stick to eating ungulates, thanks." Wanting to change the subject, I added, "And I mean it, *merci beaucoup*." I pivoted my head to take in all five of them. "I don't know how I can thank you all for what you did for me. Organizing all this must have taken every second of the day and night."

"I'll send you my Red Bull bill," said AJ. "Stefanie even drank one."

"Did not!" she said and elbowed him.

A flicker of jealously swept through me. Here AJ had helped her execute her master plan, while I lay sick in bed watching Christmas movies. And now he's even going vegan beaver on her.

Maybe she detected my pettiness, because she reached out and clasped my hand.

"We would have taken on the entire New World Order to get you back," she said, looking me in the eye.

"Yeah!" said Léo. "You know the old saying: First they came for the delivery moose..."

We all chuckled, except Mathéo. He was staring into his untouched bowl.

"We're not just saving you," he said in a voice even slower than usual. "We're saving all our futures. I don't want kids growing up in a world where they can be taken from their parents just because they have a cold or don't agree to give them vaccines or won't make them wear a mask."

He wiped his mouth with a serviette.

"And I hate seeing people hiding behind those face masks," he continued. "It's spooky. Feels like everyone is turning into, how do you say it, *les morts-vivants*?"

"Zombies!" translated Léo.

"Zombies," repeated Mathéo. "I don't understand all the science about mask pores and viruses; but my gut tells me tying a serviette around your face is wrong. And my gut never lies."

We were all silent. I'd never heard so many words come out of Mathéo's mouth at one time. And he wasn't through.

"We can't be sheep like on my uncle's farm," he continued, picking up the tempo. "Sheep don't fight back. They don't even run when it comes time for slaughter. I don't know where we're being led, but it doesn't feel right at all."

None of us responded. We just nodded our heads. We all agreed.

"Breaking you out was dangerous," concluded Mathéo, "but leaving you there would have been even more dangerous. For all of us."

The log on the fire crackled, doing what logs have done for millions of years: keeping humans warm during all their ups and downs. Tipping my bowl toward me, I slurped the last few spoonful's.

"Thanks," I said, facing Mathéo. "Your soup is a hundred times better than those microwaved dinners the hospital inflicted upon me."

"I'll let Tante Sofia know," said Mathéo. "If they ever let me see her again."

"And thank you for letting us use the cabin," said Stefanie, softly. "I'm sure it must be hard."

Mathéo pressed his lips together and nodded. "*Oui,*" he said. "I haven't been here since they died."

I bowed my head, remembering the funeral service at St. Jerome's.

"How did they die?" asked Bindu, cautiously. "If you don't mind..."

"They died here," I said, quickly, raising my head. "In the master bedroom. In their sleep. The propane heater leaked. Carbon monoxide poisoning."

"I was out back," added Mathéo. "In a tent with my brother."

"The propane heater?" said Léo with alarm, turning to Bindu. "Are you sure it's safe to use?"

"Don't worry," said Mathéo, dismissively. "My brother put in a new unit. Long time ago. And every room has a carbon monoxide detector now. It's safe."

He stood up and walked over to a white plastic device plugged into an outlet by the TV. He pulled it out of the wall. It beeped. He held it in his hands and said, "At least, as safe as life can get. In the end, we all die. Some way. Some day." He forced a smile. "Since it happens to everybody, it can't be worth worrying about."

Outside, the wind howled the way it only does when the ghost of winter has come; but the sturdy cabin, guarded by an army of pine trees, was protecting us from the frosty phantom.

Mathéo's round face smiled widely at us, as he concluded, "Every leaf falls from the tree." He plugged the device back into the wall. It beeped. "If you live a good life, then when you fall from the tree of life, you will be full of joy, like a red maple in fall."

I looked at Mathéo, my forehead puckering. "Where did you hear that?" I asked.

He smiled. "A long time ago, in a canoe." He sounded a bit perkier. Returning to his spot at the table, he began to spoon soup into his mouth.

"On the subject of someday..." I said, rising from my chair and moving to the empty couch. "How long are we staying here?" I laid my head back on a pillow. Despite only eating one small bowl of soup, I felt as energetic as a boa constrictor after swallowing a snow plough.

No one responded to my query. Léo rose from the other couch and threw another log on the fire, stirring the embers with an iron poker. Bindu sighed. Stefanie rubbed her eyes.

"I mean," I said, "it sounds like they've launched a nation-wide manhunt for us. So what's the plan, guys? Time to move to Mexico?"

AJ leaned back in his chair, hands clasped behind his neck, and grinned. "I'm afraid this is where our master plan stops looking so masterful."

103. No Mask, No Stamp

Stefanie got up from the kitchen table, walked past me lying on the couch and stood in front of the fireplace.

"We have enough food for a week. Enough grain in the van for a month. I'm sure I can bake bread in the wood stove. I just need some way to grind the grain."

"There's a blender," said AJ. "And if you need more food, there's a supermarket in Moonbeam."

"But using a debit card would probably land a SWAT team on us," I said. "They must be watching our bank transactions. At least, Stefanie's and mine."

"We all have cash," said Stefanie. "Right, guys?"

"Cleaned out my bank account," said AJ. "Wasn't going to let them get to it."

He pulled out his wallet, unfolded it on the table, and took out the thickest wad of five-dollar bills I had ever seen.

Each bill had an image of an astronaut attached to the Cana-darm floating above Earth. Stefanie had told me that the International Space Station was a hoax—all green screens, harnesses and zero-G jets. One big black hole for tax dollars, she said. I'd thought she was crazy at the time. But, now seeing how hard the government was pushing the corona hoax, I wouldn't put it past them to fake just about anything we can't see with our own eyes.

"Oh, that feels better," AJ said, rubbing his bum. "I think it was messing up my lumbar, keeping my left cheek on that pile of dough."

"Yeah," said Léo, eyeing the cash. "That's one way to make— what?—five hundred dollars look like you're some rich dude." He pulled out his own wallet, and fanned out three one-hundred-dollar bills. "I didn't bring as much. Cleaning out my account, I figured, would look suspicious."

"Hmm," said AJ, stuffing the fivers back into his wallet. "Didn't think of that."

"So that's the plan?" I said. "Hide out here until we run out of money?"

"Well, at least, you and Stefanie," said AJ, with a hint of envy. "You two are public enemy number one—COVID's own Bonnie and Clyde. The rest of us should head home soon. Maybe even report you."

I squinted my eyes at him. "Report us?"

"I mean come up with some tale," he said. "Like Stefanie asked to borrow some cash. Said she was heading out East. Or maybe Northern BC, or Nunavut, somewhere not so new-normalized. We could lead them astray."

"We can also bring you back anything you need," said Bindu.

"Yeah," said AJ, "we were thinking it would be better if one of us were here with you at all times. Every week one of us will rotate. That way when you need anything, the guy leaving can pass a message onto their replacement."

"So Stefanie and I, with nothing but one of you COVID outlaws for company, will spend the rest of our lives in this cabin watching our growing infamy on CTV News?"

"Only until May," corrected Mathéo, slowly. "My brother has already rented the cabin out for the spring."

"Assuming the lockdown ends by May," added Bindu, quickly.

"That'll give us four months to think up a new plan," said Stefanie, "unless the world comes to its senses before then."

"What about the bakery and your apartment?" I asked. "If you're not paying the rent, you'll get evicted."

Stefanie's shoulders slumped and she sat down on the couch beside Bindu. "Not likely. The Ontario Tenant Board is not allowing landlords to issue eviction notices. They say, because so many people have lost work to COVID, they shouldn't be kicked out of their homes."

"COVID squatters!" exclaimed Léo. "Haven't you heard?"

"Kind of hard for landlords to pay their bills," said Bindu, "if they are expected to house tenants who can't pay their rent."

"True," said Stefanie. "But it buys me time."

"Come May," said AJ, "if you still need to be in hiding, Father Shostakovich says he knows families back in the Ottawa Valley who will take you in. No one would suspect you were hiding out under the shadow of Parliament Hill."

I put my hands over my eyes. I felt like we were auditioning for a Hollywood holocaust film.

"But how's hiding going to stop this?" said Bindu, standing up, and beginning to pace between the couches as Stefanie had been doing. "We need to find a way to fight this."

"Sometimes it's wise to retreat," said Léo, grabbing his and Bindu's dirty dishes from the coffee table and heading toward the kitchen sink.

"Oh," said Bindu, sounding disappointed, and turning to Stefanie. "But you've been so vocal. Your YouTube channel gave me the courage to stop wearing the mask."

"Well, I still have a laptop," said Stefanie. "I can still write articles for whoever will publish them. Maybe I can start a column in *Druthers*."

"*Druthers*?" I mumbled. My eyes were closed, lying there on the couch, feeling like consciousness was about to slip away.

"It's a new print newspaper," Bindu explained, "launched this month out of Toronto. Totally independent. Media's calling it the COVID conspiracy paper. I heard the first print run hit 25,000 copies."

"How in the world are you going to submit your rogue reports?" Léo started filling the kitchen sink up with water. "You can't use email."

"I'll save them to flash drives. You can mail them. Just pick a postal box at random between here and Moosehead."

"Sounds pretty risky," said Léo.

"Ah, yeah," said AJ. "We wouldn't want to do anything risky."

"Okay, it sounds unnecessary, then," said Léo. "An unnecessary risk."

"Hey," said Stefanie, whipping around, her reddish-black hair curling even more over the dry heat of the hearth. "I'm not stopping the fight."

"Yeah, I get it," said Léo, turning off the tap. "Just seems like if you start mailing stuff, the cops might be able to trace it and ambush one of us at a mailbox..."

Their voices drifted away as I walked into a Canada Post office. There was a long line of just three people, all twelve feet apart, wearing white masks, goggles and face shields. They all had blue gloves. Along the wall I counted five giant posters. Each said "WANTED" above photos of AJ with his floppy hair parted at the side, Mathéo with his short, dark curls, Léo with his long black hair hanging loose, Bindu with her dark hair tied back and Stefanie with the long, blonde braids she no longer had.

Where was my poster?

Suddenly, as time has no meaning in the land of dreams, I was standing at the front of the line. In my hand was a white envelope, containing a Christmas card for my mother. I needed a postage stamp.

The clerk was wearing the beaver mask.

"No mask, no stamp," the clerk said through the red, motionless lips painted on the wooden surface of the beaver mask.

I gave him the envelope and he affixed a $1.07 stamp in the corner. The stamp had an image of a maple leaf. But it wasn't bright red. It was black, as if it had been burnt to ash.

No mask, no stamp, the clerk had said.

He held up a hand mirror to my face. In its reflection I saw a white mask, goggles, a plastic shield.

The beaver clerk dipped his wooden head to the side. Putting his right fist to his chest, he rotated it in a circle—the sign for "sorry."

The post office vanished. We were now standing on the frozen surface of Remi Lake. The night sky above was covered with clouds. The ice began to crack.

I stumbled backwards and fell to the ice. I hit it hard, causing a crack to form beneath my sore tailbone. The crack crawled along the ice toward the beaver clerk, where it began to split apart. Without a struggle, the masked postmaster fell through the opening, disappearing into the freezing waters.

"Nooo!" I cried, as the split in the ice crept toward me.

In the distance I could hear the sound of helicopters approaching; but when I looked up I saw instead Moonbeam's flying saucer hovering above me, ready to beam me up.

"Nooo!" I cried again. "Please, God, no!"

104. The Greatest Canadian Hero

I jolted awake, but didn't dare open my eyes. Beneath me I felt the leather sofa; not cracking ice.

Relief flowed from head to toe. It had been a dream. Just a dream.

And maybe, so had been everything else: The tasing; the hospital dungeon; the lobby escape; the Chatterjees' sandblasters; the roadside UFO; the cabin in the woods where Mathéo's parents had died.

I opened my eyes, praying I would find myself in my second floor bedroom at 211 Magder Road. Mom would be making masks in her sewing room and Dad getting drunk in the basement.

"This little cabin is but a snowflake in the vast north of Ontario," Stefanie was saying. "Ontario is three times the size of Germany."

"There's no way they'll find you," said AJ. He was now standing by the pile of firewood and peeling bark off one of the logs.

"Are you so sure?" said Léo. "I mean, this cabin belongs to Mathéo's brother. They could track you guys down easy enough."

Mathéo shrugged. "I haven't been here in so long. I don't think anyone in Moosehead will even remember my parents had a cabin."

I reached into my pocket for the cellphone that wasn't there. My phone was usually always in my pocket. It was part of me. Now it was gone, too. All that was left of my life were my friends—friends who didn't turn their back on me when the government had crossed the line of human decency.

I prayed for strength and courage; but all I wanted to do was sleep. I wished I could say the spirit was willing, but the flesh was weak. Instead, both felt weak and unwilling.

"What time is it?" I asked.

Léo picked up his tin foil wrapped phone and looked at me

with a crooked grin. "Can't tell you, man."

"It's a quarter to nine," said Stefanie, glancing at the windup watch strapped around her left wrist.

"And all is well," said AJ, as he chewed on the piece of bark he'd peeled off the log.

"I don't know about you guys," I said. "but I can barely keep my eyes open. What are the sleeping arrangements here?"

"Two bedrooms on the second floor," said Mathéo. "Bunk bed in one and a queen in the other."

"Why don't I crash here?" I said, patting the couch.

"Looks like you already have," said Léo.

"And I doubt I'll be getting back up," I replied with a yawn. "Why don't two of you guys take the bunk bed and the gals share the queen?"

"Well, that still leaves one of us stuck down here on the other couch with you, Mr. COVID," said Léo.

"I'll sleep down here," said Mathéo. "I don't want to be up there."

He grimaced. I could only imagine how it must have been for him, when, at fourteen, he climbed up that spiral staircase, to the loft, and found his parents not breathing. I remember when he came back to Moosehead—moving to Uncle Maxime and Aunt Sofia's farm—how quiet he became.

Bindu walked over to me and said, "You're not well, Vince. I could sleep down here if you want to share the queen with—"

Stefanie cut her off. "Bindu, Vince and I aren't together."

I cringed. It hurt a little to hear her say so.

"You're not?" said Bindu.

"Well, not like that," said Stefanie. She was turning red, as she threw a log into the already raging fire. "And, after all, Vince is Catholic."

Bindu pursed her lips and made the sign of the cross. "Of course."

Léo smirked, before saying, "I guess everything is a little wonky. Damsel rescues prince. Prince gets couch." He then began his way up the spiral staircase, hollering down to AJ, "Hey, Beaver Boy, first one to the room gets top bunk."

AJ tossed the bark he had been chewing into the fireplace. "Jeez, can't remember the last time I've been to bed before midnight."

"We have a long drive back home tomorrow," said Bindu. "Better if we leave early—under the cover of darkness."

AJ picked the beaver mask off the table and faced me as he put it back on his head.

"Bro, just can't thank you enough for the beaver mask," he said. "I hope it's not sacrilegious for me to be wearing it."

I shook my head. "Grandad made it for a play, not a ceremony or anything like that."

"Well, it means a lot to me. All of it. Being involved in this. I mean, it's scary as hell. But, you know, there comes a time when we have to choose to stand for something. Stand for something or fall for anything."

Years of battling dragons in the Dungeon Room of Roger Gygax's Little Shop of Heroes had given him a braver heart than mine.

I saw AJ Beaver step aside at the bottom of the spiral staircase to let Stefanie ascend first. As she came around the first loop, she glanced down at me and smiled.

I wasn't brave—just in love.

Love is a curse.

105. Vegan Beaver

Ten minutes later, all of them were in the top loft, except for Mathéo who was scrubbing the soup pots.

"Mathéo?" I said quietly, so they couldn't hear me above.

He turned, put a pot in the drying rack and walked over. "*Oui?*"

"Do you ever see your parents?" I asked. "I mean. You know, like you see..."

He shook his head. "No," he said, somewhat sadly. "Never. I can see your *grand-père* but not my own *père*."

"I'm sorry," I replied with a gulp. "Of course, your parents are in heaven."

"Why isn't your *grand-père* in heaven?"

"The Ojibwe believe it takes four days for their soul to get to the place of happiness. It's a long journey."

"It doesn't seem as if he's even started."

"No one has lit tobacco at his grave."

Mathéo nodded, as if that was somehow a satisfactory answer, and returned to the sink.

From the upper loft I could hear Stefanie's voice saying, "How long can you stay?"

"Until New Year's Day," replied AJ. "I've brought my art supplies. I'm thinking of starting a new comic book. *The Adventures of The Red Beaver*. Maybe I can turn the bunkroom into a little studio."

"Do whatever you want," said Stefanie. "It's your *dam* lodge."

"Cool!"

"I just want to say," she continued, "how grateful I am for everything you've done. You've been one brave beaver."

"Well," he responded, "it's this mask. I know you don't like masks, but this one gives me superpowers. You know, like how that red suit gave the Greatest American Hero the ability to lift up cars with one hand."

"The Greatest American Hero?" asked Stefanie.

"It was a TV show," he said. "You were probably listening to opera or something."

She giggled and said, "Well, you're becoming The Greatest Canadian Hero."

"Oh," said AJ, bashfully. "Thanks."

"No, thank you," she said.

There was a pause, and I visualized Stefanie embracing him in a big hug that left an even bigger rock sinking into the pit of my stomach.

Sounding a little shocked, AJ spoke, "No prob, Captain D. We renegade superheroes have to stick together. And, hey, if they end up jailing Father Shostakovich, maybe we can bust him out, too."

"I'd love to."

She'd love to.

I pursed my lips.

Vegan Beaver. Probably eats dandelions.

I sighed.

Greatest Canadian Hero. What a dor—. No, I promised I would not call him that any more.

Goof-ball.

So tired.

Time to retreat into my shell.

106. A Lover's Pinch

The cabin was quiet. Even the leaping flames licked the sides of the hearth without a sound. Before the fire, a figure stood with his back to me.

Mathéo?

The figure turned around.

He was short. Just a child. Dark skin. A thin face. Wore a school uniform with a green cross on the vest.

"Miskwaadesi," said the boy.

"You're young," I said.

"I'm young. I'm old," replied Grandad in the sweet and innocent voice of a child. "I'm everything."

"But you're dead."

"I'm free," he said.

"Why aren't you in heaven with Mathéo's parents?"

He shrugged, as if it wasn't important.

"Don't fear death when it comes," said the boy.

"Is death coming?"

He paused and looked at me without blinking. "Death is always coming."

Slowly, my ten-year-old grandad backed up until he was literally standing in the fireplace, unperturbed, engulfed in yellow flames. He cleared his throat, and, using a British accent, he quoted:

"The stroke of death is as a lover's pinch, which hurts, and is desired."

He smiled at me.

"*Antony and Cleopatra*," I heard him say in my head. "Act Five. Scene two."

Final act. Final scene.

And, with a flicker, he vanished.

"Here's an extra blanket," said Stefanie.

I opened my eyes. Her silhouette was above me. I had dozed off (again) while everybody was preparing for bed. My eyes scanned the first floor. We were alone, save for someone in the bathroom running the shower.

"How's your nose feeling?" she asked.

"Still hurts, but it's *nose* big deal."

She didn't laugh. Just unfolded the third blanket over me.

From the loft above I could just hear Léo saying, "You know, maybe I should check on Bindu. Make sure she's okay."

"Maybe not," said AJ. "Go to sleep, man. Or I'll break your balls."

"Hey, relax, beaver fever."

We heard a door close and their voices vanish. Stefanie chuckled and tucked the itchy wool blanket around my neck.

"You're still pretending to be that Italian nurse," I said, remembering her disguise from that morning. "I can't believe you pulled that off. Or even dared to try. You're one brave multilingual Dandelion."

She smiled. "*Grazie mille.*"

"And I'm afraid I'm still being a turtle," I grumbled. "Lying around. Moving slowly."

She squatted down beside the couch. All the lights were off. The fire cast an orange tinge over her face. "You've nothing to be sorry for. You ignored their madcap rules. You didn't let Grandad die alone. You didn't fear some genetic fragments that've been floating in the air since the beginning of time. You were there for him, and he'll always be there for you."

I felt tears begin to well up in my eyes. I swallowed and changed the subject. "But what are we doing now? We are kind of like prisoners here, aren't we?"

She shook her head. "We're not prisoners. We're living free in the beauty of Northern Ontario."

"But not free to go home," I said.

"This is our home for the moment."

"Well," I replied, "it sure doesn't feel like I have a home anymore in Moosehead. Not with my folks, at least."

The log made a popping sound. She turned her head toward the fire. I continued staring at her.

After a long pause, she said, "I couldn't bear the thought of you locked up under guard."

"No need to be jealous." I grinned. "You're far prettier than St. George Yamamoto."

MUCH ADO ABOUT CORONA – 451

"St. George?" she asked.

"Just a nickname, Dandelion," I responded.

She smiled and closed her eyes. She looked so different with three quarters of her blonde hair sheared away. But she was still the Beautiful Maid of the Mill.

"How much," I tentatively asked, "are you willing to sacrifice for freedom?"

"Freedom is everything," she replied without hesitation. "Without freedom, there's really nothing left to sacrifice."

"It's not that black and white," I said. "They haven't taken all our freedom away. And we never had all our freedom in the first place. We are forced to go to school, to pay taxes, to wear a seatbelt."

"And maybe," she said, with an edge of irritation, "if we had stood up to those violations, we wouldn't be fighting for the right to work, use a public bathroom or smile at our neighbours."

"Actually," I said, "I kind of think wearing a seatbelt is a good idea."

"So do I," said Stefanie. "But whether I wear a seatbelt or not isn't hurting anyone but me. I should have the freedom to decide, not them."

"But without any laws we'll have anarchy," I said.

She rolled her eyes. "Right now, with all these immoral restrictions, we're barrelling past anarchy straight into chaos. We can't even rely on the police or the courts anymore. Too many rules ensures anarchy."

The sound of the shower came to an end, making the old pipes rattle.

"But, hey," I said, "wouldn't you like to outlaw meat eating? If they passed a law banning the slaughter of animals, then—"

"Actually," she interrupted, "Bill Gates' Impossible Foods company is already working on it."

"Well," I said with a grin, "nice that you and Billy see eye-to-eye on something."

Stefanie shook her head. "I would never outlaw the eating of meat."

"Why not?" I said in surprise. "If you think it's unnecessarily hurting innocent animals?"

She shrugged. "Well, first off, I might be wrong. Maybe some people really do need meat. Seven billion people on the earth—who am I to say someone might not require canned ham and baloney to survive? I don't want to be responsible for other people's nutritional needs. You know that Rudyard Kipling line..."

"You'll have to remind me," I replied.

"'Trust yourself when all men doubt you, but make allowance for their doubting too,'" she recited.

"Then why are we fighting the COVID rules?" I asked

"Because they're forcing us to follow their belief system," she replied. "If masking and bankrupting your business were just recommendations, instead of mandates, I'd just shrug my shoulders. In the same vein, if I were running Health Canada, I'd only recommend people avoid eating foods that contain blood vessels; I would never force them to do so."

"But what about saving the cows?"

"I'm not willing to kill a human to save a cow," said Stefanie.

"Kill a human?" I replied. "No one said—"

Stefanie cut in with a stern edge to her voice, "When you make a law it's ultimately about life and death."

"Huh?" I said. "I was thinking you'd just fine us carnivores, not give us the electric chair."

"And if you don't pay the fine?" she replied.

"Then we'd go to jail."

"And if you refuse to go to jail?"

I exhaled loudly. "Boy, you're the vegan, not me."

"And isn't veganism about nonviolence?" she continued. "I can't condone jailing or killing a rancher, leaving his children without a father, to protect a cow that would have otherwise been viciously killed, eaten alive, by a wolf in the wild."

"Hmm," I said. "Every time I think I got you figured out, you surprise me."

"Far better," she said, ignoring my comment, her voice rising, "that the government simply stop subsidizing the meat and dairy industry. Look at the United States. Their government hands out thirty-eight billion dollars a year to the meat industry."

"Thirty-eight *billion*?" I repeated.

She nodded. "Instead, allow people to pay full price for meat. Letting beef rise to twenty dollars per pound would do more to save animals than all the laws, fines and police in the world. Leave people free to decide what they put on their plates, how often, and how much; but make the choice based on reality, not a debt-subsidized fantasy."

"I think my brain is going to explode," I said, with a half-smile.

"Sorry." She tilted her neck and cracked a bone. "I get a little riled up when it comes to freedom. I know whatever freedom we sacrifice to them—no matter how noble the justification—it only makes it easier for them to take more."

"How much freedom do you think they'll take?" I asked.

She looked at me with eyes as wide as an owl's. "As much as they can get, of course."

"Hmph!" I replied, with a grin. "Well, not while Captain Dandelion is alive and well. She's unstoppable."

She grinned and began to sing softly:

Nun wie's auch mag sein,
Ich gebe mich drein:
Was ich such, hab ich funden,
Wie's immer mag sein.[*]

Silence hung for a second, as my brain mangled a translation. Then I asked a question I didn't want to know the answer to.

"Are you willing to *die* for freedom?"

She turned toward the fire and said nothing.

107. Brave Enough to Love

After a long period of silence, staring into the fire, Stefanie turned back to me and opened her mouth. Even then it took a few seconds for words to come out.

"I saw this interview with Mahatma Gandhi once. An American journalist went to India in the 1930s and asked him the

---

* No matter what happens,
I commit myself.
What I sought I have found,
Whatever happens.

same thing. Was he willing to die for India's independence?"

"What was his answer?"

"He said..." She paused, switching to a slightly jovial East Indian accent. "'It is a bad question.'"

I chuckled. "I doubt that would ever stop you."

She planted her elbows beside the pillow under my head and leaned her chin on her crossed arms. "Without freedom, we are essentially, like Mathéo said, *les morts-vivants*. Dead while living."

"I'll take that to mean you are willing to die for your freedom," I replied, turning my sleepy head upward toward the dark ceiling.

"Mm-huh," she replied, as reluctant as Gandhi to put her convictions into words. "And you?"

"I'm not sure I'd take death over being forced to live in a Canadian Coviet Union." I turned to face her. Our eyes locked. I continued, almost in a whisper, "But I would certainly risk death to be with you."

She smiled. I wasn't sure out of appreciation or sympathy.

"Either way, we're never really safe," she whispered. "No matter which choice we make. We simply choose what will *probably* make us safer. If we refuse—like we have—to cooperate with the COVID cult, then its members will see us as their enemies. If we give in, then we become their slaves. But if we can stop this madness, then we are far safer than enemy or slave."

"Yet," I said, slowly, "you must admit, we are a little safer as their slaves than as their foes?"

She tilted her head to the left and back. "I guess vaccine roulette is safer than being on Canada's Most Wanted. So, safer for the body. But not for our minds. Our minds are what they're really after. They want us to truly believe that it really is normal to shield our faces and stand six feet apart. Once they've achieved that, they won't need tasers."

"They almost had me," I said with a sigh. "I mean, before I stumbled into your bakery, I was wearing a mask, accepting CERB auto deposits and bingeing on Netflix. If it was torture, it was palatable enough."

"Then why didn't you keep it up? It wasn't like I was paying you more than the feds."

To my surprise, I almost giggled. "Because I wanted to see your smile," I admitted, diverting my eyes away. "To help you run the bakery. Help you chase your dream. Being free myself? To do what? I went to welding school because I knew Dad could get me a job at his plant. I didn't have any dreams."

"Haven't been on a vision quest?" she asked.

I rolled my eyes, clasping my hands together between my head and the pillow. "Remember, I'm more Irish than Ojibwe."

She shrugged. "Vision quests aren't just for Indigenous youths climbing a mountain in a lightning storm. We all need to discover our purpose on earth. I can't help but feel that the reason most people were so willing to embrace this cushy battle against a made-up pandemic was because their lives had so little meaning. If we don't fill our lives with purpose, someone else will take advantage of the void."

I took a breath, relieved I hadn't coughed once.

"Well," I said, "solitary self-reflection wasn't part of my up-bringing."

"What about your grandad?"

"I think he ended up in the res school before he was old enough for anything like that. But he would tell me that every-body had a purpose in life. And that that purpose was a combi-nation of who we are, what the world needs and what we love."

"And what do you love?" she asked, looking me straight in the eyes.

"Well, there's hockey," I said. "But I don't think I'm headed for the big leagues." I chuckled. "But far more than hockey, I know that..." I paused. "I know that I love you."

There, I had said it. Aloud.

We stared at each other without another word. I, lying on my back, insulated under a thick pile of wool; her kneeling beside me. *Did she really love me?* I knew she had said it. But maybe, I thought, what she really loves is setting people free.

"Oh my Ninja Turtle," she said, giggling and covering her mouth, "what greater freedom can human beings experience than love?" I felt her hand wrap around mine. "Love is brave enough to love regardless of all the risks. It bows down to no condition. Death can't even sever it."

Was that her convoluted way of admitting that she loved me too?

I looked into her eyes. If I wasn't still on the tail end of "COVID-19," I would have sat up, leaned forward, and exercised my freedom to kiss her. And I'd hope she'd exercise her freedom to accept. But, instead, my eyelids closed again.

And then they opened. Her face was so close I could feel the air leaving her nostrils.

"We'll get through this," she said. "We may be very different people by the time it's all over. We may even have to claim asylum in Florida or Texas."

"Well," I replied, "your Texan accent is pretty good."

We both laughed, our foreheads colliding for a second.

"Things are changing fast, and so must we," she said in her Southern drawl. "We have to give up old ways, things, people, and embrace new ways, things and..."

It felt like a magnetic force was bringing us even closer. She closed her eyes and brought her lips toward mine.

Bang!

The front door swung open, slamming against the wall. A piece of the wooden doorframe hit the floor, spinning. I shot up into a sitting position, the heavy blankets falling to the floor. Stefanie was on her feet, backing toward the fireplace. From the open doorway, a blast of cold air shot around a tall, thin figure. He stood facing us, wearing a baseball cap, a black mask and a red plaid jacket.

"Oh, what a surprise," said the slurred voice of Constable Corona. "You're not social distancing."

Stefanie grabbed the iron poker, raising it back over her right shoulder to strike.

"Put it down, Joan of Arc," said Mackenzie, as he withdrew a taser from his jacket and aimed it at my chest. "Put it down or your boyfriend gets another round."

108. Mackenzie's Gift

Stefanie did not drop the iron poker, as she had been commanded, but let it hang by her side. I'll never forget how she looked, staring back at Mackenzie. Maybe it was the firelight, but I saw no surprise, shock or fear in her face—only the fierceness of a lion ready to strike.

"How sweet," taunted Mackenzie, keeping his arm extended, taser aimed at me. "Break your boyfriend out of quarantine for a romantic getaway in Moonbeam, Ontari-ari-o."

Despite his mask, we could smell the alcohol on his breath. It was even more apparent in his voice, as he began to sing "Helpless"—the classic Neil Young song that opens with the famous line about a town in Northern Ontario.

While Mackenzie serenaded us, I looked to Stefanie. I could tell she was all in her head, eyes calculating options. My heart, on the other hand, pounded so hard there was little blood flow left for my brain.

Suddenly, Stefanie shot toward him, poker before her like a bayonet.

And, almost immediately, sparks lit the dark room. I jolted back at the sound of snapping electricity. At first, I thought I had been hit. Instead, Mackenzie was pointing the stun gun up in the air, the dart still in its cartridge, letting the electricity arc across the two electrodes.

Stefanie stepped back.

"Now that I got your attention," he said, "and maybe even a little respect..."

He took a step forward. I rose from the couch, instinctively putting myself between Mackenzie and Stefanie. It didn't take any courage—for the only thing I feared more than another 50,000 volts was watching Stefanie on the receiving end of that device.

"Now, where's the other one?" he demanded, his eyes scanning the cabin. "Where's the driver?"

"We left him in Timmins," I said, without thinking.

"You didn't even go to Timmins," sneered Mackenzie. "Where is he?" He now raised his voice, yelling to the whole of the cabin. "If I don't see a moose appear in ten seconds, I will have to execute extreme measures I would much rather not." He squeezed the taser again, the air snapping with another jolt. "Ten, nine, eight—"

The bathroom door swung open and Mathéo stepped out. "Here I am," he said, casually, as if he'd been sitting in a waiting room to be called for an eye exam.

Mackenzie took a step back. Was he intimidated by Mathéo's size?

"Down on the floor!" he ordered, nervously. "Goddamn murderer. On the floor!"

"I haven't murdered anyone," said Mathéo, sounding slightly hurt.

"Not if I can help it," said Mackenzie. He waved the sparking taser at Mathéo. "Down! You self-centred prick."

Mathéo sank slowly to his knees and then into a fetal position on his side.

"Face down!" said Mackenzie, his voice bordering on hysteria.

Mathéo calmly outstretched himself, almost as if he was being guided by a yoga instructor, not threatened by a madman.

The charge in the taser began to waver. Mackenzie cursed and whipped it down on Mathéo's head. Mathéo didn't flinch. And I didn't hesitate. Seeing a chance, I pivoted forward, aiming to tackle Mackenzie to the ground; but froze when I heard the eardrum-splitting discharge of his firearm. Not another taser. A gun with a bullet. Where the bullet went, I didn't know. But I was now staring at the end of a loaded Glock 17M pistol.

"Damn," said Mackenzie, nonchalantly. "I drained my stun gun. Guess I'll have to resort to lethal force if anyone gives me any trouble." Under his black mask, I sensed he was grinning. "But, of course, you've given trouble enough already."

I raised my hands and said, "You're psycho."

"If I am, I have conspiracy nut-jobs like you to blame." He shot another bullet into the hardwood floor.

Stefanie screamed for a half second. My entire body tensed as though I had just been dropped through a fishing hole on a frozen lake.

"Down on your knees!" he yelled. "Both of you."

Stefanie stepped forward beside me. She looked at him and said with more conviction than I could ever have mustered, "I'm not afraid to die."

Mackenzie nodded and cocked his head in my direction. "Are you willing to watch him die?" He took a step back and pointed the gun shakily at my chest. "Like I watched Patty die." He brought his free hand up to steady the gun. "Slowly. Painfully.

You'll wonder if he's going to live. You'll hope he'll make it. But he won't."

"He's bluffing," I whispered, not believing my own words.

Stefanie stared into Mackenzie's eyes. He looked back, unblinking, as if he were possessed by more than an excess of alcohol.

"He's not bluffing," she said and dropped to her knees.

My love for her made me sacrifice my safety; her love for me made her sacrifice her freedom.

"You too," he said, moving the gun from my chest to hers. "On your knees."

I obeyed.

"Good," said Mackenzie. "You two are finally starting to understand."

He laughed.

"I bet you're wondering how I found you?"

Neither of us responded.

His free hand reached into his pants pocket and held out a smartphone. The display showed a green map with a white road wrapping around a blue shore labelled Remi Lake. A little to the right of the road was a green flashing dot.

"Remember how I promised you a Christmas gift?" he slurred. "GPS tracking device. It's been under your ugly yellow van since that stunt you pulled on the ice. First time shame on you. I was going to make sure there was never a shame on me. You made a fool of me then, but you're going to make me the hero now."

He began rocking back and forth, unsteadily.

"Half the province is looking for you. But it's the old fart they suspend and transfer to the boonies that saves the day."

We never had a chance. The bread van was letting him know every turn we made. I took a deep breath, suddenly feeling the pea soup pushing back up my throat.

"Once I got word of your escape, it only took a few taps to find out where you were heading, putting revenge on the top of my Boxing Day shopping list."

"Revenge?" asked Stefanie. "For hightailing it on the ice that night?"

"No!" he yelled. He fired another shot into the floor, near

where I kneeled. "No! Revenge for killing Patty."

"What?" cried Stefanie. I could hear fear beginning to creep into her voice.

"His wife," I said softly, remembering what Yamamoto had told me. "She died of COVID."

"No!" growled Mackenzie.

He rushed over to me, squeezing the back of my neck and sending me sliding forward, face first, onto the ground. My broken nose made a cracking sound. I felt the gun being wedged into my back.

"You damn anti-maskers killed her. COVID was merely your weapon."

He pressed the barrel even harder into my spine, feeling like he'd break a vertebrae.

"You just don't spread the virus, you spread lies. Sweet-tasting lies about freedom and rights and constitutions and bull crap. Bull crap that I listened to. Don't social distance! Refuse to wear a mask! Pretend to hand sanitize. And now—now she's dead."

In my chest, where my heart should have been, a hummingbird madly flapped its wings, trying to flee from this monster on my back.

"I'm sorry," I said, cringing. "People die. My grandfather just died. I know how—"

His knee came down on my lower back. My left kidney ignited with pain. An organ I had never felt before was now the only thing I knew.

"Good!" he snarled. "I'm glad the Wuhan virus got to someone you loved." I tried to throw him off, but any effort to move put more pressure on my screaming kidney.

"Killing him won't bring her back," pleaded Stefanie.

My right ear was pressed against the floor, my face looking to the left, where Mathéo's large form lay flat and still—like a hibernating bear.

"But it will stop other Pattys from dying," said Mackenzie. "That's why you *need* to watch him die so you can realize what you have been doing."

He almost sounded like he was going to cry.

"This will be my second gift to you."

And that's when the unthinkable happened.

I wish I could forget.

With speed I didn't think he was capable of, Mathéo rose to all fours and lunged toward us.

Another ear-splitting bang. The gun had fired. But not into my back.

Mathéo's bulky body, a second ago charging like a bear defending its cubs, abruptly jutted back and dropped to the floor. A short scream escaped from Stefanie and a brief moan from Mathéo.

My ears rang.

My mind went silent.

Then, as if he'd always been there, I could now see Grandad. He was old again, but strong and fit. His grey hair was braided and trailed down his shirtless back. A thin belt around his waist held a long rectangular piece of deerskin which hung in front and behind. He knelt down beside Mathéo and set his hand on his curly head.

"Mathéo!" I yelled, lifting my neck back and my head up.

Grandad turned to look at me. His lips didn't move but I could hear him in my head, "I will take care of your big friend. Me and him. We have work to do."

I closed my eyes tight, tears nonetheless seeping out.

"*Ach, du lieber Gott,*" I heard Stefanie whisper.

When I looked again, Grandad's spirit was gone.

And, I assumed, so was Mathéo's.

109. Our Common End

"I didn't want to do that," said Mackenzie, his whole body beginning to shake. "I didn't want to kill him. It's your fault he's dead." His entire body shuddered. "It's people like that who killed her. Killed my Patty."

I couldn't say anything. I just stared at Mathéo's limp form on the ground, praying that he was playing dead.

"You're sick," gasped Stefanie.

"Me?" said Mackenzie. He sounded dazed, drunk, disorientated. "Me? No. I'm, I'm... I'm the good guy stopping the bad guys from spreading the virus."

He returned the butt of the gun to my back and his knee to my kidney. My head came back down, right ear pressed against the floor, allowing me a clear view of the railing running along the loft above.

AJ, Léo and Bindu were up there. *Would they call 911?* I wondered. *Maybe Mathéo's brother?* Then I remembered all of their cellphones, wrapped in tin foil, lined up on the bookshelf.

No one was coming to rescue us. We were on the edge of the Canadian North where beast kills beast and nothing dies of old age. While we might outnumber Mackenzie five to one, he had the gun and a clear shot of anyone descending that spiral staircase.

My death, at least, now seemed inevitable. I guess it had always been. The whole world was running from COVID as though it had brought a new threat. Instead, it just reminded us of that common end we all share after the long series of events that follow our births.

"Get it over with," I said. "Just don't hurt anyone else."

If I could be the sacrificial offering, maybe the corona demon that had possessed him would leave it at that.

"No!" said Mackenzie, his voice retreating a little from the edge of chilling hysteria. "I want Joan of Arc to hope you will be spared. Just like I had hoped Patty would make it. I want her to pray, like I prayed so hard to that goddamn snake running down my wife's open mouth, moving her lungs, giving one false breath of hope after another... until finally that beeping monitor screamed that she—"

"Hurting me won't make your hurt go away," Stefanie pleaded. She was still on her knees, hands folded in supplication. "Adding more pain to this world is not going to make anything better."

"Oh, but it will, Little Miss Freedom Fighter." His voice now moving from sorrow to sarcasm. "Because you will know that you were the cause of his death. You will have to live with that; how your twisted view of reality costs lives."

His voice suddenly became drunk with regret.

"I loved her. So much. When I asked her to marry me, I knew she'd say no. But when she said yes...."

And then his voice became inflamed again.

"Seeing her die was the only thing that made me comply. Seeing him die, it will help you, like it helped me. And when others see you complying, they, too, will comply."

He wedged the gun harder into my back. I groaned, feeling acid coming up into my mouth, burning my throat.

"'Cause I know this idiot isn't smart enough or brave enough to ignore the rules. If it wasn't for a pretty face like yours, he'd be wearing his mask, staying at home and getting his COVID shot like a good little boy. But you Ayn Rands, you see it as your duty to keep everybody free to..." He began to choke on his words. "To suffer and die." He quickly cleared his throat, subduing any impending tears. "I get it. I know society, in order to be civilized, has to put up with people like you. I've spent my whole life defending law and order. But now I'm called to do the dirty work that's needed to keep everybody safe."

"You're a police officer," she shot back. "You've taken an oath."

"We are at war. Those oaths don't apply in time of war. War is never civilized."

"Then shoot me! Not him!" she yelled.

"No!" I gasped.

"Agreed," said Mackenzie, diplomatically, thrusting his weight on me again. "A pretty martyr is dangerous." His voice moved from hysteria to a deep and cold confidence. It sounded almost as if another personality had moved in. "But these idiots? Two dead sheep on your altar of freedom. That should put an end to your BS."

"You'll go to prison," she replied, point blank.

"Ha! *Me?* A cop outnumbered and ganged up on. A hero forced to defend himself."

"Patty wouldn't want you to do this," pleaded Stefanie.

"Shut the hell up!" exploded Mackenzie. He lifted his weight off my back, slightly, for a second, and then thumped back onto the kidney again, renewing the pain. His voice returned to a high-pitched hysteria. "You don't know Patty! You don't know anything!"

He took in a mouthful of air before continuing.

"But you think you know. You think you know more than the WHO, the CDC, the doctors, the scientists. And for some reason people actually listen to a freak like you. Don't trust your doctor when you got a baker on YouTube." His voice began to quaver. "That's what I did. I listened to all you whiners saying your rights were getting stepped all over. I didn't wear a mask. I didn't social distance. And now... now she's dead. And she's never coming back. We killed her. You. Me. How many have died because of us? We're despicable."

I could hear Stefanie breathing heavily. I struggled to pull in what air I could. My muscles were going limp from lack of oxygen.

"I watched her struggle," continued Mackenzie, shifting to a deranged and hopeless tone. "I watched that machine pump her last breath. And you will watch him breathe his last." He then pivoted his right shin onto the back of my neck, stopping what little air flow I had left.

"Are you ready?" he said to Stefanie. "Are you ready to watch him go?"

"Please!" she begged, rising to her feet. "Don't."

"All right," he said matter-of-factly.

He lifted his right leg off my neck. I sucked in air.

"I'll let him have one more breath."

Then he brought his left knee down again, pushing all the air out of my lungs.

"And one last exhale."

Immediately, his right shin was pressing again on my twisted neck.

Death is freedom, Grandad had said. The pain, the suffocation, the humiliation, the insanity. How many moments would it take?

I forced my bulging eyes to open. I wanted to see her. See her safe. But she began moving toward us. She looked like she was ready to pounce. Mackenzie lifted the gun from my back and aimed at her heart.

No! my mind screamed.

I tried to lift myself, but there was not enough oxygen left in my blood. My vision was blurring as I stared up toward the loft.

I'm hallucinating, I thought.

Over the loft's railing peeked a head. But it wasn't a human face that peered down. Pointed ears. Bucked teeth. It was a beaver. A Red Beaver.

"Cowabunga!" yelled AJ, as he swung his legs over the railing.

The weight on my back tripled. Ribs cracked in rapid succession like a kid crashing down on a row of piano keys. Fire shot through my entire chest, quickly followed by a modicum of relief as Mackenzie's weight toppled off me. I sucked in a breath full of pain. The lungs' cry for air deafened the screaming agony of the now broken bones that encaged them.

I stared, eyes bursting, as I watched two silhouettes grapple. They rolled over each other, halting before the raging fireplace. The Red Beaver had Constable Corona pinned to the ground. Mackenzie let out a yell and extended his foot into AJ's chest, flinging his thin body upward and backwards. He landed on his back, not with a thud, but a cracking sound. The back of the beaver mask came smacking down on the stone hearth—splitting into two halves like a walnut. Instantly, AJ's body began to vibrate, as if he were being electrocuted. His legs and arms jerked up and down. It lasted a few seconds. It lasted forever. And then another childhood friend went still.

Mackenzie stood. Rising like a dark shadow before the hearth, flames dancing behind him.

"Don't move!" screamed Stefanie.

I painfully moved my neck to see her standing, with both arms extended, hands gripped around the gun. Mackenzie began to laugh. His black mask was gone. Blood fell like thick drool from his open mouth.

"Go ahead!" he said, almost choking on his own words. "Shoot a cop! Spend the rest of your life in prison. I'll die for that!"

"Down... on... the... floor!" She had to force each word out as if her jaw were frozen shut.

"*Shoot him!*" I said in a voice full of pain. *If he got to her, what would he do?* "Shoot him!"

"Yes," he said meekly. "Please, shoot me. I deserve it."

And then he began to weep.

"Do it!" he pleaded, stepping toward her.

She stepped back. And he inched forward, again. His open mouth uttered a garbled series of pain-ridden sobs. He was the *mortes vivante*, the living dead backing her against the wall. I tried to get up, but the pain in my ribs would not let me.

She was crying, gun shaking in her hand. Did she even know how to fire a gun? Could she hold it steady? Could she kill?

"*Shoot!*" yelled the voice of Bindu from the balcony.

"*Tire!*" echoed Léo in French.

Stefanie steadied her shaking arms, let out a wail of regret and pulled the trigger.

But nothing came out.

110. The Law Mowers

They must have been waiting on the porch. Now that they knew Stefanie's gun was spent, suddenly, from the direction of the open door, I heard their boots charging over the threshold.

"Drop it!" yelled a deep, male voice.

Dots of red laser lights swarmed over Stefanie's silhouette in front of the blazing fireplace, the pistol still in her shaking hands.

Unable to lift my broken torso off the wooden floor, I turned my head toward the cabin's front door. Four figures dressed in black stood in the entryway in offensive stances—one leg forward, the other back. The two in front centre held large ballistic shields with the word POLICE inscribed across their transparent surfaces. The other two, on either side, were staring through the sights of laser-guided assault rifles. The black carbines' short, narrow barrels were contrasted by large magazines extending down in front of the triggers. The RCMP's Emergency Response Team looked like black-op military; certainly no red-suited Mounties. They wore thick helmets, each imprinted with a unique three-digit ID in white, large lettering. They wore a hundred different accoutrements around their waists, chests and legs. They wore green night-vision goggles. And they wore white, puffy face masks.

"Drop the gun!"

I heard a clang as Stefanie let the pistol fall to the floor.

"Argo!" yelled a female officer behind one of the shields.

A dog barked.

The officer with the shield stood aside and a German shepherd shot through the opening, scooting between Mathéo's and my prone bodies. The dog's handler followed, the tail end of a long leash lashing my face.

I twisted my head back toward Stefanie. She just stood there, frozen, as the canine constable barked madly at her, standing on his hind legs, while his handler tugged at the leash. Another officer came behind her, assault rifle hanging over his shoulder. He pulled her arms behind her back as Argo barked again, his fangs looking red in the firelight; his tail wagging happily as if he was playing a game.

"Good boy, Argo!" said the handler. "You did it! You know it! We got the bad guys!"

The dog handler's cheers were suddenly quenched by the voice of Mackenzie.

"The boys," said Mackenzie, standing to the side, almost blending into the dark shadows. The dog barked at him.

"Down, Argo!" said his handler. "Down."

"The boys," repeated Mackenzie, "they both need medical attention. They attacked me. I had no choice."

Mackenzie turned and knelt beside AJ and said, "My God." He turned toward Stefanie and said, "What have you done?"

"He killed them!" Bindu spoke out from above. "Mackenzie killed them!"

"The boy's still breathing," said Mackenzie, feeling AJ's neck. "Someone get me a first aid kit. Quick! Damn it!"

More footsteps on the porch.

A woman's voice spoke out, "Don't move him! He may have spinal injuries."

She came into my limited range of view. Short, dark hair, thin build, stern voice. It was the inspector from the CTV report. The one with the same surname as that dead prime minister.

"McCormick! Call in the choppers," ordered Inspector Diefenbaker.

The female Mountie with the shield ran out of the cabin, as a fifth officer entered and knelt by my side.

"Are you injured?" he said.

I groaned. "Take care of AJ, Mathéo."

Inspector Diefenbaker was already kneeling at Mathéo's side, feeling his neck.

"Help me turn him over," she ordered.

Another officer helped flip Mathéo slowly onto his back. Diefenbaker immediately began chest compressions as she looked up at Mackenzie.

"You were told that you were not to be involved," she said to him.

"It was my lead!" Mackenzie snapped back, with what almost sounded like a snarl at the end. "I didn't want them to get away. I—"

I could hear one of the Mounties asking Stefanie for her name, but getting no response.

The dog whimpered.

"Don't worry, Argo," said his handler. "You'll get a cheeseburger on the way home, I promise."

The other officer returned, carrying a white case with a red cross. He dropped to AJ's side, where Mackenzie still knelt, and popped open the lid.

Stefanie gently broke her stunned silence and whispered, "What have I done?"

"Get her out of here!" yelled Mackenzie as he rummaged through the first aid supplies, as if he didn't really know what he was looking for.

In the distance, outside the cabin, McCormick was speaking into a radio, "We have three injured—two appear critical. Requesting immediate air ambulance assistance." A pause. "The field in front is large enough."

"You're arresting the wrong person," shouted Léo, sprinting behind Bindu down the spiral staircase.

"Both of you!" barked one of the Mounties. "Hands in the air! On your knees!"

I heard Bindu gasp. I couldn't see her or Léo, but heard the sound of handcuffs sliding into place like a knife sliding over a sharpening stone.

"Him, too!" yelled the inspector. Keeping one hand on Mathéo's chest, she pointed quickly to Mackenzie, and then returned to chest compressions. "Get him away from the victims."

Mackenzie was still by AJ's side. "What the hell?" he said, rising to his feet.

"We'll sort your mess out later," she snapped back. To another officer she said, "Right now, I want him in custody. Give him a breathalyzer!"

The other officer appeared and put his hand on Mackenzie's shoulder. Mackenzie knocked it away.

"You're making a mistake, toots," said Mackenzie to Diefenbaker, his voice slurring.

"Get him out of here!"

The officer didn't handcuff Mackenzie, but merely said, "Come on, let's clear out."

The officer with Stefanie began leading her toward the door and gestured to Mackenzie to follow. She looked down at me as they passed. Disbelief, shock, horror was all our eyes mirrored to each other. My breath was knocked out of me again, as I watched her and Constable Corona being guided, almost side by side, out the front door into the cold darkness—one cuffed, the other not.

What have we done? There I lay, nearly crushed to death. Mathéo, was he dead? AJ. They said he was breathing. *For how long?*

The draft from the open door slunk across the floor and covered me like a blanket soaked in ice water. Shivering sent renewed slices of pain through my ribs.

"Can you get up?" said a constable at my side. On his shoulder were the bilingual initials "RCMP" and "GRC." His helmet displayed the digits 019.

I moaned.

"Are you hurt?"

Yes, I was hurt. So hurt. My entire life hurt.

"*Es-tu blessé?*" he repeated in French.

His head came into view. I don't know why, but I almost laughed. My blurred eyes did not see a face, but only an absurd elongated white mask which extended like a beak. A French-speaking albino duck in a police uniform.

"Chest." I forced myself to say. "Chest hurts. Cold."

He pulled the discarded blankets from the floor and draped the heavy wool painfully over my body.

Inspector Diefenbaker, still at Mathéo's side, stood up, panting. "Take over," she commanded the officer. "I'm not getting a pulse."

No pulse?

"No!" I managed to exclaim in a gasp.

Please no! They can bring Mathéo back. He'll make it. He's a bear. He's hibernating. He's big and strong and tough. He can't die. He'll digest the bullet.

The officer took off his helmet and night goggles, almost as if in solemn respect, revealing a grey crewcut. I'm sure removing his helmet must have been against protocol. He knelt beside Mathéo and continued efforts to bring a beat back to his quiet heart.

Vehicles were pulling up in front of the cabin. I could hear many voices.

But not her voice.

Joan of Arc had gone silent.

"I'll talk to the other two, first," said the inspector, now out in front of the cabin. "Put her in back."

I heard a door to a vehicle open.

"Watch your head."

And then the door slammed shut.

The *law*-mowers had finally hacked off the head of the dandelion.

And the turtle?

I withdrew into the shell of unconsciousness before the helicopters arrived.

111. An Orange Unicorn

When I came to, pain greeted me first, followed by my captor.

"Here we go, buddy," said the Mountie with the white eyebrows, the white face mask and the white digits 019 inscribed on his helmet.

He was holding the front end of the cot I now found myself strapped to, wrapped in some sort of emergency, crinkly, subzero sleeping bag. I stared up at the helicopter that awaited me. It was painted orange with a metal spike extending above its windshield like a unicorn's horn.

I'd once known a unicorn. My pain-drunk mind swayed back to that day in the parking lot behind La Papillon—the Butterfly Restaurant.

I open the back of the bread van and Cindy pokes her horn at my snout and laughs. I want to tell her what has happened to her brother. What he did for me. How much of a hero he is.

"Cindy," I mumbled, but my chest ignited with pain.

My eyes opened wide.

The side door of the chopper slid open. A thin, young lady dropped down onto a patch of frosty grass as if she were auditioning for the Nutcracker. Like the medic holding the back end of my cot, she also wore a blue face mask and a round flight helmet with dome-shaped headphones. Their bulging helmets, glowing body cams and one-piece flight suits made them look more sci-fi than medical. Their maple leaf epaulettes, however, proved they were not from the mother ship the mayor of Moonbeam reportedly kept in orbit. They also bore large name tags: "Sarah T" and "Jonathan M." Nice to be on a first-name basis with my abductors. Their name tags claimed they were "critical care flight paramedics."

The Mountie introduced himself to Sarah T. "I'm Corporal Dubois. I'll be overseeing transport of the prisoner."

Prisoner. It seemed too harsh, too hard to believe.

"Uh, I mean, accused," he corrected himself. Icy vapour escaped from the edges of his face mask as he chuckled. "You know, in the academy, we're taught to call those in our custody our 'clients.'"

"*Clients!*" exclaimed Jonathan M from behind me. "That's a joke."

"No kidding. God, I need to retire."

They all laughed in the way people do when they want to banish anxiety, guilt or confusion—I'm sure they suffered from all three.

"How're you doing?" asked Sarah T, looking down at me.

Her blue eyes were pretty, but I knew not to trust blue eyes anymore. Instead of responding, I wondered what the T stood for. Terrible? Tyrannical? Tormented?

From behind my head, Jonathan M warned, "He's a confirmed COVID case."

I decided Jonathan's M must stand for Madness.

They continued their exchange—their words drowned out by pain nerves sending nauseating signals from the fractured bones around my lungs to my exhausted brain. I moved my head ever so slightly to see around me; but all I saw were blazing headlights and the dark silhouettes of the Emergency Response Team moving around the cabin. Had they already taken Mathéo away? Was he alive? He must be. Mathéo couldn't die. What about AJ? He'd probably wake up from his concussion with those superpowers he'd always dreamed of having. Léo and Bindu? Bindu's a lawyer, or almost a lawyer, she'd show them.

And Captain D? A dandelion hauled away in handcuffs. My ribs were not the only thing that felt broken.

"Oh," Sarah T was saying, "is he the one we saw on—"

"Yes, ma'am," replied Corporal Dubois.

"Is he... *the moose?*"

"That's the other guy, I think. The one they airlifted first."

"All right," she said, "let's get him inside before we all freeze to death."

The Mountie began marching my cot toward the roaring aircraft. Eighty years ago, Mounties had captured Grandad from the bush and flew away with him. Now, they were collecting his grandson from the bush and flying away with him.

When we reached the door of the chopper, they turned the cot around, giving me my first clear look at Jonathan M. His narrow eyes and Asian features reminded me of Mr. Chung, though his accent was as Canadian as mine. He was a bulky looking guy with a wide face that I suspected only smiled when it was socially expected.

"*Un, deux, trois,*" he counted.

He and the Mountie hoisted me up. I cried out in pain. Without a pause they slid my cot headfirst into the warm chopper like a coffin into a funeral truck. Two seats were now on my right and one on my left—so close there would barely be room for my captors' kneecaps. I felt like I had become their coffee table. But instead of setting steaming mugs of holiday cheer on my pain-ridden body, critical care paramedic Sarah T removed the straps tying me to the cot, unzipped the emergency thermal cocoon and covered me with a heated blanket.

"Do you know where you are?" she asked.

"In pain," I managed to say.

"Are you allergic to anything?"

"Pain," I repeated.

"We can give you fentanyl."

I groaned.

"It's an opioid analgesic—a hundred times stronger than morphine."

Morphine, I thought. *Like you gave Grandad—so you could say he died from COVID. First you abduct us, then you kill us.*

I turned my head away to see Corporal Dubois buckling himself into the seat on my left, still wearing his black helmet with those accursed digits across the front: 019. Behind him, the rear wall of the chopper was covered with dials, gadgets, screens, drawers and storage compartments.

Jonathan M clamped an oximeter to my right middle finger, saying, "This guy's wanted across ten provinces, isn't he?"

"We always get our man," mumbled the Mountie, with no hint of pride.

"Oxygen sat is 92 percent," said Jonathan M.

Without asking permission, he began rolling up the sleeve of my right arm and quickly plunged a needle into the crux of my elbow. He repeated the same procedure with my other arm. With surprising speed, two transparent IV lines were dangling from the ceiling, running into my wrists, feeling as thick as garden hoses. All the while an inflating cuff squeezed at my right bicep.

"He's safe to rumble," declared Jonathan M after noting my exceedingly high blood pressure.

"Roger," said a voice I could barely hear from the cockpit where the pilot and his first officer sat. "Prepare for liftoff."

I squeezed my eyes shut to stop the two tears that were forming. Father Shostakovich once told us that God would never send us a cross we could not bear. If that was true, God had far too much confidence in me—for my cross was about to get a whole lot heavier.

The door rattled closed. Both medics plugged their flight helmets into a black box hanging from the ceiling. Above the ceiling, the clatter of the rotors increased.

As the copter shot up, gravity pushed down. I'd once seen a YouTube clip about ascetics in India sleeping on boards of nails. It now felt like such a board had been hammered into my chest, to serve as a platform for a six-hundred pound Indian elephant.

Air left my lungs and was replaced by so much pain it didn't matter anymore.

"Which hospital?" asked Corporal Dubois nonchalantly, as if it didn't really matter to him.

"Thunder Bay," replied Sarah T.

I choked, trying to speak, trying to tell them I couldn't breathe. A machine began to beep on my behalf.

"Dammit! O2 sat's dropping," exclaimed Jonathan M.

Did the M stand for Murder?

He looked at me. I looked back with eyes bulging.

"I think his lungs have collapsed."

112. A Dark Canvas

Finally, I thought. Death had come to usher me to Gaagige Minawaanigozigiwining—the land of happiness and joy. I'd had enough of this world of horror and pain.

The helicopter halted its ascent. The nails of pain relented but it still felt like an Indian elephant was sitting on my chest.

"Vincent, we're going to insert a chest tube," said Sarah T.

Did the T stand for Torture?

"It'll only hurt a bit."

I knew she was lying. I didn't trust her blue eyes.

"What's going on?" hollered Corporal Dubois.

"One or both of his lungs can't expand," Jonathan Murder hollered back. "An air pocket has formed somewhere in his chest." He gestured in the direction of the roaring blades above. "I can't say exactly where. A stethoscope's useless in here."

He actually sounded like he cared. My captors were performing admirably for their body cams.

"Hold his arm like this," Sarah Torture instructed the Mountie.

They brought my right arm up and back behind my head as the pain in my chest went from a ten to a twenty—but I had no air left in my lungs for a dying scream.

Snip! Snip! Snip! Hastily scissors cut away at the Orwellian T-shirt Bindu had gifted me for Christmas.

Pop! My whole body jerked as Jonathan Murder inserted something sharp and cold into the side of my chest under my right arm. When he removed his instrument, a whistle of air escaped from the bloody opening. I forced myself to watch as Sarah Torture twisted, wedged and thrust a tube through the squishy hole they had made in my side and jammed it between my broken ribs.

Sploosh, splash, splash rumbled a machine connected to the chest tube. Immediately, I felt relief from my impending suffocation as both lungs inflated slowly.

"There we go," said Jonathan M.

Maybe he wasn't Mr. Murder after all. Maybe the M stood for Mercy?

"O2 rising. 79. 80. 81..."

The copter jerked and began flying in a horizontal direction over what felt like lumpy ice rather than formless air. My chest rattled with pain. But at least I could breathe. Despite the pain, death had suddenly lost its attractiveness. I guess I still wanted to live.

"We need to okay the fentanyl with the ground doc," said Sarah T into her helmet's microphone. "Patch me through to Thunder Bay." The T must stand for Tenacity. If she could stop the pain, then maybe even Tenderness.

"Getting 180 over 120. Heart hitting 140. He's suffering from multiple broken ribs, possible spinal injury, possible renal trauma..." Sarah T was describing my condition to a doctor far away.

My condition.

A year earlier, my condition was that of a regular guy, living in a small Canadian town nobody had ever heard of, welding during the day, playing hockey at night.

"Dr. Gagnon's okayed the fentanyl," reported Sarah T a minute later.

"I'm ready," said Jonathan M. He already had a bag of the synthetic opium swaying back and forth above my body.

I'd never taken drugs before. Never even smoked a cigarette. Grandad said tobacco was for ceremonies, not recreation. My worst offence was too many Molson Canadians with Dad over lockdown.

Someone unclamped the IV line and the mega-morphine began dripping into my body. As I felt my mind slipping into an unsettling numbness, the previous six months replayed in my head:

Josh, Cindy, Walter and Ferris tossing ten- and twelve-sided dice and fighting dragons in the forbidden Dungeon Room of Roger's Little Shop of Heroes.

Léo the Bard singing his corny love songs to Bindu the Princess of Ayodhya.

Father Shostakovich defying Caesar by holding maskless Masses while his flock silently prayed for his crucifixion.

Raj proudly patting his touch-free holy water dispenser, seeking to make the Roman Catholic Church more sanitary, one font at a time.

Grandad smiling quietly on the Louis Riel Bridge, watching the sunset to the sound of quacking ducks on the French River.

Four guys slapping a puck across the same frozen river under a sky full of stars.

Watching Grandad breathe his last in the cell they called his suite.

Yamamoto being the ultimate amigo, giving up Christmas so I would be truly safe from the very people pretending to protect us.

Mr. Chatterjee spray-painting that yellow bread van into the ultimate getaway vehicle.

AJ donning his Red Beaver mask, leaping from a balcony, yelling "Cowabunga!" and saving my life.

Mathéo cooking up Aunt Sofia's French Canadian pea soup *with the ham*—his last meal before a bullet took his life.

Mackenzie watching his wife die, slowly, and then him, trying to kill me, slowly.

What horrors, heroics and humour freedom allows.

Finding an unmasked Dandelion, in a bakery, holding a mirror to my green face—waking me from *der Träume Flor*, Schubert's "veil of dreams."

Watching her laugh with such delight when I showed up for the job interview dressed as an ungulate—felt antlers, drooping nostrils and all.

Seeing her lift up the mosquito mesh in church, and wishing that it was a bride's veil.

Listening to her struggle to play *Die schöne Müllerin* on the violin in the VIP lounge at her illegal Moosehead Soup Kitchen.

Feeling her hold me tight as I retreated on ice skates along the frozen French River, her in my arms, heart pounding so hard.

Feeling my heart rate double when she told me "I love you" on the phone after being tasered, beaten, and imprisoned.

And feeling it triple with a surge of adrenaline as she raced my wheelchair down hospital hallways, breaking me out of quarantine in her Nurse Vader disguise.

And then my heart stopping as she pulled the trigger on Constable Corona.

I'd risk doing it all again.

That's how much I loved her and her insane love of freedom.

And that scared me more than anything.

It had all been worth it. She was worth it. I was worth it. Humanity was worth it.

Such feelings, so primal and, at the same time, transcendent, terrified me more than tasers, handguns and assault rifles. That frightened part of me wished that I had never gone to the bakery to pick up that loaf of bread for Grandad; that I had stayed in Dad's basement, lifting weights, drinking beer, and watching Netflix... *for just another fourteen days.*

Stefanie, Léo, and Bindu arrested. My ribs shattered. Mathéo probably dead. AJ possibly worse than dead. Was freedom worth it all ending in such darkness?

Was it?

To my left, I heard the Mountie's voice mutter, "The Northern Lights."

I opened my eyes and stared out the two windows of the sliding door at my feet. In the distance, the North Pole was unleashing a brilliant smear of red, green and blue particles—making that dark, dark night a canvas for unearthly beauty.

113. Faithful Unto Death

"Grandad?" I asked.

He was sitting on a log to my right. On my left was Mathéo. A dying fire flickered in the pit before us. Its flames fended off the toughest of mosquitos; those that endured in that cool autumn night. In the dark woods around Grandad's cabin, a symphony of cicadas were drumming their corrugated exoskeletons. Grandad looked up from the large piece of wood he was carving and smiled at me.

"Hmm?" he responded.

Behind him, between the fire pit and the cabin, stood a tent where Mathéo and I would sleep the night. We were only ten.

Speaking hesitantly, as one did when young, unsure if the question would be welcome, I asked, "When the government men came and took you and Aunt Memengwaa away from your mom and dad, why did your parents not break you out? Why didn't the village come and rescue you?

"Oui," added Mathéo. "Why didn't they start a war?"

Grandad didn't answer right away. He never did. Instead, he shuffled his feet, crunching dry maple leaves. In his hand he held the hollowed-out section of a cedar log. Slivers of wood lay in his lap. He put down his carving knife, before finally speaking:

"My people knew they would lose if we fought against the new laws. There were more government men than we knew how to count. How could my parents help me or my sister if they were dead or in prison? We could not fight government with fists."

"But you could have got guns," said Mathéo, a big grin crossing over his chubby face. He picked up two branches from the ground, and snapped away twigs until they each somewhat resembled a person—two legs, two arms and a pointy head. He propped the stickmen up on each of his knees. "Regarde ça!" he said and began making "bang, bang" noises, having them each shoot at the other, until one fell to the ground.

A hint of a smile broke on Grandad's face. "That only works if you have more and better guns," he said. "Something we did not."

He picked the knife up again and resumed scraping at the log.

"What are you making?" I asked.

"A beaver mask," he said.

"Why a beaver?"

"Beavers are resourceful. They don't destroy, they build. That's what my parents did. They learned English. They built a business. They hired lawyers to get the laws changed."

"Did it work?"

"Not fast enough for Memengwaa," said Grandad, sadly. "But now the government no longer steals children and forces them to live at schools."

"But I still have to go to school during the day," said Mathéo, glumly.

Grandad nodded.

"And there are only two choices, public or Catholic," I added. "And the government runs both of them."

"You are right." Grandad closed his eyes. "Still much work to be done." Then, switching to his British accent he quoted old Will: "'Though age from folly could not give me freedom, it does from childishness.'"

"Paul!" called out Grandma's Irish accent from the kitchen window of the cabin. I turned, but could only see the outline of her face. "Paul! It's getting late. Time to head on in."

"My beloved is calling," he said with a chuckle. "I think she misses me."

He rose and left Mathéo and me alone in the darkness.

A baton banged across the bars, pulling me out of the sweet escape dreaming provided.

"It's 10 a.m. Sleep at night!" yelled the guard, as he passed out of view.

I sat up, keeping my head tilted forward so as not to hit the bunk above me. The usual pain greeted me. Three months and the ribs still ached. At least I was off the codeine. I swung my legs out of bed onto the cold cement floor.

My cellmate didn't move. He continued lying on the bunk above, atop his blanket. He always ignored the guards. They always ignored him.

I used the frame of the bunk bed to help get me on my bare feet. The toilet was only an arm's length away. Leaning on its tank with one hand, I used the other to steady my aim. My cellmate rolled over on his left side, staring at the wall until I was done (one of the three co-habitation rules we had agreed upon). When I flushed, he returned to gazing at the cement ceiling.

I cleared my throat and enunciated slowly, "Je peux te poser une question?" *Can I ask you a question?* was one French phrase

I had mastered in the last ninety plus days.

"Oui," he responded, softly.

"Tes parents te manquent encore?" I asked. I wanted to know if he missed his parents.

"Toujours," he confirmed. "J'ai pensé que nous serions réunis quand Mackenzie m'a tiré dessus."

I repeated back in English, as I often did, to confirm I had understood: "You thought when Mackenzie shot you, that you'd finally be reunited with your parents?"

"Oui," he said. "Votre français s'améliore rapidement."

Yes, I was learning French fast. Conversing with Mathéo every day for the last three months was a life-saving distraction. It kept the mind occupied. It prevented my thoughts pushing me over the cliff of despair on which I now lived.

Mathéo said no more—for our words were infringing on a forbidden topic. Cell rule number two was that we would never talk about that night in the cabin in Moonbeam. Especially, what happened to AJ. Our pithy conversations naturally re-stricted themselves to life before COVID-19.

And, especially, before I met her.

For my third rule—*numéro trois*—was that we never men-tion Captain Dandelion. Such memories only brought regret. Regret always brought tears. Useless tears. Painful tears.

> Ach, Tränen machen
> Nicht maiengrün,
> Machen tote Liebe
> Nicht wieder blühn.[*]

Oh how I wished I could get that awful German nonsense out of my head—a silly song about the foolishness of love. Love was a curse. A curse I still bore. I still loved her. Even though that love, rather than granting freedom, had stripped it all away. Yet, somehow, she was still free—she who pulled the trigger. All I knew was she had not been sentenced. Where she was, or what

---

[*] Ah, but tears don't bring
The green of May,
Don't cause dead love
To bloom again.

she was doing, I did not know. No letters. No phone calls. The only one who ever called was Mom; but I never took her calls.

I fell into the cell's sole chair, groaning all the way down. To my right, on the triangular shelf, in the corner of the cell, below the tiny window, sat my other cellmate: a little black Bible.

When I was first brought to Milhaven Institute—the maximum security federal prison on the shore of Lake Ontario—they gave me a list of books to choose from: *The Bible, The Qur'an, the Talmud, The Book of Mormon, The Bhagavad Gita, The Lotus Sutras, The Tripitaka.*

I wanted something familiar.

It had only taken two months, but I had read every single word from the *Book of Genesis* through to the *Book of Jude*. Only one more book to go. The wispy pages of that battered Bible offered a comforting collection of stories and an unforgettable lineup of heroes and villains. It had been my only connection with the outside world—albeit, with a people who lived thousands of years ago, in a continent I had never visited, who spoke a language that I did not know. Yet, what made us all human crossed petty barriers of time and culture and language.

That morning I had already read the first chapter of the Book of Revelation, the final and most bizarre part of the Bible. I continued with chapter two:

> Do not fear what you are about to suffer. Behold, the devil is about to throw some of you into prison, that you may be tested, and for ten days you will have tribulation. Be faithful unto death, and I will give you the crown of life.

Ten days? I thought. *More than ten weeks had already passed.* The crown attorney had not had any trouble convincing the judge to give me ten years. I closed the book and closed my eyes, remembering a joke Father Shostakovich had told the congregation once about how a year to us was only like a day to God.

I slumped back in the chair; but that hurt my ribs too much, so I stood, and scuffled over to the sink. There I let water flow into my hands and splashed it on my face, wetting my shaggy beard and bushy hair. I was grateful there was no mirror to see my grisly reflection.

Mathéo sat up and let his legs fall over the side of the bed.

He wore a white T-shirt, with a small tear in the belly. His hair was curly as always, but groomed and short.

"Ils arrivent," he announced, slow and grave. *They are coming.*

I turned, walked to the bars, wrapped my hands around their cold hardness and gazed through the space between. A walkway fronted our second-level cell. Its railing overlooked the empty common area below.

"Qui arrive?" I asked.

Before Mathéo could tell me who was coming, the sound of a hydraulic lock echoed through our one-hundred-and-twenty-man unit. Not that we had that many. When the third wave hit, cells had been limited to only one person. I could hear the large metal door open at the far side of the common area, and footsteps passing through.

"I can't see who it is," I said, turning back to Mathéo. "The railing's blocking my view."

Mathéo dropped off the bunk without making a sound. He walked to my side, and then, as he often did, passed directly through the bars onto the walkway. He paused for only a second, before leaping over the side of the railing, as AJ had done that night I try so hard to forget.

A minute passed, and then I heard his voice behind me: "Two guards. And a woman in blue. A nurse."

I turned around. Mathéo was now standing in our cell again (if a ghost can be said to stand at all).

"Attention!" yelled one of the unseen guards from below. "There's a lady in the house. I expect all of you to act like gentlemen. She is here to deliver the first dose of the COVID-19 vaccine."

I felt that frightened turtle inside my heart trying to withdraw inside; to pretend this was not happening. Throughout our pod, cell doors began to rattle as prisoners began booing and hooting; swearing and cheering.

"She can stick it up her—"

"About time!"

"Is she pretty?"

"I'm not going to be a friggin' guinea pig..."

"We'll begin with the second level," yelled the guard over the racket. "Immunization is not optional. We need to all do our part to keep everyone safe and end the lockdown. We trust everyone will cooperate so that this can go painlessly."

I realized my cell door was rattling. My hands, gripping the bars, were shaking involuntarily. Mathéo walked through the bars a second time. This time, however, he stopped on the walkway and turned around to face me. Through the tear in his shirt I could see the hole in his belly, where the bullet had entered and his blood had emptied onto the cabin floor.

Footsteps were ascending the metal stairs.

I whispered to Mathéo, "What am I going to do?"

Behind him, two guards, with black masks, appeared at the top of the stairway, turning onto the walkway. Between them, walked the nurse—a woman in her forties or fifties, a little chubby, a bit short, with midnight-black, curly hair. She wore a mask, a visor and blue gloves. In her right hand she carried a white plastic case.

Mathéo grinned. "Don't worry," his slowly fading form replied. "Captain D has a plan."

<u>END OF BOOK ONE</u>
to be continued...

Green Insurgent

The great Beast of Revelation lurches
toward its global coup, the human spirit
a dandelion crushed beneath robotic boots.

Don't underestimate that green insurgent
We've seen it split open pavements, deploy
its yellow parasols on long milky necks
and carpet a dead field with new sunlight

on a morning untouched by death.

—Sean Arthur Joyce, "Cashless,"
from Diary of a Pandemic Year
(Chameleon Fire Editions, 2021)

Afterword: Help the Wordsmiths You Want to See in the World

"The wordsmith—prophet, singer, poet, essayist, novelist—has always been either the catalyst of change or, inversely, the servant of established power," writes John Ralston Saul in *Voltaire's Bastards—The Dictatorship of Reason in the West.* "[The writer] breaks up the old formulas of wisdom or truth and thus frees the human imagination so that individuals can begin thinking of themselves and their society in new ways, which the writer must then express in new language."

With the dawn of COVID-19 it was apparent that wordsmiths serving the established power had been hard at work coming up with a narrative and even a new normal language to lure people into accepting a medical dictatorship. To counter the onslaught of this well-prepared attack on the minds and hearts of humanity, I began writing this novel in March of 2020. Two years of daily effort has yielded the story you have just finished reading.

"Literature and poetry are far more than mere entertainment, or some enjoyable but unnecessary frill," writes Sean Arthur Joyce in his new book, *Words from the Dead: Relevant Readings in the Covid Age.* Instead, Joyce proposes the nobler goal of everything from "*Hamlet* to *Star Trek*" is to "stimulate critical thinking," to unearth "deep meaning" and to otherwise wake up "the public mind." Such were my aims in writing *Much Ado About Corona: A Dystopian Love Story.*

That you have finished this not-too-short tale most likely means it captivated you and that its message resonated with you. If you would like to help me help others, through this and future novels, there are a few things you can do:

1. Go to BlazingPineCone.com and sign up for my email updates. You'll get details about this and future novels that you can then share with others. (As *Much Ado About Corona* is being published, I've already completed 47,000 words of the sequel, *Brave New Normal.* I'm

485

aiming to have it released sometime in 2023.)

2. Consider buying a copy of *Much Ado About Corona* as a gift for friends and family. What better Christmas, birthday or even Valentine's present?

3. Purchase copies of *Much Ado About Corona* and send them to people of influence such as your local police chief or sheriff, your elected representatives, media (alternative or mainstream) personalities, business owners and religious leaders. Use this book as a non-violent weapon for changing the zeitgeist.

4. Leave a rating and review of *Much Ado About Corona* on the website of the retailer from where you bought it. In addition, if you did not purchase through Amazon or if it was a gift, please be sure to leave a review on the Amazon website for your region. Whether as a result of free market capitalism or tyrannical oligarchies, Amazon rules the book market, and is currently the best way to reach new readers.

5. Share your review with friends, family and co-workers, via email, social media or on your own website or blog.

6. Lastly, consider becoming a Blazing Pine Cone Patron. See the final page of this book for more details about what you'll receive as a supporting member.

If you are able to complete any of the above six items you have my thanks, and I will show my appreciation by completing the sequel as soon as possible. I also have drafts of three other novels (that have nothing to do with COVID) that I aim to complete after the Corona duology (or, possibly, trilogy) is finished. So, if you value stories like *Much Ado About Corona* then please help enable this wordsmith to produce fiction faster than the establishment's lackeys. Rather than a Great Reset, let's usher in a Great Awakening.

—John C. A. Manley
Stratford, Ontario, Canada
March 27, 202

Acknowledgements

This novel would not have reached the level of storytelling, accuracy, and detail it managed to achieve without the help of so many people. It's going to be a long list and I pray I don't forget anyone. Thank you to...

Jordan Henderson of jordanhendersonfineart.com for painting the cover that beautifully reflects the theme of the story. The process involved hours of brainstorming, many sketches, two unique paintings and many, many revisions. In addition, his feedback, encouragement, and insights with draft eight of the novel proved invaluable. In particular, his challenging suggestions are largely responsible for Constable Mackenzie becoming a deeper and more unique character.

Dr. Gary Magder of goldtadise.com for his financial contributions—made in memory of his late parents Jesse and Claire Magder—which covered most of the expense in self-publishing this novel. His willingness to back the project helped me appreciate how important and valuable this story would be to derailing the COVID-19 agenda.

Christian and Gauri "Papillon" Pillon for helping with the German (especially the Christdorn dilemma) and the Italian ("Niente sorriso, niente pane"); for proofreading the ebook version and for their generous donation toward the creation and promotion of this book.

Patti and Randy Rothwell for their financial contributions which helped cover the cost of the copy-editor and for all their prayers and support.

Michelle Qureshi for her donation toward the project, her feedback on the prologue and opening chapters, and her wonderful British accent.

Paul Jackson for his donation toward the publishing of the novel, his feedback on the Indigenous characters and his ever-witty optimism.

Wolfgang and Almut Wurzbacher of www.pfenningsorganic.ca for all their feedback on everything from maple leaves to character names; and especially for helping me craft the German characters and editing all the German words, lyrics, and whistling pigs.

Erika Lorenz-Löblein for helping me refine the character of Josef (formerly Holgar) and better reflect the COVID-19 situation in Bavaria.

Sean Arthur Joyce of seanarthurjoyce.ca for line-editing the entire novel, making many critical suggestions and allowing me to use an excerpt from his stunningly synchronistic poem, "Green Insurgent," from his book, *Diary of a Pandemic Year.*

David Hardat for beta-reading the novel, correcting my French (especially the nasty words) and making other valuable suggestions.

Alexandre Normand for double-checking David's French, offering alternative phrasings to consider, and providing feedback on the story from his nomadic minivan.

Dr. Chris Milburn for beta-reading the novel and helping me make not only the medical content more accurate, but also the residential school backstory more balanced.

Andrew Brannan for beta-reading the novel, sharing his hands-on nursing experience, and helping me make the medical content more realistic (and slightly gory).

Christine Taylor for copy-editing the novel twice and always being there to answer my grammatical queries and debate the placement of a comma.

Rosemary Frei of rosemaryfrei.ca for her tough feedback on the prologue and the first two chapters; as well as her research into the neglect and abuse that took place in Ontario nursing homes.

Dr. S. Hilary Anne Ivory for her even tougher, and more challenging critique of the opening prologue and chapters.

Dr. Éva Székely for beta-reading the novel and spending hours on the phone helping me develop the twisted subconsciousness of Constable Mackenzie.

Lisa Falcioni for beta-reading the novel and pushing me to make the first half more suspenseful.

Father Anthony Hannon of inviampacis.org for spending hours on the phone with me (from his rural retreat) going over every ecclesiastical detail of the chapters set in St. Jerome's Church.

Father Scott Murray for providing on-the-ground details

about parish life in Quebec under COVID dogma (and how to resist it).

Francine "Crane Woman" Noiseux for serving as a Métis sensitivity reader and helping me make Grandad more authentic.

Chad Curnew of takeactioncanada.ca/readmylips for serving as a deaf sensitivity reader, ensuring all the American Sign Language was accurate and that Josh's character was realistic.

Retired RCMP Constable Leland "Lee" Keane for reviewing the manuscript and spending many hours helping me understand the stress that officers are under, answering endless questions about policing, and showing me how to outwit a province-wide manhunt.

Retired OPP Constable Vincent Gircys for reviewing the manuscript, correcting many technical errors regarding policing and tasering, and being so quick and ready to help with the project.

Nowick Gray of nowickgray.com for his line-editing and formatting of the novel, all his assistance with self-publishing and his veteran support and encouragement.

Patrick Corbett for sharing his four decades of experience writing, directing, and producing movies and TV shows and pointing out the many holes in the plot that I needed to fill. (Without him, this novel would have been 40,000 words shorter.)

Pete "Typolino" Toccalino for his detailed feedback on the beta copy of this novel; then re-reading the final proof and catching all the typos everybody else missed. If it wasn't for Pete there'd still be a "flying saucer" in Moonbeam and "silts" in the moose mask.

Ron deGagne for his feedback, geological expertise, knowledge of the Greater Sudbury Area, and his Orwellian sense of humour.

Sarah Buerkle for all her feedback on the beta copy, helping with the German characters and introducing me to better translation software. Deepl.com rules!

Sonya Martin for her "hockey mom" expertise, her extensive feedback on the beta copy of the novel, and for screaming at the cliffhanger ending.

Willow Steelegrave for reviewing the beta copy and her appreciation for the spiritual undertones of the story.

Dianne and Julie Fleischauer of Golden Acres Farm for providing feedback on the prologue and opening chapters, being such big fans of this novel before they ever even read a word, and for proofreading the print edition.

Jeanette Thiessen for her eager support of the novel and for proofreading the print edition (catching all the grammatical errors most people would never have known existed).

Ted Kuntz, Gisele Baribeau, Wendy Schabrel and all the volunteers at VaccineChoiceCanada.com who made the virtual launch of this book possible.

Tash McCormick for helping on the domestic front so I had more time to finish this never-ending novel, and unknowingly serving as a model for one of the RCMP officers.

My mother, Barbara Manley, for teaching me to type (in grade two) and for proofreading this novel (catching a typo no one else spotted).

And to the **thousands of subscribers** to my email newsletter who have encouraged the writing of this novel and spread the word over the last two years.

Lastly, but always foremost, I am so grateful to my **wife, Nicole, and our son, Jonah**, who never wavered in their support over the twenty-three months and 1,100 hours of work involved in getting this novel done. They were my alpha, beta, and even delta readers—readily putting aside whatever we were reading in the evenings to hear new drafts of scenes they'd already heard before. Thank you both for your love and support.

Websites Exposing
The Truth About COVID-19

Action4Canada: Action4Canada is a grassroots movement reaching out to millions of Canadians for the purpose of uniting their voices in opposition to destructive COVID-19 policies. Action4Canada.com

America's Frontline Doctors: An association of medical professionals exposing the lies around COVID-19, with the goal of returning freedom and sanity to America through a growing collection of medical and legal resources. AmericasFrontlineDoctors.org

Andrew Kaufman MD: Duke University Medical Center graduate exposing the lack of science behind the COVID-19 hysteria. AndrewKaufmanMD.com

Awake Canada: An organization providing news, resources, and community for the purpose of awakening Canadians to the truth regarding the coronavirus deception and other global crimes. AwakeCanada.org

Awaken With JP: Short skits with comedian JP Sears exposing the blatant lies of the government and media around COVID-19 and related issues. AwakenWithJP.com

A Warrior Calls: Christopher James educates Canadians on common law, the real history and status of the corporation known as Canada and how citizens can regain their freedom. aWarriorCalls.com

Brasscheck TV: A video-based, alternative news site that has been calling fraud on the corona story since the beginning. BrassCheck.com/video

Bright Light News: Shining a light on the COVID-19 narrative. BrightLightNews.com

Canada Health Alliance: A non-profit network of healthcare professionals from across Canada whose common goal is to reclaim and protect each individual's right to health freedom through education and empowerment. CanadaHealthAlliance.org

Centre for Research on Globalization: A Montreal-based, independent research organization that has been exposing the corona hoax since the beginning of the so-called pandemic. GlobalResearch.ca

CoviLeaks: UK-based organization born in response to mainstream media propaganda and government misinformation surrounding the COVID-19 "pandemic." CoviLeaks.co.uk

Denis Rancourt PhD: Papers, articles, and talks by a retired tenured professor examining the validity of the pandemic and the measures. DenisRancourt.ca

Druthers: A monthly print newsletter distributed across Canada, sharing the truth about the COVID 19(84) agenda (that the mainstream media keeps on overlooking). Druthers.net

Dr. Vernon Coleman MD: Best-selling author and former professor of Holistic Medical Sciences at the International Open University in Sri Lanka, Dr. Coleman's "old man in a chair" videos were one of the early and clearest voices exposing the pandemic as a hoax. VernonColeman.com

Elders Without Borders: A non-profit Canadian organization dedicated to preserving the teachings of Indigenous peoples and exposing the injustice and lack of science behind the COVID-19 regulations. EldersWithoutBorders.ca

Five Times August: Indie singer/songwriter Brad Skistimas has released a series of protest songs taking aim at COVID-era regulations with "Sad Little Man" reaching #1 on Amazon and Apple Music charts. FiveTimesAugust.com

Foundation for Economic Education: In-depth articles looking at the economical and cultural harm of the government's reaction to COVID-19. FEE.org

Free Canada Media: Canadian man, a Canadian-American woman and an American man walked into a bar... and walked out with the idea for Free Canada Media. FreeCanadaMedia.com

Freedom Rising: A directory of freedom fighters and freedom-fighting organizations in Canada and abroad. FreedomRising.info

German Coronavirus Investigative Committee: Since mid-July 2020, the Corona Committee has been conducting investigations into why governments imposed unprecedented restrictions as part of the coronavirus response and what the consequences have been. Corona-Ausschuss.de/en

InfoWars: Alternative news, that borders on sensational, but is never boring, reporting on the coronavirus scamdemic and other world events. InfoWars.com

Jordan Henderson Fine Art: An artist exposing the COVID-19 agenda through oil paintings (and the illustrator of this book). JordanHendersonFineArt.com

Justice Centre for Constitutional Freedom: A Canadian legal organization and federally registered charity that defends citizens' fundamental freedoms through pro bono legal representation. JCCF.ca

Just Right: A weekly podcast analyzing the scamdemic and other issues from a viewpoint of individual rights, freedom, and capitalism. JustRightMedia.org

Laura-Lynn Tyler Thompson: Former co-host of The 700 Club Canada, Laura-Lynn Thompson's Christian-oriented talk show features interviews with guests exposing the COVID-19 agenda. LauraLynn.tv

Liberty Coalition Canada: Arming Canadians with a clarion Christian analysis of current events to diagnose the breakdown of liberty in Canada. LibertyCoalitionCanada.com

LifeSiteNews: Daily news reports on important developments in the United States, Canada, and around the world offering a more balanced coverage of the impact and validity of COVID-19 measures on humanity. LifeSiteNews.com

Mark Trozzi MD: Former emergency room doctor who quit the medical cartel, forfeited his income, and has committed himself fulltime to exposing the COVID-19 criminal enterprise. DrTrozzi.org

Mercola: The world's most visited alternative health website regularly prints well-researched articles exposing the COVID-19 deception. Mercola.com

Natural News: An uncensored, natural health organization, led by activist-turned-scientist Mike Adams (AKA the Health Ranger), unafraid to expose fraud and deception around

COVID-19. NaturalNews.com

Off-Guardian: A UK news site dedicated to open discourse and free expression, often hosting articles on both sides of the corona debate. Off-Guardian.org

PANDA Pandemics ~ Data & Analytics: A multidisciplinary group seeking to inform policy by considering explanations that allow us to count the human cost of COVID-19 responses globally. Pandata.org

Police on Guard for Thee: A Canadian group of active and retired police officers opposing the enforcement of COVID measures that violate the Charter of Rights and Freedoms. PoliceOnGuard.ca

Press for Truth: Video reporting from Canadian journalist Dan Dicks, exposing the COVID-19 agenda. Banned from YouTube. PressForTruth.ca

RebelNews: Alternative news for Canada, the UK, and Australia that looks at the facts regarding the COVID narrative, while funding civil liberty actions against the measures. RebelNews.com

Rosemary Frei: Canadian science writer publishing articles exposing the faulty science behind the COVID-19 pandemic and measures. RosemaryFrei.ca

Stand4Thee: An organization using lawful, peaceful, and effective action to end the tyranny of those who are actively attempting to take away our rights & freedoms. Stand4Thee.com

Strong and Free Canada: A grass roots organization dedicated to recovering our rights and freedoms, providing factual data and expert testimony on COVID and government overreach, and to lobbying our governments at all levels to return and respect our rights. StrongAndFreeCanada.org

Swiss Policy Research: Fully referenced facts about COVID-19, provided by experts in the field. swprs.org

TakeActionCanada: Supporting the many activists working to end lockdowns, forced masking, censorship, health intimidation, and political cancelling by aggregating all petitions, notices, fundraising activities, and events. TakeActionCanada.ca

The Corbett Report: Scamdemic-exposing journalism

presented by the witty and non-sensational investigative journalist, James Corbett. CorbettReport.com

The Daily Sceptic: Publishes essays questioning the value of lockdowns and other mandates and exploring the true motivations behind them. DailySceptic.org

The Defender: The website of Robert F. Kennedy Jr's Children's Health Defense which has been exposing political and media manipulation of the coronavirus story. ChildrensHealthDefense.org

The Highwire: High above the circus of mainstream media spin, Del Bigtree's talk show offers interviews with guests opposing the COVID narrative and mandates. TheHighWire.com

The Stew Peters Show: Interviews with a patriotic perspective on American culture and politics with a highly critical look at COVID policies and the so-called mRNA experimental vaccines. RedVoiceMedia.com/stew-peters-show

True North: A Canadian digital media platform seeking to provide fair, accurate and fact-based news reports regarding COVID-19 and other issues affecting Canada and the world. TNC.news

Vaccine Choice Canada: A federally registered not-for-profit educational society dedicated to helping families make voluntary, fully informed, and health-conscious choices about vaccination. VaccineChoiceCanada.com

Vaccine Death Report: Investigative journalist David John Sorensen and Nobel Peace Prize nominee Dr. Vladimir Zelenko present scientific data indicating that millions have died from the COVID injections, and hundreds of millions are suffering crippling side effects. StopWorldControl.com

VA Shiva Ayyadurai, PhD: The inventor of email and founder of the Truth Freedom Health movement, Dr. Shiva Ayyadurai motto is "get educated or get enslaved." VAShiva.com

World Council for Health: A worldwide coalition of health-focused organizations and civil society groups bringing a scientific and commonsense approach to COVID-19 hysteria. WorldCouncilForHealth.org

World Doctor Alliance: An alliance of healthcare professionals who have united with a view to end all lockdowns and other damaging COVID-19 measures. WorldDoctorsAlliance.com

Books Exposing
The COVID-19 Agenda

Corona, False Alarm? Facts and Figures by Karina Reiss, PhD and Sucharit Bhakdi, MD. Chelsea Green Publishing. October 2, 2020.

Covid-19: The Greatest Hoax in History by Vernon Coleman MD. September 29, 2020.

Covid Narrative Remix: Two Years of Dissent by Nowick Gray. Cougar Works. March 14, 2022.

COVID Operation: What Happened, Why It Happened, and What's Next by Pamela A Popper and Shane D Prier. Hitchcock Media Group LLC. Oct. 13, 2020.

COVID-19 and the Global Predators: We Are the Prey by Peter Breggin MD and Ginger Breggin. Lake Edge Press. Sept. 30, 2021.

Pandemia: How Coronavirus Hysteria Took Over Our Government, Rights, and Lives by Alex Berenson. Regnery Publishing. November 30, 2021.

The Real Anthony Fauci: Bill Gates, Big Pharma, and the Global War on Democracy and Public Health by Robert F. Kennedy Jr. Skyhorse. Nov. 16, 2021.

The Truth About Contagion: Exploring Theories of How Disease Spreads by Thomas S. Cowan MD and Sally Fallon Morell. Skyhorse. Feb. 22, 2021.

The Truth About COVID-19: Exposing The Great Reset, Lockdowns, Vaccine Passports, and the New Normal by Joseph Mercola, DO and Ronnie Cummins. Chelsea Green Publishing. April 29, 2021.

What Really Makes You Ill? Why Everything You Thought You Knew About Disease Is Wrong by Dawn Lester and David Parker. December 21, 2019.

Words from the Dead: Relevant Reading in the Covid Age by Sean Arthur Joyce. Ekstasis Editions. March 2022.

Music Featured in This Novel

References to songs and artists do not in any way indicate that they endorse or agree with views expressed in this book. Nonetheless, readers are encouraged to purchase and/or listen to their music to get a full flavour of why their works were alluded to in these pages.

"**Away is Mine**" by Gord Downie. Arts & Crafts Productions. 2020.

"**Cellphone Vigilante**" from the album *Torpid* by the band The Arrogant Worms. Independent. 2008.

"*Love is a First*" from the album We Are the Same by the Tragically Hip. Universal Music Group. 2009.

"**Mounted Animal Nature Trail**" from the album *Live Bait* by the Arrogant Worms. Independent. 1997.

"**Schubert: Die schöne Müllerin.**" A song cycle by Franz Schubert from 1823 based on 20 poems by Wilhelm Müller. Vocals by Ian Bostridge. Piano by Mitsuko Uchida. Warner Classics. 2006.

"**The Last Saskatchewan Pirate**" from the album *The Arrogant Worms*, by the Arrogant Worms. Festival Records. 1992.

"**The Fly**" from the album *World Container* by the Tragically Hip. Universal Music Group. 2006.

"**Helpless**" from the album *Déjà Vu* by Neil Young. Atlantic Records. 1970.

About the Cover Artist and Illustrator

The original cover painting and charcoal illustrations for this novel were rendered by fine artist Jordan Henderson. He resides in Washington State where he has completed many paintings exposing the COVID-19 deception. One such painting, *Sanity and Son,* was the inspiration for the characters Sandy and Josh in this novel. Another painting, *Safe and Sanitized,* was actually intended to be the cover of this novel, but it was just too darn scary. You can view these and other coronavirus paintings, as well as his other artwork, on his website. You can also support his work, decorate your home, and spread the truth by purchasing prints, T-shirts, greeting cards and more from his online store at:

www.JordanHendersonFineArt.com

About the Author

John C. A. Manley was born in Toronto, Ontario, Canada in 1978. His ancestry dates back to the first European settlers in sixteenth-century Canada, carrying a blend of Irish, Scottish, Welsh, and French genes (with a little First Nation from his great grandmother). He was raised Catholic, disliked school, and has been writing speculative fiction since he was nine years old.

Graduating a year early from high school, he moved to a Hindu monastery in the mountains of Southern California where he studied Eastern philosophy, practiced yoga meditation and was almost eaten alive by a mountain lion.

Three years later, he moved to Italy where he trained as a fine artist at an academy in Florence. Two years later, he found himself back in Canada, where he struggled as a portrait artist in downtown Toronto.

In 2001, he married, moved out of the big city into a small town, and began work as a freelance ghostwriter and copywriter; while penning short stories and collecting rejection slips from publishers.

In 2018, he began writing his first full-length novel, an urban fantasy set in Stratford, Ontario; but when the first lockdown began in 2020, he put down that project to pen a short dystopian story about where he saw these so-called "public health" measures going. That short story grew into the full-length novel, Much Ado About Corona.

John is currently working on the sequel, Brave New Normal, while living (and protesting) in Stratford Ontario, with his wife Nicole, and son Jonah. You can visit his website and subscribe to email updates at:

www.BlazingPineCone.com

Get Behind-the-Scenes Bonus Material Directly from the Writing Studio of John C. A. Manley

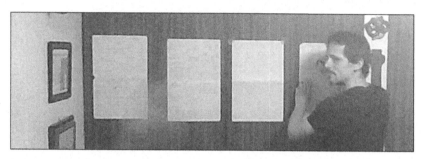

Yes, I write my first drafts, standing up, against a vertical surface. Hey, it worked for Hemingway. Become a patron of my work and you will not only be supporting my ability to produce more novels, at a faster pace, but you will also receive:

- A monthly <u>print</u> newsletter containing stories and news about my creative projects mailed to your door.
- A monthly bonus letter, giving behind-the-scenes accounts about the making of my novels, and the deeper meaning, metaphors, and intentions behind the words. Also mailed to your door.
- Monthly patron-only, live webinars, where you can ask me, and any special guests, questions about writing, my novels or the themes and controversial subjects contained within.
- Access to a digital library of previous newsletters and webinar recordings.

To find out more, or to become a patron, go to:

www.BlazingPineCone.com/patron

Made in United States
North Haven, CT
07 June 2022